HORRORS BEYOND 2

STORIES OF STRANGE CREATIONS

All stories in this anthology are original except:
"A Family Affair," *Treachery and Treason,* Penguin/Roc, 2000

FIRST EDITION
10 9 8 7 6 5 4 3 2 1
Published in October 2007

ISBN: 0-9779876-3-9 (Trade Paperback)
0-9779876-2-0 (Hardcover)

Printed in the U.S.A.

Published by Elder Signs Press
P.O. Box 389
Lake Orion, MI 48361-0389
www.eldersignspress.com

HORRORS BEYOND 2

STORIES OF STRANGE CREATIONS

EDITED BY WILLIAM JONES

2007

CONTENTS

ISOLATION POINT, CALIFORNIA

JOHN SHIRLEY

GAGE PUSHED THE DOOR of his cabin open with his booted foot, as he always did, peering inside, right and left, without going in, to make sure no one was hiding there waiting for him. He looked around, saw only the single bunk, neatly made up, with the solar-powered lamp on a small stand beside it, glowing faintly in the overcast, late afternoon gloom. Faces did stare back at him: the old magazine photos of smiling people, mostly girls, on the wall over his bunk. The wooden chair stood just where he'd left it, pulled back slightly from the metal table with its two coffee cups, long bereft of coffee, and his collection of pens, stacks of spiral notebooks, the radio. Above the table were the shelves of random books, many of them blackened at the edges, foraged from a burned library in Sweetbite. The ax leaned on the stack of firewood beside the river-stone fireplace, opposite the old woodstove, with its two pots.

It was tedious, having to stop and look around in the cabin and the out-house, before going in, day after day. But as he went inside, he told himself that the first time he neglected to do it, someone would be there to brain him with his own ax. Most of the United States was dead now — they'd all murdered one another because of the Aggfac which, God Knows, was still in force. So the odds were pretty clear . . .

He closed and barred the door behind him, saw that the fire was out, but he went immediately to the desk, and stood there, looking out the window. It was nailed shut and curtained — a risk having a window at all — but he could see the light was dimming, the clouds shrugging together for rain. The charge on the lamp was low, so he plugged it into the socket that connected to the solar-collection panel on the roof, and the lamp's charge meter bobbed to near full. He dialed up the light, and looked at the radio but decided not to try it. He was usually depressed for a while after listening to the radio and didn't want to ruin his hopeful mood.

He leaned his shotgun against the wall, within reach, put the binoculars on a stack of notebooks, and sat down at the table. He adjusted the shim under the short table leg to minimize the wobbling, picked up a pen, and wrote his newest journal entry. His fingers were stiff with the chill but he wanted to tell his journal what had happened more than he wanted to stoke up the fire.

◆◆◆

November 1st, 2023

I saw her again this afternoon, about forty-five minutes ago. She was standing on what was left of the old marina, coming out from all those burned-out buildings along San Andreas Spit, across the river's mouth from me. She was standing right where the river meets the tidal push from the ocean. That always seemed suggestive to me, the river flowing into the ocean; the ocean pushing back, the two kind of mingling. "Here's some silt" and "Here's some salt back at you." Silt and salt, never noticed how close the words were before now.

I looked at her in the binoculars, and when she saw I was doing that, she spread her arms and smiled as if to say, "Check me out!" Not that I could see much of her under all those clothes. It's pretty brisk out now, Northern coast this time of year, wind off the sea, and she was wearing a big bulky green ski jacket, and a watch cap, and jeans and boots. She had a 30.06 bolt-action deer rifle leaned against a rock. She never went far from it. She's got long wavy chestnut hair, and her face, what I could make out, seemed kind of pleasant. She's not tall. Taking into account the silhouette of her legs, she seems slim. Not that there's anyone obese left, not on this continent, anyway. She seemed energetic, confident. I wonder if she found a new supply drop somewhere. If she found it first, she could be doing well. Another reason to make contact.

But who knows what she's up to? She could be talking to men at a safe distance all over the county. Getting them to leave her gifts or something. But that'd be risky. They'll kill her eventually. Unless someone finds a cure for the AggFac soon. Not very goddamn likely.

Anyway it felt good talking to her. Shouting back and forth, really. I got pretty hoarse, since of course she was several hundred feet from me.

Said she was from San Francisco. Got out just in time. Told her I was from Sacramento. She laughed when I told her this little peninsula of mine is called "Isolation Point." Had to swear across my heart it was always called that. She said she used to be a high school English teacher. Told her, "Hey that's amazing, I used to be a high school student!" She laughed. I can just barely hear her laugh across the river.

She asked what did I used to do. Said I managed some restaurants. Wanted to be a journalist, write about America. Big story came, no one to tell it to. She said I could still write. I said for who? She said for people — you leave the writing in places and other people find it. "I'd read it!" she said. I said okay. Thinking that writing for one person at a time wasn't what I had in mind, but you scale down your dreams now. Way down.

I was running out of breath and my voice was going with all the yelling back and forth so I asked her name. Told her mine. Our ages too, me forty-three, she thirty-four. I tried to think of some way to ask her to come closer, maybe at the fence. To ask her without scaring her. But I couldn't think of any way and then she waved and picked up her rifle and walked off.

Her name's Brenda.

I was hiking back to the cabin going, "Brennnn-da! Brennnn-da!" over and over like an idiot. Like I'm twelve. Not surprising after two years alone here, I guess. It was good just to see someone who isn't trying to kill me.

Wish the dog would come back. Someone probably ate him, though. I need to check the fence again. Going to do it now. It might rain. Might get dark before I'm back. Might be someone there. I've got the shotgun. Not that I can afford to use the shells. The sight of the gun keeps people back, though, if they stay beyond the nineteen. Going now. Should stay here . . . Too antsy . . .

Gage put the pen down and picked up his shotgun. "That's right," he said aloud. "Put down the pen, pick up the gun." He had to talk aloud, fairly often, just to hear a human voice. Brenda's was the first he'd heard, except for the warning noise, for three months. "That's how it is," he said, hearing the hoarseness in his voice from all that shouting. Bad time to get laryngitis. Bad time to get anything — he'd almost died of pneumonia once. No pharmacies anymore. You ran into a doctor, he'd try to kill you. He'd be sorry afterward but that didn't do you any good.

Gage unbarred the door, and went out, closing the door carefully behind him. There was still some light. He walked out to the edge of the trees to take a quick look out at the Pacific, beyond the edge of the cliff, fifty yards away. It was steely under the clouds. He was looking for boats and hoping he wouldn't see one. Nothing out there, except maybe that slick black oblong, appearing and disappearing — a whale. At least the animals were doing better now.

He'd chosen this little finger of land, with its single intact cabin, partly because there was no easy way to land a boat. Mostly the sea was too rough around it. You could maybe come in from the sea up into the mouth of the river, clamber onto the big slippery wet crab-twitchy rocks that edged the river bank, if you could secure your boat so it didn't float away, but the current was strong there and no one had tried it that he knew of. His cabin was pretty well hidden in the trees, after all, and it didn't look like much was here. And of course, they were as scared of him as he was of them. But then, that's what his father had told him about rattlesnakes.

He turned and tramped through the pine trees toward the fence, a quarter mile back, noticing, for the first time in a year or more, the smell of the pine needles mingling with the living scent of the sea. Funny how you see a girl, you start to wake up and notice things around you again. To care about how things smell and look and feel.

The wind off the sea keened between the trees and made the hackles rise on the back of his neck. He buttoned the collar of his thick, blue REI snowline jacket with his left hand, the other keeping the Remington 12-gauge tucked up under his right armpit, pressed against him, the breach-block cupped in his palm. He was good at getting the Remington popped fast to his shoulder for firing. So far nobody had noticed what a lame shot he was. The two guys he'd killed since coming to the area — killed four months apart — had both got it at close to point-blank range. That was the AggFac for you. If people sniped at you, it was out of desperation, not because of the AggFac.

He felt the wind tugging at his streaked beard, his long sandy hair. "I must be getting pretty shaggy," he said to a red squirrel, looking beadily down from a low branch. "But the only thing I've got left to cut it with is a knife and it's so dull . . . I'm down to my last cake of soap. Half a cake really . . ." For two years, cognizant that no one on the continent was making soap anymore, he'd only washed when he could no longer bear his own smell.

The squirrel clicked its claws up the tree, looking for a snug place out of the wind, and Gage continued on, five minutes later cutting the old deer path he took to the fence. Another ten minutes and he was there: a twenty-five foot hurricane fence with anti-personnel wire across the top in a Y-frame. The fence and the place at the river where he got the fish and the crabs were two of the main reasons he'd chosen this spot. There was no gate in the fence — they'd used a chopper landing pad of cracked asphalt, near the edge of the cliff on the south side of the cape. There'd been some kind of military satellite monitoring station, here, once, and the fence, he figured, had been put up to keep people away from it. It kept bears and wolves out too. The post building had crumbled into the sea after a bad storm — you could see the satellite dish sticking up out of the water at low tide, all rusty; the cabin was all that was left. There was forage, if you knew where to look; there was river water to filter; there was a way he knew to get around the fence, underneath its southern end, when he was willing to try his luck checking the crossroads at Sweetbite Point for supply drops. But he hadn't been out to the crossroads in seven months. Previous time, someone had almost gotten him. So he stayed out here as long as he could. It was a great spot to survive in, if you wanted to survive. He'd almost stopped wanting to.

The fence looked perfectly upright, unbreached, so far as he could see from here, no more rusted than last time. Of course, a determined man could get over it — or around it, if you didn't mind clambering over a sheer drop — but it was rare for anyone to come out onto the cape. There weren't many left to come.

He walked along the fence a ways south, wondering what'd brought him here. He had a sort of instinct, especially sharp post-AggFac, that kept him alive — and usually it had its reasons for things.

There it was. The sound of a dog barking. He hoped it was Gassie.

"Hey Gassie!" he shouted, beginning to trot along the fence. "Yo, dog!" Be a great day, meeting a woman . . . sort of . . . and getting his dog back too. "Gassie!"

Then it occurred to him to wonder who the dog was barking at. Maybe a raccoon. Maybe not.

He bit off another shout, annoyed with himself for getting carried away. Shouting. Letting people know where he was.

He circled a lichen-yellowed boulder that hulked up to his own height, and came upon Gassie and the stranger — who was just a few steps beyond the nineteen. Gassie was this side of the fence, the man on the other side, staring, mouth agape, at the hole the dog had dug under the fence to get in . . .

Despite the dangerous presence of the stranger, Gage shook his head in admiration at the dog's handiwork. It was the same spot he'd gotten out at — some critter, raccoon or skunk, had dug a hole under the fence where the ground was soft, and the dog had widened it and gotten out and wandered off, more than a month ago. Gage had waited a week, then decided he had to fill the hole in. Here he was, Gassie, his ribs sticking out, limping a little, but scarcely the worse for wear — a brown-speckled tongue-drooping mix of pit bull, with his wedge-shaped head, and some other breed Gage had never been sure of.

The stranger — a gawky, emaciated man in the tatters of an Army uniform, who'd let his hair fall into accidental dreadlocks — goggled stupidly at the hole, then jerked his head up as Gage approached the dog.

Gage reckoned the stranger, carrying an altered ax handle, at twenty-one paces away, with the fence between them. Not at *The Nineteen* yet. Everyone alive on this continent was good at judging distances instantly. Nineteen paces, for most people, was the AggFac warning distance. It was possible to remain this side of psychotic — like this side of the fence — beyond nineteen paces from another human being. Nineteen paces or less, you'd go for them, with everything you had, to kill them; and they'd go at you just the same. Which was why most people in North America had died over the past few years. A couple of phrases from one of the first — and last — newspaper articles came into his mind. *The very wiring of the brain altered from within, by the nanomaterials, a machine designed to be carried by a virus. . . That portion of the brain so different victims become another species. . .*

"You're outside the margin, dude," Gage said. "You can still back up."

He knew he should probably kill the guy whether he backed up or not, on general principle. For one thing, the guy was probably planning to kill and eat his dog. For another, now that the son of a bitch knew there was someone camped on the other side of the fence, he'd come over to forage and kill — or rather, to kill and forage.

But you clung to what dignity you could. Gage did, anyway. Killing people when you didn't absolutely have to lacked dignity, in Gage's view.

"Don't come no closer," the man said. He hefted the ax-handle warningly. It was missing its ax blade but he'd found a stiff blade from a kitchen knife somewhere and he'd pushed it into a crack at one end of the handle and wrapped it in place with black electric tape.

"You were a soldier," Gage observed. "Where's your weapon?"

"I got it, real close," the man said. After thinking laboriously a moment, he said, "My partner's got it trained on your ass right now."

Gage laughed. "No one's got a partner. I saw some people try it, before I came here — watched from a roof for two days. They tried partnering by staying twenty feet away from each other. But eventually they would fuck that up, get too close — and you know what happened. Every time. You haven't got a partner — or a gun."

The man shrugged. He wasn't going to waste his breath on any more lies. He looked at the dog, licking his lips. Finally he said, "You knock that dog in the head, push it where I can get it, I'll go away for good."

"That dog's worth ten like you," Gage said. He made up his mind. It'd be pretty ironic if the AggFac had worn off, finally, and he and Brenda were staying out of reach for no reason. Of course, there was no reason to think it ever wore off. But everyone, as far as he knew, hoped it would, eventually. They didn't know what caused it, exactly — there were lots of theories, the nanotech one being the most enduring — so maybe it'd wear off as mysteriously as it came. For no good reason, the brain would revert to normal.

Yeah right. But for Brenda's sake he stepped closer to the stranger, within the nineteen, to see if the AggFac was still there in him.

He felt it immediately. The clutching up feeling, the hot geysering from the back of his skull, the heat spreading to his face, his arms. The tightening of his hands, his jaws, the background humming; the tight focus on his Enemy. And the change in the way things look — going almost colorless. Not black and white, but sickly sepia and gray, with shadows all deep and inky.

Since Gage had come within the nineteen, the stranger was seized by the AggFac too, and his face went beet red, the veins at his temples popping up. As if propelled from behind he came rushing at Gage, stopped only by the fence, hammering at the chain links with his ax handle, making that *Eeeeee* sound in the back of his throat they all made — the sound Gage might've been making himself, he could never tell somehow. Hammering the ax handle to splinters as Gage shoved the barrel of the shotgun through a fence link and pulled the trigger at point blank range . . .

The stranger fell away, gasping and dying. The AggFac ebbed. Color seeped back into the world.

Gage heard the dog barking, and saw it start for the hole in the fence. Wanting to get at the stranger's body.

"No, Gassie," Gage said, feeling tired and empty and half-dead himself. He grabbed the dog by its short tail, pulled it back before it was quite through the hole. It snarled at him but let him do it. He blocked up the hole with rocks, then started toward the end of the fence, where it projected over the cliff. He'd have to go down by the rocks, about fifty feet south of the fence's end, thread the path, climb the other cliff, to get the body, drag it to the sea. A lot of work.

But he didn't want to leave the bloody corpse there for Brenda to find. He wanted her to come to the fence . . .

So he trudged toward the cliffs.

November 2nd, 2023

My face hurts from scraping at it with that knife. Used up a lot of soap in place of shaving cream. Hope the contusions go down before she sees me up close. Not too close, of course.

Will she come? She'd be foolish to come. She doesn't know me. She can see the fence from across the river but she doesn't know if it'll keep her safe from me. I might have a gate for all she knows. She's never been out to the point.

She says she's coming. We agreed on high noon. She's got a longer-range weapon than me. She doesn't seem stupid. She'll be smart about it. She'll get close enough to take stock of the situation, with that gun right up against her shoulder, but not so close I could rush her.

I think she does understand that outside the AggFac I'm not some thug, some rapist. But she may decide not to take the chance. Or someone may kill her before she gets here. I think it's almost noon . . .

"Hi! Can you see me okay?" Gage called, spreading his hands so she could see he didn't have the shotgun. She was still about a hundred feet off, on the other side of the fence, assessing the situation from cover, like he'd figured she would, the rifle propped on the top of a big tree stump and pointed right at him.

Dangerous, not to bring the shotgun. But it was meaningful. They both knew that. Not carrying your gun was like, in the old days, bringing a bouquet of flowers.

Still, this could be a set up. She could be after his goods. She could want his cabin, maybe. She could shoot him, and Gassie, if she had the ammo. Shoot him from safety where she was. Nothing to stop her. A couple of rounds, one'd get through that fence. Down he'd go . . .

He kept his arms spread. Standing in the open, a little clearing with just rock strewn dirt on the ground, so she could see he didn't have the shotgun anywhere near — like, hidden behind a rock close to him. His gun could be somewhere in the brush, of course. But at least it wasn't in easy reach.

Slowly, she got out from behind the stump and walked toward him. She glanced right and left now and then. Looked at the dog, sitting there wagging its tail, beside him. She smiled.

"Hi Brenda," he said, when she got to about twenty-one paces, and stopped. Slowly, she lowered the gun, holding it cradled in her arms.

Then she sat down, her legs crossed, deciding to trust him that much. He sat down too, on his side of the fence. The dog put his head on Gage's lap.

"I'm embarrassed to tell you his name," Gage said, patting the dog. "It's Gassie."

"Gassie!" She laughed. "After Lassie, right?" She had all of her teeth, which was unusual in itself. Her face had lots of roundness to it, but she wasn't pie faced. Her eyes were dark brown, he saw, and the shape of them suggested she had some American Indian blood. She'd put her hair up, in a simple kind of way, and she seemed clean.

"What now?" he asked, as mildly, as casually, as much without pressure as he could.

"I don't know," she said. "I just needed to see someone up close as I could, and you seemed nice." She shrugged. "As much as anyone can be, with the — you know."

He nodded, deciding he needed to be as completely honest with her as possible. "I tried it, yesterday, when a stranger came up to the fence. I deliberately stepped closer, just to see. I always hope it might go away some time."

"I've never heard of it going away."

"No. Reports on the radio say it never has for anyone. Kids don't outgrow it, old people don't get over it. It hit me the same as always."

She nodded, not having to ask what'd happened.

"I don't feel too bad," he added. "Guy was trying to eat my dog."

She nodded again. That she understood too, both sides. "You fish?"

"Sure." They talked a long time about practical things like that. He told her about his water filter, the crabs, the fish, the wild plants he knew — she knew them too — and about the forays to the food drops.

"They'll drop food to us sometimes, the foreign people," she said, "but they seem to have just . . . given up on curing it. Unless — you said you had a radio? You heard anything?" About the AggFac, she meant.

He shrugged. "If it's true. One guy — hard to get the signal, I think it was from the Virgin Islands, I had to move the radio around — he said the Japanese had confirmed it was some kind of self-replicating nanotech-creation that got out of hand, like an artificial virus, was supposed to alter your brain wiring in a good way, does it in a bad way instead, jumps from person to person."

"The glories of high technology."

"Whatever it is," he went on, venting, "you'd think someone would make some damn progress by now. If the nanodevice is self replicating and virus-carried then they should be able to do a vaccine. No vaccines, nothing. It is like they're just waiting for us to die. Won't let anybody come to their perfect little countries. That blockade in Panama. And they shoot down our planes . . ."

"Can you blame them?" she asked.

He knew what she meant. The world had watched, as the "Aggression Factor" rolled over a hemisphere; as millions of people had killed one another: people in North America and Mexico, all the way to the geo-quarantine at the Panama Canal; the world had watched as millions of longtime neighbors had killed one another; watched as an unthinkable number of husbands had killed their wives, and wives their husbands; as unspeakable quantities of children were murdered by parents, by siblings, by friends; as others murdered their parents. As women throttled babies freshly plucked from the womb — and then wept in utter bafflement. He remembered a boy walking through the ruins of Sacramento, weeping, "Why did I kill my Mom? Why did I kill my Mom?" And then the boy had come within nineteen steps and . . . without meaning to, Gage had put him out of his misery.

"Nah. I don't blame them. I just . . ." He didn't have to say it. She smiled sadly and they understood one another.

"Nice not to have to shout."

"Yeah. I . . . have some dried fish for you, if you need it. I'll leave it at the fence. I thought maybe I'd loan you my solar radio, too, if you wanted. The dog dug a hole under the fence a ways down. I could push it under there . . . leave it for you to get later. You can see me walking a good quarter mile off from there."

"That's so sweet. You look like you carved your face up a bit . . ."

"Best I could do with what I had."

"You're still a nice looking guy."

Probably not when the AggFac hits, he thought. But he said only, "Thanks."

"I'll borrow the radio, I promise to bring it back . . ."

November 6, 2023

I've seen her every day but yesterday — I was really worried yesterday when she didn't come but she had to duck a guy who had gotten wind of her. He was stalking her. She finally managed to lure him up to a hill she knew real well and she shot him from cover. Smart, cool-headed girl. I'm crazy about her. Of course, I can't get within 19 steps of her but . . . I'm still crazy about her.

She told me about a girl who'd lived down the street from her, they talked from rooftops, sometimes. The girl would trade a look at her naked body to guys who'd come around, look at her naked up on a second floor balcony. She had a gun up there in case they started up. They'd leave her food and stuff and they'd look at her naked and masturbate. It worked for awhile but of course some predator got wind of it, some guy who was always more or less AggFac, even before it came along, and he busted in and jumped her. Killed her, of course, the AggFac won't be denied, but I figure her body was still warm afterward. Lot of bodies get raped now.

Why did Brenda tell me this story? Maybe suggesting we trusted each other enough to get naked, if only from a distance? I'm too embarrassed to masturbate even if she's doing it too. That desperate I'm not.

I wrote her some poetry I'm going to leave for her. She might blow me off for good after she reads it, if she's got any taste . . .

"Feels like it might snow," Brenda said, hugging herself against the morning mist, the occasional gusts of cold wind.

"Kind of cold. I could go back, get you a blanket, toss it over." They were sitting in their usual spot, fence between them.

"Oh it'd probably get stuck on the wire," she said.

"I could send Gassie over again to keep you warm."

"Last time he came over he humped my leg."

"He did? I didn't see that." He was only momentarily tempted to say, I don't blame him. Even now he could be slicker than that.

"There's something I wanted to talk to you about," she said. She chewed her lip for a moment, then went on, "Look — you ever hear about someone being cured of, like, a phobia, before the AggFac, by getting used to whatever they were scared of, little by little? Scared of flying, they made you go to airports, sit in a plane, but then get off the plane before it flies, look at pictures taken out a plane window, till you're ready to fly . . . all that kind of thing. You know?"

"Yeah, I forget what they call that. But . . . you don't think the AggFac would work that way. It's not a phobia."

"No it isn't. But it's a kind of compulsive aversion for people . . . when they get physically close. Right? What if a person could sort of inure themselves to the presence of another person within nineteen steps — by slow degrees? Make the brain accustomed to the other person . . . the wiring of the brain itself acclimated to them."

"How? It's so powerful that even if your eyes are shut and you can't see the person, soon as you know they're close, the AggFac hits and you kill them. Whatever you do, the murder reflex comes out. I mean — I could probably find a way to restrain myself, somehow, for awhile, so I couldn't get loose too easily. So you could get close — but then, let's face it, *you'd* kill *me*. I mean, mothers killed children they loved all their lives . . ."

"Sure. But . . . suppose we both restrain ourselves somewhat. With rope, whatever, the weapons off somewhere, we keep the fence between us at first . . . but we're basically within reach. I don't think I could even bite you through those links. But we could have some contact . . ."

The idea made him breathless. His blood raced as he thought about it. But then he shook his head. "Even if we didn't hurt one another — we'd hate one another, within the nineteen. There'd be no pleasure in it — just rage."

"Our brains would feel that way — at first. But our bodies! Our bodies would . . . I think they'd respond. It'd be a kind of . . . counter force in the brain. Maybe enough, after awhile, to . . . Oh Gage I can't take this distance from people much longer. I'm . . . I've got skin hunger. It's bad. I have to try something."

"Hey. Me too. And I really, really like you. I'd have liked you before all this stuff, I swear it. But — even if we couldn't hurt each other, how would the encounter ever end? We'd be smashing at each other through the fence!"

"That's the risk. There has to be some risk. There always was some risk. But Gage — I want to try. I think that . . . if I'm starting to hurt myself against the fence, I'll finally manage to back off and the AggFac'll go away. Then we can try again. We can *inure*. We can *accustom*. We can . . . acclimate. Maybe you'll stop seeing me as . . . the other. Maybe I'll be, like, an extension of you, after awhile, so the AggFac won't come any more, at least when it's me."

"You mean . . . you want to get naked, on either side of the fence . . ."

"Yeah. Well, I'll keep my coat on, and some boots. Won't look too elegant but . . . I'm burning to touch you. I want to love you. I want you to love me . . ."

She was crying now. Finally he said yes.

November 11, 2023
The weather cleared up some, and, partly naked, we tried it. We each had our guns put way out of reach but where the other could see it. She had

some rope, left some for me — she'd pushed it through the mesh, inch by inch, while she was waiting for me. We took turns, measuring it out carefully. The rope went from a tree behind me to the fence, just enough so I could press against it, but restraining me so I couldn't start to climb over it easily. My arms were tied to my sides. That was tricky. Had to work with our teeth, use a fork in a tree to pull a knot taut, stuff like that. Laughing a lot back and forth as we worked out how to do it, all alone, each on their side of the fence. Of course we knew it was still possible to get out of the rope but it would take time and the other could get away or get their gun . . . We thought maybe we'd be too frenzied with kill lust or the other kind to really work out how to attack the other person with all that stuff in the way. The AggFac isn't about thinking or planning, god knows.

I used up the last of my soap, getting ready for this. She had cleaned herself up too . . .

We came close, the fence between us, the rope restraining us. The AggFac hit and there was no remembering how we'd said we'd loved each other, there was no remembering how we wanted to trust . . .

He tried to snap at her nose through the mesh, envisioned tearing it off in his teeth, but couldn't reach her. She tried to bite into his chin, couldn't reach it.

But their skin touched, through the links, *and he did get a hard-on under the rope* — it was roped to his belly, no way it was going to be free to go through that fence, she'd bite it off for sure. They writhed and snapped and snarled and then she managed to back away . . .

Still, I swear something did get through the AggFac, some other feeling — it really did get through. Just enough.

We both got bloody on the fence but we're going to try again. We have a plan, a way to try it in the cabin.

His heart was slamming in his chest, so loud he could hear it in the quiet of the cabin. He just lay there on his bunk listening to his heart thudding, trying the ropes, hoping the self-restraint system he'd worked up was going to hold him long enough. He could get out of the ropes, afterward, but it'd take time. The dog was tied up in the woods. He was ready for her to come. Maybe she wouldn't show up. He'd lie here like an idiot and some son of a bitch would climb over the fence and find him here, before he got loose, and he'd be helpless. Then dead.

Big risk, trying it in the cabin this way. Risk from her too. She said she was getting some control over the AggFac, but how long would it last, in close proximity?

He knew he couldn't bear it if he killed her. If she killed him, well, it wouldn't matter.

The door opened and he looked up and saw her there, inside the nineteen, almost naked. Her hands were all muffled, tied together and smothered in big thick home-made boxing gloves, and her mouth was gagged, she'd gagged it herself, to try to keep her from biting him.

The color drained from the room. The *Eeeee* was building up in the back of his throat; was trying to get out of her too. He could see her struggling to keep it back. But the other thing, the distance from the AggFac, that they'd worked on, built up through the fence, that was there too. He was able to look at her, like a man close to the sheet of flames in a forest fire — feeling the heat painfully but not quite so close he was burned yet.

She waited there for a moment, looking at his ropes. Then she started toward him. He tried to hold onto the memory of her touch, through the fence, the desire he felt for her, but the AggFac rose up. He writhed against the ropes.

She rushed him, her face reddening with AggFac, leaped on him, straddled him . . .

It was funny how the two feelings were there, right close, so distinct. Kill. Love. Almost intertwined. But not combined. Like, alternating. I just kept trying to drag my mind back to the love feeling. I looked in her eyes, saw her doing the same thing. Whole moments of close, intimate sanity, each one of those moments — impossible to explain how precious they were. Impossible.

The AggFac was still there but somehow, for a few moments, they were in a kind of blessed state of betweenness. She was there, so close, her breath on his cheek, the feeling of her closeness like a hot meal after a week of hunger.

Something in him, something that went to sleep during the Aggression Factor, quivered awake and brought color back to the room . . . Their eyes locked . . . hers cleared . . . She stopped shaking . . . .

She stopped pounding at him . . . and slipped him into her, pumped her hips, working the gag out of her mouth, chewing the gloves off her hands so she could touch him.

There was intimacy; after so much privation, there was rapid mutual orgasm. Then he drew away from her, instinctively, as he came, and the AggFac returned, and he started thrashing against the ropes, trying to kill her, and her own Aggression broke free in response, and she started clawing at his eyes, snapping at his throat. She bit hard, she tore, his blood began to flow . . .

Some of his rope gave way. Enough.

He seized her by the throat and — just to get her hands from his eyes — threw her off him, to the floor. He tore loose as she scrambled to her feet, turned snarling to face him. He reached out with one hand, scooped up the chair, threw it at her — it felt light as cardboard to him in that moment. It struck her on the side of the head and she fell backward, crying out. He still had ropes around his ankles and jerked them loose, looking for another weapon to kill her with. Stunned, confused, she crawled to the door . . .

She turned and stared dazedly at him. He hunkered, ready to spring at her. Panting, they stared at one another. She was within nineteen. He wanted to kill her. But a second passed and he didn't spring. Neither did she. The betweenness was in her eyes. But it wouldn't last, not now.

"Run!" he managed, huskily.

But she hesitated . . .

And then the moment passed.

February 2, 2024.
I've met someone else. Her name is Elise. Pretty soon I'm going to tell her about the fence and the process. I'm going to try again. I have to try again.

There was that one second, when I was free, and didn't attack. Seeing the humanness in her eyes, too, for a moment. It gave me hope. That one second could telescope out to a lifetime of forbearance . . .

Some day I'll get control of it, and then I can be honest with Elise. And show her Brenda's grave.

SERENADE

LUCIEN SOULBAN

THE WOODEN STAIRS PROTESTED their burden with a groan and all conversation seemed to die on that one stroke. The two army officers entered the quiet second-story hallway with its solitary, naked bulb, and surveyed the row of weathered doors. They were strangers to the apartment building's crushing poverty. A carpet-bagger, his frayed clothes still heavy with Kansas dirt, walked past the silent pair. Once out of prying earshot, the two officers resumed their discussion, almost in mid-sentence.

"Nightmares?" Second Lt. Adams asked, securing the manila envelope under his arm. He was all Black Irish wrapped in a Bronx accent.

First Lt. Samuels shrugged. "That's how I heard it. None of these guys was right in the head after that," he said.

"How?"

Samuels offered a knowing half-smile that sent out a ripple of wrinkles across his leathery face. He removed his beige cap, long enough to run his fingers through his mane of silver before wedging the cap on tight. "You'll see," he said, knocking on the worn door of apartment 214.

"What if he ain't home?" Adams said.

"He's here." Samuels squatted and slipped a ten dollar bill under the door before standing again. "There's more of that, Mr. Abernathy," Samuels said, calling through the door, "if you open up."

The door creaked open, revealing an old man aged prematurely by the day's sorrows. He was clean-shaven and dressed in cream-striped cotton pajamas and slippers. His green eyes were sharp enough to pinch both men with his stare.

"What d'you want?" Abernathy said

Samuels leaned in close. "Uncle Sam has a job for you," he whispered, "and unless you want every Dust Bowl vagrant in this lean-to hearing you're earning scratch . . . ."

Abernathy considered it for a moment before opening the door.

The apartment was in disrepair — books piled on shelves and more stacked in boxes — threadbare furniture and a small pile of broken chairs stripped for a cold night's fire. Water-stains mottled the faded yellow wallpaper and dust covered everything in generous coats. It was easy to spot the roaches. Still, Abernathy did enough to keep the place tidy, if barely.

"Isn't much to look at," Abernathy admitted without a shred of embarrassment, "but it keeps the rain out." He walked past the coffee table where a chessboard sat, and sank into the armchair, leaving his guests standing.

"You said you had work?" Abernathy asked. He studied the two men carefully. "Don't much have time for family — Uncle Sam and I aren't on civil terms." He chuckled at his own wit.

"The Department of War has a small job for you."

"Now they need me. How much they paying?"

Adams tossed Abernathy the manila envelope.

"You have a week to complete it," Samuels said. "We pay you $100 now and another $100 next week."

"What if I'm done before?"

"You have a week." Samuels repeated.

Abernathy unwound the envelope's string and emptied its contents on his lap: Crisp ten dollar bills that would carry him for a couple of weeks, an empty pad, pencils and a sheaf of papers. He quickly pocketed the money and studied the black lettering typed across the marked pages.

"What's this?" Abernathy said, shaking the papers.

"It's the code," Samuels said.

"I know that. What's the language of origin? Can't help you if I don't know the language."

The two army men said nothing for a moment before Samuels responded: "English."

"Brit or American?"

"You have a week," Samuels replied.

The two officers reached their car, a blue Studebaker, but Samuels looked at the black Lincoln parked across the street. He nodded. Two men, fedoras pulled tight on their brow stared back and nodded in return . . . all business.

Scratching his bald scalp, Abernathy studied the text. He moved to the window and pushed back the blanket with his elbow; sunlight pierced the filthy glass. Abernathy normally preferred the dark.

The apartment was a sty by his Princeton standards and a hundred pounds heavier for all the dirt; too poor to even waste garbage by throwing it away. Abernathy squandered nothing, from the thread-worn blanket to the preserves tins under the sink that he used as a poor man's china. The little cannibalized furniture that survived winter's firewood stock wasn't fit for a beast, but he'd stopped caring. His delight was a rare bit of golden escape called whiskey, which provided him with all the sense he needed — when he could afford it. Truth be told, he didn't care much about working for Uncle Sam, the same kin who tossed him out in 1928. But work was work, and his ego sorely needed something to fill his days. Abernathy had a desperate itch that needed tending. It craved challenge, the opportunity to stretch its legs.

Abernathy hadn't tasked his mind for some time. The rusty cogs of his brain struggled to budge even though he relished the notion of drinking away the money and showing nothing for it but piss.

There wasn't a finer "thank you" to Uncle Sam that Abernathy could imagine.

The government marooned him, after he slaved for the Black Chamber, deciphering their codes and enduring nightmares . . . they fired him. At least the nightmares were finally gone; no more trying to decipher the code scratched on the teeth of a dog whose jaws were at his throat. The alienation and isolation never left, though. It lingered with a sour stink. It was all he could do to shave in the morning or keep the apartment proper. These small actions had become reflex now — something to wile away the day in a world that no longer wanted him.

Abernathy needed purpose. He needed structure.

A knock at the door startled the old code-breaker. It was quick and light, a hummingbird's rap. Abernathy smiled and opened the door for the young, soot-faced ten-year old from next door — Jonathan. Jon was black-haired and had too much lip for his age. He smiled — which meant his pops hadn't disciplined him today — and he wore his "lucky" knickerbockers and wool tweed cap. He called them lucky, though Abernathy suspected he only owned two pairs of clothing.

"Hi, Mr. Abernathy," Jon said. "Saw them leathernecks knocking at your door."

"They needed help," Abernathy said. He dropped into the armchair and waited for Jon to sit down for their daily chess match.

Jon noticed the envelope and papers. "They bring that?"

Abernathy smiled. Jon was a bright kid; would be brighter if his old man didn't dull him with a regular tarring.

"What they bring?"

Abernathy handed Jon the papers. He could read, but this was way above his head. Jon stared at the code, mouthing the words, juggling them on his tongue.

"This some foreign language?" Jon asked. His brows furrowed and he studied the text, part frustration and part curiosity all rolled into the intense scrunched-up face of a 10-year old.

Something about the text demanded uttering, it seemed.

"Ayụn, Cthulhu akhŭ́d e' akul," Jon said.

The words looked hard, but they slipped off the boy's tongue with ease and swelled inside the apartment. They danced through Abernathy's ears and back out his mouth; he had to utter them himself. The words rolled on his tongue with the friction of mercury, like he was born to them. His lips parted, eager to repeat them, but hesitated. He recognized that particular version of stage-fright, the moment the actor takes the still stage before his voice becomes the first thing the audience hears. Mouthing the words, Abernathy's lungs filled with air. The words took root in his breast, but he said nothing.

"What's it mean, Mr. Abernathy?" Jon asked.

Abernathy took the paper and pushed away the chessboard. He set the paper on the table. Somehow, this seemed for more interesting than their weekly match. "Let's find out, shall we?" Abernathy offered. He picked up the pencil and pad. He felt strangely elated . . . useful, directed, for the first time in years even though the code seemed relatively easy. At first glance, it appeared an almost straight monoalphabetic substitution, one alphabet set replacing another.

"They didn't hide the spacing, punctuation or even word frequency," Abernathy said.

"This like spy stuff? Hot dog!"

Abernathy half-smiled, but the text would not be ignored. It ran its fingers along his jaw and pulled his gaze back to the page. Several words repeated over and over again, mostly flanked by the same sets of letters.

"It can't be this simple."

"What, Mr. Abernathy?"

"Here," Abernathy said. "The spacing and high frequency of repeated words must be part of the code, or — a red herring."

It surprised Abernathy how easily the process came back to him. Within moments of studying the text, he was breaking it down, taking tallies of each letter, their spacing, their relation to other letters and the intervals between repeated words. There was something inviting about the text, like slipping your cold hand into a warm glove. He forgot his anger, his isolation. Only the words mattered now and, despite their simplicity, they possessed a seemingly infinite scope of nuances that Abernathy could only imagine.

When Abernathy looked up again, Jon was gone, and the sun slanted low in the sky, skipping its light across rooftops. Abernathy panicked and raced to the window.

It's dusk. How many hours had passed? When did Jon leave? Abernathy looked around the apartment, but he was indeed alone. He shook his head and rinsed his face in the sink. He flicked away a bold roach from the countertop.

Abernathy always lost track of time while working, but it was never this severe. He felt bad for ignoring Jon, but the ease with which the text engulfed him poured the cold water of fear through his intestines. There was something strange about the code. It had taken him half the pad before he concluded the text was some strange cipher using multiple alphabets. Still the frequency of the letters confused him, as did their cadence. Maybe they had mathematical values ascribed to them, or–

"Maybe they used beats as part of their code." Abernathy tried reading the text while tapping his foot, but it didn't carry the rhythm well. In fact, the count seemed deliberately jarring; Abernathy found his cadence tripping over itself every time he settled into a rhythm. It also didn't help that his neighbor's radio rested against the wall, warbling distorted tunes from the *American Album of Familiar Music.*

"Damn it, Celia," Abernathy said, cursing the wall. He stopped using the tempo. It prodded him in all the wrong ways, agitating and unsettling him. No, the code surpassed the transitory, hollow notes of today's music, but they were words to sing; at least that seemed certain.

The sleeping hours had settled in but Abernathy read by the open window. There was a gnawing familiarity about the code, like he was on the verge of understanding one word, or perhaps all of them. It was a suspended revelation — Damocles holding his breath — a moment when everything would emerge into the light, a moment just outside of his reach. He waited for the revelation to come (*arrive*) but it lingered beyond his grasp. He wasn't owed this pleasure yet.

Abernathy remembered several lines of the text without prompting. He paced around the apartment, reciting the sentences, burning them into his brain with the frenzy of a tent-revival preacher memorizing passages from the bible. He was fervent and holy in his works. He belonged again, though the "where" of that statement eluded him.

"Mgh'rib lgan' Cthulhu Cthulhu m'nakul," Abernathy said, uttering the words for the pure pleasure of them alone. "Cthulhu akhùd."

My God, he thought. *How the words carry power.*

Cthulhu m'akhùd e' akűl

Abernathy awoke on the couch, startled by the voice, the one closer to him then his own hammering heart. His arms swept the black void before he even remembered his own name.

A soft hiss filled the room, a chorus of vipers singing their serenade through the walls. Old Celia had left on her radio again; probably asleep in her armchair. She coughed, a wet, puckered affair by the sound of it. Abernathy calmed down.

I just dreamt the voice, that's all, he thought, *the words plucked from the static sea*. Still, Abernathy heard distorted voices on the radio. He got up from the legless couch and shuffled over to the wall. The voices grew stronger, but incoherent still. It seemed like a parade of consonants. He could almost understand the words . . . .

Mgh..lgan . . . Cthul . . . Cth . . . u m . . . kul

Abernathy shook his head. He was imagining things. He didn't know the time, but it was probably well after 2:00 a.m. No program played this late. Yet, there it was, or rather, there he was, moving to the wall, full of excitement and anxious butterflies. He reached out to touch the wall — his fingers stumbled across a glossy black cockroach almost invisible in the dark. It skittered away.

The voices were stronger, but still warbled.

Abernathy pressed his ear against the wall.

The static stopped. Abruptly.

Cockroaches, hundreds to the wall, skittered off in mad directions. Some raced down and away, into those cracks that only roaches knew existed. Others ran over Abernathy's hands and head.

Abernathy screamed and flailed his arms, throwing and brushing away unwanted passengers. A few scurried down his undershirt and up his pant-legs for safety. Abernathy danced in mad steps and dervish spins, trying to remove his clothing, trying to remove the roaches.

The phantom brush of tiny, hair-like legs raced over Abernathy's body, even in the hours after his brisk night walk. Their ephemeral stroke never really left him, and occasionally overwhelmed his resolve; Abernathy's hand shot to the offending spot, brush-slapping away the specter touch till skin stung and turned red; until his flesh was too numb to feel anything. The only refuge he found was in the code. In fact, he left the apartment that evening, with the pad and code in tow, half-aware of the late-hour. What did he care, though? He didn't belong among civilized society.

So why am I beholden to its rules?

Abernathy forced himself to stay out, despite the pull, the need, to return back home. The outside was abrasive and harsh, not like the comfortable womb of the four walls he knew. But he felt uneasy about the roaches and his growing desire to stay home worried him. Return he did, however, the next morning, a scrawl of dead-end theories, frequency charts, failed mathematical assumptions and even musical notes and word beats covering the writing pad. He felt invigorated nonetheless, closer to some startling revelation. Still, he needed a break; he spent the morning searching for roaches in the cupboards, under piles of clothing, in the sink, bathroom and every dark corner where they normally hid and schemed. Nothing. No roaches to kill or drive away. Nothing to remind him of last night.

Abernathy stockpiled the furniture and everything from his living room and kitchen into his rarely-used bedroom. The endeavor cost him precious daylight, but by dusk, the living room was almost empty save for the couch where he slept . . .

. . . the couch where Jonathan now sat very still, mouthing the words to the code.

Abernathy suddenly realized Jonathan had arrived that very morning. He'd forgotten that Jon was even here, and vaguely remembered him mumbling: "Couldn't sleep" when he walked in. His eyes were swollen and dark, as though stung by his nightmares.

"Hey there," Abernathy said softly, touching Jonathan's shoulder. "Aren't you hungry or something?"

Jonathan shook his head.

"Shouldn't you be going home?"

Jonathan nodded and shuffled to the door. He turned, scratching an encrusted patch of white skin on his elbow. Abernathy found it growing on the back of his own neck and gingerly tore away flakes whenever he was alone, or thought he was alone.

"Mr. Abernathy? What's cthonic mean?"

The question caught Abernathy off-guard.

"It means infernal. Why? Where did you hear that word?"

Jon shook his head, uncertain.

"Jon?" Abernathy asked, sensing that it somehow pertained to the code, "where did you hear that word?"

Jon kept his back turned. "In my dream," he said. "The bugs were singing that word before . . .."

"Before what?"

Jon looked back. His eyes were bloodshot and bruised. "I can't remember," Jon said. "They sang a lot of stuff — before they ate my eyes."

Jon shuffled out, leaving the door open.

It must have been Saturday night. Snippets of big band tunes filtered through the wall late into the evening, a live broadcast from Lucille's, a local nightclub. Abernathy enjoyed the throaty brass notes the best — made it easier to ignore his neighbor, Ed McCarthy, who was beating "sense" into Jon. For the first time, though, the boy didn't cry out. That seemed to infuriate his father even more, who shouted, "Stop staring at me, goddammit!"

The living room was blissfully empty, and Abernathy could absorb its entirety without distraction. This stark, Spartan simplicity brought him a calm comfort, like no other worries mattered. It felt good to be free of mortal clutter; a tranquility to the openness; a sense of purity and possibility waiting in the faded wallpaper and warped floorboards. Abernathy couldn't explain it, but somehow, pushing away everything felt like renewal; rejection of the world that turned its back on him.

If Abernathy was happy tonight, it was also because of his handiwork. It seemed a fitting tribute to the code whose meaning eluded him. He felt like the artist given a chance to sketch the nude of a woman he secretly loved. During the day, he purchased sticks of compressed charcoal, which he used to transcribe the pages of code across one wall, the one covered with roaches the night before. The code now veneered the wall from ceiling to floor, but seeing it all here, in one glance, felt right. Abernathy had difficulty unlocking the text because it was scattered across several pages. The words carried a grand weight, too large for mere paper. They represented a greater whole of something, something Abernathy wanted to partake in; something Abernathy knew was best read in one glance. Still, even here, on the wall, it was like trying to appreciate the enormity of the cosmos through a magnifying glass.

Abernathy pulled the couch to face the wall, and sat there, absorbing the immensity of the code. The words ran off his tongue, wet and slippery, and drank his skin with ice-water cool on a hot day. He was intimately familiar with the phrases . . . knew them by heart. Staring at the wall, he pawed at another charcoal stick, and wrote on the floor before falling asleep.

"Mgh'rib lgan' Cthulhu Cthulhu m'nakul," Abernathy muttered, and dreamt of deep stone vaults hidden beneath fog-drenched, country towns. And throughout all his terrible journeys, he felt connected to greater things than his own growing estrangement from humanity.

Static drifted into the room and the cockroaches on the wall sat patiently. And they watched.

Abernathy ignored the knocking at the door at first. It was distant, like hearing it on the radio. Only when it became incessant, a stream of interruptions, did Abernathy answer.

He opened the door a crack. He didn't want anyone to see the room, the marked floor, the walls, the ceiling. Nobody could appreciate this. They didn't deserve it.

"What?"

"Mr. Abernathy," Samuels said, trying to look into the room. Adams stood behind him. It was obvious in Adams' expression that he saw some change in Abernathy that horrified him. Perhaps it was because Abernathy's irises had leaked, the green yolk of two cooked eggs hemorrhaging onto the white plate of the sclera. Maybe it was the eczema covering his arms and neck. Samuels, however, didn't react.

Panic welled in Abernathy's throat. He'd lost track of time. "Is it a week already?"

"No, not yet. You still have two days. May we come in?"

"No!" Abernathy said, then blinked at the hard bite to his voice. He softened his tone. "I don't like being disturbed when I'm working."

Samuels nodded, measuring Abernathy in quick glances. "Just asking."

"I'm fine."

"You — uh — don't need nothing?" Adams asked. "I got a fresh pad here."

"No. I'm fine." With that, Abernathy closed the door.

"Okay then," Samuels said, calling out. "Two days."

The two men walked away, their footsteps fading. Suddenly, an impulse struck Abernathy and he yanked the door open. Samuels and Adams turned around.

"I wanted to ask. The code. Where's it from?"

Samuels shrugged. "It's just a test, Mr. Abernathy. Why?"

Abernathy shook his head and retreated back into the doorway. He didn't vocalize his concerns because it would acknowledge a suspicion and reveal some crucial truth to the two men: That the code didn't sound like a code at all in his head.

It sounded like chanting.

Two days passed. Abernathy ate only when hunger pierced his stomach and drank only when his dried lips split. He scratched at the strange crust on his body that cracked when he moved. He was a mystic hermit in his personal corner of the Sinai Desert. He hadn't seen Jon in days.

The code covered the living room — ceiling and floor included — and Abernathy walked between the words, in the negative spaces, out of some unfathomable reverence, the kind where fear and fidelity lost their distinction. His footsteps felt like punctuation to the sentences, and any misstep would interrupt the sentence in the wrong place.

Abernathy spent hours on the floor naked, staring at the ceiling — his arcane, alien sky. There was no longer the pretense of deciphering the code, because, Abernathy realized, there was no language to understand. The code was brilliant. It embodied concepts, not facts, and each word contained a terrible infinity in their uttering. That was their cruelty and blessing. Transcribing the code from paper to wall helped encompass the entirety of the text, but now, even the room proved an inadequate canvas.

The code would not be contained.

It spilled through the walls, into the adjoining apartments. It touched upon Abernathy's neighbors, irrevocably overwriting them with its nature. Abernathy no longer heard the distinct steps of the upstairs neighbor, Mr. Ansel. Instead, Mr. Ansel shuffled about, dragging a dead, wet mass across the floor. Abernathy could even see water stains spreading and growing across his own ceiling. McCarthy was also different. He cried all the time now, afraid of the unblinking little boy he locked in the closet, afraid of the scratching at the door that would soon claw its way out. Even Celia changed. Her radio did little to mask her beleaguered wheezing with each drowning breath, and the radio played only static now.

Mgh'rib lgan' Cthulhu Cthulhu m'nakul, akhüd'ana Cthulhu akhüd'ana . . .

Mostly static.

Abernathy moved to the wall, listening. He could barely hear the radio, but the words filtering through were unmistakable. It was the code, leaking out from the room. It could not be contained and Abernathy needed to hear more.

The voices chanted, but their pronunciation differed from his. More now than ever, Abernathy believed he was close to comprehending the text, to grasping its inky, slippery significance, but . . . but he couldn't hear the radio well enough. It faced away from the wall, toward Celia, who didn't deserve the honor of listening. Uncle Sam gave *him* the code. It was intended for *him* alone. She was eavesdropping, a pitiful insect . . .

. . . a tick on a God's ass.

Careful not to step on the words, Abernathy jumped from one clear spot to another on his way to the door. He left his apartment, unashamed by his naked and encrusted body, and knocked at his neighbor's door.

No answer.

He hammered again, a furious fusillade that sent his shoulder into the door in a moment of sudden rage. It broke open with a terrible wooden crack and Abernathy stumbled into Celia's apartment.

The dwelling was a modest affair with all the humble, but proud trimmings of poverty; plain wood furniture, faded drapes and unimportant knickknacks adorned the shelves. Celia sat in the living room, on a simple chair, her once sharp, bird-like features distorted. Her pale flesh held the consistency of melted tallow and her face hung several inches from her skull, stretching her features. She coughed and wheezed, her esophagus loose and filling her airway with folds of overlapping flesh. She was melting slowly, both inside and out. Celia moved, sending ripples across drooping skin. She tried speaking, but was too weak to move her sagging lips or contract her stretched, flaccid muscles. A pitiful hiss escaped her lips. She tried looking at Abernathy, but her eyes merely hung in the loose slings of her eyelids.

On the common wall between the two apartments, Abernathy's code appeared in mirrored reverse of what he'd transcribed, a greasy stain eating its way through the wallpaper. The radio was also there, chest-high, blocky and veneered in dark mahogany. A bronze statue of a robe-draped woman lay atop the radio. No noise issued from its speaker grill, however, neither static nor voice. Puzzled, Abernathy approached, ignoring Celia's pathetic, desperate mewling. The radio's wood façade was smashed, as was the speaker. She'd broken the dials and ripped out its entrails.

The radio was dead; had been for days.

"What have you done?" Abernathy reached for the cold bronze statue and approached the old woman. Standing over her, he raised the statue high above his head, a naked Neanderthal ready to slaughter his kill with a heavy rock.

"What have you DONE!"

The man in the fedora was a bruiser by all accounts, thick in the neck and thin on civility. He stood on the sidewalk next to the black Lincoln, a cigarette cradled in the corner of his mouth. He stared up at the second floor, catching telling hints of movement. Blood hit Celia's window. Unperturbed, the man bent down and spoke to the Lincoln's driver though the open window.

"It's time. I'll call Samuels."

Abernathy stumbled back into his apartment, blood-splattered and barely aware of himself. The code had obliterated his name, but he didn't care. He stepped clear of the words on the floor without even looking and lay down in his small, untouched island, staring at his arcane sky. He could still hear the static; the reception was much clearer, now — more distinct.

Mgh'rib lgan' Cthulhu akhüd'ana.

The written words trembled and a dozen roaches broke free from formation, skittering elsewhere and forming new words with their black, glossy bodies, new lines to the ever-protean code. At first, the roaches scared Abernathy, but they proved docile, even willing, when he picked one up, then spelled out his first word using their bodies. One by one, he placed them until they acted on their own to denote the text. One by one, they stayed in place, changing only to reveal new portions of the puzzle. Now Abernathy understood how the code could not be contained, and even spilled out into life itself.

And so Abernathy lay there, listening to the static and the text submerged beneath ... words that surfaced like a great leviathan of the starry oceans that only breaches the waves with its mountain-like fins. More roaches appeared through cracks in the floor and walls, and formed new sentences, filling the lines between lines and covering every available space. They ran and skittered over Abernathy's naked skin, forming words and sentences across his body, incorporating him into the code. Abernathy sank into the floor, melting away any distinction between himself and his surroundings. He didn't mind.

The wood planks sent splintered shivers into Abernathy's raw organs and impaled his flesh. Iron nails pushed through his skin and pressed slowly into his brains and lungs, becoming part of him. He could taste the wood and iron. Abernathy opened his eyes once, to see one cockroach on the bridge of his nose. Its antennas twitched, searching for the right frequency to break through the static. And it sang to Abernathy, joining the chorus of roaches filling the room, their voices a choir of static . . . their serenade to the chthonic ancients . . .

. . . his radio to the Gods.

And they welcomed Abernathy. Welcomed him home.

Adams pulled alongside the black Lincoln and stared up at the building. It was night, but he could see a crawling, writhing black mass covering Abernathy's windows.

Samuels leaned forward, looking through the car's windshield. He saw it, too. He rolled down his window.

"He killed his neighbor, an old dame," the Lincoln's driver said.

"That would be Celia Macula," Samuels said. "Any others?"

"Apartments above and below his are acting queer. We checked on his other neighbor. The kid–" The driver, choked; he had some difficulty finishing the sentence.

Samuels nodded. "Save it for your report. We're done here. Torch the building. Nothing gets out. I want everything in cinders. Use the petrol."

The two goons nodded and drove away slowly, to an adjoining alley.

Adams looked at Samuels, his mouth screwed up in a question that needed asking, his manner apprehensive.

"Spit it out," Samuels said with a sigh.

"I know we ain't supposed to ask questions."

"Ask."

"Are they actually gonna use the code, sir? I mean we know it works pretty damn good, now."

"What do you think?"

"Yeah . . . I guess — I just feel sorry for the poor code-breakers they use this against."

"It's one way of dealing with eavesdroppers."

Adams stared up at Abernathy's window.

"What?" Samuels said.

"What — what if it gets out, like it did in New England?"

"It'll only get out when we need it to, and even then, only piecemeal, like with Abernathy."

"You certain?"

"Yeah," Samuels said, confident and full of Army steel. "We got it contained."

WYSHES.COM

RICHARD A. LUPOFF

THE REASON MOST CLICHÉS are clichés, I think, is that they express an idea well. Once some clever bozo formulates the idea to perfection there's no reason to concoct another way of putting it, so everybody hops on the first guy's phrase and away we go.

Away we go.

Right.

See, I do it myself. I guess we all do.

For instance, "Be careful what you wish for, you just might get it." That, or minor variations on it, have been around for years, and I'll bet a nickel that no day goes past without some pundit using it for the title of a newspaper column or some screenwriter putting it into a script. You doubt that? Paste it into your search engine and see how many hits you get.

And as for me, I was tired of living in the 'burbs. Sunnyvale strikes me as an up-scale, latter-day Levittown for the technologically hip and the economically ambitious. I bought a house there for my family when my wife and I were still getting along and our very little girl was a daily ray of sunshine for us both.

Well, fifteen years and one divorce later, the dotcom boom and bust have swept through our happy little suburb, my daughter wants to go live with her mother because men just don't understand women (and she's right about that one!), and I manage to sell the house for a decent price. Enough to get me into a new condo on Drumm Street in San Francisco and even put a few bucks in the bank. I can see the Bay

Bridge and the Bay itself and the lights of Oakland and environs from my living room window.

For a while I made a decent living, most of it by telecommuting, although I must confess that business has been slow of late and I've been casting worried if not panicked glances at my bank account. I do enjoy the variety and color of the city instead of trying to play Jim Anderson of the old *Father Knows Best* sitcom with my own daughter as innocent young Betty. I tried hitting the singles bars briefly but I quit that when I discovered they were full of twenty-year-olds and forty-year-olds trying to look twenty. I didn't want to fall into that pit!

Online dating was something else, and I was amazed at the women I met there. People my own age who shared my attitudes and interests. It was easy to sort out the ones who just wanted to get laid — not that there's anything wrong with that — and the ones who never wanted to get laid — and before I knew it I was hooked up with a lovely, mature, intelligent woman. She had her place, I had my place, we enjoyed each other's company, and it looked as if the relationship was actually going to have legs.

The only problem, in fact, came from her name. Martha Washington, would you believe it? She's some kind of remote cousin, many times removed, of Our First President. The surname was tough enough but her parents apparently thought it would be fun to name their child for the First, First Lady. After enough years of ribbing and a couple of marriages and divorces (and who am I to criticize on that score?), she decided to take back her maiden name and make it a point of pride rather than an embarrassment.

Well, good for Martha, says I. Besides, she loves good music, she cooks well (as do I), she makes fascinating conversation, and we please each other in bed. A lot.

So it looks as if I came out of my divorce really well, not even hating my ex or being hated by her, and living the pleasant life of a middle-aged single in the first decade of this the twenty-first century.

Then Ed Guenther phoned.

"Can you come in for a meeting, Webster?"

I asked him what about.

"We've got a project we'd like you to consult on."

Okay, that meant at least a day's pay at a fat hourly fee. It would mean renting a car; I'd dumped my faithful Saab when I sold the Sunnyvale house, but I'd hit Ed for the rental. If my business had been booming I would have played hard to get, but revenues were down and I was, to put it mildly, starting to feel uneasy around the money belt. Even so, I wanted a little more info before I agreed.

"You had that experience with the Dreems.biz outfit, Web."

I grunted.

"I know you were pretty upset by the end of it. Felt they were doing some dangerous stuff."

That was an understatement. Dreems.biz pretty well scrambled my brain, and I don't know how many others. The Feds got into the act and the company quietly disappeared and its founding guru and CEO, a sharpy named Carter Thurston Hull, did the same. Where was he now, St. Elizabeth's? Guantanamo? Rumania? Just try asking, but if you do, don't blame me for what happens to you next.

"We know you were pretty upset by the end of the gig, Web."

"Sure, Ed, if you call six months in the bin alternating between ultra-high-dose tranks and intensive therapy sessions being pretty upset."

"Well, but you know what that stuff is like, and we think you can give us some important help with a new product." He paused for effect. I knew Ed Guenther well enough to know that he was sitting with his eyes closed, counting down, ". . . four, three, two, one . . ." And then he would open his eyes, inhale sharply, and get rolling again. I also noticed that he was bouncing back and forth between *I* and *we*, another favorite trick of his. Was he talking for himself or was he talking for Silicon Research Labs, Inc? *I* or *we?*

Good old Ed. I'd worked with him before and he was a pretty good guy. Pretty good. But I wouldn't exactly trust him with the only can opener on the island if we were marooned with a case of canned goods and no other source of nourishment.

"Actually it's more than a product, Webster. It's an important new tool. It's really exciting. I think you're going to love this one."

A quick glance at the calendar, a mental calculation of my bank balance and current cash flow, and I made an appointment to spend a day at SRL, Silicon Research Labs, Incorporated, and find out what Ed Guenther had up his sleeve.

The car I rented was a hybrid. I figure I can't reverse global warming — I wish I could! — or even stop it but at least I can limit the damage that I personally do to this planet. I cruised down 280, pulled into a visitor's slot at SRL, and told the five-year-old receptionist that Mr. Sloat was here to see Mr. Guenther.

Ed bustled into the lobby, curly iron-gray hair in need of a trim, five o'clock shadow on his jaw even at ten in the morning, striped sleeves rolled up, and grabbed my hand in a paw the size of a catcher's mitt. He put his arm around my shoulders and practically carried me off to a conference room. There were half a dozen Silicon Valley types there. A couple looked old enough to have survived the big meltdown. The rest were members of the new generation. I felt a rush of relief that I wasn't making the Union Street singles bars, trying to compete with the likes of these kids. They looked as if they belonged on the campus at Stanford or Berkeley but I knew they were already looking over their shoulders at the next generation of grads.

Before we got started, Ed delivered a little lecture on the fact that we were going to be exposed to classified information and under penalty of fine or imprisonment and yada-yada-yada. There was nothing there I hadn't heard a dozen times before, and I signed the confidential disclosure form with my trusty Cross ball-point that I'd got from a onetime employer for completing five years of honorable service.

There were carafes of coffee on the table, fake leather folders with the SRL logo emblazoned on the covers, and freshly sharpened pencils for all. Obviously, they were out to impress good old Webster Sloat. Frankly, it made me apprehensive. I opened my folder, trying to look casually curious, and found nothing inside but a fresh pad of lined paper with a different logo ghosted in the middle of each page. It was an abstract sketch that might have been a spiral nebula crossed with a happy face with just a suggestion of God as we know and love Him from Michelangelo's Sistine Chapel painting. The lettering WYSHES.COM ran across it.

Ed Guenther introduced me to the gang. Most likely they'd been briefed in advance. That's the way Ed worked. But he went over my sterling credentials, credited me with heroic public service in the Dreems.biz affair, considerately overlooked the fact that I'd wound up in the cuckoo's nest after it was over. Then he turned the meeting over to the genius whose work I was supposed to support.

Her name was Miranda Nguyen. She squinted through Harry Potter glasses. Her face was makeup-free. She was as tall as I was and must have weighed sixty-five pounds. She was wearing a Xena Warrior Princess tee shirt that had clearly seen better days. I'm sure she washed her hair on occasion but I wouldn't want to guess how often that occurred.

When Miranda stood up I was afraid for a moment that she was going to topple over. She righted herself, flicked on a computer-fed image projector, switched off the overhead lights and started to lecture.

She did not lose me with her first word, or even with her first sentence, but by the middle of what must have been her first paragraph I was floundering and before I could finish a cup of hot SLR Custom Roast Mocha Java I realized that I had no idea what she was talking about.

Well, almost no idea. I'd made my living for the past decade turning the jargon of programmers and circuit designers and systems engineers into at least semi-literate and somewhat understandable prose. I bore down and managed to get at least the gist of Ms. Nguyen's pitch. She had reverse-engineered the software that my old buddy Carter Thurston Hull had used to make his *dreems* seem realer than real. Apparently Miranda knew that he'd also come within a hair's breadth of wrecking my brain, and God knows what he did to how many other customers. But Miranda Nguyen had developed some *mixed-ware* — circuitry plus programming — that she claimed would work better than Hull's and would be perfectly safe for the user.

I believed her, every word.

And there's that nice new Bay Bridge they're working on at this very moment, and if you'd like to buy it from Yours Truly, I'm sure we could strike a really attractive bargain.

Ms. Nguyen sat down to a smattering of applause from her colleagues and Ed Guenther introduced the next genius. Alberto Salazar. Alberto Salazar from NASA Ames, a few miles up the freeway from Silicon Research Labs. Alberto was Mexican from the top of his glossy black hair to the tips of his tan fingers. Mexican, yes, but I had a feeling that he was a full-blooded Mayan or something close to it. He had an accent you could cut *con una cuchilla.* And he was living proof that we need all the smart immigrants we can get, *con documentación o sin.*

And he didn't mince words, accent or no accent.

"There are aliens," he said. "They're not here, they're not little greenies or busty blond princesses or monsters who want to cook us for dinner, Rod Serling and Damon Knight notwithstanding."

He paused and I guessed it was my turn to contribute something, even if it was only a question. "They don't zip around in flying saucers or abduct fishermen from Mississippi, then?"

"Nope. We're not sure where they are, but they're probably very far from Earth. There's some debate in NASA as to whether they're on the other side of the galactic disk or in another galaxy altogether."

"Are they a threat?" I asked.

"As far as I know they're totally unaware that we even exist."

"Then why trouble trouble?"

"Good question." Alberto smiled. "Again, some of our people say we should just pull our heads in and hope they never notice us. Others think we need to go out and say hello, take a risk if we need to, see what happens."

"What do you think, Alberto?"

"Who, me? I'm just a humble astronomer. My ancestors had the chance to wipe out their first European visitors and they didn't. So it's risky, I can't deny it. Still, Mr. Sloat, it's a basic philosophical question. Do we want to be *tortugas o iguanas?*"

"You lost me," I said. "I know what an iguana is but what's a tortuga?"

"Sorry," he said.

I didn't think for a split second he was sorry.

"Sorry," he repeated. "That means *turtles or iguanas.* Do we want to pull our heads in, hide in our shells, and hope nobody notices us, or do we want to get out there and move, make friends if we can or fight like hell if we have to. That was the mistake my ancestors made. They were ready to make friends but they weren't ready to fight, and they wound up in chains. But enough of that. What do you think about playing *Let's Make a Deal* with alien critters?"

"Not my field," I told him. "You want the SETI people, don't you? Or maybe Spielberg?"

"No, Mr. Sloat. We want you."

I felt my brain racing. All I could do was ask the obvious question. "Why me?"

"Because you've experienced *dreems* and lived to tell the tale. You emerged from the experience with your sanity intact." He shot a glance at another of the conferees, a black-skinned guy in a suit, the only one I'd seen at SRL.

The only suit, that is, not the only black-skinned individual.

The suit nodded almost imperceptibly, emphasize *almost*, and Salazar kept on going. "You'll hear from Mr. Armstrong shortly. But for now, I'll just beg your indulgence. Okay?"

"Okay." I don't think he caught my Señor Wences impression. "Before you go any further, suppose you tell me how you know these Martians or whoever the hell they are, are out there."

Salazar said, "Miranda?"

Okay, it was Miss Saigon Olive Oyl's turn again.

The giant stringbean put a picture on the screen. I had no idea what it was, a neutron bomb detonator or a new model can opener. There was even a caption underneath the schematic that told me nothing.

"In attempting to resolve the Einsteinian FTL dilemma and achieve tachyonic acceleration," Miranda Nguyen piped — did I tell you that she had a reedy, almost incomprehensible way of speaking? — "we felt that a first modest attempt at ultra-high-speed data transmission would be a suitable preliminary to sending matter through a Hawking-Murray-Disch destabilizing filter."

"Good for you," I muttered under my breath.

"We were unable to achieve our goals," she told her tee shirt — anybody else who wanted to listen in, could — "but the Law of Unintended Consequences kicked in and we picked up signals. At first we thought they were random radiation, just as early researchers thought that cosmic rays were messages and our friends at SETI did when they first turned on their giant arrays and got instant results. So we were very cautious about what we were getting, but after a while we were able to translate them into visuals."

"Don't tell me they were old *I Love Lucy* episodes." I know I was being nasty but by this time I couldn't help it.

"No, Mr. Sloat." She didn't bat an eye. Go figure. "They were not old *I Love Lucy* episodes. Not even early *South Parks*. I'll show you what we got."

She tinkered with her Power Point gadget and the screen lit up with something that looked vaguely like two bright pink pool balls and something that I couldn't really describe except that it looked a little like an ebony marble, all in a row. Whatever the something was, my eyes, to be honest, just couldn't deal with it. Or maybe my brain was incapable of processing the signal that came zooming up the optic nerve.

"What do you think of that, Mr. Sloat?"

"Deponent knoweth not what he see-eth," I told her.

"It's a complex star system," Salazar put in. "Three stars locked in a gravitational gavotte."

"I see two pink objects that I suppose could be stars," I conceded, "but what's that — that other thing?"

"We're not quite sure. Most likely it's a neutron star. We've consulted with some of the best brains in the world, even got to Coleman at Harvard. Lots of suggestions. No certainties. If it's a neutron star, it must have gone nova at some point in time. And if that's the case, it should have destroyed its two partners. Obviously it didn't."

"And you got this image — how?" I asked.

Miranda Nguyen actually flashed me a grin. "I picked it up and decoded it. And we have plenty of others, Mr. Sloat. Treat yourself to a gander at this one."

Treat myself to a gander. Right.

She flashed through a rapid series of images, finally settled on one that showed the two pink stars much more faintly than I'd seen them before. "This took a lot of tweaking," she said, "but we were finally able to get this far."

The image on the screen showed the two pink stars and the I-had-no-way-to-describe-it thingumbob, and several tiny disks apparently caught in mid-flight between them.

I asked, "Are those planets?"

Alberto Salazar said, "Probably."

Miranda Nguyen played with her tinker toy a little more. The two pink stars and the thingumbob grew still fainter, the things that Salazar said were probably planets grew larger, and some specks no larger than single pixels appeared, dancing like dust motes in a sunbeam.

"Jesus."

"You got it, Web." Ed Guenther switched on the overhead lights. "End of slide show. Our Trip to Yosemite, preserved for the ages." He paused and looked around. I hadn't made so much as a doodle in my nice leatherette SRL folder.

I said, "I'll bet I can guess what Wyshes.com does."

Ed Guenther said, "I'll bet you can."

One thing about SRL, they don't skimp. It was time for a lunch break and our hosts treated us to limp sandwiches on balloon bread and bottled water, followed by coffee or something that I guess was supposed to be coffee. Was it stale or just weak?

As the great Nero Wolfe used to say, *Pfui!*

The afternoon session was at least shorter than the morning had been. The star performer was Robert Armstrong from NIMH. Since everybody else in the room knew each other before I arrived, I wasn't surprised when Armstrong reached across the table to shake my hand and repeat his name.

"Any relation to Carl Denham?" Golly, I thought I was being clever. Either he'd never heard that line before or he was an expert at keeping a poker face. I guessed it was the first and pretended I hadn't heard myself, muttered, "Pleased ta meetcha," and sat back down.

"I've studied Mr. Sloat's file and I want to remind everyone present that Mr. Sloat's privacy rights are very important to the United States government and must be respected by us all."

What the heck?

"Mr. Sloat is unique among the 14,293 known cases of persons victimized by the *Dreems.biz* disorder, in that he apparently achieved a level of complete psychotic dissociation and has fully recovered from said break. Of the other cases, well over 13,000 went into psychic shock as a result of their experience, and emerged with little or no damage but also with little or no memory of their experiences."

Fourteen thousand? I wasn't so egotistical as to think I was the only sucker to fall for Charles Thurston Hull's nasty game, but I had no idea there were that many fools.

"Approximately 1,000 individuals," Armstrong went on, "to be precise, 857, suffered serious damage. Of these, 294 committed suicide, 18 became violent and were killed in accidents or by law enforcement officers, and the remaining 549 remain hospitalized. Their prognosis is not encouraging."

He looked around the table, smiling brilliantly. You'd have thought he had just won the lottery. "Mr. Sloat here, you see, is uniquely qualified to become the subject, should I say the operator, of our newest investigative tool."

"Which," Ed Guenther put in, "we call Wyshes.com."

Guenther had risen to his feet. I don't know why but suddenly he appeared to be at least six inches taller and eighty pounds heavier than anyone else in the room.

After the session I headed back toward San Francisco. Before I pulled onto the freeway I used my cell phone to check calls on my home answering machine. There was one from Martha Washington so I called her back.

She asked if I was busy tonight.

I told her I was not.

She said, "How about dinner out?"

I said I was feeling jangled and had a lot on my mind and could I have a rain check.

She said she thought as much from the sound of my voice and invited me to her place instead. "I'll whip something up, we can drink a glass of wine and listen to some music. I bet you'll feel better."

How could I refuse?

She lives in a restored Victorian in Noe Valley. Built right after the 1906 quake-and-fire, amazing gingerbread trim, bright yellow paint with white trim, high ceilings, cut glass, carved and polished wood. Amazing. Makes my condo look like a Motel 6. Or maybe the Bates Motel, with Tony Perkins ready to jerk back the shower curtain at any moment.

Did I mention that Martha has amazing powers of empathy? She could read my mood like a book. (There, how's that for a cliché?) I showed up on her doorstep after surviving the freeway back from Silicon Valley without even stopping at my condo for a clean-up and fresh clothes. I knew if I tried that I would have flopped on my bed between shower and dressing and that would have been it for good old Webster Sloat.

Another thing I love about Martha is her amazing talent for irony.

She met me in the vestibule of her Queen Anne. Of course, nobody has built a house with a vestibule for seventy-five years at least. She was wearing a satiny copper-colored hostess gown that set off her rich, auburn hair and that showed plenty of cleavage with a tiny diamond-and-pearl pendant just above her sternum. She held a glass of pinot noir from a winery we'd visited together up north in Ukiah. The house was illuminated by candles and there was music playing.

Music.

We'd been exploring some difficult composers for the past couple of months, downloading their works and listening to them — *really* listening to them — at her place or at mine, then trying to find live performances to attend. Not easy when you're into Ives, Schoenberg, Edgar Varese or late John Coltrane from his "sheets of sound" period.

But tonight she had put on a Mozart clarinet concerto. Cool, melodic, just involving enough, not too challenging.

You see what I mean? Hostess gown, candles, wine, Mozart. It was just perfect and it made me feel something in my chest that I didn't think I'd ever feel again, after my divorce. But did Martha have her tongue in her cheek, just a little bit?

I didn't worry about that. I took her in my arms, gave her a warm (not hot) kiss, and accepted the glass of wine. We strolled into her Victorian parlor arm-in-arm and made ourselves comfortable. She must have sensed that I wasn't ready to talk about the day's events so she went first. She works in the Mayor's office and she dotes on City Hall gossip the way a soap fan relishes the latest convolutions of a favorite daytime serial.

The Sewers and Streetlamps Commissioner had her nose out of joint because her most recent boyfriend had left her to take up with her former boyfriend, whom she had lusted after so dearly that she had abandoned her own former girlfriend to be with him. Her former girlfriend had even offered to undergo a sex change if it would just keep her steady squeeze in her bed, but the course of true love was clear, leaving a playing field strewn with angry exes and one couple — was it the Commish herself and her new sweetums? I couldn't quite keep up with the comings and goings — reportedly indulging in a nightly sexual circus that would make the Mitchell Brothers blush.

The whole sequence of events had left the San Francisco political community in a state of sexual confusion.

Martha laid out some *hors d'oeuvres* and we snacked on them, finished the bottle of pinot noir, and kissed and cuddled for a while. The Mozart ended and was replaced by Tchaikovsky's Sixth, a transfer of the old 1959 Carl Maria Giulini version. Somewhere along the way Martha disappeared into the kitchen and returned carrying a cold ahi tuna salad and two forks. How we got from there to her bed I cannot tell you; I think that Tchaikovsky may have wafted us through the air.

We made love, and rested, and made love again, and I was finally ready to talk about my visit to Silicon Research Labs and Wyshes.com.

And Martha was ready to listen. By the time I'd reviewed the events of the day, Ed Guenther's butter-wouldn't-melt-in-his-mouth performance and the pitches of the various bigdomes, Martha was interjecting little hmm's and mm's and mm?'s every time I paused for breath. She seemed particularly intrigued by Robert Armstrong's actions. Why would the National Institutes of Mental Health care about Wyshes.com?

I reminded her that Dreems.biz had walloped almost 15,000 people's sanity, with a variety of outcomes ranging from apparently complete recovery — me — to those poor souls who just couldn't deal with Carter Thurston Hull's nasty gift and took their own lives. Nearly 300 of them.

Martha was sitting against the headboard of her bed by now. She was still naked after our love-making and the flickering candlelight in the room cast a deep shadow between her breasts. I leaned over and planted a kiss right there and she laughed and wrapped her arms around me. She is not a fragile flower.

"Web, I don't want to sound stupid but after everything you've told me I still don't know exactly what this Miranda Nguyen's — what did she call it? —"

"Mixed-ware."

"— what it's supposed to do. And what was that Salazar genius from NASA all about? What do they want you to do? I guess that's the main question, what the hell do they want you to do, Webster?"

"They want me to be the first of a new breed of astronauts. They want me to go play footsie with the aliens. Or potsy. Or poker. Something."

"Not in a spaceship, though." She shook her head. Her medium-long hair swung around her shoulders and made a screen between me and the rest of the world. I wanted to stay inside that screen for good, but I knew that wasn't in the cards.

That wasn't in the cards. Charge one more to my cliché account.

"That's where the Hull events come in." I pushed myself up and stretched. "I'll be right back, Martha." I climbed out of bed and padded to the kitchen. I brought us each a cold mineral water with a slice of lime.

I climbed back into bed with Martha. Jesus, I had a hard time keeping my mind off sex when I was a randy teenager but now that I'm a middle-aged ex-husband with graying hair and the beginning of a pot belly I'm worse than ever. What the hell is the matter with me?

"Okay." I ordered myself to concentrate. "You know, I'm not supposed to talk about this. We could both wind up in the slammer."

"Bull shit, Webster. Come on, spill." Martha is not a blushing rose, either.

"Armstrong says that NASA has been trying to develop an ultra-high-speed communication system. They're serious about sending people to Mars and they don't want the long delay in radio transmissions. Even talking to moon bases involves a little delay, but they can live with that. But once you get much farther away from Earth, it's a serious problem."

I paused to gather my thoughts.

Martha waited.

"They've been trying all sorts of things to get around the speed-of-light problem. Looking for wormholes, trying to produce fourth-dimensional paper-folds, searching for tachyons."

"Science fiction." Martha grinned.

"No," I said. "They're serious about it, and when they set up an experimental transmitter and receiver they started getting messages. I mean, messages that they hadn't sent. Scared the bejesus out of 'em."

Scared the bejesus out of 'em. Rack up another one.

Martha said, "What kind of signals?"

"Visuals." I told her about the three-sun system. I was starting to think of 'em as Big Pink, Little Pink, and Gingrich the Neutron Star. I told her about the planets that didn't so much circle any of those stars as weave among them in a wildly complex dance. And I told her about the dust-motes, if that's what they were, that appeared to weave among the planets. And of course they weren't dust motes. Oh, no. They were certainly not dust motes.

"I ask again, Webster, although I have a feeling I already know the answer, I'll ask you again anyway, What do they want you to do?"

"They want me to go there."

"By super-high-speed wormhole tachyon express?"

"Nope. By Miranda Nguyen's mixed-ware gadget. By Wyshes.com."

Martha swung her legs off the bed and stood between me and a candle. All I could see of her was her silhouette. She said, "You're going."

I said, "You're way ahead of me."

"I'm not trying to influence you."

"I know it. It scares the piss out of me, but I'm going."

Scares the piss out of me. Ding!

"And this will be something like your Dreems.biz experiences?"

"Not very much."

First, Carl Denham's — I mean, Robert Armstrong's — people at NIMH had to run me through every mental health and stability, does this guy have a firm grip on reality, etc., test in the book, plus a couple that I think they made up just for my personal benefit. I won't say that I came through with flying colors but Armstrong did finally sign off.

Every test in the book. Flying colors. Two for the price of one. Whoops! Two for the price of one. Call that a bonus point.

I saw Rorschach blobs variously as grasshoppers, butterflies, Satanic faces, and vaginas. Once I got to vaginas I think Armstrong let a small smile escape. I associated *mother* with *love, rain* with *wet, pencil* with *paper* and *alien* with *Roberto Salazar.* I think that last one upset Armstrong until he decided I was pulling his leg. I balanced on one foot, admitted that I'd experimented with weed and acid and coke in my wild youth and denied that I'd used anything illegal in the past couple of decades. I told him that I'd masturbated as a teenager, had sex with approximately thirty women in my life and with one man. Didn't like the latter and never repeated the experiment. I told him that I thought maybe there was a God and maybe not, I really didn't know.

Oh, was it ever fun.

Armstrong decided I was sane, or at least sane enough to put at risk once I signed the release form that Ed Guenther kindly provided.

I had to pass a pretty rigorous physical, but nothing excessively demanding. After all, I didn't have to sit on top of a giant firecracker and get launched into outer space. I was going to travel by — what? Might as well be honest and go all the way back to Madame Blavatsky and her gang of wild and crazy partiers and call it astral projection.

Miranda Nguyen personally showed me her wonderful gadget, the Wyshes.com device.

Have you ever had a CT Scan? Computerized Tomography? I did, a few years ago. One of my internal organs blew up and the docs at the Cal Pacific Med Center decided they needed a good look at my innards. First I had to drink a cocktail with some kind of gunk in it to make my insides show up. It came in banana and chocolate flavors. I asked the refugee from Romper Room who ran the dispensing station which one she recommended and she said, "Doesn't matter, Mister. Whichever one I suggest you'll drink it and get mad at me because no matter how bad the other one is, this one has to be worse."

Actually I had to do the do a couple of times, once before a surgeon went in and fixed my plumbing and once after he was finished. I tried the banana once and the chocolate once and they were both worse.

Anyhow, Miranda Nguyen's Wyshes.com device looked something like a CT Scanner. There's a big doughnut-shaped thingumy with enough flashing lights on it to make George Lucas wet his pants. You lie down on a powerized gurney and an operator plays Phantom of the Opera at a futuristic looking control panel. The gurney rolls into the giant doughnut and if you're strapped to it, as I was, even for a dry run, you feel as if somebody made a mistake and sent you to the Fisher and Sons Mortuary for cremation.

It took a couple of weeks for everybody to brief me on what to expect and how to react. Then everybody from the cafeteria manager to the corporate comptroller had to sign off. Then they had a little party in my honor, complete with SRL baseball caps and Wyshes.com tee shirts.

And then there was no more putting it off. I sent a text message to Martha Washington's Blackberry, handed the keys to my rented hybrid and my condo to Ed Guenther, transmitted an Internet greeting card to my daughter in care of her mother saying that I loved her, and told my courtiers, "I'm ready."

One of the guards slit the bottoms of my trousers, the chaplain read a few verses from the Bible, and we went a-strolling to the little green Wyshes.com room.

Just kidding.

But it was a creepy feeling. Maybe more like old Boris lying on Dr. Frankenstein's operating table and getting hoisted into the storm than Bogey getting fried in a Warner Brothers gangster epic. Once I was settled comfortably on the gurney, they had to blindfold me and block my ears. An all-out sensory deprivation tank might have served better, but Miranda Nguyen's super-doughnut wouldn't have worked under water. And lying on soft padding pretty well damped out tactile sensations.

So there I was locked inside my skull with nobody for company but myself and nothing to play with but my own thoughts. I tried to imagine the lights flashing and the micro motors whirring, electrons flashing and data gates opening and shutting in Miranda's mixed-ware. I tried to see that picture that Alberto Salazar had showed me of those three stars, Big Pink and Little Pink and Newt, and the planets that wove among them and the dust motes that floated from one to another.

Except I knew they weren't dust motes.

And then I was out of my head. I don't mean crazy, although upon further review maybe I was at that. I didn't feel myself leaving my body and there was none of the light show folderol that Carter Thurston Hull's Dreems.biz provided. It was more like falling asleep, where you're not aware of the transition between waking and dream states. Just that, there you are lying in your bed gazing up at the ceiling or maybe at the inside of your eyelids, and then you're walking on the beach in Maui with a lovely naked maiden, the surf is crashing, the breeze is wafting the odor of jasmine to you and — and how the hell did you get from Smallville, Kansas, to Maui?

No idea, right? No sense of transition, certainly no sensation of travel. Just — you were in one place and then you're in another.

I knew where I was, too. I was out there at Big Pink and Little Pink and Newt. I knew where I was but there's no way I can tell you, exactly. I mean, I wasn't at Betelgeuse or Alpha Centauri or Beta Reticuli or NGC 9999 or any other star that we've cataloged and named.

Oh, no.

If you went all the way to the center of our galaxy, tipped your hat to the black hole that's been sitting there gobbling up matter for the past several billion years, continued to the far side of the galaxy and then jumped off, you would just be starting to go where I was. You'd have to hopscotch over a couple of galactic clusters, hang a couple of sharp curves through the third, fourth, and polka-dot dimensions, reach down your own throat until you came to the inside of your great toe, grab hold and pull with all your might.

You would hear a loud *pop!* and you would have a slight idea of where I was.

Or you could just click your ruby slippers together and say, "I wish, I wish, I wish I was in Kansas!"

Hey, worked for Dorothy Gale, didn't it?

How long did it take me to get there, wherever *there* was? I don't know whether *I know* and can't tell you, or I don't know myself. You know how time passes in a dream? It was a little bit like that. I could have been floating in that sensory-deprived limbo, wondering what the hell I'd let myself in for, for a few seconds or for ten thousand years. Ten million years. It just doesn't make sense. And it wasn't like a Dreems. biz dream, oh no, this was one of Miranda Nguyen's wyshes. Very different. Very.

There they were, Big Pink, Little Pink, and Newt.

Alberto Salazar had given me a crash course in star types. As far as I could make it out, Big Pink was a Type M red giant. A huge thing, nearing the end of its stellar lifetime, with a relatively low surface temperature of a few thousand degrees Celsius. Little Pink was a red dwarf. They were both variables, Big Pink with a long period and Little Pink with a much shorter one.

Newt was indeed a neutron star, its diameter not much more than five miles. If you stood on its surface and if you could move you could walk around the mother in a day. But of course its substance was so dense and its gravity so strong, you'd be squashed into a kind of Flatland creature in a fraction of a second, and even if that didn't happen you'd be held down so you couldn't lift a foot no less walk around the star.

I tried to figure out who or what I was. In Carter Thurston Hull's dreems I'd been able to flit from mind to mind and from person to person. I'd been Stu Sutcliffe at Candlestick Park, Robert Oppenheimer at Alamogordo, and Howard Lovecraft sitting at his desk in Providence, Rhode Island. Did I have to be somebody to function in Miranda Nguyen's wysh?

I tried looking at myself, you know, the way you hold your hand in front of your face in a dream to make sure you're alive, but there was nothing there. At least, there was nothing there for a moment, and then there was. Yes, there was the good old familiar Webster Sloat *mano* that had lifted a thousand brewskis and fondled a hundred derrieres.

Then I blinked.

My hand was changing. The knuckles became smaller, the fingers more tapered, the skin smoother. I looked down and there was the generous cleavage of my squeeze, Martha Washington. I picked up a mirror and . . .

Okay, where the hell did I get a mirror?

If I knew the answer to that one I would be totally willing to tell you.

I picked up a mirror, no, I sat down in front of a mirror, no, I stood in front of a mirror and I was Martha Washington. I was starkers except for that tiny diamond and pearl pendant and I won't deny that I was fuckin' gorgeous, baby.

Nice rounded shoulders, but even as I stood there looking at myself I felt myself changing again. I held out my arms and they grew longer and longer until I could hardly see my hands. I was getting taller, too, and my head — Martha's good-looking head — was morphing into something a little bit like a goddamned pteranodon.

A pteranodon? Fuck me, what the hell was that about? I barely knew what a pteranodon was, some kind of amazing aerial reptile that lived in the age of dinosaurs and disappeared from the Earth fifty or a hundred million years ago.

What?

I turned my head and looked at my arm, now something like a batwing with clawlike fingers and thin, hollow bones holding up an impossibly thin membrane. The membrane was pinkish in color, or maybe it was colorless and picked up the glare of pink light from around me.

Okay, calm down, Sloat. You're here, wherever the hell here is. You are a pink pteranodon.

Yiiiiiiikes!

Did I just say what I thought I said? Talking to myself, okay, that's not as crazy as it might be, "thinking out loud" (ding!) isn't that far from talking to yourself, is it? Okay, Sloat, *You are a pink pteranodon.*

This was a lot crazier than anything that happened to me in one of Carter Thurston Hull's dreems. God bless Miranda Nguyen!

Calm down, calm down.

All right, maybe this is another kind of dream, or dreem, or wysh. If I'm a — don't say it again, just let it go, Sloat — okay, if I am a whatever-the-heck, if that is *what* I am, then *where* am I? Okay, okay, I came out here courtesy of Guenther, Nguyen, Salazar, and Armstrong. Sounds like a high-price downtown law firm but in fact it was my committee of pals at Silicon Research Labs. I'm someplace near Big Pink, Little Pink, and Newt, somewhere in some galaxy someplace in this great big friggin' universe of ours.

Look around, Sloat. Look down. Look at your feet.

Gaak! Big scaly things with claws like the pigeons in Golden Gate Park. Okay, never mind that, what are you standing on, buddy?

A pink surface, pink or maybe white or a sort of colorless translucence picking up the light from Big Pink or Little Pink, whichever one that star up there is. Hey, I can see both of those old red stars up above, and I can even see Newt the neutron star in the distant sky.

Newt the Neutron Star, a picture book for ages three and up, by Webster Sloat. Might be salable. I'll have to look at that when I get back to California.

When I get back to California. Lots of luck.

I can see down into the earth — well, of course it isn't "Earth, earth" but what the heck, close enough for federal work — I can see down into the earth a ways but then things get jumbled and confused looking. I can reach down with my claws, the ones that used to be hands, I think, and feel the surface I'm standing on.

Is it sand? Feels kind of like sand. I pick up a claw full and let it sift through my, er, claws. There's a wind here and the sand, if that's what it is, drifts away. Except it's awfully cold. I pick up some more and hold it close to my eyes. My eyes seem to work very, very well today. This is one pteranodon who doesn't need specs. The stuff is grainy like sand, all right, but I have a feeling it's something else, maybe ice.

The wind is getting stronger and sure enough the sand or ice is getting swept up off the ground (?) ground (?) ground (?) and swirled through the air (?) and it stings as it collides with my skin (?) or membrane.

Just for the heck of it I try running into the wind, spreading my wings, my membranes, and then I jump and I can glide pretty well. I don't land quite so well. In fact I tumble head over ashcan (ding!) and bounce and roll over the icy terrain. But I am undaunted and I give it another try and do better, and then after a while I try flapping my wings once I'm airborne and I discover that, by golly gee, I can actually fly.

Soon I'm soaring over an eerie pink landscape of swirling ice-sand dunes. I can do an Immelmann. I can do an inside loop. I am one hell of a fine pteranodon, I'll tell you that. But am I really a pteranodon? Is this something that I conjured up out of my fevered imagination (hey, "fevered imagination," ding that!) at the behest of Miranda Nguyen, or is it really a native life form here on Pink, whichever Pink, actually on a planet that wandered between the Pinks and Newt, that I somehow morphed into when I arrived courtesy of Wyshes.com?

Pumping for altitude soon gets me high enough to see a hell of a lot of landscape, if that's the right term, for miles and miles and miles of ice. Rocky ice, tumbled ice, ice dunes, ice plains.

Oh, boy!

Here comes something else.

One, two, three, many specks in the sky. They're moving in formation. My first thought is that this is a sign of intelligence. Then I think of the Canada geese who love to nest in Lake Merritt over in Oakland, to the delight of local ornithologists and the dismay of joggers and picnickers whose ideas of sanitation do not quite harmonize with those of the geese.

Intelligent? Well, maybe, but certainly not in any sense that implies you could sit down and discuss cosmic philosophy with them. Or even exchange clichés like *Pleased ta meetcha* and *Have a nice day.*

At the same time that I spot the specks the specks spot me. I'm playing at being a kite in the chilly breezes. The specks are already arranged in a chevron and their leader has obviously decided to take a closer gander at me. He-she-or-it does a sharp nose-over, pumps his-her-or-its wings, and comes zooming down at yours truly at a frightening rate. The rest of the formation follows.

There's no way I can fly away from these critters and I don't want to stay there and parlay with them because they seem to be equipped with nasty beaks and claws. I also know that I'm not experienced at this pteranodon business. This situation looks very damned scary, and I don't know whether Ed Guenther, Miranda Nguyen and Company would be more upset to get me back in bloody chunks or not to get me back at all.

And I think Martha Washington would be dismayed. And despite her teenaged rebelliousness, I do believe that my daughter likes the idea of having a father and would not take kindly to being told that I'd been, ah, *Wyshed* off to an alien world in a galaxy far, far away, only to be torn to shreds by a flock of flying pink dinosaurs.

No, this is not good.

At this point some circuit buried deep in my brain takes over. I'm not being modest. I was, to coin a phrase, scared witless. I did not know what to do. Those scary critters were rocketing at me and there couldn't be more than a few seconds before they sampled their first Sloat-kebob dinner.

And then they disappeared. What the hell? I swiveled my reptilian neck looking for them, and there they were, looking comically confused, a couple of thousand feet *below* me. What had happened? Had I jumped to a higher altitude just as they approached my lower one? Or, more intriguingly, had I *time-jumped* a few seconds into the future? I think that's what happened. I think I disappeared from my spot in the Pink firmament just as the nasties were about to reach me. They continued downward and I popped back into being, right where I'd been before, but they had zipped right through momentarily empty space.

You may get a giggle out of this. I automatically moved my arm — except that it was now a wing! — so I could get a look at my wristwatch. It's a genuine counterfeit $10,000 Rolex Oyster, by the way, that I bought over the Internet for less than thirty bucks, and beat that if you can!

The predators tried another couple of passes at me, but pretty soon they gave it up as a bad job and went squawking and quarreling away through the sky. I have a feeling that there was going to be a leadership shakeup in that gang before very long.

If there were predators on this world there had to be prey, and if there was prey there had to be something for the prey to live on, too. I'm no expert on ecosystems, but it's just common sense that everything has to eat something. I dropped to a lower altitude. Keeping a watchful eye for more dive-bombers, I started a survey of the region.

After a while the ice dunes gave way to something truly remarkable. There were fields of something vaguely grassy or grain-like. This had to be damned hardy stuff, to thrive under these conditions. I doubted that its metabolism or biochemistry was much like life on Earth, but I also remembered something that an evolutionary biologist named Stephen Jay Gould had once said at a Silicon Valley tech session. Somebody in the audience had asked him to talk about extraterrestrial life forms, and Gould had modestly pointed out that he was not an exobiologist. But then he'd added, "It seems to be a law of nature that, wherever life *can* exist, it *will* exist."

He also added that the range of environments in which life had been found, even on Earth, was truly astonishing. I wondered what he would think of life on the Pink planets!

The fields of grain — apparently wild grain — gave way to forests, and in the forests I detected an astonishing variety of wildlife. There was a slithering, snakelike creature that must have been a couple of miles long and at least a hundred yards across, but not much more than a quarter of an inch thick. It had a face at one end, or something that I guess was a face. It moved through the forest, apparently scooping up small vegetation and any slow-moving creatures that got in its way.

It left behind perfectly round, flat objects that inflated to globular shapes and then sprouted trunks and limbs and leaves. What the heck kind of thing was that? A snake that gave birth to Frisbees that turned into volleyballs that turned into trees? And I suppose there would be little birdies building their nests in those trees. Yeah, sure.

Except there were, only they weren't birds, they were little flying dinosaurs, miniature versions of the current "me."

Oh, Ed Guenther sent the wrong guy out here. He should have recruited an exobiologist. This expedition alone would have brought home enough data to keep a dozen research institutes busy for the next twenty years.

I came to a river that flowed pinkly through the woods. Ahead there was a highland area, obviously the source of the river. I followed the river until it fed into a body of water that had to be a sea if not an ocean.

Pink, too.

There was plenty of marine life doing its stuff in that body of water. I flew out over the surface looking for ships or islands or any sign of civilization. I didn't find any but I was so focused on my search that I didn't notice a storm coming up. No, I didn't notice until I was buffeted by violent, swirling wind and smashed into a roaring wall of pink. I'd hit a waterspout.

I had a feeling that I could die in this world, in this Wysh, and if I did I would really be dead. Die in a dream and you'll really die, right? That's an old wives' tale (ding!) and I didn't take it seriously, but die in a Wysh? I didn't want to find out.

I tried to beat my wings and fly above the waterspout but I didn't have the strength. Things were looking desperate and then that old smart part of my brain took over again. Before you could say Jack Robinson (ding! ding!) I found myself swimming away from the storm. I couldn't see myself very well but I could feel my body, my organs, my beak.

Hot damn, I was a giant squid. An Architeuthis. Hey, don't ask me how I knew what those big guys are called. Must have learned it before dozing off in front of the National Geographic Channel one night. I was one big son of a gun! (Okay, ding!)

But as much fun and adventure as I was having on this world, I wanted at least a quick peek at a couple of other worlds in this cockamamie system.

Back at Silicon Research Labs I'd seen the pictures that Alberto Salazar had brought to our little clambake. They weren't exactly photographs, not exactly CGI's, certainly not drawings. But they were something, and they'd shown specks moving between the planets of the Pink System.

What were those specks?

Okay, subconscious brain, take over. I'm just a-squiddin' along here, happy as a — thought you'd get me, hey? — so let's see what you can do for good old Webster Sloat.

And — *wham!* — ask and it shall be given to thee! I was way, way above the planet, so high that the sky was black, the world was round, and there was hardly any atmosphere at all. I was back in my pteranodon persona. I guess that's a good shape. But this time I was far bigger than I'd ever been before. I was easily a thousand miles across, and I was so thin that a kid's toy balloon would have looked like a fat blob of pancake batter compared to me.

I was so thin, in fact, that I could maneuver in the solar wind coming from Big Pink and Little Pink. I was able to fly or sail or whatever you want to call it, and I as I tacked I surveyed no fewer than sixteen planets that wove and danced among the three stars of the Pink System. I could write a book about the things that I saw, the marvels and the monsters of those worlds and their moons and their inhabitants. Hey, come to think of it, maybe I will. Write a book, that is. Why the heck not, it should sell plenty of copies and it'll be a lot more fun than editing software manuals and getting paid by the hour.

The seventeenth world that I visited was a water world, at least when I was there. I realized that those planets must experience amazing changes in their climates as the three stars of the system engaged in their eternal gavotte, and as the planets pirouetted around their primaries. A planet might be frozen solid at one point in its orbit and turn to a boiling hell at another.

This world was cold but not frozen. A global ocean covered it. It was pink, all right, but I hope I haven't given you the impression that the dominant color of the Pink System was that sweet pink that doting parents swathe their darling baby girls in. No, it was an angry pink, a raging magenta that tore at the eyes. Or at least that was the way it made my eyes feel.

And this world was populated by every manner of marine life, animal and vegetable, from microscopic algae to crustaceans and predators that would scare the daylights (okay, you got me) out of Clive Barker on a bad night. There were even flying creatures, the this-world equivalent of amphibians. They could swim to the surface of the world-ocean, use their version of a blowfish's inflatable membrane until they were, are you ready for this, living blimps, then propel themselves into the air and go merrily seeking their dinners.

There I was, just about ready to start packing it in and head for home if I could just figure out how to get back to dear old Earth, when I spotted the first sign of intelligent life I'd encountered on seventeen worlds.

The first thing I saw was, well, I guess you could call it an aircraft. Nothing like a Boeing 777 or a MiG-29 or a Bell helicopter. It had wings, maybe it resembled one of those B-2 stealth bombers just a little bit. But that would be like saying that Arnold Schwarzenegger resembled Eddie Gaedel.

Yeah, Eddie Gaedel. You could look it up, but I'll save you the trouble. He was the only officially recognized "little person" ever to play major league baseball. He was a pinch-hitter for the 1951 St. Louis Browns, wore number 7/8 on the back of his jersey, used a toy bat, and drew a walk in his one and only appearance in an American League game.

He was later murdered and the case was never solved.

I am digressing, am I not?

This thing that looked like a cross between a mechanical sting ray and an artificial chiropteran was droning through the sky. I don't know where it came from and I didn't wait around to find out where it was headed. I abandoned my shape as a giant solar sail and tried something vaguely sharkish. I plunged into that global ocean. I tried to sense any kind of artificial activity and almost at once, there it was.

Beneath my fins was the largest city I had ever seen or even imagined. If it had been on Earth you could have dumped Tokyo, Beijing, New York, London, Paris, Rome, and Rio de Janeiro into one corner of it and hardly made a splash.

The ocean must have been two hundred miles deep, surrounding an icy core. The buildings of this city were easily twenty miles tall. Their shapes were jagged, projecting into the waters above them like angry, voracious mouths. The pressure must have been immense, but as Stephen Jay Gould had said, where life *can* exist . . .

I swam above the city. To the creatures who inhabited it, I imagine the heavy, cold water was as air is to the inhabitants of any city on Earth.

The denizens of the metropolis were clearly the product of the same evolution that had inspired their flying craft. They had bat-like wings and they swam with them, or in a sense flew through the water as aquatic rays seem to fly through the shallow seas of Earth.

Now I came to something that I can only compare to an outdoor amphitheater on Earth. It was immense, on a scale with everything else in this strange civilization. It must have held — I tried to calculate — no fewer than twenty million of the bat-winged rays. In the center of the arena thousands, no, tens of thousands of similar beings were — were — I can hardly bring myself to say it. They were staked to the ground.

I tried to get a closer look at them, suddenly realizing my peril. If these hideous monsters discovered me, captured me, there was no telling what my fate would be, but I knew it would be terrible. I used my shape-shifting ability to make myself into a tiny creature, so small and inconspicuous that I could observe the proceedings unnoticed.

The rays that were staked to the ground were clearly close biological relatives of the ones looking on, but there were small, subtle differences. Their cranial development was not identical. One species had a small triangular protuberance in the center of what I can almost bring myself to call a forehead. The other species had slightly longer claws on its batwings. The one species were a slightly paler shade of angry magenta, and mottled with irregular blotches; the other, a slightly darker shade, and solid in coloration.

Which were the more hideous? Which were the more terrible?

How could such monstrous conduct take place among such an obviously intelligent, obviously advanced race as these bat-rays? At first I was baffled but then I remembered the legendary sport of Vlad the Impaler, the Transylvanian ruler who gave rise to the legend of Dracula.

I thought of the death camps of the Nazis and the killing fields of Pol Pot and a hundred other monstrous, cruel slaughters that my own species had carried out against its own.

No, there was nothing surprising here. These monsters were no worse than humans.

And gradually I realized that they were beautiful. They were lovely creatures, and the staking of their victims to the floor of the arena was an act of artistry. The occupants of the front row of the audience swept from their places and swooped down upon their struggling, staked victims and began to have sport with them. They tore at their bodies with their claws and their teeth, they ripped bits of flesh and tossed them back and forth like playthings before devouring them. They danced, they sang. They mated, mated on the writhing bodies of dying victims.

It was glorious.

I used my power to assume a shape like theirs. I plunged into the melee. I gorged. I cavorted. I–

Miranda Nguyen was standing over me, and Robert Armstrong was standing beside her. Armstrong had his hand on my wrist, clearly feeling for a pulse. Nguyen was fussing with the controls of her mixed-ware gadget.

For a moment I thought I was still a bat-ray, that I was surrounded by the magenta waters of the planet of those horrible beings. No, not horrible. Beautiful. They had found the full joy of life. Murder. And I was one of them.

The gurney was rolling out of Nguyen's machine. There were medical personnel there. I struggled to get free. I wanted to sink my teeth into their flesh, into their throats, to gorge myself on their blood.

Then Martha was there. How had they known of our involvement? How had they located her?

She was standing with Ed Guenther. There were tears on her face. She was trying to get to me but Guenther was holding her back. She called my name and I replied not with words but with a savage roar. That was the way to communicate. With roars and screams and death.

And death.

And death.

5150

Gene O'Neill

WE GOT THE CALL Friday night at 11:45 p.m.

"Car 3256, we have several reports of a black male acting oddly, highly agitated, scaring people . . . repeat, a code 5150 on Leavenworth between Post and Geary."

A 5150: A psycho, someone behaving in a threatening and irrational manner; or a situation gone completely ballistic, everything dangerously awry — a call every cop dreads more than testing positive for an STD.

"God Al-migh-ty," I panted under my breath, closing my eyes, the iceworm awakened in my gut and feeding now in an enraged frenzy, each electric crunch sending a bolt of icy pain tearing through my body. The *iceworm*, my special name for the ferocious little demon burrowed deeply into my lower intestine–

I gasped loudly.

But somehow, ingrained habits kicked in automatically: I sucked in a long, deep breath, squeezed my eyes even tighter, concentrated on a bright white dot for several seconds, then let the air trickle back out of my mouth, and regained some degree of control. Blinking away the tears of pain, I reluctantly responded to Central Dispatch in a shaky, hoarse voice: "Yeah, 10 . . . 4, this is car 3256 responding to the 5150, over and out."

My partner, Benny Tomaho, stomped the brakes on our patrol car, spun a fishtailing U on busy Geary Street, and headed back toward Leavenworth, hitting both the siren and flash bar, and narrowly missing a long-legged, tranny hooker stepping off the median. She gave us the finger as we sped by.

With a trembling hand, I reached under the car seat, pulled out the Crystal Geyser liter bottle, and took a long pull. The high-proof, cheap vodka made my eyes water, and it wasn't the first or second drink of the shift even counting by fours. The huge hit of fiery liquor burned all the way down, the anesthetizing wave working itself out from my gut into my legs, arms, fingertips, and toes. For a moment or two I thought even my nose numbed. But I knew from past experience that the relaxed feeling from the jolt of vodka wouldn't last long, not permanently stilling the famished devil. No, the iceworm was locked-in deep inside me and no amount of booze or anything else would ever kill or dislodge it. At best, I could hope for only temporary respite, pray that it would be knocked out and stay asleep for a while.

"Motherfock," Benny said, oblivious to my pain, as he worked his way through the Tenderloin traffic. We were still a couple of blocks away from the location. "Only fifteen friggin' minutes until end of shift, Skipper; then we would've busted out for two days, free from this miserable, sleazy, smelly armpit of the city."

Forget that weekend respite shit, small potatoes. I was close to permanent relief, 24/7. Two weeks — ten working days — until retirement from the San Francisco Police Department. Man, I was shorter than a mosquito's pecker. So, *please*, I pleaded silently to a higher power, not some crazy-ass crap, not now, just a few nights before my escape from this ongoing nightmare–

"Wow, look at the size of the mob milling about, gawking," Benny said, his higher-pitched-than-normal voice interrupting my reverie of self-pity. He braked a half block up Leavenworth from Geary near Post Street, in front of the crowded alley entry. "Yeah, somebody has got to be down. C'mon, Skip!"

Benny jumped out of the car, pausing a few seconds to attach his baton and adjust his equipment belt.

I hung back long enough to scrunch down partially out of view of the crowd and take another snort from the water bottle. I wiped my eyes and coughed. The little hit didn't help much, the fucking worm fully awake now and chomping away sharply.

But with an effort of will I forced myself out of the car, my weak knees almost buckling under me. For a moment I steadied myself against the side of the patrol car. Then, letting Benny take the lead, I followed, shouldering slowly through the crowd clustered at the mouth of the dark alley, noticing thankfully the lack of any immediate gunfire. Still, I moved stiffly, scanning left and right, 5150 repeating silently in my head. In short, *showing a lotta white eyeball,* as the guys back at the station said, describing a rookie on an edgy call–

"Yo, Skip."

I glanced down, where I had almost stepped on the legless black guy resting on his scooter board while tugging at my pants leg.

"Hey, Double S," I said sheepishly, reaching down and tapping my knuckles against Short Stuff's fist, relieved to see someone in the crowd I knew well. "What's up, dude? We got a 5150 a minute ago from dispatch."

Double S was a hustler, knew everything that happened on the street in the 'loin; and you could bet a bundle he'd know what had gone down here.

"Yeah, it be the Prophet got hisself hit, Skip," Short Stuff explained in a low whisper as I watched my partner continue working his way through the gawkers, finally dropping alongside a man stretched-out on his back in the alley. "He hasslin wunna Big Leroy's ladies, Lil Sister, and her john. You know his line, calling the dude somepin terrible, a . . . a forn-i-cator this time. Then on with his usual pocket-leaps rant, swearin that shitstorm be hittin the 'loin real soon. The dead be raisin' up, rippin-n-runnin like a mob of dope-sick junkie muthah-fuckahs lookin foh a quick fix. Ya unnerstan what I'm tellin ya here, Skip? The dude was goin off big time, barkin and spittin and pokin his finger in this here john's face."

"Yeah, I hear you, Double S," I replied, nervously checking the crowd, especially keeping my eyes open for anyone looking hostile or coming my way with his hands jammed in his pockets.

"But the Prophet ain't lettin it go, man, shakin it lak a pit bull wif a mailman's trouser leg in his mouf," Short Stuff said. "He callin that john a whoremonger and Lil Sister a jezebel, bof big time sinners in this here modern-day Sodomy and Gonorrhea, which was gonna bring on that pocket-leaps shit any day now . . ."

Double S paused to take a breath and spit in the gutter and look around furtively, before continuing. "Dick-shriveled the trick big time, ya know what I'm sayin? John jus turned away from Lil Sister and hauled ass outta there, like my man, Carl Lewis. And Big Leroy jus up the street glarin, hearing ever word of that rantin and ravin boolshit by the Prophet, jus as plain as bad bref on a wino behind a Sterno binge."

"Pissed off Big Leroy," I said, peering over the heads of the crowd, searching and not spotting the giant pimp's shiny head, before finally taking another look over at my kneeling partner. Benny was busy on his shoulder phone, obviously calling in the EMT troops.

"That crazy dude's *bad*, man, no one to fuck wif," Double S continued, when I glanced back down at him. "Big LeRoy pushed the Prophet inna alley, then he growled, 'Fool, I gonna make sure ya'll member inna mornin when ya look in the mirror, member *not* to ever mess agin wif my bidness–' Then his hand was a blur, leavin a black line from jus unner the outside corner of Prophet's lef eye cross his cheekbone to the corner of his mouf. Din't bleed foh almos half a minute, ya know how a real sharp cut do. Then I see it open a bit and spot white cheekbone, jus foh it gush red. Mean, nasty-ass cut. Ya unnerstan what I'm sayin here, Skip?"

"Yeah, you're saying Big Leroy slashed the Prophet's cheek open with a straight razor, purposely marking him for costing Leroy business," I repeated, a little too loudly.

The legless man grimaced as if I'd struck him with my baton on one of his stumps and glanced about anxiously to see if anyone had overheard me, before nodding slightly, confirming my blurted-out accusation.

I slipped him a couple a bills. "Hey, thanks man, get yourself a snack and some joe up at All Star Donuts."

Short Stuff took the money, grinned, and scooted off, up Leavenworth toward Post Street. Of course I knew he wasn't buying no doughnuts or coffee with that bread.

Uh-uh. My man was dabbling with the glass pipe.

When I got closer to where Benny kneeled over the Prophet, I saw that my partner had given the injured man a clean handkerchief to staunch the flow of blood down his left cheek. The frail-looking, old, black man was propped up on a stack of cardboard now, pressing the red-soaked hanky against his slashed face, deflecting the last of Benny's questions. Not looking too bad really, all things considered.

He nodded at me as I kneeled.

"Yo, Skip," the old man said like a ventriloquist, trying not to move his mouth much.

I nodded back, smiling wryly.

We'd known each other for maybe . . . I guess about five years, ever since he'd showed up in the Tenderloin. Back then the Prophet wasn't a religious nut, just plain ole Gent Brown.

"Got yourself in a little deep with Big Leroy?" I said, not really expecting him to acknowledge his attacker.

"Jus preachin the Word, Skip," he said with an effort, chopping off the sentence as if he were short of breath, the hurt obvious in his dark eyes. "Bad times is comin, jus round the corner for all the sinners here in the 'loin," he pressed on in spite of the pain. "The Man be comin back. I see it clearer and clearer–"

I held up my hand as he warmed up, having heard his apocalyptic rant a number of times, including two weeks ago after a pair of teenage crack dealers beat the shit out of him with a piece of garden hose and a toy bat down on Taylor Street. He'd apparently broken up a sale with his spiel. "Okay, save your breath, and take it easy, Gent, the ambulance will be here any minute now." I patted his shoulder, lit up a Winston, and gave it to him, knowing the cigarette would keep him quiet for a moment or two, hoping the EMT guys would hurry. The old guy was cut pretty deep, Benny's handkerchief sopping wet with blood now, but Gent was not really in shock or anything — his eyes were clear, he was alert and coherent. A tough ole geezer, I thought, shaking my head with grudging admiration.

They got here about a minute later and I nodded goodbye, as they loaded Gent Brown into the ambulance. Wouldn't've done much good to press and get a statement from him, because he wouldn't implicate Big Leroy — preacher or no preacher, Gent Brown wasn't into suicide. Benny and I would just have to catch the giant on the street sometime, try and shake him up, which wasn't too likely, the mean-ass pimp tougher than a piece of stale beef jerky.

Anyhow, the iceworm was resting, maybe even asleep; and I felt pretty relaxed myself now that the 5150 was resolved. Just absently watching the ambulance take off and the crowd disperse, able to think back on the Prophet's transformation.

I had first met Gent Brown responding to a shoplifting call up on O'Farrell near Van Ness, about five years ago. He was a common wet head back then, a Tenderloin stumblebum. He'd tried snagging a liter of red from the Korean liquor store. *Big* mistake. Mr. Pak had thrown down on Gent with a .44 magnum cannon that the Korean kept within reach under the checkout counter, stopping the old bum from leaving the store with the shoplifted bottle and keeping him frozen in place staring at the open end of that scary handgun, as Mr. Pak called 911.

I didn't think too much about it, just took Gent Brown outside for a get-yourself-cleaned-up lecture before I dropped him over at St. Anthony's for something to eat — an overcrowded jail wouldn't have helped him at all.

But the same kinda no-account life went on for Gent Brown, for the next four years, the old boy stumbling around the 'loin, panhandling, shoplifting, doing whatever it took to keep himself full of anti-freeze. Feeling sorry for him, I even slipped him an occasional buck or two at the end of the month when his Social Security was long gone. Then about a year ago something odd happened to him, one night around midnight in an alley, where he had his cardboard tent set up. The next day, he told me he'd had a vision, that he'd got *The Call* from a skinny-ass transvestite named Angel, who a month previously had died of AIDS. Which I guess makes you kinda wonder about the Big Guy's recruitment staff.

Anyhow, whatever really happened, Gent Brown cleaned up his act overnight. Got a room in the Reo residential hotel on Hyde, lived exclusively off his Social Security, quickly becoming one of the good guys around the 'loin — volunteering at St. Anthony's, handing out clean needles and condoms to junkies, helping homeless folks hook up with needed social services, and preaching on the street. He became known around the 'loin soon after that as the Prophet.

But about six months ago his preaching turned to hardcore fundamental sermons, and lately they were laced with hard-edged fire and brimstone rants about the evils of the city, the Prophet going off about all the sinners and the coming of the Apocalypse. He'd turned away from helping poor people to getting in their faces over their weaknesses and vices, becoming a major pain-in-the-ass to a lotta folks down here. Almost a low grade 5150, usually drawing an audience of little more than parking meters, folks scattering when they saw him coming.

But this was all too much for me to worry about tonight, because I had a six-pack of troubles of my own.

On the way to my apartment on O'Farrell, I picked up some taco chips, bean dip, a quart of vodka, and a twelve pack of Bud: dinner, the bean dip my concession to health food.

Inside the shabby digs, I flicked on the TV — Steve McQueen movie, one of my favorites, the Devil's Island one — and settled into my easy chair, popping a can of beer, relieved that the call hadn't turned shitty, not like that fiasco at the *Bluenote* four years ago last month.

Michael James, my long-time partner back then and a good man, took a .22 hollow point in the head after we'd rolled on the 5150 and walked into the open door of the seedy bar over on Jones. Homeboy, dusted-up good with PCP, had his piece out and capped Mike, who had strolled in a half step ahead of me. At the sound of the gunshot, I had hit the deck and dug in, with my equipment belt twisted around and my holstered piece trapped underneath me, staring into Mike's frozen expression, shaking like a dog shitting peach pits. The bartender had finally slipped out from behind the bar and subdued the perp with a baseball bat up against the back of his head.

Man, for months after that night I had nightmares, seeing Mike's surprised face with that innocent little blue-ringed tiny hole in his forehead oozing just a drop or two of blood, then waking up in a clammy sweat, getting up close and personal with some serious boozing. Calling in sick often, or showing up for work hung-over, and of course drinking on the job. Before that I had always been a decent Blue, cited twice, a half-ass hero on one occasion, having saved a toddler in a hostage situation. But that all changed when Mike bought it. After that night every 5150 froze my shit.

Then, a little over two years ago, the *ball buster*.

We'd responded to a 5150 at a neighborhood market down on Hyde, my heart hammering, my pulse racing, my asshole puckered up, and my judgment messed up, Big Time.

Latino, wearing a blue bandanna around his forehead, had bolted out the front door of the market, just as we pulled up in front.

My partner jumped out of the patrol car, weapon drawn, and shouted, "Halt! Halt! Halt!" He fired off a warning round in the air. Following the book, SOP.

The guy came to a stop after that, not quite a half a block away; and he turned to face us, wearing a gray Pendleton shirt outside his baggy tan pants and the blue headband.

It turned surreal at that moment, everything moving in super slow motion, like I was detached from it all, watching an NFL replay on Sunday. My partner ordered the Latino to raise his hands. Instead of obeying, the guy smiled goofy-like and reached inside his Pendleton near his belt and brought his hand up and out, holding something dark–

Suddenly the Latino flew backward a step or two, looking startled, a big, wet, crimson flower spreading across the front of his gray Pendleton; then his knees gave way, as the strength drained from his legs, and he collapsed.

I looked down in disbelief at the gun clutched in my sweaty hand. God Almighty!

In shock, I shuffled closer to the crumpled figure.

My partner bent over and lifted a black comb from the guy's hand.

Turned out, the dead Latino was a twelve-year-old kid from the neighborhood, who after sniffing glue with a pair of friends, had entered the grocery and scared the owner with his erratic behavior. The frightened storekeeper called 911. As we arrived, the boy bolted out of the store right into us. Confused, only reaching for his stupid-ass comb, an apparently nervous habit. Man, all I saw was a .38 Special.

Of course there was an IAD investigation and hearing; but I was eventually cleared after two months. I took an additional two months off after that, not getting much from the visits with the head doctors. Just sitting around home, often fighting with Diane, mostly getting acquainted well with various brands of cheap vodka and shaking hands with a steady supply of Bud tall boys. I checked out all the HBO and Showtime movies, seeing some of them two, three times in one day, remembering nothing. Eventually economics forced me back to work. Tried several times to transfer out of the Tenderloin. No luck. Stuck with a series of rookie partners like Benny, who would be moving on soon — nobody wanting to partner up steady with me.

I got up from the chair, stumbled across the room, and flipped off the TV — McQueen was floating away to freedom on a raft. I really liked that final image. Half a dozen empty beer cans were sitting on the TV tray I used as an end table next to my Easy Boy recliner. The chair was about the only piece of furniture I brought along when I'd left Diane and our Sunset place a couple months ago.

She'd come home last April with the bad results from Doctor Serra at Kaiser. They said colon cancer, inoperable; but of course I knew better. She had the iceworm, same as me; must have infected her sometime before that doctor's visit.

So I left Diane, not wanting to watch her die. Or maybe just to get away from her nagging about my drinking. Who knows? My thinking not too clear at that point. In any event I'd moved into this studio dump on O'Farrell on the edge of the 'loin. Oddly, the medical experts at Kaiser could find nothing wrong with me even after several G.I. probes and X-rays with that barium crap — the fucking iceworm only burrowing deeper, able to hide from the doctors and the tests. Hibernating sometimes. For sure, the damn thing wasn't killing me fast like Diane.

I sighed and shuffled into the tiny bathroom to take a piss, glancing at my mug in the mirror over the toilet. It said 52 on my California D.L., but my reflection was a stranger, some beat-up old guy, at least 65. "Man, hang on," I instructed the reflection, "two more weeks, dude."

At that moment, the front door burst open, startling me.

A familiar voice: "Hey, Skippy, you home?"

It was Nicki Machado, my roommate.

"Yeah, Babe, in here taking a leak."

She peeked around the corner, trying to raise her eyebrows like Groucho Marx and leer lustfully at my johnson. But she was a little worse for wear, her mascara was smudged, her lipstick not quite centered on her usually attractive full lips, and only one cheek had been rouged, making her look clown-like silly, not sexy.

She frowned uncharacteristically. “Couldn’t find Smoky anywhere again today,” she said, referring to her kitten that had disappeared two nights ago. Of course I knew what had happened to the cat. In a drunken frenzy I’d tossed it down the old, empty elevator shaft at the end of our hall, through the doors permanently stuck apart eighteen inches or so, the deep shaft a garbage dump for the other residents. It hadn’t made a peep, just a sickening, echoing wet *splat* sound. So I’d restacked the two big, cardboard boxes in front of the open shaft — management’s idea of hi-tech security, the boxes maybe too heavy for a toddler to move, but easily scooted clear by the three elementary-school-age Asian kids who sometimes played out in the hallway. So far the owners hadn’t been cited for safety violations, or if so management ignored the citations.

Nicki had probably done most of her searching this evening down at *The Greek’s* around the corner.

My roomy was in her late forties, a cop on disability for the last year or so — shot up in a botched liquor store robbery over in the Haight. Still had a trim, smooth, athletic body, except for her two extra belly buttons — the ugly, red 9 mm scars near her navel. Actually dark, sexy, good looks when she was sober and dressed nice, which wasn’t too often anymore.

She had spotted the groceries and vodka on the counter. “Hey, Skippy, fix you a drink?” she asked cheerily, sampling the taco chips and bean dip.

I nodded.

We each had a couple of generous hits from the bottle, then Nicki got friendly. Kissing me. Exploring the inside of my mouth with her tongue. Placing her hands under my tee shirt, caressing my chest and stomach, tentatively edging her hand inside my shorts. She broke apart, and whispered huskily, “You wanna do the short yo-yo tonight, Skippy?”

I nuzzled her neck. Yeah, not a bad idea, I thought, it had been quite awhile since a one-on-one.

A few minutes later, the radio station K-FOG played back up to our rassling match. The two of us naked and sweaty on the bed, Nicki on top like she preferred, pinning my shoulders down with her hands, moving her hips slowly in time to the Eagles’ long instrumental introduction to “Hotel California,” her eyes closed, her expression dreamy . . . As the song ended, Nicki bucked, shuddered, moaned, blinked, and smiled; then she kissed me sloppily on the lips.

Breaking apart, she rasped, “Skippy, you’re a stud, you lay right there and I’ll get you a drink.”

It had indeed gone better than usual. Last couple of times, Nicki had been too dry, and by the time she returned from the bathroom with the KY Gel, I had lost interest; too tired, or too old, or too limp, or just too fucked-up from the booze to work up enthusiasm again — often the iceworm reawakened by all the sweaty activity, gnawing away like mad and ruining everything.

She got up, not trying to cover up with her hands her slight girlish breasts with huge, dark aureoles, the nipples still engorged and standing out almost half an inch, or even hiding her thick, unruly, black pubic thatch, damp now. Unembarrassed. No false modesty with Nicki. Something else I kinda liked about her.

"Got a letter from Ray today," she said, her voice slightly slurred, smiling and handing me the drink of vodka — three fingers neat.

Ray was her son, a computer whiz, working in North Carolina. He'd been concerned about her welfare after the shooting, wanting her to come out and stay with his family. But Nicki had resisted his calls and letters to date, telling me that Ray had a young wife and a two-year-old to care for. He didn't need a boozy old lady hanging around; and, besides, she was going back to work real soon, right after she got her act cleaned up.

She was probably right about the old lady part, but deep down we both knew she wasn't going back to police work ever again. And it would've been so easy for her to give in, let her son take care of her. But she still had a little pride left — something else I envied. And she wasn't any trouble living here in the tiny apartment, even with her kitten.

I felt a little surge of guilt well up into my consciousness over snuffing ole Smoky just because he'd been meowing loudly to get in at the same time the iceworm had reared up and been gnawing away unmercifully . . . But I managed to easily force the feeling to the back of my mind; something I was getting pretty damned good at ever since coming back to work after whacking the Latino kid.

I got up, and joined her for another drink, both of us sitting around and chatting drunkeningly in our birthday suits, not much giving a shit how we looked — a couple of worthless, broken-down ole cops, trying to provide some needed comfort to each other.

Late that same night, Nicki awakened me with a loud groan. Sitting up next to me in bed, then doubling over in pain. Through clenched teeth, she described an icy gnawing sensation deep in her stomach. "Maybe scar tissue broken loose, Skippy," she whispered weakly, rubbing the two scars near her navel, her face contorted with pain. "Or even an ulcer. I been hitting the juice pretty hard ever since the shooting, you know."

I nodded, making no comment.

She described the sharp biting pain in detail, between gasps for breath.

I nodded, got up, and gave her the last of the vodka mixed with a little milk from the fridge. "Maybe this will help."

She grimaced, but managed to get the mix down. In a few minutes the pain lines in her face eased up. "I feel better. Thanks, Skippy." She smiled and kissed me gratefully on the lips.

I kissed her back, forcing a fake smile.

Of course it wasn't scar tissue or an ulcer that had wakened her in the middle of the night. Uh-uh. No way, man. It was the fucking iceworm. I'd probably infected her by having unprotected sex, just like I'd done with Diane. What an asshole. I had to do something to help her, for chrissake.

But how ? What could I do? I couldn't even drown the hidden devil in my own gut.

10:00 p.m., Friday night: One week from retirement now, everything slow and easy in the Tenderloin. If it only holds for another week, I prayed, as we patrolled along the upper fringe of the 'loin. Just cruising along relaxed-like, absently checking out the hookers, junkies, and dealers along the street, nothing really unusual happening, nothing out of line.

Then, we spotted Gent Brown signaling us over to the corner of O'Farrell and Hyde. Benny braked the car and double-parked.

"Yo, Skip, got a minute, man?" the Prophet asked, gesturing for me to step out for a private moment.

I nodded, figuring he was ready to give up Big Leroy. Even though I was nervous anywhere near the Hyde Street store, I got out of the patrol car and moved closer to the old man. That's when I noticed his face looked funny, stitches out already, barely a scar noticeable on his cheek, everything healed up good, too good — weird, because that had been a bone-deep razor-cut only a week ago.

"What's up?" I asked, squinting and checking his healed wound a little closer. Yeah, just a slight red mark now, little more than a shaving burn.

"It's you, man," Gent Brown said, pointing an accusing finger at my chest, his tone not sharp or strident as usual when lecturing someone, but soft, gentle, like the expression on his face.

"Me?"

"Yeah, Skip, you gotta get your affairs in order, man. Time is runnin out–"

"Hold off, Gent," I protested, bringing up both hands in the stop gesture.

He just smiled, ignored my protest, and continued, "I'm serious, man, you only got a coupla days at most. You need to get rid of that ex-cop girlfriend; your wife needs your support right now. You need to make amends, because the Grand Judgment Day beckons soon." At that point, he placed his hand on my shoulder in a fatherly gesture.

Whoa!

It felt like I had been touched with a live 440 volt wire, the electric shock traveling the length of my body, and transporting me to another place.

I was home back in the Sunset, in our bedroom, looking down at Diane stretched out on our king-sized bed. She was pale and skinny, asleep, but gasping for breath, her bald head partially covered with a bright green kerchief.

The view shifted, and it was like time running backward: I saw Diane and myself, both younger, in the back yard barbecuing with friends at a 40th birthday party for me; and an even younger Diane in a new dress, dancing at *The Top of the Mark*; and earlier in our first apartment in the Mission, making love, frantic and slippery, a couple of eager youngsters; our wedding day: All happy times in the distant past, with hopes for the family that never came.

I shuddered and moaned, breaking the man's electric grip on my shoulder, the vision disappearing.

Gent Brown just nodded, as if privy to all I had seen. "Hurry, make peace with her now, or you will be sorry on Judgment Day. Time to act is short. Give up the juice. Go home for good, Skip, leave the 'loin behind *now*." His tone had taken on a sharper edge, moving up in pitch, his eyes clear and shining brightly.

I pulled away from him, feeling weak-kneed, stunned by the shock to my system and especially the vivid vision, or hallucination, or whatever the fuck it was. Sweating now, I nodded as if agreeing with the Prophet, but quickly retreated back into the patrol car.

"Let's get out of here," I whispered out of the side of my mouth to my partner, "now, man, now!"

Benny dropped the car into gear and drove off. Glancing over at me, he asked, "What happened back there, Skip? You look like you've seen a ghost."

"Maybe I did at that," I answered weakly, remembering how

bad Diane looked. Automatically, I reached under the seat for my Crystal Geyser bottle, the iceworm awake now and beginning to feed in my gut.

Saturday night I awakened in a cold sweat.

"What's the matter, honey?" Nicki sleepily asked, glancing at the bedside digital clock: 2:37 a.m.

"Nothing, Babe, just a bad dream, go back to sleep," I said dismissively, but shaken because I had experienced the first part of the vision again, updated: Diane obviously dying, looking even worse than the first vision the other day when the Prophet grabbed my shoulder; her older sister at her bedside now.

I got up, went out to the kitchen and drained a Bud, idly glancing out the window at the signboard on the roof of the building across the way. A blue neon message was flashing in the foggy night: NOW, SKIP! NOW, SKIP! NOW, SK–!

I blinked and the signboard was dark as usual at this hour.

Holy shit!

The booze had finally gotten to me.

I was going around the corner, Big Time, hallucinating; and Gent Brown had packed my bags.

I paced about for a few minutes, finally focusing on the real cause of all my trouble.

Man, it wasn't Gent Brown or even the booze.

No, not really; it was the fucking iceworm!

I had to do something about it for the sake of all three of us. Diane was dying, Nicki was hurting, and I was being driven crazy by the damned thing. Standing there in the dark at 3:00 a.m., I knew what I had to do . . .. Okay, I thought, smoothing it all out in my mind, dividing it into three steps.

A few minutes later, with no one up yet in the building, I dressed. Then I slid my Glock 9mm in my belt in the hollow of my back, concealed under my tee shirt, and took a long, deep breath. Finally, I awakened Nicki.

"Babe, get up. I heard Smokey crying. I think I know where he is."

"Wha–? Smokey?"

She struggled up, confused, but finally grasping my meaning

"Yes, now slip on your stuff."

Nicki pulled on her jeans and a tee shirt, running her hands through her hair. Then she looked at me expectantly, her expression still dazed. "Where is he?"

"C'mon," I said, beckoning her follow me out into the hallway.

The building was graveyard quiet.

"This way."

I led her down the hall to the old elevator shaft. As hoped, she meekly followed me, not asking questions, still half-asleep and anxious about the welfare of her kitten. At the shaft, I pushed aside the boxes, exposing the gap in the elevator doors. "He fell down there," I said, pointing down into the blackness, the smell of something rotten almost making me gag.

"Smokey? Smokey, baby, you down there?" Nicki said, kneeling and leaning forward into the shaft.

I blinked, my eyes tearing up, my hands shaking as if I had Parkinson's. Do it, now, man, I told myself.

But I hesitated drawing my gun, thinking it would be easier to just give her a quick nudge . . . But she might survive the fall; then what?

Nicki glanced back at me. "God, what is that smell?" she said, rubbing her nose. She peered back down the darkened shaft. "You sure Smokey is down there?" she asked, her voice tight, mixed with both hope and dread. "Smokey?"

"Yeah," I replied, resigned to the original plan, pulling the automatic out from under my tee shirt, my hand trembling. I eased the weapon up, sucking in a deep breath. "He's down there, Babe, I promise." Then through my blurred gaze, I picked a spot just behind her left ear, steadied myself, and squeezed the trigger; the shot echoing loudly down the elevator shaft.

Instantly, Nicki tumbled forward, disappearing into the darkness.

Splat, then silence.

"He's there, Babe," I said, my voice a barely audible, scratchy whisper. "You found your Smokey." I wiped my eyes and runny nose on a hanky before tossing it down after Nicki, then added, "And the fucking iceworm ain't going to hurt you no more either."

I turned away, fighting back the tears, and hurried down the hallway to the stairwell, as I heard people in the apartments beginning to stir, awakened by the echoing gunshot.

A little later, still very early in the morning, I found the extra key on the nail partially driven into the back porch overhang, where it was always kept at our place in the Sunset. After letting myself in quietly, I tiptoed down to the spare bedroom, everything happening in slow motion, as if I was watching some dark movie, with time somehow geared down.

Diane's older sister, Robin, was asleep, snoring loudly. She was a PA, recently retired from the ER at UCSF. As I thought, she'd moved in and been taking care of Diane, at least the last week or so.

I tiptoed down the hall to the master bedroom.

Diane was asleep, hospital-room bottles hanging on supports on either side of the bed, one probably morphine, the medicine dripping down lines into shunts taped on the backs of both her hands, her breathing labored but steady, her lips chapped and flaky, her face emaciated and chalky pale. Skinny under her nightshirt.

The iceworm was eating her alive.

"I'm sorry, Ba–" I whispered, a huge lump rising in my throat choking off the rest of my apology.

Well, I would take care of everything now, I thought, sucking in a deep breath, resigned to completing the second part of my plan.

Choked up, teary-eyed, but able to move on automatic pilot, I bent over the frail woman, who I had once loved dearly; and I pressed a pillow over her face.

She struggled frantically, but I pushed down with all my weight. Her feet made a few weak cycling movements, kicking off the sheet . . . Then nothing. Diane was gone. She wasn't going to suffer anymore.

I tiptoed back down the hall and past my sleeping sister-in-law, then let myself quietly out of the house, the neighborhood still asleep in the early morning fog.

Back in the apartment in the 'loin, still dark outside. Sitting, sipping a Bud, thinking about the plan.

Feeling better about doing something good for a change, helping both Nicki and Diane, their iceworms stilled. I sighed and looked down at the table, the 9 mm Glock wiped clean and just sitting there waiting next to my beer. I reached, picked up the can and drained the Bud. Surprisingly my devil had been quiet all morning, ever since Nicki tumbled down the elevator shaft. "Uh-huh, running a low profile, you shitty bastard," I said aloud, grinning wryly to myself. "Well, it's too fucking late, boyo!" I picked up my gun, jacking a round into the chamber. Time to take care of step three . . .

But I faltered, an intense wave of fear washing over me, speeding my heart rate and pulse, my eyelid twitching out of control, hands slippery and shaking badly.

"You can do it, man," I whispered unconvincingly, barely able to hold onto the Glock, my grip baby-weak.

That's when I heard it.

A faint *scratching* sound at the hallway door.

Then: a familiar *mewling.*

"No way," I whispered, shaking my head in denial, but lacking any real conviction.

I stood up, slipping the gun into my belt under my tee shirt, and crossed the room, nervously easing open the front door.

Smokey, tail standing up, walked in and brushed himself against my right ankle. He looked exactly the same, maybe a little scuffed-up and dirty, but unhurt.

Shocked, I remained in place for a few moments, rubbing my eyes, the kitten purring around my ankle. Man, what the fuck is going on? An icicle stabbed into my gut, the iceworm awakening in a frenzy. Momentarily ignoring the pain, I leaned out into the hallway, peering left down toward the shaft, half expecting to see Nicki–

Nothing!

But the cat was here, no question about that.

Suddenly, it took off running, back out the door and into the hallway.

"Wait, Smokey!" I shouted, following the gray kitten down the stairwell.

Out on the street, I pulled up short, stunned and gasping for breath–

The whole frigging Tenderloin appeared to be on fire from where I stood, smoke and flames leaping up from the nearby buildings into the pre-dawn darkness.

And sirens wailed in the distance.

A fire truck appeared, sliding around the corner, then pulling up in front of my building, spilling out its crew, who pulled off their fire hoses, hooking up to the nearby water hydrants.

A screaming patrol car braked just up the street.

Looking that way past the firemen and cops, I spotted Smokey, who had ran out . . . and was now lost in the crowd, folks from nearby apartments milling in the street, many only half-dressed, peering around wide-eyed at the inferno raging around them.

On some silent cue, everyone began to move en mass downtown.

I followed the crowd for several blocks. At the corner of O'Farrell and Market Street, I paused, looking both ways, watching what looked like all of downtown San Francisco spilling out from the nearby streets that fed into Market — hundreds, perhaps thousands of people.

What is going on?

9/11 flashed into my head.

Another terrorist attack?

Maybe one of those suitcase nuclear devices going off around here in a building, setting everything afire, people lit up with radiation.

I noticed that some of the crowd did look kinda funny, not glowing with radiation, but peculiar, stunned expressions, clothes dirty and scuffed up, and shuffling along, as if they'd stepped out of one of those George Romero movies.

At that moment the ground bucked and the street in front of me cracked open with a loud snapping *pop*, the sidewalk rolling, as if it had turned to Jell-O, knocking people to their knees.

I grabbed the closest parking meter and hung on, looking up in awe as streaks of jagged lightning ripped across the sky . . . and lower, just above the building tops, neon-blue balls of psychedelic fire were tumbling over and over, the giant balls of burning gas rolling westerly in the direction of the Civic Center. And accompanying the spectacular light show was an orchestra of chaos: thunder — boulders crashing into nearby canyons; more sirens wailing from every direction; sporadic explosions in buildings; debris tearing away overhead and crashing down onto the street; cars braking and colliding; and frightened people shouting, crying, some struck down by falling objects and screaming out in pain.

Still clutching the parking meter as an anchor, I looked around at ground level, trying to take it all in.

That's when I spotted *them*, down by the Ferry Building: Black-cloaked horsemen astride ebony steeds thundering up Market Street, the magnificent beasts' eyes crimson, nostrils flared and snorting fire, the riders scattering the crowd as they galloped by four abreast toward Civic Center–

"Yo, Skip."

Stunned by the whole phantasmagoric scene, I finally dropped my gaze, looking down at the foot of the parking meter.

It was Short Stuff.

I couldn't speak for a moment, but eventually managed a raspy whisper, "What's happening here, Double S?"

He wasn't wearing his normal laid-back, half-ass cynical expression. Instead he looked kind of whacked-out, awestruck himself. Still he spoke calmly in spite of all that was happening around us. "Hey, this gotta be the shitstorm the Prophet been rantin bout."

"Shitstorm?" I repeated, as fragments of building material crashed just a few yards away from where we stood, flattening a Volvo station wagon parked on the street, and covering us with a thin layer of dust.

"Yeah, ya know, that pocket-leaps jive he been preachin bout," the crippled man sputtered, wiping his dirty face on his sweatshirt sleeve. "Dead raisin up . . . Thas them mothafuckahs out there, ya know, the stupid-lookin, scuffed-up ones, shufflin along like a chain gang."

I looked where he was pointing, out into the crowd, every other person indeed looking stoned, marching along in lock step, zombie-like. But arisen from the dead? Whoa!

"Oh yeah, Skip, the shit done hit the fan, ya unnerstan what I'm sayin?" Double S continued over the hubbub, snorting and spitting mud out into the gutter. "Uh-huh, and check *him* out, now. Guess he ain't jus a prophet, no moh. Uh-uh, he gotta be, Da Man!"

I glanced in the direction of his gesture, the crowd gathering back in the street after the horsemen galloped by, coalescing tightly around a nearby figure.

It was Gent Brown!

All dressed-up in a flowing golden robe, so bright it made me squint. He sure didn't resemble any Tenderloin wet head or stumblebum now, nor any street preacher either. No way. He was drifting up Market Street, gathering people behind him, the crowd moving in the general direction of Civic Center–

Holy shit!

Close behind Gent, in the middle of the crowd, was Nicki, wearing a dazed expression, shuffling along in step with the others. "Hey, Babe," I shouted and waved uselessly, as she disappeared from view, lost in the hubbub.

"C'mon, Skip, guess we bettah fall in our ownselves. Maybe get the word at Civic Center, ya hear me?" Double S pushed off on his scooter board, not waiting for my response.

At that moment the iceworm reared up, thrashing about in a frenzy, doubling me over. I grabbed my stomach, the pain incredible, and looked down, half-expecting to see the devil explode out of my body like that gut-wrenching scene in the movie, *Alien*.

God Almighty!

I had indeed gone around the corner, Big Time, for sure. The iceworm driving me crazier than a shithouse mouse. This must be some kinda crazy-ass shit, an elaborate, grand delusion. No, I wasn't following any hallucination to Civic Center or anywhere else. And even if they were real, I was going to do what was right. Finish what I'd started with Diane and Nicki. Take care of the iceworm *now*, once and for all, worry about salvation and resurrection later.

Sweat soaking my shirt, vision tunneling, heart thumping, pulse hammering in my ears, right eyelid going bananas, dry mouthed, hands shaking worse than if I had Parkinson's Disease, choked up big time, ragged breathing. Bad shape.

The revelation hit me hard: *I could not do it.* No way.

As I had suspected earlier, before Smokey's scratching distracted me, I just did not have the stones to go out the traditional cop way. The admission brought tears to my eyes.

"You lousy, fucking pussy–"

Wait!

Maybe, just maybe, I could still go out stand-up. A good chance *if* all this was bogus, just happening in my head.

With heavy legs, I stumbled past the debris on the sidewalk to a corner phone kiosk, and dug two quarters from my pocket, hoping the damn thing still worked. Amazing, a dial tone.

I called dispatch at the station, and, surprisingly, someone picked the phone up on the first ring. After identifying myself and giving my badge number, I laid it on them, the whole maryann.

". . . That's right, a total 5150 going fucking ballistic on lower Market . . . I'm at the corner of O'Farrell . . . Yeah, armed," I finished in an exhausted voice, letting the phone slip out of my trembling left hand. I slumped down on my butt, back against the phone stand, and waited, the Glock resting in my lap. Something crashed nearby behind me, covering me with a thick coating of dust.

I didn't turn, just squeezed my eyes shut against the pain in my gut, took several long, deep breaths, and concentrated on the white circle, blotting out everything around me . . .

Quiet now, real quiet.

Shitstorm gone.

Iceworm still.

THE SIGNAL

PAUL S. KEMP

NOT ALL STORIES END well. Hank had told me that often enough. I'd always laughed the words away until a demon had torn off his head and made him a prophet.

Hank's words were the last thing on my mind when Lucy Booth's shadow darkened the door of my windowless office.

Too bad for me. I could have used the reminder.

I had not seen her in over three years, not since my final bout in the ring with Young Stribling, but I still recognized her silhouette. No mistaking that. Even her shadow cut a nice figure. I turned off the RK radio I kept on my desk to listen to Yankee games. It died with cheers as Lefty Gomez put strike three past Luke Appling.

Lucy hesitated in the dimly-lit hallway, her curves plastered on the misted glass of my door. My stenciled name cut right across her heart — *Gustafsson Occult Investigations.* I'd finally had Hank's name removed a week earlier.

I ran my palm over the stubble on my cheeks and chided myself for not shaving, then chided myself for caring. Lucy Booth was in the past.

And in the hall.

She opened the door and the scent of her perfume filled the room. She looked exactly as I remembered — plenty of curves, long curls, and long legs wrapped in a crisp blue sport suit.

My heart punched my ribs almost as hard as had Stribling but I kept it from my face and tried to sound casual.

"Surprises never cease. Long time, no see, doll."

Her cheeks reddened and I could tell from the little crease between her eyes that she was in trouble. She looked at me for only a moment, then looked over and past me. The brick wall must have been interesting.

"Hello, Abe. It's . . . been a while."

I leaned back in my chair.

"That it has."

Her eyes fell on the empty space where Hank's desk had stood. She'd known Hank, too.

"I'm sorry about Henry."

The papers claimed Hank had been chewed up in a screw machine while investigating a series of disappearances. I did not see any need to disabuse Lucy of the mistaken impression.

"Sit?"

I indicated the chair across from my desk.

Her heels sounded like gunshots as she crossed the floor. She lowered herself into the chair, a pretty face in a sea of blue, and looked around at the walls of my office: the Golden Gloves trophies, the pictures of me and Hank, the framed newspapers articles that reported on our work, the bookshelves filled with books on the occult, the radio on which I listened to Gehrig and Ruth bombard the rest of the American League.

"I've never seen your office," she said.

"You wouldn't have," I answered, and left it at that, but she took my point.

Lucy had left me for a Wall Street financier while I was still in the hospital from my final bout. Her desertion had hurt more than the beating Stribling had put on me. Money had been her demon and watching me bleed onto the canvas in the third had made it clear to her that I would never have much of it.

So, while I recovered in Saint Mary's from the surgery that had left a steel plate in my head — to fix a soft skull, the surgeons had told me — she had dined at the Waldorf with one Herman Keene, of the filthy rich Keenes. Herman Keene had kept his fortune even through the Crash of '29; no one knew how. The society pages said Herman and Lucy would marry soon.

I snapped a pencil between my fingers and she pretended not to understand the significance. The whir of the ceiling fan tried to fill the silence.

"You look good, Abe," she lied.

I chuckled. I didn't look good. I looked like I always looked — a big Swede with a punching bag for a mug.

She reached into her blouse pocket for a cigarette, but came away empty and mumbling. I had a pack of Lucky Strikes in my shirt pocket. She saw them but I did not offer her one. She took that point, too.

"What are you doing here, doll?"

"Do we have to do all this, Abe?"

I raised my eyebrows, all innocence. "Do what, doll? I'm only asking a question."

She could not hold my eyes. She looked away and stared at my trophies while she spoke.

"It's like this, Abe. I need help and you're all I've got."

I tried to keep the resentment from my tone but could not. The ceiling fan dispersed it through the room, poisoning the air.

"Since when? Have Herman Keene help you. Have Herman Keene *buy* you help. That's what he does."

Anger turned the crease between her eyes into a ravine — I knew the expression well — but she did not get up to leave. That showed me something. She *was* in trouble. And Herman Keene and his money could not fix it. She still stared at the trophies, at the articles, at nothing.

"Karl is missing, Abe."

That hit me below the belt. I leaned forward in my chair and frowned. Professor Karl Booth was Lucy's older brother, the chair of the newly endowed Occult Studies department at Columbia. He had first introduced me to Hank and got me interested in the Occult, in the world that only a few of us saw. He'd taught me backgammon. I owed him a lot. I'd lost touch with him after I'd lost Lucy.

"Define 'missing,' Lucy."

She looked everywhere but my face.

"Missing as in disappeared. He was helping Herman–"

"*Helping* Herman? Karl?"

Karl respected only the intellect (which made his affection for me all the more inexplicable). Not money. Not status. Not Herman Keene.

Lucy licked her lips and finally held my eyes for a moment. "Herman is one of the backers of the Empire State Building construction. The most important backer, really."

The Empire State Building. I had seen the artist's rendering in the *Times*. They'd torn down the Waldorf to build it. I figured that monstrosity had about the same chance of being built as someone breaking the Babe's homerun record. Man was not meant to hit more than sixty homers in a season, or to build something that brushed the clouds.

"A dozen workmen have died on the job," I said. "Herman's running a sweatshop. The paper said they suspended building pending investigations."

She nodded and her blond curls bounced.

"Herman will get things going again."

I had little doubt. A little money went a long way with city inspectors and cops.

"What help could Karl be to Herman Keene? He's not an engineer."

Lucy shook her head. "I don't know. But . . . often I heard them talking. Several times Karl said the word 'Astiroth.' He seemed frightened."

The name rang a bell. Astiroth — one of Lucifer's crew. Things were serious, then. I decided all at once to help her.

I reached into my pocket and tapped out two Lucky Strikes, lit, and passed one to her. She gave me a grateful smile, took it in a shaking hand, and had a long drag.

"What is Astiroth?"

"It's a name," I answered. "I haven't seen anything about Karl's disappearance in the press."

She nodded. "Herman has kept it quiet. He's worried about more bad press. He . . . he doesn't know I've come to see you."

I did not let on how that pleased me. I tapped some ash into the glass ashtray on my desk. "You and Karl weren't close, Lucy. Why the stir?"

She regarded me with eyes as cool as December. "He's my brother, Abe."

I nodded. And he was still my friend, or at least an amiable acquaintance. That was enough.

"I'll help you, doll. Let me do some research. Meet me back here tonight, say eight. You have a key to Karl's place?"

She nodded.

"Bring it."

After she'd gone, I pulled copies of *Van Koorl's Guide to the Netherworld* and Jameson's *Demonology* from the office bookshelf. Age and use had yellowed their pages. Hank's handwritten notes filled the margins. He'd usually been the one to do the research, the brains to my brawn. He'd always derided Jameson as a poor translator of the Dark Speech. I didn't know enough to complain. No one would have ever described me as bookish. Thuggish, more like.

Still, I did my best imitation of Hank, found a few references about 'Astiroth,' and learned what I could. Even those snippets made me worried for Karl.

Lucy returned at eight sharp, still beautiful, still dressed in blue, but in flats rather than heels. I'd just finished my Chop Suey from Lee Ho's.

I pushed back my chair. "Got the key?"

She nodded.

"Good."

I walked past her to the coat rack and pulled on my jacket. Hank's black, felt fedora still hung on the rack. I looked at it a long while, then put it on. A bit small, but tolerable. I could not fill his shoes, but I could fill his hat.

"What is going on, Abe?" she asked my back.

I turned around and played dumb. "Doll?"

"I want to know, Abe. You're not telling me everything."

I stared into her pretty face and saw the resolve. I sighed, pulled out two cigarettes, lit them, and handed one over. She'd need it.

"Should I sit?" she asked.

I blew out a cloud of smoke. "Up to you."

She stood her ground and held my eyes. I gave her credit for that. I decided to be straight, bad news first.

"Astiroth is a demon, doll. A demon of the earth."

She looked startled but asked no questions. I credited her for that, too. I went on:

"You know a bit about demons from Karl, but demons are not what you think. And this one is even less so. It hasn't had a body since Sumerian times but its cults have thrived for centuries. It had a good following among the Indian tribes hereabouts. Lucy . . . ," I exhaled another cloud of Lucky Strike, ". . . Astiroth demands human sacrifice."

Specifically, Jameson had provided that Astiroth required sacrifice of 'mind and body,' whatever that meant. I could have used Hank.

Lucy put her hand to her mouth.

"My God! We have to find him, Abe!"

I nodded. "We'll start at his place. See what there is to see. Maybe he left a clue."

Another time I might have gone straight for Herman Keene and grilled him. But I was wearing Hank's hat. And Hank would have gone to Karl's first. He would have called it being thorough, being cautious, being prepared. After all, Herman could have been involved. I was going to do this Hank's way, slow and sure.

We took the trolley uptown, then fought our way through the street traffic of automobiles and people until we reached 101st street. The dim streetlights illuminated a row of three-story brownstones, Karl's among them. A full moon crested the roofline.

The windows of Karl's place were dark. I checked the street, saw nothing suspicious. We crossed to the door and Lucy gave me the key. I fumbled with the lock in the dark, cursed, and finally got it. I opened the door and stepped inside.

A punch to the side of my head put sparks behind my eyes and sent Hank's hat flying. I whirled and lashed out with a wild backhand right. Enough of my fist met jaw to stagger my attacker. Another man grabbed at my arm and tried to wrench it backward. His mistake; he did not have enough strength. I twisted free, pulled him before me, unloaded another left, and sent him careening toward the door.

Lucy screamed as the man tumbled past her, down the porch, and into the street. His companion darted past me and after him.

I shook off the effects of the blow to my head and tried to gather my bearings. Neither thug was much to look at — unshaven men in cheap worker's dungarees, one bleeding from the nose, the other from his mouth. They looked like stonemasons.

I stepped out onto the porch, fists clenched.

"You boys should have brought some more friends."

They looked at me, at each other, at Lucy, and high-tailed it down 101st. One of them said, "Astiroth will have you!" as he fled.

I cursed, chased them for two blocks, and lost them in the press of people and automobiles. When I returned to Karl's, I found Lucy waiting for me on the porch.

"I was worried, Abe. Are you all right?" She gently touched my head.

I ignored the thrill her touch sent though me.

"Fine. I took harder punches than that when I was fighting for nothing in Crown's Gym. Lost 'em, though."

"Too bad." She put her hands over one of mine. "You're still handy with your fists. I'm glad to see that."

"Not something you lose," I answered softly.

"No. I guess not," she said.

I would have kissed her, then, but heads poked out of the windows of some of the adjacent brownstones and the moment passed.

"Come on," I said, and together we walked into Karl's home. I retrieved Hank's hat, put it on, and turned on a light.

The thugs had rifled the place — chairs overturned, Karl's collection of first editions and antique books tossed haphazardly about, drawers thrown open, working papers scattered like leaves. If there was a clue about Karl's fate there, we'd never find it.

"He has a safe," Lucy blurted, and waded through the destruction for the small library. I followed. She put her shoulder against a small walnut desk and slid it across the hardwood, then threw back the Persian carpet on which it sat to reveal a floor safe.

"You know the combination?" I asked.

She nodded, knelt, and set to work. In moments she had it open — I saw cash, a few passports, some gold artifacts, and . . . a book on demonology by someone I'd never heard of. I grabbed it and flipped through the pages. Karl had dog-eared a section on Astiroth. I skimmed over it while Lucy continued to examine the contents of the safe.

Demon of the earth, I read. *Preferred sacrifice is strength and knowledge.*

I puzzled over that. It differed from Jameson's translation, which would not have surprised Hank. I read on:

Devouring maw. Veins of the earth. Night of the full moon.

"Lucy–"

"Abe, look."

Lucy pulled a roll of paper from the safe — blueprints — and slowly unrolled it.

"The Empire State Building," I said, recognizing it from the drawings I'd seen in the paper. Lucy spread them out on the floor and we studied them. Karl had written the word 'Astiroth' across the building's foundation. Next to it was the word 'receiver,' dotted with an exclamation point.

Now I knew why the thugs had been in worker's dungarees. They were not stonemasons. They were construction workers.

Lucy must have made the same connection. She looked up at me, eyes wide. "They found something while digging the foundation of Herman's building. That's why he needed Karl."

"Come on," I said to her, and pulled her to her feet. "We've got to get to the construction site. Now."

"What is it, Abe?"

"A full moon," I said, and headed out into the street. I cursed myself for not bringing my gun or my knuckledusters.

By the time we crossed town to the construction site, the moon had risen above the rooftops to glare down on the city. The construction site was deserted. The whole block felt hushed. The distant ring of the trolley's bell carried from another world.

"Where's the security?" I asked.

Lucy shrugged.

"We should get the cops," I said, channeling Hank through his hat.

Lucy looked alarmed. "Abe, Herman can't take anymore bad press. It will sink the project. All his money is tied up in it."

And all your money, I thought but didn't say. Like I said, money was her demon.

"We can do it ourselves," she said. "Please, Abe. What if there's nothing? Let's at least look."

I looked into her face, bit my lip, and nodded. Hank would not have approved.

"If it gets any hairier, we find a cop."

She nodded and patted my arm in gratitude.

A chain link fence surrounded the site, which took up half a city block. Mounds of dirt and rock, wheelbarrows, picks, shovels and other equipment lay in neat piles here and there. I turned to Lucy.

"You should wait for me here," I said to her.

"No, Abe. We do it together."

I knew that tone and did not waste time arguing.

"Up we go, then," I said, and we climbed the fence, the moon casting dim shadows on the earth.

We picked our way through the site. I was not sure what to expect so I grabbed a crowbar along the way and handed Lucy a hammer. As we drew closer to the center of the site, I started to hear voices, chanting.

I looked at Lucy and put a finger to my lips. She nodded, eyes wide. We sneaked forward in a crouch until we reached the top of the foundation pit. The papers said that Herman Keene had three hundred men digging in two shifts and I believed it. The hole was already fifty feet deep and three times that wide. It might as well have been a quarry. Herman Keene had burrowed through the flesh of the earth to reach its bones, onto which they would graft his building.

"Demon of the earth," I muttered and stared down into the darkness.

"Devouring maw," Lucy said, rapt.

Twelve figures stood in the moonlight at the bottom of the pit, chanting. They wore black robes and surrounded a circular black hole, like a well, or the mouth of the beast. I thought I recognized one of the cultists, the tallest, who held a long knife in his hand.

"Christ, is that Herman Keene?" I asked.

Lucy edged closer to me.

Karl Booth lay stretched out and naked on the ground within their circle. He was not moving and I figured him unconscious or already dead.

The cultists swayed as they chanted. Herman stood threateningly over Karl. A dark gas issued from the mouth of the well, from the maw. That well must have been there long before the site had been chosen for the building. Keene had probably known it, had probably set his crews to work to dig it up.

"We've got to get down there, Lucy," I said.

"A scholar and a warrior for Astiroth of the Earth," she said.

Her tone was strange. I started to turn to her and she coldcocked me in the head with her hammer.

I swear I heard a clang like a church bell. My vision went blurry and I started to fall. I lost consciousness cursing both Lucy Booth and Jameson's poor translation. *Body and mind, my ass.* Astiroth wanted a warrior and a scholar, and now it had both, in the form of me and Karl Booth.

Hank would have laughed.

The chanting brought me back to consciousness. Lucy had hit me squarely in the skull, right on my metal plate; otherwise I'd have still been out cold.

I kept my eyes closed, so as not to tip my condition, and took stock of my situation. I was lying on my back on stone, presumably at the bottom of the foundation pit. The cultists encircled me. A smell like rotting meat filled the air. I presumed it issued from the unholy well. A voice said, "This scholar is offered to you, Asitoroth of the Earth, to hallow this ground, on which we build your edifice."

The chanting intensified and I heard the sound of something sliding down the well. I imagined Herman Keene dumping Karl's limp body into the demonic maw while Lucy looked on, chanting and swaying.

Her own brother.

I had no gun, no crowbar, and a dozen cultists around me. I knew I could not win a fight, but I'd entered the ring many times knowing that, and it never stopped me from giving hell before I went down.

I heard Herman Keene standing over me. At the very least *he* was going to bleed.

"And this warrior, Astiroth, is offered to you–"

Hands closed on my arms and legs and I lurched into motion. Two left hooks and a straight right in rapid succession had me on my feet and two surprised cultists bleeding and staggered.

Herman Keene recoiled with shock. "What the–"

I kicked him in the stomach and ended whatever he might have thought to say. He dropped the knife and I kicked it down the well.

Lucy shouted, "Kill him! Astiroth hungers for a warrior!"

A moan issued from the well and the stink of a graveyard issued forth. The knife must not have agreed with it.

"Come on!" I shouted, fists raised, turning a circle.

The cultists looked about in shock. The men wore glasses, had paunches. They looked like bankers, not demon-worshippers, and none closed on me. The two I'd put down crawled away over the rocks.

"Not a one of you with any guts?" I challenged.

Herman Keene stripped off his robe.

An excited murmur went through the rest of the demon-worshippers. Lucy looked on with glowing, eager eyes.

"We're long overdue for it, Keene," I said.

He lunged at me and I let him have it. He surprised me by taking a few punches and giving a fair account of himself. But I'd been beaten by heavyweights, by the best. Herman Keene was neither. My lip was bloody and my eye dotted before I finally put him on his back for good, groaning and bloody. I daubed my lip and looked around at the rest, ready for any other takers. They weren't looking at me. They were staring down at Herman.

"Go on, Abe," said Lucy, eyeing her husband-to-be. "We have our warrior."

I looked at her, at Herman, and understood.

Like I said, money was her demon. And Astiroth.

I didn't give them time to reconsider and high-tailed it out of there. I heard Herman Keene's screams as I ascended the pit, but I did not look back.

Lucy must have been in Herman's will, for she continued the construction after his "disappearance." And with the demonic foundation laid and the maw sated, I watched the Empire State Building rise into the sky in a mere eighteen months. What would soon become the tallest building in the world was built on a demon's shrine and consecrated in the blood of Karl Booth and Herman Keene. My dread grew as the metal, stone, and glass skin wrapped around the girders. Anytime I walked the streets, I felt it looming over me, over the city.

I never told anyone of the events in the pit. What good would it do? They won't shut the building down and no one would take the word of an ex-palooka.

I never saw Lucy Booth again and she enjoyed Herman's money for only a short time. She vanished the day the building was opened to the public. Whatever happened to her, I hope it was awful and prolonged. She deserved no less.

For a long while the building's purpose plagued me. At first I thought maybe Astiroth was trying to build his way back to Heaven, using the Herman Keenes of the world as his puppets. But that did not seem to fit. I kept thinking again and again of the word Karl had written at the bottom of the blueprints: "Receiver."

It hit me one day in my office, while I was listening to the Yankees beat the Dodgers on my old RK.

A receiver.

The Empire State Building was only incidentally a building. First and foremost, it was an antenna, a receiver through which the demon at its root received unseen signals from . . . somewhere or someone and distributed them through the veins in the earth.

I hear the signal in my dreams and wake up sweating, screaming. I can never recall what it says. I'm glad for that.

I am concerned more and more about what might be coming. *Van Koorl's* speaks of something called the Hellstorm but I can no longer trust what I read. That's what got me into this. I miss Hank, especially now.

This is what I know: more and more skyscrapers are planned in cities around the world. And if even a fraction of those spires clawing their way into the sky turn out to be antennae, well . . . I fear we're in for a hell of a broadcast.

FRACTAL FREAKS

A. A. Attanasio

"All things in this world have a mystery of their own."

—*Zohar* 2:16a

Psycho Macchina

IN THE SUNSTRUCK FOYER, a bronze torso of a nude female mounted on black marble gigantically occupied a space of high skylights, sinuate empty walls in pure white, and no furniture. The visitors, two elegantly dressed men, stood baffled before the colossal bronze until a young, strawberry blonde wearing a crushed silk shirt and gray slacks approached smiling. "Bevan Powers — Motassem Razori — please, come in, gentlemen. E. Randolph will see you shortly."

E. Randolph Rayne, gallery owner and executive art dealer, knew more about the secret world of vampires than anyone on the planet. For that reason, Bevan Powers had sought him out here at *Psycho Macchina*, Rayne's exclusive art salon, reserved many months in advance by corporate clients seeking monumental, contemporary chef-d'oeuvres. But he had not expected to wait. An aggressive arbitrageur with a majestic net worth, he moved through circles where people usually waited for him. Today, however, he *would* wait, because four nights ago he had met his first vampire.

"I'm Jenne Prosper." The strawberry blonde led the men around the mirroring torso to a placid, vacant space of curly heart pine floorboards with a single desk of smoked glass and a stainless steel chair. A flat screen monitor and wireless keyboard shared the desk with nothing else, no telephone, no pad, not a pencil. "Please, sit." She motioned to a low bench of laminated birch and took her own seat. "Something to drink perhaps?"

Both men declined and sat. With a flagrant murmur of silence in the air and nothing on the blank, undulant walls but slants of sunlight, they stared at their bespoke shoes. Motassem Razori reached inside his jacket pocket, removed a small pad and began to scribble. Bevan Powers flexed his hands and, in the singing silence, remembered why he was here.

Four nights ago, when the trill alarm in his mattress had gently awakened him, he had groggily noted the time on the nightstand's digital display: 2:49 a.m. Razori's voice quietly informed him on the intercom, "Sir, I find your daughter at the gate."

A week earlier, sixteen-year-old Ivy Powers had disappeared from the hospital where her doctors had admitted her for treatment of lymphoma. The disease had manifested suddenly and aggressively, resistant to therapy. She would be dead in six months, and he hadn't blamed her for running away to die somewhere else on her own terms. "Let her in, Razori."

"She will not, sir. She would speak with you at the gate."

"She knows I'm here." Olivia Fairleigh-Powers sat up in bed beside Bevan. "That's why she won't come in." Olivia, his third wife, a tall, striking woman of honeyed skin, frost hair and razor blue eyes possessed a face of stern beauty. "She despises me."

Bevan did not refute her. He put on a kaftan and hurried out of the bedchamber. As he passed through the dressing room, he glanced at himself in a cheval mirror. Blue-black hair stood out stiffly. His very pale face and dramatic hazel eyes hovered like an apparition in the focal light, and he startled himself. Sleep creases marred his boyish, heartbroken features. Quickly, he swept fingers across his scalp and rushed to the stairwell.

Razori met him in the security office on the first floor. The front gate monitors showed a midsize car, empty except for Ivy in the driver's seat. He asked her to come in and opened the gates, but she refused. In exasperation, he agreed to come out. Razori gave him a disquieted look. Perhaps Ivy had not run away from the hospital. Perhaps she was a lure. In Bevan's business, underworld figures sometimes made trouble. And that's why he had hired Razori, a former Iraqi intelligence officer and Sunni thug with a falcon's furious face.

Razori drove Bevan out to the gate in the Peugeot, and when they arrived, sure enough, there was a big man with a shaved head sitting next to Ivy. "Stay, sir." The trained killer got out of the Peugeot and approached the midsize, hand in his jacket gripping an M11 compact pistol. "Miss Ivy, please, come from the car."

Ivy got out. She didn't appear as emaciated as she had in the hospital, where she had shrunk to her skeleton. In the metal halide floodlights, she looked implausibly beautiful: spiky midnight hair in perfect disorder, surly teen features pallid as if a cutout of moonlight. She spieled some long speech about how she was all right now and had decided to live on her own and didn't want her father worrying about or searching for her.

While she rattled on, Bevan exited the Peugeot and gradually approached, intending to grab her and haul her inside, away from that big stranger in the passenger seat wearing ski sunglasses in the dark. The stranger stepped out, and Razori drew his M11. What happened next . . .

EVOLVING DOOR

What happened next? Bevan dizzied at the memory and stood up. "May I look around?"

Jenne Prosper peered over the flat screen with a pensive pout. "The installations are in the east wing. Some are mechanical, others electrical. For your safety, Mister Powers, be sure not to touch them."

Razori moved to rise, and Bevan motioned for him to stay. "Finish your poem, Razori. I'll be fine."

Sunlight bounded off the Peroba Rosa floorboards in the hall effervescent as champagne and instilled Bevan with sufficient well-being to remember the horrid details of what had happened four nights ago when Razori aimed his pistol at the stranger with Ivy. The big, bald man — or the thing that looked like a big, bald man — seemed to *flow* through space as he or it moved across the drive. It had features that must have been broken in hell and then fused to silence, for surely that was more mask than face. Razori never got off a shot. It collided with him violently, slamming the bodyguard against the wrought iron gate, and its mask burrowed against his neck. Razori cast up his eyes, which filled with radiant pain, and he cried a lustrous song of agony reveling in every twisted syllable. Bevan wanted to delve that desperate scream out of his memory.

"He's a vampire," Ivy had explained, stepping closer, speaking with a sweet chill in her voice. "And I'm going with him. Do you understand?" He didn't. He couldn't.

Morning occupied the east wing. The installations there loomed large as house frames. He approached one that struck him as a revolving door set on a platform of blue lace agate. When he bent toward the small identifying tag on the stone base, he expected it to announce: *Door to Nowhere.* Instead, he read, *Evolving Door.* A cage of white mice stood at one corner of the agate platform. Despite the front desk's admonition — or perhaps out of spite for making him wait — he worked the aluminum lever that opened the cage like a shutter, releasing one mouse into a chamber of the Evolving Door. He pushed a glass pane of the door to let the mouse out, so he could catch it and return it to the cage, and stood back with surprise at how easily the door swung around. The door swept the wee creature through an entire rotation counterclockwise. For a moment, the brass panel at the bottom of the door hid the animal from sight. When it came back around and reached the open threshold, not a mouse emerged but a sizable amber insect — a water bug!

He inhaled a small, reverse laugh, a sucked-in gasp of amusement. Intrigued, he repeated the action, this time pushing the door clockwise — and, instead of a mouse, a red squirrel rushed out. The bushy tail flurried around the exhibit hall and disappeared through a small swinging door beneath one of the tall, narrow windows. Bevan stood at the window and watched the spry creature bound across the lawn and swirl up a tree trunk. Delight propelled him backward several paces, and he almost began to laugh before he recalled why he was here.

The vampire had dropped Razori like a bag of sawdust. The Iraqi's eyes inked up, clouding like squid smoke. The jackhammer jolts of Bevan's heart used all his blood, and he couldn't move. He stood transfixed, gaze jittering between Razori and Ivy, afraid to see but needing to see if she, too, was a vampire. "Bernie's not like other vampires, Dad. He's a twice dead thing. He kills vampires. You'll see."

Bernie . . . Bevan raised his eyebrows. *What kind of name is that for a vampire? Or a . . . what was that? A twice dead thing?*

He waded through a wash of sunshine toward the other installations in the east wing of *Psycho Macchina.* The gallery lived up to its name. Each art piece dominated space like a stupendous machine. A gargantuan robotic armature attached to a vaguely anthropoid figure with prismatic visor looked about to rape him.

Another work displayed a severed head bouncing twice in an endless tape loop rolling through a circular series of LCD monitors. Was that *his* face on the bounding head? He glanced around for the camera capturing his likeness and imposing it on the projected head.

Monumental titanium gantries enclosed contraptions he couldn't decipher at all: a kinetic Möbius ribbon churning madly inside the hole of a blue glass torus crisscrossed with laser rays. Tetrahedron gadgets of hypnotic strobes and flickering keypads slowly gyrated atop mirror-faceted fulcrums. Cantilevered, compound pendulums of steel beams rhythmically floated among each other with massive weightlessness. The labels identifying these works displayed binary code, making no sense to him.

Nothing had made sense since the vampire. That hideous night after it had dropped Razori, Ivy had informed him she was leaving with Bernie for good. He had looked on horrified as his personal guard convulsed upright with a blurred face and outer space eyes. "Your tough guy's a vampire now, Dad. He's the undead. You see?" He didn't want to see. He reached desperately for Ivy, and she backed away. "Watch. Watch this now." Bernie gripped the undead Razori by the back of the neck and mashed something into his gaping mouth, something like dirt. "It's the ash of a twice dead thing. It completes the fractal blood soul and gets rid of the vampire virus. It happened to me, Dad. It cured me. I'm whole now. You understand?"

Understand? Not at all! That's why he was here. He decided to return to the front alcove and see if E. Randolph Rayne was ready to receive him. But first he had to find out how the Evolving Door switched animals. So, he entered and pushed through it clockwise, looking for the exchanging mechanism.

He was still searching when he came around and stepped out. His brain outburst orchestrated chaos. Instantly, he perceived that everything fit together meaningfully, every detail of his awareness large as his heart was keen, everything succinctly fusing into his pleonastic mind of mind.

Two Bounces of a Severed Head

Now, he understood. This whole hominid world was an attitudinal problem. Anthropocentrism embedded in biocentrism nested in chronocentrism distorted reality. Who could blame the humanimal for believing consciousness required a brain? In the experience of sapiens, everything living was a slippery complexity of chemicals. And chemistry floated adrift on a one-way current of temporal flow, the thermodynamic river bound for the vast Entropic Ocean. Everything decipherable had to fit in the neural net of the brain — or it didn't exist for the humanimal.

Bevan pivoted, dazed at finding himself so transformed. Simply the radiance of the gallery astonished him, charmed light wobbling off the edges of things. Valence electrons spitting photons from reflective surfaces entertained him a moment. The anonymous One observed from beyond the resonance cells of spacetime, impulsing him. Without thought, he eased mind toward the beyond-me, and the anonymous One undulated awareness from off the chromosomal ribbons whose protein kinesis generated his consciousness, an epiphenomenon linked to existence and all its biophysical illusions. Time centered.

He sensed the archons. These sentient entities intersect the worldsheet from 5-space the way physical objects meet two dimensions with their shadows. Their beauty touched him as a raw dreamy feeling. They noticed him while egressing across the worldsheet. He noticed himself. His anti-self moved as a shiver in the radiant room. Death closed in.

This perception collapsed to the egocentric awareness that he didn't have any idea what was going on here — but he knew he didn't have much time.

Joy in the flesh moved him around the east wing. These so-called sculptural installations he immediately recognized as devices. He wasn't sure yet what function each machine performed. He did recognize the Evolving Door as a transdimensional machine, a hypervectorization contraption that had rotated him into this world from a parallel universe where evolution had more expansively convoluted the hominid neocortex. *Clever quantum gate appliance!* He admired its elegance. *Who constructed this?*

At a colossal mechanical rotor coil affixed to a giant cataphract with prism eyeshade — the humanlike armorial figure that he had originally thought looked about to violate him — he read the label in binary code: *Backhoe in the String Theory Landscape*. He knew about the Landscape, the mathematical space whose values are the 'fields' that make up the physical laws and constants of any particular vacuum or what the humanimal commonly called a 'universe.' The many possible sets of physical laws and constants generate stupendous numbers of vacua or universes, with less than 1% capable of evolving observers with consciousness and imagination. In most universes, there could be no observers, because the fundamental conditions for observation — spatial dimensions that differentiate things and permit subject-object relationships — don't exist. This device could tunnel between vacua. It had excavated the passage to a compatible parallel universe that the Evolving Door then used to deliver him here.

But why?

Earth has many replicas in the Landscape. In this one, he had a daughter — Ivy. Morphogenetic field memories fit snugly in the similar yet more convoluted crannies of his brain. He 'remembered' the nightmare of four nights previous. The experience did not frighten or baffle him. He knew about the fractal aspect virus with its recursive self-similarity to the genome. Its incompleteness required that those infected feed on self-similar blood. Bernie, the big stranger with the shaved head accompanying Ivy, was not a typical vampire. Bernie had obviously discovered that a dead vampire was a "twice dead thing" and its remains canceled the fractal aspect virus of the undead. Bernie had infected Razori with the vampire virus by biting him — and then, right in front of Bevan's eyes, cured the bodyguard with the cremated ash of a twice dead thing. Ivy had wanted him to see that, to know that she was herself cured and on a crusade to exterminate vampires.

Bevan's anti-self shivered closer, a tremor in the air like thermal wrinkles from a radiator. The archons circulated closer, faithless to the gallery's geometry or his biology, just pastels of mood coloring him with transparencies of anxiety. He — or actually his self in this world — had come to *Psycho Macchina* because his best investigators informed him that E. Randolph Rayne knew a great deal about vampires. Looking around the east wing, at the ominous machines disguised as artwork, Bevan realized E. Randolph knew a tremendous amount more about the boundaries of reality than simply the history of the undead. Perhaps, as the gallery owner's acronym E.R.R. suggested, coming here was a mistake.

Too late now, the anti-self insisted. Too bad, the archons imposed with their glare of foreboding as they portaged upstream into a past of their choosing from some future roaring off a cliff-edge into vaporspace. He thought of calling out to his bodyguard. *No.* The vampire bite and the cure had transformed Razori from a stonehearted killer to a Sufi poet. He sat now in the front office composing a love song to his soul. This mystery would have to disclose itself without him.

Bevan studied the powerful and mysterious devices on display in the sunny gallery. He stood before the array of LCD monitors showing his lopped head spinning blood as it rolled. When he bent over to read the binary code tag — *Two Bounces of a Severed Head* — he glimpsed the colorless chromatics of his anti-self closing on him and knew in that instant the injured truth, that his arrival in this more primitive parallax of his origins fulfilled his destinal limit. A scything fin of volcanic glass large as a propeller vane dropped from the ceiling, guillotining him. The glass fin slid through a floor notch, tripped a mechanism that sprung open a trapdoor and plummeted the beheaded body down a chute that quickly clicked shut behind.

The severed head bounced twice as it had in many symmetric vacua of the Landscape. Bevan's rotating perspective whirled across the enamel platform, a birling, blurring arc that jolted abruptly when a hand seized his hair and hoisted his dizzy head.

Eidolon Agglomerator

"'Sup, Mister P. Gettin' a*head* of yaself?" An African face assessed the severed head, a chiseled Oromo face with cavernous eyes, broad nose, and proud lips bent to an ineffable smile. "The mind takes us far away. Don't it? Even across universes. But the heart, man — the heart, it always brings us back."

"ReShawn, why must you talk to the heads?" A short, narrow man of gaunt, unshaven countenance with a sinister scar across his thick nose pulled himself from a hatch in the String Landscape Backhoe. His dense mane of coarse, shoulder-length hair shone dully as steel wool, and a smoldering Drina cigarette dangled from reptilian lips, smoke leaking from that harsh mouth like an escaping soul. "They hear, you know."

"I know that, E." ReShawn dropped the head in a plastic bag and zipped it shut, careful to keep the streaming blood on the enamel pedestal. "Straight up. They listen. That's why I speak."

"Install him, will you?" E. Randolph spoke impatiently, shutting the hatch with thick hands bulging with veins, tattoos in Serbian on four square knuckles: *kuga* — plague, pest, infection, death. "Hurry — before he's meat."

While ReShawn carried the plastic-wrapped head to the glass torus of latticed laser rays, E. Randolph lowered a hideaway desk built into the curved wall. He knelt in a fold-out transformer chair, wrists propped on a slender white laminate desktop and began typing across the surface touchboard. His input slowed the Mobius ribbon rotating in the torus. When it stopped, a box drawer slid out from the installation's blue epoxy platform, and ReShawn unbagged the head and seated it in the drawer's cradle of open-cell black foam. Immediately, the drawer slid closed, and the Mobius ribbon spun again with a deep ascending whistle that abruptly resolved to silence. A moment later, the laser rays in the torus realigned, and a holoform eidolon of Bevan Powers stood upon the epoxy platform.

"E. Randolph Rayne gone see you now, Mister P." ReShawn offered a hand to the eidolon. "Thanks for waitin'."

Bevan hopped down from the dais. He eyed the splattered blood on the enamel pedestal and snorted with derision. *Modern art.* Then, he assessed ReShawn in denim jumpsuit, scuffed work boots, black bandana wrapped over his long skull and turned his attention to the seated man with the scarred nose and two day beard. "You? *You're* E. Randolph Rayne?"

Above his flat Tartar cheekbones, E. Randolph's thin, red-rimmed eyes with their muddy irises and tangled capillaries smiled. "Емил Радован Радмило — Emil Radovan Radmilo." His speech, fully modulated, carried no hint of accent. He dragged on his cigarette, blue-whiskered chin upraised, the dimple at its center deep as a nail hole. "E. Randolph Rayne better suits an art gallery owner, don't you agree?"

"But you're not a gallery owner, are you?" Bevan stepped closer. Despite his coarse, unshaven countenance, Emil Radmilo wore Gucci jeans, scarlet Berluti loafers and a black V-neck silk t-shirt. "This is a front, isn't it?" He tracked his gaze around the sunlit gallery while ReShawn unlocked a transformer chair from the wall and unfolded it for the financier to sit. Bevan touched the unusual chair with his fingertips, testing its stability, and sat. "You're a vampire expert. That's right?"

"Oh, yes. And gallery owner as well." E. Randolph waved his cigarette through curlicues of smoke. "These installations sell to corporations worldwide and finance my research."

ReShawn's deep eyes widened, noticing that the back of Bevan's head and neck blurred to smoky plasma wisps. In moments, his entire skull would vanish. Behind Bevan's back, he gesticulated frantic concern to E. Randolph.

"You research vampires?" At the edge of sight, Bevan caught a glimpse of scintillant fumes, sparkling confetti of his vaporizing eidolon form.

"Fractal freaks." E. Randolph typed furiously at the touchboard. The Mobius ribbon yawed slightly, and Bevan's head reconstituted itself. "You know about fractals, Mister Powers?"

"I know about vampires," Bevan responded, his voice hollow and stiff. "I saw one four nights ago. It attacked my bodyguard and ran off with my daughter."

ReShawn hissed in disgust. "Yo, that is cruel!"

"ReShawn, the installation in the south wing, CryptoCyborgCipher?" E. Randolph exhaled smoke-jets through his nostrils. "The movers are picking it up today."

"On it, E." ReShawn gave Bevan a comradely slap on the back while surreptitiously nodding satisfaction to E. Randolph. "Easy, Mister P. This the right place. E. will do for you."

E. Randolph dragged on the Drina while ReShawn ambled off. "He's an Oromo chief's son, from Ethiopia. Vampires claimed his family. I brought him here when he was a child."

"Okay." Bevan bobbed his head impatiently. "You rescued him — can you rescue my daughter?"

E. Randolph gave a gravelly laugh. "She doesn't need rescuing, Mister Powers. You do."

Bevan hunched over. "Excuse me?"

"Your wife — the girl's stepmother — she is a mighty pythoness." He stubbed the butt in a shagreen cigarette case and drew another Drina to his lips. "The pythoness is the most dangerous fractal freak."

Bevan stared at him as he lit up with a gold lighter. "How do you know I even have a wife?"

E. Randolph returned the stare, leisurely exhaling tobacco fumes through his mouth while inhaling them through his nostrils.

"All right, you did some homework." Bevan remained flat-faced. "So, tell me then. What's a fractal freak?"

"Your wife, the pythoness." He pointed his whiskery, nail-hole chin to morning in the windows. "Your daughter Ivy's boyfriend, Bernie, the twice dead thing."

"Enough! Listen–" Bevan paused, weighted with anger, the vein down the middle of his brow darker. "I don't care about your strange ideas. I want straight answers. I want the truth."

"Ah, Mister Powers." E. Randolph shook his shaggy head morosely. "Do Gödel, Heisenberg and Wittgenstein mean nothing to you? Hmm?" An accusatory squint tightened his smoke-raddled eyes. "You are a 21st century man. You should know. There are no straight answers about the truth — only many, many wonderful questions."

The Afterlife Machine

Bevan focused on the thin windows that framed wind wafted trees. From a low bough, the red squirrel that had escaped the gallery gnawed an acorn. "Okay, look. Something . . . *horrible* happened at my home four nights ago. I need you to explain it to me."

"There is a secret and sublime world of profoundly broken people carrying on with their aberrant lives outside the society of ordinary human beings. They are fractal freaks." E. Randolph spoke to his cigarette. "A fractal is a geometric pattern that repeats at endlessly smaller scales. Bear in mind, fractals were first known as *monster* curves."

"So?" Bevan groaned.

"This original intuition proves uncannily accurate, because fractal humans *are* monsters." Wafting the lit end of the Drina under his nose, the art dealer faced his new client through a swirling veil of blue smoke, his haggard, damaged visage a caricature of the monstrosities he described. "They are not whole. Their DNA is broken, as the name fractal implies. When the fractal aspect virus inserts itself into the human genome, people become inhuman — vampires, werewolves, demonic creatures like your wife. Fractal freaks."

"What makes you think my wife is . . . one of these monsters?"

"As you say, I did some homework." After a brusque puff, he confided, "A cosmic battle rages, Mister Powers. Angels and demons. They have been fighting since the origin of the cosmos. Angels built life from the elements. They are Fire Lords, and for them life is a complex machine and the human brain a quantum computer that will eventually figure a way out of this cold, dark void into which angels and demons alike have fallen. The human brain will find a way back home, to hyperspace, whence the cosmos originated and where all opposites are reconciled beyond good and evil, life and death, Fire Lords and Dark Lords." He squinted through another puff. "Dark Lords believe that's nonsense. They are convinced there is no way back. They want only to attain to the void and the serenity of formlessness. For the Dark Lords, life is an execration. They are the ones who inserted the fractal aspect virus in the genome — a monkey-wrench in life's creepy, slimy works."

"And you're on the side of the angels."

"No, Mister Powers." E. Randolph continued in a low-keyed yet serious voice. "I take no sides. I am a scientist. Observation and data — that is my methodology. I experiment with the world as I find it."

Bevan's jaw pulsed. "That sounds unlikely, Mister Radmilo." His voice hung from the edge of his nerves, and he seethed with indignation, watching this Euro-trash art monger coolly smoking, calling himself a scientist while Ivy romped somewhere with an abomination. "I can't imagine any reputable scientific journal publishing your findings about fractal freaks."

"The research I conduct is strictly for my own purposes." E. Randolph spoke off the back end of a long drag, his tone soft and neutral. "Knowledge is power. And I have accrued extraordinary knowledge."

"Do you know how to get my daughter back?"

"Yes. But you would not live to see her return." He inflected his words with an ominous timbre. "The pythoness tried to eat your daughter, and the pythoness knows now she has failed. Worse for you, she knows you know. She will devour you."

"Hold up. The pythoness — you mean, my wife — Olivia?"

"Yes." One word crammed with horrifying certainty. "You married her eighteen months ago. Your daughter's lymphoma began shortly thereafter."

"That's crazy."

"What you witnessed four nights past, was that not crazy?" He lifted bold eyebrows. "Perhaps you are crazy."

"Maybe I am." Bevan pushed to his feet. "I made a mistake coming here."

E. Randolph sighed, resignedly. "Before you go, there is a strange device you will find edifying." He snuffed his cigarette in the shagreen case, snapped it shut and stood. "Come."

Briskly, the small man crossed through optimistic swathes of sunlight to a gargantuan titanium scaffold housing a slew of pyramidal metallic gizmos. Some small as thimbles flickered with dichroic pinpoint crystals. Others bulky as compact cars flashed mesmeric strobes from chromatic pendant keypads and electroluminescent rotary cams. Each tetrahedron reeled slowly on a pivot of faceted mirrors. "This is the Afterlife Machine." The gallery owner reached into the array and manipulated a backlit spherical input device. "This will reveal your destiny when you die."

He's crazy mad! Bevan fully realized and muscled down the impulse to flee immediately. "So . . . my *destiny* — when I die? You're referring to heaven and hell?"

"Those who serve Fire Lords are recycled. Reincarnated." E. Randolph let his words hang in the softly tremulous air while he took Bevan's hand and placed it on a palm sensor set in the gantry frame. "Waveforms of individuals useful to the angels are reinstalled in quantum computers — in human brains — repeatedly, with the promise of ascending to hyperspace once humanity designs a way out."

"And the Dark Ones?" Bevan dragged the words out, reluctant to encourage the madman. "What do they do with souls?"

"This." As E. Randolph stepped back, the mirror planes of the fulcrums darkened, and a ghostly reflection of Bevan, naked and terrified, pirouetted in each of them. His wraith spun in empty space, hot fragments spitting off him. Incandescent bits congealed in the void to fiery peels as though his phantom twirled on an invisible lathe. Though the apparition whirled in dark silence, his contorted expression of flapping g-force cheeks and piggy eyes translated shrieks of hideous suffering. "Dark Lords deconstruct human waveforms to ores of silence and slag of stillness. The hellish process occupies a dilated time span of aeons.

And that is your fate when the pythoness you married devours you."

Bevan snatched his hand from the palm sensor and staggered backward. "You are insane," he uttered in stricken monotone.

E. Randolph shrugged — *it is what it is* — and Bevan saw the truth of it in his face.

THE GARDEN OF EVIL

"Bevan may be a while." Jenne Prosper spoke to the scribbling bodyguard while speed typing. When he didn't reply, she pushed back from her glass desk and spoke louder, "Motassem? Would you like to view our garden?"

Razori, beating a paradiddle on his pad with a pencil, lifted a look of murderous despair that was actually fathomless poetic reverie. "Your pardon?"

"The garden is beautiful in morning light." Jenne swiveled out of her chair. "Would you like to see?"

"Perhaps sir will need me."

"He can find us in the garden." She extended a pale hand of trim, unpainted nails. "Come on."

"This is poetry." Razori moved to her side gracile as a panther, displaying a page filigreed with Arabic script. "A song of silence."

Jenne took the pad and read aloud as she led him to sliding glass doors fronting a garden of coppiced hedges studded with roses, "'Unfurl your heart and expose the wound that blossoms at the center. Then, your dreams are pollen for ecstatic bees, your nightmares attar for the Friend's honey.'" She returned the pad with a sadly illuminated smile. "This is poetry of tragic beauty."

Razori stood transfixed. "You read Arabic."

"Several languages." Jenne slid aside the glass door and stepped out among spasming butterflies. "I'm a linguist. That's partly why E. Randolph hired me for the front desk." She closed the door behind Razori, a movement that brought her close enough to ask in a dazzling whisper, "؟ رعَ شل ا بتكت ا ذ ا مل"

His face of irreversible fury broke to a grin of flawless teeth, instantly depleting the threat of his dangerous features. "Why do I write poetry?" His transient smile tightened, then vanished, leaving no discernable trace. He strolled onto a path of cinnamon flagstones, eyes dark as drill holes, head slung forward, swiping glances sideways, a prowling predator searching among thorny hedges for an answer. "It is a must."

"You are in a dark world seeking light." Four stone benches violently green with moss convened around a sundial footed in larkspur. Jenne sat. "Poetry illuminates your darkness."

Razori stopped stalking his shadow and turned around. "Yes. I think this is so."

"That is the strength of poetry." She motioned casually for him to sit. "Made with intensity from nothing, poetry is fragile — and ruthless."

Razori stood staring at the white modular building with its transgressive swerves of green glass through which he glimpsed giant kinetic sculptures menacing as rebel angels. "My English is bad. I cannot say what is poetry." He sat opposite her, and from across the sundial fixed her with an expression devoid of all consolation, a visage like a hatchet. "What I say to you is this. I am not fragile. And I am ruthless. Many have I slain with these hands. Slowly. With much suffering. Now, these very hands — all these very hard fingers — make poetry. And poetry makes the soul's propaganda. Yes? You understand?"

"ىتم تأدب يف ةباتك ا لشَرع ؟"

"Speak English." Razori flung a brutal stare at thorn hedges splashed with crimson roses. "This is dreaming. We speak English while dreaming with the beautiful American. Okay? So, you want to know this. When do I begin writing poetry?" He upheld a dark hand, thumb tucked against a beige palm. "Four days now."

"Since the vampire attacked you."

"You know this?"

"E. Randolph informed me." Jenne's voice floated light as air, as if this were a dream indeed. "You understand what happened to you?"

"You are to tell me?"

"You're transformed, Motassem. Forever changed."

His cubical head nodded. "I am not the same man."

"You have come forth from darkness into light — from a hard life to a fragile one." Her eyes, green as imperial jade, insisted. "You must flee from this place. Immediately. Go far away."

"Why?" His voice got small, meant to fit only her ears. "Why do you say these things?"

"A vampire killed you, Motassem. Do you remember?"

"Yes." Terror banged from inside his eyes before he yanked it back. "That is why we find your boss."

"You died once already." She spoke with vigorous precision. "When next you die, you will become a twice dead thing — and your dead body will be useful to those who hunt and kill vampires. You are far more valuable to them dead than alive."

"Such a hunter of vampires is your boss."

"E. Randolph would never murder an innocent. Not even to exterminate vampires. He lost everyone dear to him in '92, during the Bosnian conflict. Those four letters on the knuckles of his right hand spell *death*, because he fights it with all his strength." Her voice got so quiet it could have been telepathic. "But there are others who will kill you for your flesh."

"I cannot *leave*." He stressed certitude far beyond his will. "My boss requires me."

"Your boss is doomed. His wife is a demon. She will kill him. And you, as well."

"Mrs. Olivia?" His cheeks puffed. "No. You have a mistake. Mrs. Olivia cares only for shoes and parties."

"Mrs. Powers is a pythoness — a priestess of the demons. She discards time and people's lives the way a snake sheds its skin."

"I do not understand." He addressed her, stare into stare. "Why do you tell me these things?"

"You are not a killer anymore, Motassem. Something terrible — something truly horrible is going to happen. It should not happen to you."

"In Iraq, I had my family. All are dead. I have nowhere to go. Now my life is here."

"Then, take this." In her ivory palm, she proffered a large ring, platinum and subtly mirror beveled so that it lucidly captured the world around them compacted to a darker, nether dimension, a precise and miniature spyhole into a garden of evil. "It will lead you to the vampire that killed you. Find him and you find Ivy Powers. Bring them here, and we can protect them. And you."

"And my boss?"

She shook her head. "Your boss came here to save his daughter. Here is your chance to do that. But do not go home with your boss. You will die — and then Ivy will die."

Lair of the Scream

Driving back into Manhattan with Razori at the wheel of the Maybach 62, Bevan noticed the thick, platinum band on his personal guard's right thumb. "Where did you get the ring?"

"Beautiful American." Razori's mind had been hurrying since they left *Psycho Macchina*, rushing through every possible way of warning

Bevan without offending him. "She liked poetry."

Bevan threw him a wry smile. "You're going to find that a lot of beautiful Americans like your poetry."

"This one says we are not to go home." Razori looked to his passenger, wanting to search into his eyes. But Bevan gazed out at dirty sunlight filling the cross streets like ginger ale. "I am unhappy to say, she insists Mrs. Olivia is . . . dangerous."

"Sure, right. Radmilo told me the same thing. Called her a pythoness."

"What is this — pythoness?"

"A witch."

"She calls her a demon."

"That's all nonsense," Bevan declared with disenchanted ire. "We were misinformed. I wasted a whole morning there. We're going to have to look elsewhere to find out what happened to Ivy — and to you." He returned his attention to the filthy morning squeezed between the buildings. "Let's not talk about it anymore."

During the following hours at the Manhattan office, the wide platinum band trilled silently on Razori's thumb. He ignored it and applied himself diligently to his poetry. *I am weaving ghosts into a rope of memories, a lariat to throw about the tossing head of the wild stallion, the black stallion death rides.*

When they returned to Bevan's Connecticut estate, sunset identified the western sky with flaming arrowheads among shaggy conifers. Olivia Farleigh-Powers awaited them in the porte-cochere where Razori dropped off Bevan. She seemed congealed of twilight, all amber hues and gold highlights, the chandelier lanterns reflecting fiery facets from her diamond accessories, enveloping her in an opalescent aura. As Bevan ascended the cut stone steps, he berated himself for letting that Bosnian hoodlum play him.

"What's the occasion?" he asked, meeting the metallic stare under the auburn horizon of her eyebrows.

"Where were you today?"

"Office." He kissed her, like embracing a manikin, and quickly went in the front door, speaking over his shoulder. "We restructured that collateralized debt obligation I told you about."

"Before that. This morning." She closed the door and leaned back against it. In her crushed velvet blue pantsuit with gold brocade at the ankles, she looked like a tall belle esprit, which is why he had married her. Aggressively elegant and serious in the most sensual way, she was good for business at the many high society functions his work entailed.

But, for the same reasons, she was difficult to handle when she got mad. "You met with him."

He tugged loose the knot of his tie, making room for the lie generator his larynx had become. "What are you talking about?"

"The Scar. You saw him about Ivy, didn't you?" Her bruised expression said she knew it all. "I told you it was drugs. There are no vampires, Bevan. That man Ivy was with. He drugged Razori. You should have your poet tested. You'll see."

"Let's not go on about this." He moved quickly through the double stair foyer, past the elevator, toward the living room bar and the promise of a bracing drink. "Have you eaten yet?"

"What did the Scar tell you?"

"Who?"

"Radmilo."

He tossed his jacket onto the antique fruitwood lounge chair and went directly to the liquor cabinet. Over his shoulder, he gave her an inquisitory frown. "How do you know about him?"

Her stiletto sandals clicked across the lustrous oak floor. "I know what my husband does when he's not with me."

"Olivia, I don't like the way you're talking." He turned around slowly, hiding his discomfort in a snifter of cognac.

"How should I talk when you're sneaking around behind my back?"

"I'm not sneaking around. I went for a consult. About Ivy." He sunk into an English club chair as she closed in. "And why do you call him the Scar?"

"That's how he's known in our circle."

"And what circle is that?"

"You know. He told you." She approached somberly. "He said I gave Ivy cancer."

"I don't believe a word of it. He's a con man. My researchers misled me. It was a mistake meeting him." He was talking too fast he realized and sucked cognac through his teeth.

"What did he say about me?" She gazed down at him with scorching anger. "Bevan. What did he say?"

A sigh fluttered out. "He called you a witch."

"A witch?"

"A snake lady." The cognac swirled. "A pythoness. He spoke nonsense. That's why I walked out." His heart felt like an untethered balloon as he stared up into her umbrageous features. He'd never seen her so outraged and reflexively went on the offensive. "How did you find out I went there? Only two people at the office know. They wouldn't have told you." They wouldn't have told her what he had eaten for lunch — and he immediately regretted pressing her.

She placed her hands on the arms of the chair, scarlet and ebony manicured nails indenting the maroon leather, and her severely lovely face pressed close, crooked with rage. "I *am* a pythoness."

A deep silence came over the room. Bevan's inner voice rose up full of omen — *This is it!*

And it was. Olivia's carnelian painted mouth stretched to a Mesozoic grin, a slime-maw of serried teeth. Cognac scattered like a cloudburst. Bevan emitted a molten cry before dagger teeth chewed his face. His body convulsed in elastic throes of agony, then vanished as monstrous jaws of stretched saliva slammed shut on nothing.

Olivia leaped back from her fatal bite, acetylene eyes taut in their sockets. For a wrenched instant, she stood disoriented, forked tongue running against the back of her fangs hard as a striking match. Then, she understood. The Scar had tricked her with an eidolon.

From the lair of the scream, her wrath ran free.

The Maiden and the Vampire

Razori dropped his pencil. The panes of the security bungalow twanged like gelatin, and a bellow akin to low-flying fighter jets occupied the burly pine walls. The array of flat screens monitoring the grounds blinked out, and for a pitch black nethermoment, susurrous, erotic breathing tickled his brain. His heart slid across his ribs like a spider dancing on silk struts. The beautiful American had warned him. Bevan Powers was dead.

Old instincts flexed, and Razori dropped to the polished floorboards and slithered out the door, M11 compact pistol in hand. What was he doing running through the moonless night under shuddering stars, gun held down against his leg, when moments before he had been scrawling his soul's secrets? *The soul's boat is the heart, bobbing toward horizons of tempest on a sea of blood . . .*

Something sinuous slinked his way across the great lawn. Why hadn't the emergency generator kicked on? Where was the groundskeeper? The household staff? The patrol dogs? Gripful darkness throttled his senses with palpable threat. He aimed the M11 at the slippery silhouette closing on him, and the platinum band on his right thumb jerked his gun hand aside and pulled him toward the garage.

His former self, the intelligence officer, would have reconnoitered the house. The aberration in his blood, the vampire's blessing that had made him a poet and brimmed his soul into the chalice of his heart, said no. And he obeyed. He dashed for the garage.

When the garage door rose and the Peugeot's headlights flared, what he saw in the driveway heaped shrieks through him so rapidly he couldn't breathe. The groundskeeper, the cook, the housemaid and the dogs weirdly ripped together, a gory collage of jammed limbs, tangled entrails and gibbering masks helplessly alive and vomiting yells in a whorled meat sauce sploshed toward him!

He floored the accelerator, and the crazy screaming carnal mess of knotted bodies splatted across hood and windshield. For a sick second, a smashed face thrived flat against the glass crying imbecile sounds. He swerved, weaved and tore down the drive and through the barely opened gate. In the rearview, out of the spongy mess of torn carcasses, something abhorrent rose, lithe as an arachnid with a pair of eyes.

Squinting past blood weldings the wipers couldn't remove, he drove wildly. His right hand steered, guided by the thick thumb ring, abruptly cutting corners. A morse of fear pulsed loudly in his ears as he sped through the night. At dawn, blood hummed like the remnant buzz from the Big Bang, and he rolled to a stop shrouded by pastels of haze deep in the Pine Barrens.

A girl with blurred stars for eyes stood in the road. He gouged clarity into his sockets with his knuckles and recognized Ivy. She looked as though she expected him. Against the chill, she wore an oversize brown leather jacket torn and shredded as if by claws. But she seemed whole in her red halter top that exposed her midriff, tight tapered jeans, and those big hiking boots her stepmother abhorred. He scanned the misty woods for the large vampire.

"Mister R." Ivy greeted Razori with a desultory nod as he unfolded from the Peugeot. "Bernie said you would find us."

Razori held onto the car door, his knees gelatinous. "*Bernie* — he is here?"

Ivy looked into the dismal woods. Then, she redirected her gaze to the grille of the car. "You hit something."

Razori stepped around and gazed with a mortified scowl at the placenta of bloody orts gumming the front fender. The snout of a dog and several fingers had wedged in the grille. A magnetic pull from the thumb ring turned him to face Ivy and her mile deep stare. "Your father sends me to take you to safety." He heard his voice going flutey and took a deep breath. "Bernie comes too."

"Okay." She led the way through violet fog and writhen pines where sunrise glowed like rubies in the branches. They moved among milk-weeds and burdock growing in rectangular frames imprinted in the earth, foundation shadows of a ghost town. Ahead appeared four bleak stone walls roofed with mats of honeysuckle pitched steeply off saplings risen from a foundered interior. "Don't let the sun in," Ivy warned sliding through draperies of woodbine.

Razori entered the ruined house crabwise. In the umber dark, odor of loam and wood rot packed the small enclosure. Moonlight burned in a corner — *no!* — a shaved head shining, and, staring from under a thick bone brow, crater eyes of final darkness. The vampire rose, tall, heavy-shouldered, and with a scurrilous visage carved in florid, luminescent cicatrices.

Fright pierced Razori. He stepped back, tripped on his own feet and sat with a grunt.

I'm sorry I took your blood. The vampire stared down into Razori's eyes, and the skin on the bodyguard's soul shivered at the night color of that voice. *You were going to shoot me.*

"I am changed." Razori nodded vigorously. "I would not now shoot you."

I know. The vampire exuded a supple fragrance like a balmy breeze escaping fruit trees. *Now you are a twice dead thing. You know death is not simply emptiness.*

Amazement lifted Razori to his feet. "Who are you?"

I'm not sure anymore. The vampire turned his shining head and looked off. After an engrossed silence, his voice returned from its sorrowful excursion into memory. *I was human a few days ago.*

"Vampires attacked Bernie and his lover." Ivy gazed at Bernie with jazzed eyes. "They both died."

We both died. My lover lost his soul. And I lost my body. Because I went back into it and burned it.

Razori leaned forward. "Such a thing is possible?"

"He's here, right?" Ivy sounded sad. "He used the ashes of his burned body to cancel the vampire in his lover's flesh."

And now I occupy my lover's body.

"I do not understand."

Nor I.

Indulging the Gorgon

Razori moved next to Ivy, the bitumen eyes of the vampire watching him closely. "How have you come together?"

"Bernie showed up at my hospital looking for transfusion bags." Ivy combined a grin and a frown, woefully amused by the hulking vampire. "He needed blood, but he didn't want to kill anybody. So, he asked me to help him sneak into the hospital and steal . . . "

With a drastic shriek, steel winds shredded the honeysuckle canopy, and sunlight cauterized the stone walls. Bernie collapsed howling, caustic fumes raying off him in sooty jets right through his clothes. Ivy threw herself atop him, shouting, "Get us out of here!"

Razori swooped over the fallen vampire, lugged him half upright and, tugged by hysterical Ivy, lumbered through a skewed backdoor. He dared a glance over his shoulder and saw a barbed silhouette of a gruesome, flame-pinioned thing against the sun. The midsize car that had conveyed Ivy to the gates of the estate five days earlier waited in the flaring grass, trunk lid open. He uphove the fuming body, face inches from the vampire's raving muzzle. The whirling fumes stank of hostile death and opened a dungeon of coma in him. Gasping, he fell back on his haunches, and Ivy slammed the lid shut.

On all fours, he scrambled for the driver's door, a stark shadow fallen over him. Clutching at the door handle, he looked for Ivy, needing the ignition key, and her tormented gasp hitched his gaze upward. Big boots kicking, tattered jacket flapping, Ivy's narrow body vanished into the bedazzling eastern sun above the treetops, where a jagged goblin shadow of lizard jaw and tissue paper wings frenzied. Thunder fury exploded, and the fierce apparition burst to blusters of glittering diatoms, emerald volts that jigged briefly in the solar wind before festering to blue nothing.

Ivy woke cradled in the buttery leather passenger seat of the Maybach 62. Olivia drove north on the Garden State Parkway with breezy, detached ease, paisleys of Mozart's Rondo in A minor shivering in the frosty climate control. The disheveled sixteen-year-old ran a shaky hand through her patchy, chemo-thinned hair, eyeing with churlish incredulity her stepmother's perfect maquillage, aureate coiffure, and black plissé turtleneck. For a disjunct instant, she thought she had dreamed not only her raptor-claw abduction but the whole vampire escapade that had cured her lymphoma — all of it a nugget of annulment coagulated from taxol and pain in her cryogenic soul.

"Don't even try fooling yourself, you little bitch." Olivia glowered, eyes all pupil like the punched windows of an old forsaken house. "You're alive now only because I need you to get Bevan." The space between them quivered, tense as thermal emptiness, their intermixed destinies clashing with nightmare strength that rent the worldsheet to a sickening sideglance of the Dark Ones and their grinning parabolas of deadfall void. Ivy jolted. Through the incense of warped time, she faced her stepmother's true visage: a crazed tremor of iridescent bluefly flesh musclepacked over an agitated maw and iguanid eyesockets swiveling in opposite directions, crystal ball lenses eerily populated with protozoic entities of oozing light each with its own unblinking foetal eyes peering into the mystery of things, searching out horizons of her future and the coming night of death.

Olivia's human countenance jarred back into place, and Mozart restored order to spacetime. Ivy gagged. "What *are* you?"

"Why, dear, I'm a pythoness." Olivia fought off a sour grin, checking her makeup in the rearview. "I am visited upon this world by the Dark Ones. We are come to end this disgusting odium of incessant hunger and lust. It's a mercy killing, you understand." She grimaced as if swallowing a razor. "Life! That monstrous shape I showed you — doesn't it mock organic horror very well indeed? I designed it myself."

Ivy stared impassively at the thing beside her. "What do you want with my father?"

"Is that a question — or a challenge?" An acid laugh sizzled between her painted lips. "I indulge myself with you, Ivy. I feel a need to declare my purpose. I must remember why I'm enduring such misery. This is so horrid being here, wearing this atrocious shape. How else to carry on? You know, actually I am nothing. Really, I am. Oh, well, as close to nothing as something can be. A mist mote. A diaphanous condensation in the nowhere. And the less I become, the more serenely annihilation curls on me. It is the Way, Ivy. The Dark Ones are the Way. All else is atrocity. But can I really expect understanding from you, a bag of hormones and feces, a nematode with limbs, voracity incarnate?"

Ivy chewed her thumb with a vexed look. "Why don't you go back to nothing?"

"That's what I'm doing," Olivia answered brightly. "I'm on a mission. And not my first. Each time I succeed, the Dark Ones carry me closer to the start of void, the incubation of unbeing, the only joy." Her head bobbled with reminiscent happiness. "To complete this mission, I need a lot of money, enough to help fund the deconstruction of civilization. But a pre-nup protects Bevan's money. Unless you both die, I get nothing. And I need it all."

"Where is he?" She spoke faintly to the window. "Where are we going?"

"To find an old nemesis." Anxiety cadenced a trip of the heart, tightening of the stomach, and Olivia regretted again taking this assignment. The Scar had frustrated her before. What was he up to this time? She forced herself to focus and spoke aloud, delivering her attention to the traffic flow and the pulsing signal of the device the Scar had given Bevan's bodyguard. "Razori will lead us there. But you needn't trouble your befuddled head about it. I've indulged myself enough. Little monster, go to sleep."

When Ivy woke next, she stood in peachy sunlight before a monolithic sliding door of brushed steel. The door glided open silently.

The Door in the Wound

"Ivy!" A rangy strawberry blonde with startling green eyes cheerfully took the young woman's arm and drew her into the sunny interior. "We've been expecting you."

Casting an anxious look behind, Ivy noticed the Maybach 62 parked at the curb, menacingly empty. The steel door slowly closed, and in the narrowing aperture she spied her car nearby with Bernie in the trunk. The skyline of Manhattan slid away, a treasure trove hoarding the afternoon in a million coins of window glare.

Armpits dewing, she let the slim blonde lead her past a black granite cube upholding the bronze torso of an athletic goddess. "Where am I?"

"*Psycho Macchina* — a private art gallery." They entered a capacious space of sweeping blank walls and luminous skylights. "I'm Jenne Prosper. Something to drink?"

Before she could reply, before she could utter a syllable of warning about the pythoness and the terrifying mayhem that had delivered her here, an indigo shadow swathed her. Her joints unlocked with a snickety noise, and she plopped onto the polished floorboards with a deep groan that bulged through the giant room like an iceberg suffering a loss.

The violet shadow condensed to a purple polyp pulsing in midair. *Am I dreaming?* She watched Jenne spin on her heels. The polyp burst with a nuclear glare that inked the fleeing blonde's shadow onto the white wall. When vision knocked back into her skull, Ivy slid backward on the glossy floor, a hockey puck slammed with terror.

An archnoid lizard bride occupied the room veiled in fiendish wings furling black and unfurling gossamer gray shot with rainbows. Sprawling wingbeats made the air cringe like heat. The muscular maw with many teeth, each a sharp yellow flame with a blue root, gnawed Jenne's head and dropped her body under a plume of blood.

A talon hand swung out swift and lissome and snagged Ivy by the collar of her ripped leather jacket. Swinging like clumsy luggage, Ivy accompanied the striding hobgoblin queen. The terror's meathook claws clacked on the wood floor quickly and loudly, chitinous, backward bending legs scurrying down the corridor into the east wing. Swivel eyes scanned the gallery of syrupy sunlight, raking the chamber in spectral and thermal wavelengths for everything living among the titan machines disguised as art installations.

She sighted Razori crouching in a shivering ball behind the gantry frame of the Afterlife Machine, M11 pistol trembling in his hand. Two other neon bodies glowed through the wall that curved into the south wing. In an apocalyptic voice, the pythoness commanded, "*Come forth! Or I spill the child's bowels.*" A red-tipped wing hook poised its threatful promise before Ivy's pale, ossified face.

Razori emerged at once and gently placed his pistol on the floor, staring up with a lachrymose expression at the jawbone slaver of razor teeth laid bare. A blurred swipe of a satanic wing sent him on a horizontal flight to thudding impact with the far wall.

"Enough!" The Scar strode into view followed meekly by a lanky African in denim overalls. "ReShawn, attend to Mr. Razori."

Scampering to the fallen bodyguard, ReShawn appraised with frazzled eyes the saurian mutation on its crableg pylons.

"*Where is Bevan?*"

The Scar's coarse voice rippled with exasperation, "First, put down the girl — gently."

"*First, die!*" A black-tar leg long as a lance impaled the Scar, and he slumped with a gargled cry and skittering eyeballs.

"*ReShawn — where is Bevan Powers?*"

ReShawn, flustering over a dazed Razori, gestured without hesitation to the Eidolon Agglomerator.

A barb-tipped wing pulled at a drawer in the Agglomerator's blue epoxy platform, and it slued open, revealing Bevan's severed head encased in green aspic. The pythoness dropped Ivy, who scuttled away mewling. Knife-curved claws and prehensile wing-hooks reached for the cockeyed prize.

Abrupt mechanical whirring danced the spiderlegged creature full about. The String Landscape Backhoe wailed to life, prismatic visor lighting up, revealing the cataphract's interior, where Bernie, with a face like scorched diamond, worked controls. The prodigious robotic armature aimed its accelerator tube at the dragonish monstrosity. In one sliver of a second, the pythoness rocked back with the migraine realization she had scanned for the living but not the undead.

The colossal rotor coil bansheed a whitehot strobe, and the Dark Ones' half ton phantasmagoria splintered to a cubist mirage that shimmered on the skin of the void before a hyperdimensional undertow whisked it into some unimaginable reality.

"Whoo-ee!" ReShawn drew a utility knife from the pocket of his denims. "That is so wack it rapes my head!" He squatted over E. Randolph, who was writhing in puddled blood, and swiped the knife across his throat. Razori and Ivy shouted with horror. Before their cries dimmed, E. Randolph's corpse blinked to nothing, every corpuscle of blood gone.

"Hey, E. ain't dead." ReShawn skipped to the Eidolon Agglomerator, clenched Bevan's head by the hair and tossed it into the Evolving Door. "They just hidin' out in some weird dimension I don't wanna know nuthin' about." He punched a code into a chromatic pendant keypad, and two other drawers sighed open. ReShawn extracted the heads of E. Randolph and Jenne Prosper and tossed both into the Evolving Door. "But after seein' that *thing*, I wished I was on Pluto!" He strolled to the glass door and shoved it counterclockwise, rolling the decapitated heads out of sight.

Bevan staggered out the Evolving Door with wide, sober eyes, features soaked in sorrow. "God! What happened?"

ReShawn nodded sharply. "That is the straight dope question, Mister P."

Ivy collided with her father, breathing too hard to speak. Razori gazed at them from his depths, then retrieved his gun and limped over to the Backhoe. He opened the cataphract and spoke into the darkness, "Thank you for us all."

No problem.

E. Randolph and Jenne, mussed hair in their flushed faces, bounded through the Evolving Door, exhilarated. "Was that for real?" Jenne laughed from a chest hollowed out by wonder.

With a diffuse smile and a sigh, E. Randolph shrugged, "Fractal freaks."

GHOST LENS

STEPHEN MARK RAINEY

VIC KOHAN INTENDED TO receive full credit for the discovery of the Ghost Lens.

He knew that qualified scientists and physicians needed to research the object thoroughly, to study its potential long-term effects, both positive and negative, first on nonhuman subjects and then on volunteer patients. But he was not yet ready to relinquish it, for he feared being cast aside or forgotten as the lens passed farther up the chain, into levels of bureaucracy he could not yet foresee. Hell, with a property as radical as this, he wasn't even certain where the official process should begin.

The object was a convex, crystalline disc, approximately five inches in diameter and an inch thick at its center. Its color he could scarcely describe: a soft pink-violet-azure-amber, a lustrous, vibrant conglomeration of shifting hues, sometimes so brilliant that it seemed to encase the essence of sunlight, other times so pale and silvery that it appeared softer than moonglow. In pitch darkness, though the thing did not actually shine with a luminosity of its own, it seemed to absorb ambient light and transform it into a supernal radiation that one actually *felt* rather than saw.

Obviously, the lens had been manufactured — for what force of nature could have ground the unknown material into such a perfect circle, polished it so smoothly that its perpetually warm surface felt almost distastefully slick and oily? Manufactured, yes, but its maker, he thought, must reside somewhere beyond the stars the Ghost Lens so closely resembled.

That's what he called it, the Ghost Lens; for though the thing had substance, it seemed ethereal, mysterious — unearthly, even, despite the fact he had found it half-buried in the scorched ground. In the aftermath of the recent forest fire, he had seen it flickering in the sunlight like an ember that refused to die, long after the last remnant of the blaze had grown cold. At first, he was intrigued, then enthralled by his discovery, and after carefully inspecting the thing to verify that it was neither too hot to handle nor terribly fragile, he had carried it back to his parents' old mountain chalet.

Kohan had come out to the north Georgia mountains three weeks earlier, just as summer began, to find the peace and solitude he needed to finish his PsyD thesis, which he had been struggling with for over a year. His subject was "The Scientific Study of Dreams: Neural Networks, Cognitive Development, and Content Analysis," and it hadn't been going well. Twice he had formulated test procedures that he considered both novel and effective, but in both cases, he had learned that other researchers already had developed similar, if not identical procedures, one of them only a few months earlier. He decided that spending time in an isolated environment, one he considered picturesque and conducive to introspection, was exactly what he needed to restore his focus and rekindle his enthusiasm for the project. Twice a week, he still made the trip to Argosy University in Atlanta for supervised counseling with clients, but otherwise, until the end of summer, his time was officially his own.

He could hardly have counted on a forest fire — and his subsequent discovery — turning his plans upside down. Thanks to an intervening river and some timely rain, the fire had halted at the base of Birch Mountain, over a mile from his chalet, preventing him from having to evacuate, and sparing the investment his parents had made when he was a young teen. As a habit, he walked a good two miles daily, often in the deep woods, and the fire's passage had provided him with a captivating landscape, altered from the recognizable one he had known, to explore on his regular excursions. After finding the Ghost Lens, he had reconnoitered that area thoroughly but found nothing else of similar nature or that gave any clue to its origin.

At first, he had considered it little more than a curiosity; an odd trinket, or perhaps some aircraft component that had fallen from the sky. Only when he began viewing things through its convex face did he realize it was something beyond unique.

Most strikingly, the lens did not enlarge or distort objects as he would have expected. If anything, it seemed to illuminate their contours with prismatic highlights, almost as if it were shining a beam of multihued light on them. Then, the longer he looked, the more he realized that background objects appeared to become insubstantial, *ghostly,* almost as if they were fading into some other dimension of space, while the object of his focus assumed a new, peculiar clarity.

Inevitably, he placed his hand in front of the lens, and as he studied its familiar structure, he began to see textures that he knew he should not be seeing: networks of capillaries, veins, and arteries; striated cords of muscle; pale envelopes of clumped fat; lengths of coarse bone, and even strands of dark marrow within them. These images were neither blurry nor in any manner abstract; they were as detailed and brilliantly colored as a computer-generated anatomical map, perfectly three-dimensional. He found that by shifting his concentration, he could adjust the depth at which he viewed the *interior* of his hand.

He moved the lens up his arm, down his legs, to his feet. The thing's magical power peeled away his clothes and shoes every bit as precisely as it surgically removed his flesh to reveal what lay underneath.

Jesus!

For the coming weekend, he had been considering inviting his sometimes-girlfriend Debra Shelton from Gainesville for a visit, but instead, he immediately phoned his best friend, Joe Samacicia, who was a pre-med student at Emory, and told him to get his ass up to the chalet faster than immediately.

Unswayed by Kohan's excitement and cryptic hints of things bigger than big, Samacicia agreed to come the following afternoon, rather than miss a morning meeting with his faculty advisor that might have career-making consequences.

Kohan spent the rest of that evening putting the lens to every piece of furniture, every appliance, every assorted item he could find in the house. The spectral eye penetrated virtually any object he selected, to an almost unlimited depth, though only to its opposite surface; it would not reveal other objects placed behind the first. Eventually, he found his way to the rear deck, which overlooked the forest to the south, and peered through the lens at the three-quarter moon, which afforded him an uncanny spectacle: to his surprise, rather than the X-ray view he half-expected, he saw a series of concentric haloes around a hotly glowing, golden sphere, far larger than the moon as it ordinarily appeared. After a thrilling few minutes studying this phenomenon, he realized that, in the center of this fiery orb, something was moving.

He quickly lowered the lens, only to see the cool, gibbous eye peering blankly back at him, no different from any other clear night, sans halo or other atmospheric distortion. Replacing the lens, he again saw the haloes, the golden fire, and something indistinct but distinctly *there,* slowly pulsing and writhing, like a dark embryo swimming in a globe of blazing amniotic fluid.

Of all the wondrous things the lens had shown him, this struck him as the most dramatic and exhilarating, yet somehow *dangerous,* as if, despite all warning, he had stared too long at the sun. That thought prompted him to view the lens with a new sense of caution. Suppose the thing were radioactive, or perhaps subjecting him to some totally unknown, but no less deadly emission?

He returned inside and scanned the great room for something — anything — that might serve to ease his mind. There. In the corner near the front door, he found a potted cactus his mom had kept for God knew how many years, apparently healthy — insofar as he could identify a healthy and happy cactus. He placed the lens in the pot next to the spindly, quilled trunk, feeling a tad silly about it, having not the slightest idea what the thing would do to a cactus if it *were* radioactive. But the glittering device now enthralled him considerably less than it had a short time ago, and he left it in the pot without looking back, figuring he wouldn't fiddle with it further until Samacicia arrived the next day.

Before retiring for the evening, he went out to the deck to inspect the moon a final time. It had fallen lower in the sky and barely peeked above the trees that pressed close to the chalet. The oblong disc appeared entirely innocuous, its silver light painting the Chattahoochee National Forest a mottled greenish-gray, a faintly luminous mist crowning the treetops. Off to his left, far in the distance, he could see the hazy lights of Tynan, the little town that nestled in the valley between Birch Mountain and Bell's Ridge. The night air felt cool and pleasant, but something was causing him to shiver, so he went back inside and locked all the doors.

He went to bed, half-exuberant, half-apprehensive, and it took him an hour to drift off to sleep.

"This," Joe Samacicia said, "is beyond amazing. And you just found it on the ground?"

Kohan nodded and motioned out the window. "A little over a mile from here, right at the edge of the burn. Half-buried in ash. I've been back there a couple of times already, but no sign of anything else like it. Or any hint of where it came from."

They were seated at the kitchen table, a half-full beer bottle in front of each. Samacicia, who answered only to "Joker" (an epithet Kohan had given him years earlier because of his exceedingly lame sense of humor), held the lens to his eye and studied the inner workings of his wristwatch. Then he turned and gazed through the lens into Kohan's eyes. "It's keyed to organic tissue," he said. "I have to focus long and hard to get it to penetrate the watch, and then everything is a bit hazy. However, the inside of your head comes clear immediately, even through your thick skull."

"Maybe it's just the density of metal versus flesh and bone."

Samacicia shook his head. "No, if you've noticed, even the cushions on the couch are more opaque to it. My guess is that this was designed for viewing living tissue."

Kohan shrugged. "But *who* designed it? There's no technology on Earth that could produce this. None that I'm aware of."

"No," Samacicia said, shaking his head thoughtfully. "But we're seeing exactly what we think we're seeing. It's no illusion. So it's obviously possible for someone." He rose from the table, went to his suitcase, which he had left on the great room couch, and retrieved his digital camera, a Canon A520. "I want to try something. When we look through the lens, we have to adjust our vision — or rather our concentration — to see into an object. Let's find out what the camera tells us."

Kohan took the lens and held it a few inches away from his chest. The cactus had survived the night with no visible detrimental results, a fact that eased his mind only slightly; ever since glimpsing that unsettling vision in the sky, he felt as if he were jumping out of his skin.

Samacicia positioned himself a couple of feet in front of him, crouched slightly, and focused the camera's eye. "Bring the lens down a couple of inches, if you would," he said, squinting through the viewfinder as he framed the shot he wanted. Then he paused. "So, Vic. You have any problems with acid reflux or pain in the stomach area?"

"A little."

"You have a hiatal hernia. Not too severe. Hold the lens very steady, please." A moment later, he snapped the picture, and then reviewed the image in the small pane on the back of the camera. "Well, there's a shock," he said and handed the camera to Kohan.

The miniature picture revealed the clear outline of Kohan's stomach and esophagus against a backdrop of stippled red. He could see a small, irregular bulge where the esophagus joined the stomach and a dark shadow on the left-hand side of the frame that suggested the shape of his liver.

"Let's try another one," Samacicia said, taking the camera back and directing Kohan to return to his previous position. This time he took several shots, and when he stopped to look at the results, his features brightened with excitement. Kohan could barely get him to relinquish the camera.

Each photo revealed a different layer of Kohan's abdominal cavity, from his liver and gall bladder to his transverse colon to his spinal column and lower ribs. Not ghostly, amorphous images such as those generated by an Ultrasound, but clear, incredibly detailed pictures that, at least in the small pane, appeared truer than even the best MRI image.

"Son of a bitch," Kohan said, shaking his head in amazement. "I would have guessed that the images are actually being processed in our brains rather than in the lens — because the level we see depends on the intensity of our concentration. But this proves otherwise."

"Do you realize what could be done with this?" Samacicia said. "Medically, I mean. This is revolutionary."

"Of course I do. But not knowing where this came from, or who made it, we don't know what other effects it might have on our tissue. I don't even know what it's made of. That's not glass or plastic."

Samacicia sat back down, placed the lens on the table in front of him, and leaned close to study its convex surface. "You've noticed that it's warm, almost the same as our body temperature. That would suggest it isn't inert matter."

Kohan nodded, sitting down beside his friend. "I wonder. Was it designed for the very thing we're doing, or something different altogether?"

"You have a knife, like an X-Acto blade or something?"

Kohan stiffened. "What for?"

"I'm curious about this substance."

"No way," Kohan said, chilled by the idea of even scratching the lens. "Look at it. It's flawless. Perfectly round, not a blemish on it. No way, Joker."

"It's going to have to be analyzed at some point."

"But you can't analyze it here. What if its properties depend on its surface being unmarred? Ruining it before it can even be used. That would be just great, wouldn't it?"

Samacicia sighed and nodded. "You're right. We certainly can't do any meaningful analysis here. But I think it should go to Emory. I could take it to Dr. Lassiter, my department head. He's the best person I know of to start the wheels grinding."

Again, Kohan felt a cold stab in his gut. "Well, maybe *we* can take it to Dr. Lassiter. I'm not letting it leave my possession. Not yet."

"What are you going to do with it? It needs to be tested under controlled conditions. Don't you agree?"

"Of course I do. But I'm not ready to give it up. *I'm* not finished with it."

Samacicia gazed at him, thoughtfully but coolly. "All right. So what else are we going to do?"

"Anything but damage it."

"Well, we've got the weekend. Then I propose we take it to Lassiter on Monday."

Kohan mulled over the idea. He wasn't certain why the idea of losing the object to the scientific bureaucracy riled him so. It *had* to happen, he knew that, and putting off the inevitable only reinforced his attachment to the thing. "All right," he said at last. "But I tell you this. I'm going to put together a set of conditions for my releasing it. I'm not going to let them take it over and write me out altogether."

Samacicia chuckled sardonically. "You sound as if you invented this thing yourself. You didn't."

"You're trivializing the situation. When I turn the lens over, it's going to be with as much meaningful data as we can come up with. And this is *my* investigation."

"I think you don't want to get trumped before you start — again."

"Don't make it sound so crass, Joker. *I* found the lens. I'm entitled to get something for it."

Samacicia raised a placating hand. "Calm down. I'm not trying to steal your discovery. You know that. But you did ask me here to help you."

Kohan glared sharply at him before relaxing somewhat. "Okay. Yeah, I want your help. So let's find out if there's more that this thing can do, even if we can't figure out where it came from."

Only the waxing moon shining through the great room window told Kohan that night had fallen, his attention having been fixed on matters too significant to include the time of day. Yet at the end of it all, he and Samacicia knew little more than they had previously — except for one new, staggering fact: not only was the Ghost Lens capable of revealing specific infirmities within the human body, it also had the power to heal them.

Samacicia had been closely studying Kohan's hiatal hernia, and after a short time, he noticed that the bulge at the join of the stomach and esophagus had diminished visibly. Directing Kohan to remain absolutely still, he focused the lens on the hernia for a full ten minutes. At the end of that period, the portion of the stomach that had protruded above the diaphragm had returned completely to normal.

Kohan had desperately wanted to protest, his fear of what the thing might actually be doing to his body boiling in his veins like magma; nevertheless, when Samacicia had finished, the easing of the familiar, persistent burning in his chest offered considerable solace and half-convinced him that his worries were baseless, even childish.

"There's something else I want us to try," Samacicia said. He lowered his head, as if embarrassed. "I want to find out if this will also cure a chronic syndrome, as opposed to physical damage."

"How so?"

"I've never said anything to you, but I've got Crohn's Disease. Right now, it's not all that serious, but it gets worse over time. Most people with Crohn's end up having a portion of their colons removed, but the disease still tends to come back. I want you to focus that thing on my colon, all right?"

"What will I be looking for?"

"Inflammation or ulcerations, mainly on the right side. You may not see much 'cause I don't think there's major thickening of the intestinal wall yet. Even so, I want you to do a full scan for several minutes. I may be able to tell just by sensation whether it's working."

"Are you in pain?"

"Not too much. Three on a ten-point scale. But it's pretty constant."

At first reluctantly, and finally resolutely, Kohan focused the lens on Samacicia's lower abdomen, on the right side as he suggested. As a portion of the ascending colon came into view, he concentrated on its interior — and a few moments later, sure enough, he could see a patch of thick, red tissue that partially obstructed the passageway.

"Got it."

As he peered through the lens, he could see the tissue very gradually diminishing in thickness, its angry red color turning to pale pink.

"God, I can feel it," Samacicia said, his face beaming. "Stay on that area for a few minutes, but then go all the way around, right to left."

Fifteen minutes later, Samacicia signaled him to stop, and Kohan put the lens aside, feeling both exhilarated and exhausted, as if the process had enervated him.

"It's all the more important that we get this into the right people's hands," Samacicia told him, his tone ecstatic. "This thing is going to revolutionize medicine."

"There is one thing we haven't considered," Kohan said. "The lens was obviously designed by *someone.* Suppose . . . whoever . . . should decide to claim it, after all we've learned? What would we do?"

"I don't think anyone would actually misplace something like this. Now, I'm not saying I subscribe to the idea that it might actually be extraterrestrial. But you found it in the ruins of a forest fire. It might have been there for a long, long time. If the lens were very important to its creator, something tells me they wouldn't have allowed it to fall out of their possession."

"That brings something else to mind." Kohan led Samacicia out to the elevated deck. "Hold the lens up to the moon," he said, "and tell me what it looks like."

His friend gave him a curious glance and then raised the disc to his eye. "Interesting," he said at last. "The colors are a little strange. Sort of a greenish-gold. But it looks like the moon to me."

"Let me see." Kohan took the lens in a hand that had begun to tremble. "That's not how it appeared last night."

When he examined the moon, he saw that it bore no sign of the haloes he had previously seen, nor of the shadowy shape writhing in its fiery heart. He nearly dropped the lens, wondering why, instead of being relieved, he suddenly felt as if a frigid hand had squeezed all the air out of his lungs. The darkness surrounding the deck seemed sullen and inhospitable, and the feeble moonlight failed to penetrate the layers of deep shadow beneath the treetops; scarcely different from any other night in his experience here, yet somehow more foreboding. When he handed the lens back to his friend, his hand was shaking visibly.

Samacicia looked at him thoughtfully. "What's wrong? For someone who wants to leave his mark in the scientific community, you sure seem leery of your discovery."

After a long, uncomfortable pause, he said, "I don't know. Something just doesn't feel right."

"My friend, you're our resident psychiatrist. You have issues, maybe you need to be the one to sort them out. You think?"

He chuckled half-heartedly. "I doubt I could afford to pay myself for the first session."

Samacicia laughed. "Celebrate, man. I'm going to get another beer. You want one?"

"In a minute."

As Samacicia disappeared indoors, something dark and heavy seemed to settle over the chalet: a fetid, murky cloud that smothered every erg of the excitement that, by rights, he ought to be enjoying after the success of their experiments. His body, healed by painless but unimaginable means, felt as physically sharp as it ever had, yet he was damn near distraught over that very fact.

Something about the moon. Why did it all go back to what he had seen in the sky?

Because, of all the things the lens had revealed to him, that seemed to be the one thing it shouldn't have.

As he stood at the railing overlooking the silver-crowned trees, he felt a faint vibration beneath his feet. It only lasted a few seconds, then diminished to absolute stillness. No breeze stirred the branches, and barely a cloud marred the starlit sky. Distant thunder, he thought, that's all, and despite the fact that, deep down, he knew it *wasn't* thunder, he somehow forced his mind to accept that explanation, however reluctantly.

Another beer would help, so he turned his back on the moon as if it were an angry lover whose gaze he couldn't bear to meet and went indoors to rejoin his friend.

He had lain in bed for two hours, unable to go to sleep. His nerves were frazzled, his mind on overload, and the darkness was no longer the comforting blanket that ordinarily watched over him by night, but a mysterious, impenetrable cavern in which something sinister seemed to be skulking, just beyond his range of vision.

For a while, he had listened to Joker's slow, rhythmic snoring from the other room, but it had since fallen silent, and now a tomblike stillness filled the chalet, disturbed only by a periodic vibration that seemed as distant as the moon itself, yet as threatening as a whirling funnel cloud descending on the house.

Woven in with his discomfiture was a nagging, prodding urge to retrieve the Ghost Lens and keep it close to him. Despite every instinct that warned him against it, an equally powerful possessiveness gripped him with implacable fingers, a *jealousy* that had taken hold of him the first time Joker picked up the lens. Samacicia had been right about one thing: Kohan simply could not abide the idea of being trumped again and denied credit for something that he, by right, deserved. He had spent countless hours working on his thesis, so many of which had gone literally to waste, and he wasn't about to suffer such ignominy again, not when the lens had the potential to make up for all of that and more.

He wanted to believe that his sleeplessness was due to mere anxiety, but every time he began to buy into the idea, that low, distant vibration set him further on edge. Whatever it was, in all his years of coming here, he had never experienced anything like it. He had always felt safe and relaxed at the chalet, for it represented a haven from everything that troubled him. But not tonight.

The next vibration had the distinct timbre of thunder, and he sat up in bed, listening intently.

When he placed a bare foot on the carpeted floor, he felt it *creeping* beneath his sole, as if the hardwood boards beneath the soft fibers were shifting rhythmically. He refrained from pulling his leg back and burying himself in the bedclothes but clenched his teeth and slipped out of bed, determined to conquer his fear, to convince himself that the vibration was only distant thunder reverberating through the chalet's foundation and framework.

On the kitchen table, right where he had left it, the Ghost Lens gleamed faintly in the darkness like an amber-tinted moon, its face reflecting his features from several feet away. He picked it up, disliking its warm, slippery surface, and carried it with him out to the deck, where his eyes sought the moon. But it had already slipped behind the walls of trees that surrounded the house, leaving only a faint glow in the midnight blue canopy to the west. Out here, though his ears detected nothing, he felt a distinct tremor beneath his feet, and suddenly, the impression that something was actually moving underneath the house took him in a chilling, viselike grip.

Disregarding the alarms in his head, he went inside to retrieve a flashlight, and when he came back out, he was determined to descend the stairs to the backyard and peer beneath the deck, solely to prove his fears unfounded. However, before he could reach the stairs, his legs locked up on him, paralyzed by an involuntary, defensive reflex impervious to conscious effort. He had only once experienced a similar sensation: when he was in high school, having experimented with pot for the first time. He had been sitting by a window at a friend's house, and the paranoid notion that someone might hurl a brick through the glass, cutting him to ribbons, gripped him so powerfully that he had ducked behind his chair, incapable of moving for a full fifteen minutes, until the nonsensical, drug-induced fear left him.

He was now rendered similarly immobile, the great difference being that he was not presently under the influence of anything so mundane as cannabis. His body stovepipe-rigid, another tremor passed through the boards beneath his feet, and he felt himself rocking slightly, then teetering, until the loss of balance forced him into motion. To avoid toppling, he dropped to his knees, his eyes falling on the half-inch gaps between the boards of the deck flooring, through which a dense, liquid darkness seemed to be seeping up from the empty space below. With a trembling hand, he switched on the flashlight and aimed its beam into the void beneath, lowering his head to peer down after it.

Nothing. Nothing but empty space and a floor of dirt some ten feet below.

He moved the flashlight from gap to gap, his eyes searching the illuminated stripes for any sign of *something,* his mind half-relieved but still disbelieving. When he switched off the light, he felt as if he had gone blind, the darkness too complete, the night bearing down too heavily on his back. Then he reached for the Ghost Lens, positioned it over the widest space between the boards he could find, and peered into the deep well it presented to his eyes.

The thing he saw was *almost* a face. A wide, flat surface of pallid hue, with hollow eyeholes and a gaping mouth, from which something — a tongue, perhaps — extended like a fleshy rope in the direction of the chalet, passing beyond his view into the depths of impenetrable shadow.

He might have cried out, but he felt himself scrambling backward, toward whatever safety the indoors might offer. The lens no longer in his hand, forgotten, he clambered to his feet and bolted through the great room to the guest room where Samacicia slept.

"Joker!" he shouted, shoving open the door and stumbling to his friend's bedside. "Joker, wake up! Outside, there's . . ."

His hand fell into something warm and wet, which stopped him where he stood. His other hand now trembled its way to the bedside lamp, and with his heart in his throat, he turned the switch and gagged, already backing away from the ruin in the bed.

There wasn't much left of Samacicia's body. An empty envelope of flesh, its internal organs liquefied and drained, a chaotic mosaic of dark stains on the pastel sheets. Even the bones had mostly disintegrated, the face now a loose, gaping mask that retained only the vaguest semblance of familiarity.

Out of the corner of his eye, Kohan detected a movement, and he swiveled his head in time to see the faintest hint of a long, snakelike shadow slipping back into the ventilation register — a mere ghost that would have escaped the notice of any eyes other than those already acutely aware of its existence. His horror temporarily overcome by sheer rage, he lurched to the rectangular vent and screamed into it, his voice becoming a tortured howl that gushed through the network of ducts to ring like a dirge through every room of the mountain chalet.

But the moment the scream spent itself, Kohan felt the boards beneath his feet starting to quiver, and another sound crept back through the vent: an eerie echo of his own mournful cry, reflected mockingly back to him by something with no voice of its own — at least, no voice that human ears might perceive.

In one stark moment of realization, his body nearly melted into the floor, incapable of supporting both his weight and the burden of bleak certainty that now clambered like a dexterous boulder onto his shoulders. Hope fled with one exhalation, yet his legs somehow propelled him through the door, into the dimly lit great room that had once been the heart of his most cherished haven. He found his car keys in his pocket and he made his way out to the driveway, where Samacicia's car sat morosely beside his own, as if aware of its owner's passing.

Unhurriedly, he slid behind the wheel of his trusty old Camry, started the engine, and turned the car around carefully to avoid dinging Samacicia's Element, whose unblemished surfaces served as a final reminder of his friend, a once-whole being, possessed of so much vitality and human dignity. The driveway passed beneath a long archway of pine boughs, and his headlights carved a bright tunnel through their shadowed depths, revealing only void beyond the brigades of pillar-like trunks. He did not speed, for wrecking the car here would only shorten whatever time remained for him in this life.

He had left the Ghost Lens behind, so he probably would not see the thing when it eventually came for him. Or perhaps, if he kept alert, he might glimpse a ghostly shadow creeping toward him at the last.

He didn't know which was worse. But the answer lay in the none-too-distant future, when his quest for knowledge, which had taken such an unexpected detour, reached its inevitable, logical conclusion.

All he hoped for now was that, after he had passed, his parents were not the ones to find the lens at the chalet. But whether they did or didn't, its efficacy had been proven, and it *would* turn up again somewhere. For someone.

Someone doomed, as he was.

DEAD AIR

DAVID NIALL WILSON

NO TEARS FELL FOR Abner Brody. The sky seemed unable to contain its sorrow, and no sun rose to dry away its tears. The damp, chilled air hung heavy and dead. The air waves were dead. No more Brodymania. No more morning crew to stir up trouble for the nervous management at WROQ.

When Abner had been alive, they'd been nervous about what he might do — what he might say between paid advertisements and classic rock tracks. Now they were nervous about their future, because without Dear Abby Brody, they were going to have to scurry about like the little bureaucratic rats Brody had dubbed them just to stay afloat. He might have been an asshole, but he was all they'd had.

Now he was gone. The morning show had fallen on the drooping shoulders of Eddie too-much Tequila Braddock and his propensity toward fat-lady jokes. No one was listening. No one had come to the funeral, either. Abner Brody had been a great entertainer, but he'd not made any friends in the business, or out. Everyone hated him equally.

The tomb he'd had erected was an oddity unto itself. The four corners of the squat stone monument were in the shape of radio antennae. The stone box was wider at the foot and narrowed to a triangular point at the far tip. One of Brody's best weeks in the ratings had come the week he'd had the work done on this final resting place. He'd claimed that they would never shut him up — that the mindless, witless morons who tuned in day after day to hear him insult them would never be rid of him.

It appeared he'd been wrong. It appeared that no amount of haranguing the public for not reading a book when they chose to listen to him berate yet another idiot could make a difference. The radios clicked on like clockwork. The morning show blared through so many speakers it seemed you could walk from building to building or car to car and never lose a moment of it. It was everywhere — BRODY was everywhere — and now the air was dead.

Slack faced graveyard employees heaved the lid of the stone vault into place, raising it on hydraulic lifts that had been disguised for the day with black draping cloths and garlands of flowers from admirers and family too tired or apathetic to attend in person. They might as well have slid him out of the bed of a dump truck and backed over him with a load of fill dirt. No one would have been the wiser.

Still, the lid slid into place. The stone was sealed. Things *clicked* as Brody would have put it, grinning into his microphone and leering at a world only connected to him through his voice.

Veiled in layers of stone, purchased with hours of sweat and hours of words, copper wires met as the stone lid sealed tightly. The sound of stone scraping on stone was blurred for just a moment with a loud crackle of energy, and swallowed in a steady hum. No one noticed. With the lid sealed, and rain threatening, those left behind to seal him away departed. Brody was alone, and the current started to flow.

He'd not spent all his hours on the air. Not all hours alone are wasted. Power surged down lines laid over three bottles of Jack Daniels and five nights of hard labor. Wires spiraled up a pole near the fence of Shady Acres Cemetery and into the darkening gloom.

At WROQ, the sour stench of Tequila fouling the air in the booth, Eddie Braddock wrapped his long bony fingers around Abner's microphone. At WBNT TV-10, Elena Roberson wound up her knock-em-dead smile for the morning traffic report. At All-Com cable, 101 channels of dreck pumped like a molasses pulse through miles of cable, numbing minds across a tri-city area. The sheep were in the pasture, but the shepherd had departed the building.

Power surged. Underground batteries, charged and waiting, poured life into circuits born to the moment. The damp air around Abner Brody's grave crackled with energy. Then, with a snap, switches tripped, and church was in session.

Eddie Braddock leaned in close, slurring an introduction to the million and tenth spin of *Freebird*. There was a quick flash of lights as a panel to his right, a panel he'd never paid a moment's thought, burst into lightning-bright flame. The tequila on his breath probably ignited seconds before his greasy hair. It didn't matter — the glass doors leading out of the studio worked on an electronic slide assembly. The electronic slide assembly no longer slid. The WROQ lines were lit. Except for the dancing flame and a howl with no wire to travel, no one was home.

At WBNT the power was going out. It didn't flash out, like the radio station had done. It slowly melted. The heat rose, the current rushed through circuits no longer fuse-protected, but spliced by rolled balls of aluminum foil. Transformers bubbled, the oil melting from their cores. For a few moments, Elena Roberson smiled at the world. Then the signal fizzled, flickered, and died.

At All-Com three small electrical units popped. A one, and a two, and a three. Pop pop pop — nothing. Dead air.

Fifteen minutes to the second after Abner Brody's grave was sealed, the city fell silent. It took Eddie Braddock a few moments longer than the rest to grow still, but eventually the flames caught his clothing, and he stumbled into a rack of dials and knobs and compact discs, slipping toward the floor with a drunken lurch. His head struck the corner of a bench, and stars ushered him to oblivion.

Televisions paid silent homage. Radios crackled, a few dragging in the alternative rock station from down the coast — just for a moment — before the final pre-set explosion fused the power company's main transformers into a modern-art tribute to Rock 'n' Roll. Until the voice of Abner Brody spoke in deafening silence to the sheep, herding them along as always.

Tommy Murphy, last caller to be brow-beaten by the King of Radio, stared at his stereo in silent amazement. The hiss was mesmerizing. For some reason, he felt the weight of eyes on his back, and he spun, but no one was there. No one to share the moment. Falling back into one of his kitchen chairs, his hand curling reflexively around his coffee cup and raising it to his lips, Tommy turned.

On the shelf over his stereo, a short row of books sat. Books he'd not noticed in forever, and he wondered why he'd never read them.

Across town, Mary Phelps glanced out her window, the weather from the television dead, and the need to see for herself overwhelming.

For that short moment — the time between times when all was dead air and silence — the sheep awoke. In his bed of stone, it is said, Abner Brody smiled.

THE BIGGER THEY ARE . . .

C.J. HENDERSON

"My name is Ozymandias, king of kings;
Look on my works, ye Mighty, and despair!"

—Percy Bysshe Shelley

"IT WAS A BEAUTIFUL wedding . . ."

"Ya. Dey make a lovely couple, don't dey?"

Director Aikana and janitor Swenson looked at the young couple gliding across the dance floor, both of them wondering when either of the scientists had ever found the time to learn how to dance so gracefully. Of all his widely lauded accomplishments, however, from his discovery of the Jiffy-Pop Cancer Cure to the invention of the Spray-On Whoopie Cushion, Dr. Wendel Q. Wezleski was at the moment most admired for his being able to woo the fair, well really, the beautiful, all right, the darn right ravishing Linda Ginderhoff, the woman voted the Wonderful World of Science's favorite pin-up girl three years running.

But, despite the fame, glamor and mountainous chests of gold the pair had earned for her beloved Pelgimbly, director Aikana's eyes did not stay on the newlyweds for long. Try as she might to be in the moment, still she was the steel rod and biting whip of the Pelgimbly Center for the Advanced Sciences, and as such her attention was constantly attracted to whichever person, endeavor or whimsy might best next strengthen the walls of her venerable institute.

Thus the director could hardly be blamed in taking the occasional glance out over the crowd. Yes, of course, she recognized the couple's many co-workers. There to the left were the irrepressible Drs. Jones, Kimbreubo and Trillingham spiking the punch with either Trillingham's new Love Potion, or Jones' riotous "Temporary Flesh-Eating Virus," the disappearing ink of the bio/chem research set. And, to the right, she saw Associate Brodsky leading his highly-sought-after all-chimp orchestra, switching them from the melodic strains of the love ballad from *The Poseidon Adventure* to the theme from *Jaws* polka with barely a noticeable ripple in the tempo.

But far more was there to be seen that day in the crowd besides mere prank-oriented and rhythm-happy scientists. Everywhere one looked the glittering and the powerful were in attendance. The director had insisted the young couple allow the Center to pick up the tab for their nuptials, telling the love-struck pair it was far more important to keep them busy in their laboratories than allowing them to waste precious research time on such trivial matters as ordering flowers or inviting guests — especially when their address books were more likely to be filled with unnecessary types such as friends and relatives, rather than those whose presence would ensure further benefits of all manner for those wackiest of walking IQ machines who called that most bruised, battered and yet somehow still dignified edifice known as the Pelgimbly Center "the ol' work house."

In every direction kings, theologians and entertainers of the highest caliber could be spotted. The venerable Sultan of Si'chenba; the CEO of Hells Angels; Kendell Winkley, author of the wildly popular, if not terribly effective, new best seller *The Buttered Pork Diet — with Cheese!* right next to a gaggle of senators, governors, big city mayors and other unhorsewhippable rouges, all otherwise known as Aikana's kind of people.

But, even as she armed herself with two waiters laden down with free champagne and headed into the thicket of loose money, in a near perfect triangulation from the ever-creative director and the dancing couple who were, of course, the natural center of interest that evening, there stood two gentlemen quietly sipping drinks, barely noticed by the rest of the gala. The nearly Zen-like Professor Philip Morvently and his long-time friend and colleague, the far more excitable Dr. Maxim Ginderhoff scanned the crowd without actually being a part of it.

This was common enough for the venerable pair of researchers known affectionately to many as the Mutt and Jeff of the Pelgimbly Center, and most thought nothing of it, despite the fact that Ginderhoff was the father of the bride. In fact, those who knew the history of the pair at all, who understood Ginderhoff's deep and abiding dislike for the groom's slovenly research habits, his annoyance at the fact the man was recognized hands down as the world's greatest scientist despite his flawed though brilliant reasoning, his near-pathological hatred for the hunk of male flesh that, having taken every scientific accolade Ginderhoff had ever desired was now taking from him the only thing he considered more precious, deeply appreciated the wisdom of staying the Hell out of the scientist's way on that particular evening.

"So, Doc Ginderhoff, big night, ehhhh?"

The good doctor looked down his nose at the speaker, one Wheatley Glover, a research assistant Ginderhoff had taken an instant dislike to some months earlier when the nitwit had been involved with nearly collapsing the universe. Rumor had it the nincompoop had briefly had a chance to speak with God, but had merely stammered something about gratitude for Classic Trek. Ginderhoff had no idea whether the rumor was true or not, but the project had involved Wezleski, so he had decided to detest the sorry little graduate student on principle. When all he received for his attempt at communication was a frosted glare, Glover asked;

"Freshen your drink for you, sir?" This suggestion met with Ginderhoff's instant approval and brought about something akin to a slight thaw in his attitude. Indeed, as father of the bride, and considering the bride's father's well-known feelings about the bride's choice in husbands, it had been the most popular ice breaker he had heard that evening. And, thus far, whenever hearing it, Ginderhoff's answer seemed to always settle on something along the lines of;

"Yes. The quicker the better."

Glover asked what the professor was drinking, was given the curt answer of "whatever's closest," and departed to discover what that might be. In the meantime, Dr. Morvently, moving a touch closer to his oldest friend, opened his eyes a bit more against the crushing weight of fifteen Quarter Deck cocktails and said;

"I think you're going to have to accept the fact, Max, old boy. They're married now." Shaking his head in much the manner of a bull terrier attempting to throttle a piece of meat free from a bone, the esteemed professor of thermodynamic physics reached down into the bowels of his soul, then shouted;

"*Never!*"

"That's a very, very long time, Max."

"Yes," responded Ginderhoff, "it is. As is the amount of time that it took for mankind to realize the world was round. Or for the glaciers to roll relentlessly, irresistibly down from their Arctic strongholds to the beckoning warm seas of the south. That was a very long time, too. Or the amount of time dinosaurs ruled the Earth, now *that* was a very long time. But–"

The professor interrupted himself long enough to accept the Beauty Spot Cocktail brought to him by Glover, down it with a victorious gulp, and even enjoy the fascinating interplay of sweet and dry vermouths against the tastes of orange and pomegranate as they worked feverishly to pummel the drink's gin into submission, then threw back his head and roared;

"But there is no passage of time possible to equate with how long I shall despise, loath and forevermore spit upon the name of Wendel Q. Wezleski!"

Professor Ginderhoff was in a full-blown mad, and for once his old friend and companion had no idea how to curb his blood boil. His problem was that the vast intake of alcohol molecules into the bloodstream was not what was creating his friend's anger, only what was releasing it. Ginderhoff really did hate Wezleski with all the passion of a New Testament saint at the moment of epiphany or a Hollywood producer who had finally been green-lighted to begin his remake of *Citizen Kane* with two sit-com stars, four pop singers and a self-help guru with really nice teeth.

It was not that Wezleski had done anything personally or maliciously to the professor. It was only that every time Ginderhoff was about to achieve the next staggering step forward in scientific evolution, or reach for the last doughnut with both chocolate sprinkles and baby marshmallow creme swirls, there was that darn Wezleski, just a half step ahead of him.

Sliding down the wall, his body simply oozing under the weight of his depression, Ginderhoff sagged the sag of the damned and settled into a human puddle on the floor. Fishing through his pockets for the tiny airline bottles of alcohol he had wisely hidden about his person for just such an emergency, he twisted the top off a two-inch replica of a fifth of Old Mr. Boston Sloe Gin and then flipped the cap off into the darkened hallway beyond. Holding it before his eyes, trying to focus on the tiny Elizabethan face on the bottle, he said;

"I'm not a bad man. I wasn't a bad father. I'm a highly respected scientist . . ." The words trailed off as he continued to stare. After a moment, however, he suddenly turned his head to his friend and shouted;

"Why?!"

"Oh, I'm afraid," offered Morvently, "I really wouldn't know. I mean, actually, er ah, ummmm . . . why *what?*"

"Why, Philip? Why does Wezleski get the grants and awards? Why of all the bipeds with an extra ped crawling across the face of this world, why did he had to be the one my sweet baby girl had to fall in love with? How do such monstrous tragedies like this happen?"

"Gee," interrupted Glover quite by accident, not realizing how inappropriate it was for a research assistant to cut into a full professor's external monologue, "you really hate Doc Wezleski, don't you? And I'm betting for more than just that dinosaur thing — huh?"

And in that horrifying moment of moments, all was suddenly made clear to the besotted Ginderhoff. Pushing himself to his feet with the anger of a last place sports team's home town, the professor roared;

"By God, that's it!"

"What's it, Max?"

"The damn dinosaur, that damned dinosaur Wezleski let loose in the Institute, the one that chased us — you and I — up one son-of-a-bitching hallway and down the other. The only living dinosaur to ever smell the air of the twenty-first century. The one who almost had us for lunch! Do you remember that one particular dinosaur, Philip?"

"Well, now that you mention it," admitted Morvently, staring longingly into the bowels of his thoroughly empty cocktail glass, "yes, I do."

"That was where it all began. That day — that moment, when he let loose his masterstroke, turning us into objects of ridicule and scorn, leaving us to run like frightened schoolchildren from his escapee from the Mesozoic . . ."

Everyone at the Pelgimbly Institute for the Advanced Sciences remembered that day, of course, that sad, regrettable Tuesday when one of Wezleski's little adventures allowed a formidably-sized young velociraptor access to the venerable halls of their esteemed workplace. Half the staff had a reptilian encounter before that day was over. But sadly for Ginderhoff, he could not help but take the event far too personally.

Letting out a hollow sigh dripping with ennui and a longing for bigger bottles, he drained both his Jack Daniels Green Label and a pink and black affair covered with Chinese writing and a warning label about the danger of removing the cork near an open flame. Then suddenly, after a burp so prodigious it actually hurt his eyelids, he snapped his fingers and shouted;

"Eureka — that's it!"

Caught off guard by his friend's sudden enthusiasm, Philip Morvently could only watch in surprise as the heavy-set Ginderhoff leapt to his feet and began running down the hall. Starting after him a moment later, half-running, half-lurching under the crushing weight of his fifteen Quarter Decks, the quite confused professor of non-linear philosophy shouted;

"What's it, Max? What's it?"

"I'll beat Wezleski at his own game," shouted back Ginderhoff. "He wants to ruin my reputation, make me look like a fool, running away from dinosaurs. I'll show him . . ."

Pushing open the doors to the Chronology Department, Ginderhoff worked his way with amazing speed for a blind drunk through the regrettably all-too-lax protocols of Wezleski's time travel machine. Then, as the familiar pop-snapp — whiz-bing — fa'wuubabu of the chronos circuits began to chatter, Morvently entered the chamber just in time to hear his colleague growl to himself, in different voices, no less;

"Set the Wayback Machine, Sherman."

"For how far, Mr. Peabody?"

"Sixty-five goddamned million years, boy. I just figured out what killed the dinosaurs, and I want to see it happen."

"Really," exclaimed Morvently. Hanging onto the doorframe, his alcohol-soused body winded and reeling, he called out in honest scientific curiosity;

"What, Max? What was it? What killed the dinosaurs?"

"Me!" Ginderhoff shouted the word in wild-eyed triumph, "*I* killed the bastards — and now I'm going to go back and watch me do it!"

And, with those words formed, Dr. Maxim Ginderhoff vanished from sight, leaving behind only the echo of his final snarled sentence, and the feeling in the air that the idea of drunken time travels was not something to be taken lightly.

Ginderhoff awoke sixty-five million years earlier, marveling that he could travel back so incredibly far before his evening of non-stop drinking and still have such a world-class hang-over. It must have been a world class hang-over, he reckoned, for he was in such complete and utter agony he seemed to have gone — in the ever-so-refreshing slang of the American Hobo, circa 1933 — booze blind. He must have, he further reckoned, for although he was holding his eyes wide open, he could see absolutely nothing except a complete and unrelenting darkness.

His concern was not misdirected. Indeed, by all the scientific evidence at his disposal, he might very well be blind. He felt a slight breeze on his face. Warm and wet, it indicated to him that he was out-of-doors. But, when he aimed his head upward, he saw no stars, no trace of the moon — nothing. Of course, turning his head skyward made it throb all the more, and he was forced to return it to resting on his chin and shutting his eyes in an attempt to alleviate the pounding on the sixty-six little men he felt within his head along with their sixty-six little drums.

As he did so, he noted that his back seemed to be propped against a flat surface. Reaching behind him, his fingers encountered what his senses told him must be stone. In fact, as he probed the surface more closely, he found his never-ending cranial drum roll dissipating as he murmured;

"Now that's most curious . . ."

Not trusting a simple running over of the fingers, Ginderhoff heaved himself around and began moving his hands quite carefully over the surface against which he had found himself propped. Even there in the unrelenting darkness of the Mesozoic, after all, research was still research. Placing his cheek against the surface, he mumbled to himself;

"Interesting . . . cold to touch . . . perfectly smooth . . . no ripples, no sharp edges, not a waver or a fleck out of place . . . no, this isn't a volcanic out-throwing, nor obsidian or some other glass . . . no . . ." Standing, still running his hands over the absurdly smooth surface, he added;

"This is cut stone. Cut and polished. But who in the name of all the gods could have cut it?"

"That," came a slightly mechanical, somewhat alien voice, "would be me."

If Maxim Ginderhoff had ever shown surprise in his life, he showed it most clearly in that moment. To understand the situation, one must understand Wezleskian time travel. Dr. Wendel Wezleski, when he tinkered together the ability for people to propel themselves through the millennia, over a drunken weekend solely because his even drunker frat brothers had wagered he could not do it, had decided to create the most luxurious, care-free and idiot-proof method of time travel there could be.

If you needed to be inoculated against a certain disease before you could travel freely wherever you were going, his machine made certain you were inoculated. If you needed skin of a certain color, hair of a mandated length, clothing of a blend-in-able fashion, a nose that curved a particular way — whatever — all was arranged during the instant you disappeared from the present and the one where you reappeared somewhen else. Conversely, if understanding a certain language when you arrived wherever it was you were going was going to make things easier for you, then understand it you would.

Now, anyone knowing Ginderhoff well knew two things about him. One — he hated Wendel Q. Wezleski with a passion. And, two — he would allow nothing whatsoever, not even his deepest passions or desires, stand in the way of truth. Dislike Wezleski or not, he still was not fool enough to dispute the simple facts of the man's invention. He knew where he was. He was at the end of the Mesozoic. He had to be, because that was where he had told Wezleski's infernal device to take him.

Worse yet, in his drunken state he had indeed asked to be taken to the absolute, complete and very end of Mesozoic. By rights, he should be standing at ground zero, looking up to see a giant meteor plunging down toward his position from one angle or another. The dinosaurs should all be looking up, the sky should be sizzling, and he should be seconds from death.

Since none of that was happening, however, Dr. Maxim Ginderhoff had no choice but to accept that something was very, very wrong. And, while he was at it, he apparently also had to accept that if he was sitting on, standing on, and running his hands over cut, polished stone, and that there was a voice telling him that they were indeed the stone cutting and polishing type, that he was going to need a great deal more information, or at least liquor, to get through the morning. Patting his pockets, counting only some twenty, twenty-five more tiny bottles, he found he had no choice but to ask;

"And, where are you?"

"I'm right here in front of you." Since Ginderhoff could find nothing in front of himself except a stone wall, one of highly exceptional quality, but a stone wall nonetheless, he repeated his question. To which the reply came;

"As I said, I'm right here in front of you. And, of course, to either side. You are also standing on me."

At this point some, small but leading clues began to show themselves to the good doctor. Also, the passage of time and the calming of his initial alarm over the prospect of having gone blind had given him a previously overlooked fact. It was not completely dark everywhere. Off to the distance, in the opposite direction of the stone wall, he could see light along the far horizon.

In fact, as he began to adjust to the world of sixty-five million years before his own, he began to realize that there were stars in the sky after all. He simply could not see them for although he was outside, he was standing upon, and next to, something of such immense proportions, that it blotted out most of the sky.

"You . . ." Ginderhoff paused, the reassuring clink of his tiny bottles clanking against one another in his pockets the only sound to be heard. Crafting his question as carefully as he could for a man who had consciously so far only used seven words of the language within which he was communicating, he asked;

"You aren't the same as me . . . are you?"

"No."

"Could you, if it's not too much bother," asked Ginderhoff, "expound upon those differences for me?"

The slightly mechanical, somewhat alien voice returned its opinion in short order. As compared to the human Ginderhoff, it was longer lived by a great deal, of a much greater consciousness, size and stature. It considered its place in the universe as much more significant than the doctor of thermodynamic physics could ever even hope to understand, let alone obtain. It was merely stating facts, it insisted, but it did also offer Ginderhoff the chance to dispute its findings.

"It has been made clear to me," the voice freely admitted, "that facts can often change radically when one is given new facts to put against what one already has. For instance, I knew for a fact there were no living bipeds with opposable thumbs and even rudimentary tool-making ability anywhere on this planet. But you come from a primitive species nicely evolved to a practically conscious state. I grant you the right to argue with my findings since you are an anomaly to me."

And, in that moment, Maxim Ginderhoff froze to the core of his intellect. Instantly was he sober. Immediately did his limbs clear of fatigue, his nerves and mind free of static. They had to be, for he had no time for weakness. He was a man of science — more — he was a Pelgimblian. He was expected to rise to the occasion.

"Come, being . . . talk to me."

In rapidly split seconds, information poured in from every direction, all of it advising the good doctor on which course of action to take next. How to best approach the coming situation — whatever it was. How to figure out what to ask this unknown thing, the existence of which had never been evidenced by history or any of those who lived it. From the Greeks to the CIA, from ancient Mesopotamia to the halls of his own beloved Institute, never had even the wildest madmen of science ever seriously proposed such a thing.

What, he wondered, could he had possibly wandered into.

And, more importantly, he thought, how to wander back out again.

"I'm waiting . . ."

"Oh, my apologies," responded Ginderhoff delicately. Taking keen note of the actual impatience in the voice, he added; "it's just, well you see, I didn't think you would mind waiting a moment. I mean, who would think omnipotent beings could be impatient? You know, to be the one precludes being the other."

"Are you suggesting that you believe I am omnipotent?"

"No, no," argued Ginderhoff slyly, he hoped, "I'm suggesting I believed you must be omnipotent — for that moment, anyway."

"And why would you be willing to believe so?" asked the voice.

"Quite simple. You see . . ."

Ginderhoff raised his hand, his index finger pointed skyward, when suddenly he realized he was glowing — or at least, that his hand was glowing. Immediately his brain assured him he had been glowing for quite some time. Off and on, actually, and in different colors.

Egad, he thought, whatever I'm communicating with, we're not talking, vocalizing . . . we're modulating hues at each other.

Rapidly Ginderhoff realized that it had been his head that had done the majority of the glowing, but that when he had begun to add hand gestures for emphasis, that his hands had begun to glow as well. Suddenly, the implications of his situation staggered the good doctor.

Sixty-five million years in the past, he told himself, I run into an intelligent life form made out of cut stone, that cut the stone itself, that communicates through flashing colors . . . and the damn thing blots out the sky and thinks itself as supremely more important than a human being–

And at that moment, Ginderhoff's mind froze. What was he doing, he wondered. What was he speaking to? Why was it perched there at the end of the Mesozoic? What was it up to?

"What you are doing, of course, is up to you."

The good doctor's eyes bugged within his head, his mouth opening just enough for him to make a hissing noise that would have frightened any number of small children, had there been any small children present to be frightened. His thoughts, he realized, were not his own. Whatever he was talking with, it had "heard" everything he had just "said."

"As to what I am, I am a Time Anchor, the most sophisticated mining tool ever created. I was placed here in this time to oversee the strip mining of this world."

"Huh?" The noise was not the good doctor's most articulate moment, but it was enough to prompt the alien voice forward.

"My creators, the race known as the Mi-Go, first colonized the planet Yuggoth, ninth world in this solar system, some millions of years back. They have been mining their way through to the system's gravitational star ever since. Do you not know of Mi-Goian mining techniques?"

"Let us pretend I don't," answered Ginderhoff weakly.

In short order, the great stone wall explained to the good doctor that it was an anchor in time, one which served as a beacon for a mining operation from the other side of the universe. Although they were happy to take anything they found which was of use to any advanced civilization, of course, what had attracted the Mi-Go to the Earth was its incredibly rich copper deposits. The notion that the universe was not lousy with cupric and cuprous compounds was quite shocking to Ginderhoff, but not nearly as shocking as the fact that the Mi-Go mined a planet backward through time.

The furthest the Time Anchor could send mining parties forward was somewhat less than a billion standard Earthly years. At that point in the future, even as they spoke apparently, Mi-Goian miners were stripping the planet of all its desirable natural resources. When they were finished, however, they would not simply leave and go home like any other rapacious force. No, at that point they would simply fall back in time to a moment previous to the beginning of their first onslaught of the Earth, and re-dig up all the materials they had already mined all over again. This process would be repeated over and over until the miners had arrived back in the Mesozoic, where they would ravage the world one final time and then ship off to Venus to see what they could find beneath its sea or poisonous clouds.

Ginderhoff sat down in a crushed and gurgling heap, his mind reeling from what he had learned. His brain, metaphorically gasping from the consequences, struggled to find a corner to hide itself in which was not more frightening that the reality it was witnessing. Fortunately for the good doctor, his imagination, coupled with his overt pessimism, was sufficient that he could formulate something more terrible in every direction in which his trembling mind tried to hide. Having realized that by forcing himself to speak, he could mask his thoughts from the color-sensitive sensors of the Time Anchor, he said aloud;

"It's like the science in really bad sci fi, like L. Ron Hubbard, or *Space: 1999.* Then again, as Arthur C. Clarke said, 'Any significantly advanced technology is indistinguishable from magic.' Very well, if they think they can do it, they probably can. The problem is, what are you going to do about it, Ginderhoff?" Used to having conversations within his mind, to hearing the various tracks of his mind argue like any rational being, the good doctor answered himself, saying;

"What can I do?"

The good doctor took a moment to ponder that question. As the

Time Anchor had flashed its hues at him, he had seen within his mind the Mi-Go. Huge they were, resembling monstrously large, winged crustaceans with vast, egg-shaped heads. Their weapons were as astounding as the rest of their technology, and their sense of purpose absolute. In fact, he could see no way to disturb it. When the Anchor had mentioned the Mi-Go to him, it had told him everything about them in that one simple, two syllable burst of yellow and indigo. What it had told him the good doctor had found vastly depressing.

The Mi-Go mentality, it seemed, was practically unfathomable to the human mind. The race, if he understood what had been flashed to him correctly, purged its minds of any information if did not need for its immediate purposes. It was a strict need-to-know type of mentality, one that denied the human impulse toward creative thinking, but which kept them far more focused that any human could ever hope to be.

"The Mi-Go," he flashed to the Time Anchor, "swell guys that they are, their thought processes, they can't be distracted, can they?"

"It is not believed to be possible."

"You can't confuse them with logic, mess them up with metaphysics, twist them up in Nietzschian knots — can you?"

"Unlikely," agreed the machine. "But being a mere creation of theirs, I would not be able to say for certain. Of course, you could ask them yourself."

And then, as if things weren't bad enough, as the rays of the rising sun began to creep over the horizon, there lumbering toward the good doctor along the vast expanse of the Time Anchor were three dangerous-looking shapes he knew could be nothing else but a trio of Mi-Go. And, for the third time that morning, Ginderhoff's mind settled into an Arctic stupor.

Staring at the advancing aliens, the good doctor was as close to surrender as he could possible get without having him put on a beret and sing "La Marseillaise." They were armed, and he was not. They were three, and he was one. They were big and he was small. They were sober and despite his miraculous rallying of his inner spirit, he was still half in the bag. No matter which way he looked at his situation, from every angle, the Mi-Go seemed to have the unbeatable advantage.

And yet, if he let them incapacitate him, if he did not somehow conquer these invading aliens, stop their insidious machinery, and bring about the destruction of the dinosaurs, all life as he knew it on Earth, everything he held dear, even his precious daughter, Linda, would wink out of existence.

Would never come to be.

"Big problem," flashed the indifferent Time Anchor. "Much like wrestling with the Wezleski."

And with that, Ginderhoff realized that just as the Anchor had revealed all there was to know about the Mi-Go simply by mentioning them, he had revealed all about himself to it somewhere along the line. But far worse, the damnable machine had dared to compare its paltry invading alien race and their unfathomable, relentless mining operation and solar system-shattering offensive to the gut-wrenching poison that was Wezleski. It was saying he had no chance against them, that they were unstoppable. That he had no choice other than to fail.

Just as if they were *Wezleski!*

The sun just passing the edge of the horizon, the three approaching Mi-Go were clearly shown in all their otherworldly horror. Their clawed hands were monstrous, any one of them large enough to snap Ginderhoff in two with the slightest "snap." And, with the distance between them only a score of yards, it was obvious to the good doctor he had but seconds to act. Instantly submerging his anger, fear and inability to walk a straight line in the metaphysical liquid oxygen of his mind, he reached into his deepest bag of tricks, pulling out the last-ditch, sure-fire tactic of the truly evolved, he shut his mind to the facts that he was too old, too fat, too bald, and asked himself;

"Goddamnit — what would James T. Kirk do?"

As the Mi-Go continued to approach, the forward pair of the trio began to unlimber their sidearms when Ginderhoff threw up his hands and glowed;

"It's about time . . ."

Not recognizing his species, the Mi-Go were naturally somewhat suspicious. Voicing this fact, however, only brought from the good doctor that they did not recognize him because that information had been downloaded from their brains before their mission.

"In fact," he flashed, "we have a terrible problem because far too much about this operation was omitted from your initial information upload. Oh, it's terrible. Just terrible. The Time Anchor, it's in the wrong spot. It has to be moved. Has to. Simply has to. And the diseases this planet holds, the myriad deadly spores and pollens you were never inoculated against. It staggers the mind."

"W-W-What should we do?" asked one with a nervous flicker.

"Well first," responded the beaming doctor of thermodynamic physics as he fished in his pockets for every loose bottle he could find, "you've got to drink these, ah, antibiotics. As much as you can. As fast as you can."

"And then you did what?"

"Well," said a no-longer-glowing Ginderhoff, "after I got them sufficiently lubricated, making them a tiny bit more open to suggestion, I simply told them the Time Anchor had been set on its side instead of its base. They immediately set to work with some very impressive hydraulic jacks. Toppled the thing over on its side in no time."

"And so," asked a nearly sober Morvently, "it was the falling over of this stone computer, not an asteroid, that raised the dust cloud that killed the dinosaurs?"

"Created all the mountain ranges in Mexico and the Rockies, too, I believe," added the good doctor drily.

"Dad," said Linda Ginderhoff Wezleski, stepping forward to give her father a loving kiss on the cheek, "only you could save every human being who ever lived since the beginning of time with two pocketsful of itty-bitty liquor bottles."

"Hell of a story," added her new husband. "I mean, all I ever do is sit around and invent things. That . . . man alive . . . that was an adventure."

"A two-fisted adventure in science," shouted Glover, his face beaming with an admiration and longing not seen since Mr. Watson figured out what it was Alexander Graham Bell actually needed.

Ignoring the youngster for the moment, Ginderhoff looked over into Wezleski's eyes, searching the younger, far-less-bloodshot orbs for even the slightest hint of insincerity. Finishing his inspection and finding nothing but what appeared to be honest admiration, however, the good doctor felt something deep within him snap and melt away. Deciding that it might be time to accept his physician's advice and stop inviting a stroke, he allowed his blinding jealousy of the man who was now his son-in-law to evaporate against the warmth of his present good feelings. Sticking out his right hand, Ginderhoff amazed most everyone present then by saying;

"It was, indeed, son, it was, indeed."

And then, while the crowd attempted to recover, the good doctor made a beckoning motion to Glover and said, "So, my boy, if you think that was something, did anyone ever tell you of the time Phil Morvently and I piloted a blimp to the Andes in a search for the lost transistors of the zombie prince?"

Glover, who had only heard rumors of that most magnificent of tales, shook his head with the eager anticipation of a acne-festooned teenager as his fingers suddenly come in contact with printed matter under his father's mattress. Accepting the tall, frosty mugful of Ballard's Bitters from the impressionable young research assistant, Ginderhoff started;

"It was the year the dead began to walk in Peru. I remember because of the marguerites . . ."

THE MARGINS

ROBERT WEINBERG

1.

In 2001 (the most recent year for which statistics were available) 840,279 people (adults and juveniles) were reported missing to the police and entered into the FBI's National Crime Information Center (NCIC). The FBI estimated that 85-90% of missing persons were juveniles. Thus, in approximately 725,000 cases (or 2,000 per day) the disappearance of a child was serious enough that a parent called the police. Of this number, only a handful of children were ever located.

THE CLOCK HAD JUST finished striking eight when the phone rang. Looking up from the book he was reading, Jake Rosenberg frowned in annoyance. Thursdays were his night off. No calls, no assignments, no nothing. As a police detective, he rarely saw his wife and kids as it was. He needed the down time and the captain knew it. Hopefully, the call wasn't for him. Though Jake knew it was.

So did the two little girls sitting on the couch next to him, one on each side. Cute kids, twins named Kimberly and Kate, with long blond hair in pigtails, they resembled their mother much more than their dad. Just as well, as Jake was no movie star. He was six-two, two hundred and twenty pounds, with dark brown eyes, thick brown hair, and a four-inch scar that circled his right eye. The perils of being a cop, Jake called it. Damned lucky was all his wife Cindy would ever say.

"Jake," called Cindy from the kitchen where she was just finishing the dishes. "It's Phil."

"Tell him I'm out for the evening," said Jake, annoyed with his partner. Phil knew how much Jake looked forward to these evenings home with the twins. "Tell him I went out for a drink with a bunch of dancing girls and you don't know when I'll be back."

"Sure you did, sailor," said Cindy, walking the receiver into the living room. "Then he'd know for sure I'm lying. Take the call, honey. You know Phil wouldn't interrupt your free night unless it was an emergency."

"Yeah, I know," said Jake. Carefully, he closed the big picture book and shooed the kids off the sofa. Disappointed for only an instant, the twins followed their mother back to the kitchen where cookies waited. The girls knew better than to bother dad when he was talking police stuff.

"What's up?" he asked when they were gone.

"Another murder. Several more victims," said Phil Ketchum, his fellow detective and thirty-year veteran of the force. Phil's words were slurred, as if he had indulged in a few drinks before making the call. Knowing the case, Jake wouldn't have been surprised. "Same as always. Apartment locked from the inside. No signs of forced entry. Security system on. Blood everywhere. The usual stuff."

"How many stiffs?" asked Jake, dreading the answer.

"Two, we think," said Phil. The slur in his voice was worse. "*We think,* for jesus sake! We don't *know* for sure. Ain't easy for the guys in forensics to piece together the body parts scattered all over the apartment. It's hell, Jake. It's hell on Earth."

"I know, Phil. I know all too well. Give me the address. I'll be there as soon as possible. Try to stay loose till I arrive. Whatever you do, don't talk to the press."

"I'm not crazy," said Phil. "Besides, they'd never believe me. Sometimes I don't believe me myself."

"Have some coffee, Phil," said Jake, "and stay clear of the body parts. Try to sober up a little before I get there. Drinking ain't gonna crack this case."

"Nothing's gonna crack this case," repeated Phil. Phil started crying on the phone. "It ain't right. It ain't right."

Five minutes later, Jake, wearing his trench coat, packing his guns, was ready for the night. Cindy stood by the door, an apprehensive look on her face. She knew just enough about this latest case to be worried. The twins hung onto her apron.

"Don't wait up for me," said Jake. "Who knows how long this latest investigation will take. I might be gone all night."

"I'll leave a plate for you in the fridge," said Cindy.

"Daddy, daddy, when will you read us the rest of *Sleeping Beauty*?" asked Kate.

"When, when?" echoed Kimberly.

"Tomorrow," said Jake. "I promise girls. Tomorrow."

"Jake," said Cindy as he stepped over the threshold and into the hallway leading to the garage. "Be careful. Please be careful."

"I always am, honey," said Jake. For the briefest instant, he leaned over the girls and kissed his wife gently on the lips. "You're my one and only. I'm not going to do anything risky while you're around."

Jake meant every word he said. He had met Cindy on a blind date seven years earlier and it had been love at first sight. Jake sold his motorcycle in a week, and moved out of his low–rent bachelor pad in a month. His drinking was limited to a few cold beers once a week after the night shift with the boys. Otherwise, he walked the straight and narrow. Marriage and family had straightened him out big time. Which was one of the several reasons he hated the case he was working on.

"The Cut and Run Killer" it was called by the tabloids. And they didn't know half of it. The truth was too terrifying for all the details ever to appear in print. Bodies had been found inside apartments and homes, all locked and bolted from the inside, with no evidence that anyone had exited the premises. But, in every location, two, three, sometimes four or five bodies had been found. All dead, all cut up into pieces. Chewed into pieces, as if done by some huge animal. Chewed, with blood, lots and lots of blood everywhere, done by a beast with a mouth bigger than nearly anything on record. See any escaped lions in the neighborhood lately? Ones that entered a locked room, killed the inhabitants, and then disappeared, leaving no fingerprints and the doors still locked and bolted? Twelve people dead in the past two weeks with nothing to link them together other than the strange method of their murder. It was a field day for conspiracy theorists and wackos of all stripes and persuasions. The worst of it being that for all Jake knew, one of the wackos might have it right.

Jake stepped out of an elevator on the tenth floor of an expensive high-rise apartment building on Chicago's near north side. Places around here cost three or four times as much as his two bedroom bungalow on the south side. In Chicago, you paid for location. Carefully, he walked down the hallway, avoiding forensic detectives working on the glass walls and shag carpet. Fifteen feet from the elevator was a doorway, 10-C, that had been kicked in. The CSI man examining the lock didn't even bother to lock up when Jake walked into the apartment. Jake knew already that there would be no fingerprints. Whoever the perp or perps were, they never left fingerprints. Not even a smudge. Jake stepped into the living room. Nice. A huge hi-def TV hung on one wall. Across from it was a white leather couch, two marble end tables, and some lights. The carpet was light blue and matched everything perfectly. Several crime-scene people were examining the furniture. His partner, Phil Hale, was questioning a middle aged couple, most likely man and wife, probably the neighbors. Jake knew what they would say. No fight, no noise, no nothing. After waiting for the people inside to open up the door for one reason or another, they had gotten frightened and called the cops. The police, already on alert due to the previous silent kills, had broken down the door and stumbled across this. The perfect apartment, in near perfect shape, no evidence of violence anywhere, but with large pieces of the owners scattered across the floor like pieces of modeling clay dropped by a hurried child.

Phil, his face beet red, closed his notebook and nodded his appreciation to the people he had been interviewing. "Thanks for your help. Please do us one favor. Keep everything to yourself. We wouldn't want to start a riot."

The big, burly cop turned to Jake. "Sorry I had to interrupt your night off. I know how much you like to spend time with your kids."

"No problem, partner," answered Jake. He saw no reason to remind Phil of their phone conversation. His partner seemed to have sobered up remarkably well. This case did that. "It comes with the territory. Where's the bodies?"

"In the bedroom," said Phil, dropping his voice to a whisper. "We thought it best to keep the pieces in there. The hell with moving them before the coroner arrived. Too many outsiders see the remains we'd be in deep shit. Need a riot squad to break us out of here."

Jake said nothing, as there was nothing to say. He hated violating department policy, but Phil was right. One look at the corpses would freak out the country.

The bodies, or at least the pieces of them, were in the bedroom. There were eight sections total. A foot, wearing a shoe, attached to an ankle, with a sock on, attached to a leg that extended almost up to a knee. Where it came to an abrupt halt, an ending. Bitten off cleanly, one cut from teeth as sharp as razors. A leg, ripped from a torso, with a pool of dark blood beneath. What animal had a bite so powerful and so deep that it could just cut through a body at the thigh on both sides? And what sort of animal ate flesh in such huge chunks?

Next to the foot was a hand comprised of four fingers and a thumb, a palm, and the beginnings of a wrist. That was all that was there. Again, the cut was sharp, as if done by a razor. Layer upon layer, flesh then tissue, then bone. Sliced off the arm, which was nowhere to be found. Blood, pools of it, quarts and quarts of it everywhere. A hand and a foot, an arm from elbow to shoulder. Part of a torso, with most of it missing. A head with half the skull off. It was grotesque, frightening. It was unholy.

Jake lifted the head by the thick wavy hair growing from the scalp. For an instant, he stared directly at the head, trying to see some clue that the rest of them had missed. It was at that instant, both of the head's blue eyes popped open and seemed for a second to look at Jake in absolute shock. With a screech that nearly woke the dead, Jake dropped the head back on the bed. On the blanket, the eyes blinked, once, twice, and then were still. Rushing to the nearby bathroom, Jake threw up his supper.

"Sorry about that," said Phil. "The bodies are cut so sharply that sometimes the reflexes still seem to work. Even hours after death. The hand over there was still twitching when I arrived on the scene twenty minutes ago. Reflexes I guess."

"Right," said Jake. "Next time, remember to warn me in advance not to pick up any stray heads. I'll be lucky if I sleep in a week."

"What do we tell the press?" asked Phil.

"Same as before," answered Jake. "No comment, no comment, we're working hard on these cases and expect a break any time now. No comment."

They made it back to their police car with a minimum of fuss. More than a dozen reporters had converged at the front entrance of the condominium, and they were all anxious for answers. Something, anything to tell their viewers beyond the usual "no comment." A pretty, young woman from CNN was the most determined.

"Detective Rosenberg, is it true that the police don't have any leads in this murder investigation? Are you any closer to finding the Cut and Run Killer? How can there be twelve people dead without one clue?"

"No comment," said Jake.

"Eye-witness reports indicate that only parts of the bodies have been found at the crime scenes. What do you say to that? Is some jungle beast killing Chicagoans?"

"No comment," repeated Jake.

"When will the police comment on these crimes?" the girl finally asked in frustration.

"No comment," said Jake.

2.

On November 25,1809, an Englishman named Benjamin Bathurst vanished, inexplicably and utterly. He was en route to Hamburg from Vienna, where he had been serving as his government's envoy to the court of what Napoleon had left of the Austrian Empire. At an inn in Perleburg, in Prussia, while examining a change of horses for his coach, he casually stepped out of sight of his secretary and valet. He was not seen to leave the inn yard. He was never seen again.

Stepping on the gas, Jake pulled the police car out into traffic. Sitting next to him, Phil scribbled notes onto a small note pad.

"Sooner or later," said Phil, "the public is going to learn the truth. The city will explode."

"Not our problem," said Jake. "Let the chief handle the publicity."

"People see those body pieces, they're gonna go nuts. Close down the zoos. Demand all the animals be shackled to their cages."

"Not if we find the killer first," said Jake.

Jake glanced over at his partner. Phil was starting to show his age. His face was beet red, with small rivulets of sweat trickling down his cheeks. His breaths came in deep, measured gasps. He really shouldn't be in the field anymore. Phil belonged behind a desk, shuffling paperwork. His presence on this case indicated how desperate the chief was to find the "Cut and Run Killer." Every able-bodied man in the department had been assigned the case. With absolutely no results to show for it.

"Cindy said you were reading to the twins," said Phil, shifting subjects.

"Yeah, right," said Jake. "The girls really have grown the past six months. You need to stop by for dinner some time. They'd be thrilled to see their "Uncle Phil."

"Sure," said Phil. "Once this case–"

Suddenly, the car radio burst into sound. "All cars, all cars. Armed robbery in progress. Fourteenth and Madison, the *Lexo Grill*. Suspect is described as armed and dangerous. Repeat, armed and dangerous!"

"Fourteenth and Madison," repeated Phil. He reached into his jacket, pulled out his service revolver. "That's only six blocks from here. Coincidence?"

"I hope not," said Jake.

Holding the steering wheel with one hand, Jake reached down and grabbed a portable police siren from the floor. He attached it to the door and cued in the siren. Phil was already on the hand-mic with the dispatcher. "We're on the way!"

The restaurant was located on the corner of Fourteenth Street and Madison Avenue. It was a big wooden building that filled most of the lot. Lots of fancy glass windows, well landscaped, to Jake's eyes it looked fancy. Not the type of place where a maniac starts firing into a crowd. Twenty years ago, the patrons of the place probably all dressed in suits and dresses. Now, the crowd outside was wearing jeans, men and women both, and tank tops and muscle tees. The only thing certain in the world was change.

Revolver drawn, Jake only half-listened to the establishment's owner who was busily jabbering away at Phil. "Don't know where the guy came from. One minute he wasn't there. The next, poof, there was this weird popping noise and he was standing on a table, waving around this funny-looking gun, demanding food. Crazy, I tell you, crazy. Why my place? Why not the the dump down the street? They handle crazy people all the time. Me, I got standards. We don't let no crazy people in our place."

"Right," said Phil. "Where's the suspect at the moment?"

"In the kitchen," said the owner, his hands fluttering in the air like lost birds. "He's in the kitchen. With my chef, Pierre."

Phil looked at Jake. Jake nodded. They both had their guns drawn.

"A guy that appears out of nowhere?" said Jake.

"You don't think–" said Phil.

"I don't know what to think," said Jake. "All I know is that I'm not waiting for backup. This guy might disappear back into nowhere before they arrive."

"Sounds like a plan to me," said Phil. "Let's go."

Cautiously, making as little noise as possible, the two officers entered the restaurant. The place was a mess. Tables and chairs overturned, dishes and glasses scattered everywhere. Food on the floor. The obvious result of a mad, panicky rush for the exit. Beyond the dinning room, from the kitchen, came the sounds of raised voices. Checking to make sure the safety was off on his revolver, Jake edged up to the swinging doors that led into the kitchen. Phil was a step behind him.

"Three, two, one," mouthed Jake and burst through the doors into the other room. He was on his feet, his gun pointed out in front of him, his finger steady on the trigger.

"NYPD!" he announced. "Nobody move! And I mean nobody."

The kitchen was crowded with metal stands, sinks, burners and refrigerators. There was food on most every bare space. In the center of the room was a large preparation table loaded with half-completed meals.

To one side stood a tall slender man dressed in a white chef's apron and chef's cap. He had curly black hair and dark terrified eyes. His face was whiter than his clothing. His hands were high in the air.

"Do not shoot," he said, his voice trembling with emotion. "I am an innocent bystander. Please, do not shoot."

A few feet further on was a short, elderly man with long white hair and a bristly white moustache. Even his eyebrows were white. Blue eyes stared at the two policemen. He said nothing, as his mouth was crammed full of a dinner roll. He was dressed shabbily in an old pair of blue jeans and a gray sweat-shirt. In one hand he held what looked like a futuristic, stubby weapon that closely resembled a pistol. The weapon, if it was one, was pointed directly at the chef.

"Lower your weapon," said Jake, taking in the entire scenario in an instant and deciding the old man was the most dangerous foe they faced. "Lower that weapon *now*!"

"You're making a terrible mistake," said the old man, gobbling down the last of a roll. "I'm not your enemy. Really, I'm not."

"Right," said Phil. "That's what they all say, pops."

SCRE-E-ECH! The sound was so loud, so intense that for a moment, Jake forgot where he was, what he was doing, and why he was doing it. His mind went numb, his eyes glazed and his hearing ceased to function. Then, his senses returned and he found himself staring at horror unimaginable.

"The Hounds," cried the old man. "Maureen must have followed you here. Gentlemen, if you value your life, don't move. Don't move a muscle. Motion attracts them. If you remain still, they'll leave you alone."

The creatures, the Hounds according to the old man, were emerging like immense drops of water through what appeared to be a foot-wide black hole directly in the top right corner of the room, where the walls and ceiling all intersected to form a corner.

Each creature appeared to be about four feet long, with an extremely narrow, hairless body, and a huge head, with a incredibly wide mouth bristling with immense teeth. Legless, armless, the things wiggled like gigantic worms through the air, their gigantic jaws opening and closing like steel traps. They resembled nothing on Earth. Colors rippled across their bodies. Gray, brown, black, magenta, pearl. The monsters pulsed like some gigantic living strobe light. Their bodies rippled like gigantic snakes wiggling across a floor. They were the most grotesque, most horrifying things Jake had ever seen.

Jake blinked, shook his head, tried to clear his vision. Dust motes, stirred up from the floor and table, hung in the air in front of his eyes.

Unmoving, unchanging dust motes. Spurred by a sudden hunch, Jake looked down at his watch. It was 2:15 a.m., and the second hand was no longer moving. Yet Jake had the terrible feeling that the watch wasn't broken. Instead, he sensed, he knew without any other evidence, that the appearance of the creatures had frozen time. They had emerged from a place where time did not exist and brought a small piece of their darkness with them. Reality for the moment had broken down.

"Mother of God," whispered Phil.

"What the hell are they?" asked Jake.

"Four-dimensional Hounds," said the old man. "Gigantic appetites with teeth."

"Can we kill them?" asked Jake. "Will our bullets harm them?"

"No," said the old man. "They don't belong in this dimension and nothing here can hurt them. Fortunately, when the hole in space through which they entered closes, they'll die. They can't exist in real time. The trick is to stay alive until then."

"Your crazy if you think I'm staying here with those things," cried the chef, almost forgotten in the horror of the moment. The dark haired man grabbed a kitchen cleaver and swinging it back and forth in front of himself, started backing up to the door leading to the dining room.

"Stop, you fool!" the old man cried. "They're attracted by motion."

Jake gasped as suddenly all three of the monsters zapped like wasps across the room. They headed straight for the chef. Jaws opened wide, nearly doubling in size. Cursing, the chef swung his cleaver at the first of the Hounds. Moving faster than the eye could follow, the creature circled around the swinging blade and chomped down onto the arm holding the cleaver.

The entire room seemed to jerk, as if hit by an earthquake. Teeth gnashed against teeth. The chef's hand, fingers still wrapped around the handle of the cleaver, dropped to the floor. Blood spurted like a fountain from the man's arm, sheared off from the shoulder like a piece of roast. On the floor, the chef's fingers still twitched with life.

The chef shrieked. He was missing an arm all the way up to his shoulder. His limb was gone and blood was pouring out of his wound like a fountain. He only had seconds to live, if that. But he didn't die. With no time, there was no death. "Where's my arm?" the chef screamed. "Where's my arm!"

There was no answer that made any sense. The second of the three creatures darted forward and buried its teeth into the chef's chest. The man in white fell backward, looking exactly as if a gigantic ice cream scoop had ripped out a section of his torso. What little blood still remained in his body trickled out onto the front of his uniform. His limp form, cut nearly into two separate pieces, folded inward like a shell with the center removed. The upper portion hit a table, slid a few inches on the blood, then held. Stuck. The chef's eyes were still open. In this state of limbo, he couldn't die.

Buzzing like some gigantic bumble-bee, the third Hound hovered over the chef's head. Tears trickled down the man's face as the huge jaws only a few inches above him, opened, revealing dozens of inch-long razor-sharp teeth.

Blam, Blam, the sound of bullets caught Jake totally off guard. Two blotches of darkness suddenly appeared on the Hound's face; otherwise it seemed unharmed. But distracted. Ignoring the chef, the creature spun around, searching for the cause of this sudden annoyance.

Phil stood ten feet away, his revolver drawn, a wisp of smoke drifting from its muzzle. He looked frightened but determined. Before the Hound could move, Phil fired again. This bullet caught it square in the mouth. Nothing happened. In a three-dimensional world, the Hounds were invulnerable to physical objects.

Jake pulled out his gun. He wasn't going to let his partner down, even if it meant trying to stop the unstoppable. All three Hounds were swarming toward Phil. Not even bothering to aim, Jake just pointed and fired. And fired. And fired.

The Hounds disappeared an instant before their jaws could close upon either of them. Jake knew they had been incredibly lucky. Their guns had been totally useless against the monsters. Only the closing of the hole from which the creatures had emerged had saved them. He glanced back down at his watch. The second hand was moving again. It was 2:16 in the morning. During the time the Hounds had been in the room, time had stopped.

"Damn," said Phil, his face bright red as a tomato. Sweat was pouring down his cheeks. "That was close."

"Too close for the chef," said Jake, holstering his gun. There, on the floor, was the unfortunate cook, in several pieces. Dead, in a widening pool of blood, exactly like the people they had been finding in the locked apartments for the past week. That mystery was solved. Though explaining the solution and the Hounds to the captain might take some doing. At least they had the old man to back them up. He seemed to know a lot about what had happened.

Thinking of the old man, Jake looked around. Just in time. A dozen feet away, the white-haired man had his gun pointed at a wall and jagged lines that looked like electrical static were coming out of the nozzle.

Forming on the wall was a hole some three feet in diameter, filled with the same dark nothingness from which the Hounds had appeared.

"Hey," shouted Jake, taking a step forward. "Hey you!"

"Jake, I don't feel so good," said Phil, gasping for air. The big man's eyes glazed over and without another word, he crumpled to the floor.

The old man looked at Jake then stepped into the shadowy hole in the wall. He was gone, disappeared, before Jake could even blink.

Jake hesitated but just for an instant. He needed to help Phil. But first he had to catch the old man. Otherwise, no one would believe a word of what had taken place here tonight. And Jake very much wanted them to believe.

Running forward, Jake leapt for the circle which was quickly shrinking to nothing. "Come back here," he yelled and plunged into the shadows. Unfortunately, the hole closed so fast that the toe of his right foot didn't make it through in time. The circle vanished, and Jake's toe, still in his shoe, dropped like a stone to the kitchen floor.

"Jake," gasped Phil, "Help me, Jake!"

But Jake was no longer there.

3.

On November 5, 1872, the brigantine, Mary Celeste set sail from New York harbor for Genoa, Italy. On December 5, a British naval ship, the DeGratia, discovered the ship derelict, floating in the middle of a calm sea, and boarded her. Everyone aboard the Mary Celeste was gone — her captain, his family including a young daughter, and its 14-man crew. The ship was in perfect order with ample supplies and there was no sign of violence or trouble. Nor was anything unusual marked in the Captain's Log. The fate of the crew remains unknown.

Jake was in no position to help anyone. Eyes wide open, he looked around at nothingness. Wherever he was, scenery seemed unimportant. The world was empty of anything. He stood in nothingness, surrounded by nothingness. Behind him, words that no longer had any meaning, the hole was gone. Whatever method he had used to arrive in this place, that method of travel was no more.

"Where am I?" he asked. The words seemed to vanish into the void, without the least trace of an echo or vibration.

"What the hell is this place? Some sort of underground prison? Where's the old man? Where's anybody? Anything?"

No answer. He stared at his watch. The second hand had stopped again. Wherever he was, it was outside of time. If that made any sense.

Jake stepped forward. At least his body still seemed okay. Nothing wrong with that. Then he noticed his right foot. And remembered an instant of pain just before he entered this place. The leather on the end of his foot was gone, and his big toe was missing. Fortunately, it seemed that being chopped off by the gateway had burned the wound closed. He wasn't even in pain, though he suspected it would be a long time before he ever walked barefoot again.

Carefully, he took several deep breaths. He wasn't sure what he was breathing, but it seemed safe. Despite his missing toe, his foot felt okay. Tentatively, he took a step forward. Then another, and another. He was walking in nothingness, but somehow the nothingness supported him.

Looking around, he spotted what appeared to be a series of dark smudges on the horizon. Not knowing what to do and knowing that doing nothing would drive him crazy, Jake began walking in the direction of the markings. Surprisingly, it only took him a few minutes to arrive at the first dark spot. Distances were different here.

He found himself looking at what appeared to be a gigantic bubble. Though it was totally transparent, he couldn't claw his way through, though he tried and tried. The outside material was stronger than steel. Inside the container he could see the kitchen of the restaurant he had just been in. Evidently, only a few seconds had passed since he had gone through the hole into somewhere. Phil was lying in a heap in the middle of the floor, both hands clutching his chest. His breathing was harsh, labored. Jake could hear every sound.

"Phil," Jake cried. "Hang in there, old buddy. I'm here, on the other side of this barrier. I'm here." Phil gave no indication he had heard a word.

A half-dozen men, wearing SWAT jackets, poured into the room. The lead officer looked around, spotted Phil. Saw the remains of the chef.

"Officer down!" the SWAT leader cried.

"Medic, we need a medic in here immediately."

"Hey, guys, it's me," Jake shouted at the top of his lungs. "Me, Jake Rosenberg, I'm outside the bubble. Hey, hey!"

No one heard him. No one saw him. It was as if he wasn't there.

"I'm not crazy," Jake said aloud. "I'm not crazy." But he was no longer so sure.

He soon discovered another bubble, not far from the first. There were dozens of them, hundreds of them, stretching out for as far as he could see. Same size, same shape, but inside each was different. Jake found himself looking at his living room. At Cindy. Talking to an inspector from the department. It was later, hours later. The clock on the mantle said 5 a.m. He had been awake all night but he didn't feel tired. He was hungry, but not terribly so. Still, he couldn't help wonder what he could eat in a place like this. Or even if there was anything to eat in a place like this?

"No," said Cindy, a horrified look on her face. "I-I don't believe it. He can't be dead. He just can't."

"I'm sorry, Mrs. Rosenberg," said George Pryor, the department spokesman. Jake knew George pretty well. They were friends. George would never do this to Cindy. Never. "The only thing left of Jake was his right toe. Whatever horror devoured the chef must have eaten Jake too. I'm sorry. It's too grotesque to even believe, but we have no choice. The evidence doesn't lie."

"Devoured?" whispered Cindy. "Devoured? What kind of monster devours policemen in high-class restaurants and then disappears without a trace? This can't be true. It can't be."

Jake howled in anguish. "Cindy, I'm alive. I'm alive! Don't believe this insanity. I'm alive!"

Yet even Jake wondered if he was or not.

It was later, much later. Jake wasn't sure of the time, nor did he care. Nothing really mattered in this universe of absolute emptiness. He was perched on a bubble, another one of the uncountable number of bubbles that existed in this strange place. By now, he felt so depressed, so filled with despair, that he hadn't bothered to check what was inside. Why should he care? He was trapped outside, and there was absolutely nothing he could do about it. He felt very alone. Very very alone.

"Hey, you up there." It took Jake several seconds until he realized whoever was speaking was speaking to him. Someone speaking to him, not inside a bubble. Not a product of his imagination. Another person, here, in nowhere, talking to him, seeing him. "Are you that cop, Jake Rosenberg? The one assigned to the Cut and Run murders?"

Jake raised himself on his hands, peered over the side of the bubble. He wasn't dreaming. A middle-aged blond woman, dressed in a fairly conservative brown suit, with a beige blouse, and a thin gold chain dangling around her neck, stood about ten feet away. She had blue eyes, hard blue eyes. As a cop, Jake had long ago learned to judge people by the look in their eyes. He didn't like what he saw in this woman's eyes. Even less, he didn't like the things that swirled around her feet. Hounds, the old man had called the monsters. Smaller than the ones who had slithered through the hole in the ceiling, through the crack in reality. More like worms with mouths. Mouths that were full of gigantic, sharp teeth. Nearly a dozen of the hounds swayed and danced around the woman's knees and ankles. She paid them no heed.

"Are you deaf?" she asked, a nasty sound to her voice. "Or just dumb? Are you or are you not Jake Rosenberg?"

"Sure," he said, standing up on the bubble so that he towered over her like some giant Goliath confronting the boy, David. "That's me. Who wants to know?"

"Dr. Maureen Trevor, if it matters," said the blonde. "Not that it will do you much good to know. I'm the person behind the Cut and Run killings. Me and my pets, that is."

"You confess?" said Jake, momentarily confused. "I don't get it."

"Of course not," said Maureen, laughing wildly. For the first time, Jake got a look at her teeth. They were huge, longer than any human teeth had a right to be, and filled her mouth to overflowing. They were the same sort of teeth as those possessed by the Hounds. Whatever Maureen Trevor was, she wasn't entirely human.

"Get him, my pets," she commanded and pointed at Jake. "Tear him to pieces. Tiny little pieces I can put in a box and mail to his grieving wife."

Hissing like snakes, the Hounds floated upward, their thin bodies twisting back and forth, propelling them forward straight at Jake. Suddenly realizing his peril, he turned, scrambled to the other end of the bubble, only to be confronted by more Hounds. They were everywhere, dozens and dozens of them. Slipping and sliding through the nothingness toward him. He was trapped, no place to go.

Then, with Jake thinking nothing more could surprise him, a three-foot glowing circle appeared on the surface of the bubble only a few feet from where he was standing. The circle turned silver, then gray, then black. Out from its center appeared a man's head. The old man Jake had chased into this bizarre place.

"Do you want to live?" the old man asked.

"Of course," replied Jake, as the Hounds came slithering ever closer.

"Then grab my hand," commanded the old man, raising one hand out of the circle and into the nothingness. "And don't let go."

Jake grabbed. The old man yanked, hard, and Jake went flying. With a clank, he smashed hard into a sheet metal floor. Above him, a hole into nothingness disappeared.

4.

The disappearance of New York Supreme Court associate justice Joseph F. Crater is considered one of the most baffling mysteries of the 20th century. For years after, Judge Crater was known by the phrase "the most missingest man in New York." The Judge was last seen on the night of August 6, 1930, leaving out of a Manhattan restaurant. Crater was a tall, heavyset man who liked good clothes. He looked particularly svelte that night as he left the eating establishment, waved his goodnights to some friends, and then slipped into a taxi-cab for a ride home. He never arrived. Judge Crater was never seen again. Leaving people to wonder how a man as powerful and prominent as a Supreme Court judge could disappear without a trace?

"Where am I?" Jake asked, not entirely sure if he wanted to know the answer. He appeared to be in a huge circular chamber composed entirely out of painted red sheet metal. He estimated the room to be twenty feet in diameter and ten feet high. He was half-lying, half-sitting in the center. The old man was a few steps away, staring into something that resembled a computer monitor. On it, Jake could see an image of a very angry Maureen Trevor. She was screaming at several dozen hounds clustered around her feet. The monstrous creatures appeared to be cringing in fear.

"Hell hath no fury like a woman," said the old man.

"A woman scorned," said Jake.

"In this case, a woman is enough," said the old man. "I assume you are hungry? Yes. Then we will eat. After, we will talk."

"My wife," said Jake. "I've got to call my wife. Tell her I'm not dead."

"I understand," said the old man. "But I would strongly advise not. Maureen Trevor has you on her mind. Until you bring her reign of terror to an end, contacting anyone, anyone at all, would be the same as pointing out their location to Maureen and her hounds. Remember what happened in the restaurant? Now, think of the same events taking place in your house. I know it sounds unbelievable, impossible, but think of what you've just experienced. Then, tell me if anything is impossible?"

That little speech silenced Jake more effectively than a fist to the mouth. He followed every order the old man gave, did every chore as fast as possible. In less than a half-hour, they sat outside in the late afternoon sunshine, feasting on steaks and beer. The one thing Jake did notice was that there were no sharp angles anywhere nearby. None.

"My name is Beckham Salt," declared the old man, snogging down a bottle of dark beer with one fluid motion. "I'm retired. This is my country estate, in Chicago's northwest suburbs. I taught at University of Chicago for twenty years in the Advanced Math department and was pretty well known throughout the country. After the death of my wife, I left teaching and did some traveling. Finally, I ended up here.

"One day, a little more than a year ago, I received an incredible letter. It was from a mathematician I had met in Germany. In the letter, my colleague claimed to have discovered a fairly simple method to enter the fourth dimension. It was going to be the subject of his next book and he had no doubts that it would win him the Nobel Prize in Physics. He wanted me to read the manuscript, checking it for errors. I agreed, then waited for the book to arrive. And waited and waited. Months passed and I heard nothing more from my friend, Ziegfried. I started to worry. While his discovery was fairly esoteric, it could have military uses. I made some inquiries and learned nothing. So I flew to Germany to see what was what.

"I could find nothing about Ziegfried other than that he had died in a fire in his apartment a week after he had contacted me. No one knew about any manuscript nor anything about his project. The only one who seemed to know anything about his studies was his assistant, a very plain but pleasant woman named Maureen Trevor.

"I gathered up Ziggy's notes and decided to try to duplicate his experiments. Maureen proved to be a great help and it wasn't long before I felt sure I was on the verge of making the same breakthrough as my old friend. I know, you are wondering why I never suspected Maureen of being involved with Ziggy's death. Call me a foolish old man, but it never once occurred to me that Maureen could be a killer.

Until the night that I actually tested my inter-dimensional pistol. It worked perfectly. That's when Maureen congratulated me and pulled a gun. She had killed Ziggy but his plans had proven too complex for her to understand. So she waited for me to come along and provide her with the weapon she needed. Fortunately, she was a miserable shot. I escaped and ran to the police. Being not entirely a fool, I told them that Maureen was a student trying to steal a secret government project I was working on for the Chinese. They sent a squad car to my house, but it was too late. Maureen had used the inter-dimensional pistol to open a hole into the fourth dimension and had escaped there, along with most of my equipment."

"When was that?" asked Jake.

"A little more than three weeks ago," answered the Professor. "A little investigating on my part turned up the fact that Maureen was actually a quite dangerous psychopath. She had a list of enemies with hundreds of names on it. Persons she had met over the years that had slighted her in some imaginary manner. Armed with the gun and access to the fourth dimension, she started killing everyone on her list. And continued to kill them, until I finally realized that I was the only one who could stop her. When you stumbled across me in the restaurant, I was on that mission. Not succeeding I must admit. I am not a killer."

"Better back up a few paces," said Jake. "I understand all about Maureen. But explain to me the part about the fourth dimension. I'm a little hazy on that. My last math class was in high school. I always thought there were only three dimensions, length, width and height. What's the fourth? Time?"

"Some scientists think of time as an extra dimension," said Salt, "and a measurement of duration that is important in every dimensional map. But, it is not the dimension of measurement like the one I mean. A single dimension can be represented by a straight line . Two dimensions, length and width, placed at right angles form a field, a two dimension surface, a square or a rectangle. Three dimensions, require three lines placed at right angles to each other. Using three lines, we can form a cube, a body of width, length, and height. Adding a fourth dimension would consist of merely adding another line at right angles to the first three. In a three dimensional universe, such a direction is impossible. But in a multi-dimensional universe, it does exist."

"Space curves in four dimensions," said Jake, trying to remember what little he recalled of high-school physics. "That fourth dimension is called hyperspace."

"Exactly," said Professor Salt. "The easiest way to understand the curvature of space is to think of an auto race. The two cars race along what seems to be a straight track. The one that goes faster wins. However, we know the Earth is curved, so therefore the race track is on a curved surface even though that's not noticeable to us. If a car went directly from the beginning of the track to the end, following a straight line from one point to another, much of its straight route would plow through the earth. That's the curvature of space. Apply the same example to the real world of three dimensions, and it becomes obvious that the shortest path between two objects in three-dimensional space is to travel on a curve through the fourth dimension,"

"Yeah, but what does this have to do with the murders?" asked Jake.

"All in good time," promised Salt.

"We live in a three dimensional world, Jake. At least it seems that way to us. But as we proved with the race, what we see isn't always everything. Our space is curved in a fourth dimension. The entire universe is curved. We just don't have the right senses to see that fourth dimensional curve. Every object in three dimensions has an extension in the fourth dimension. An invisible part of them, in a world never seen."

"I still don't get it," said Jake.

"Think of the 2nd dimension again. A perfect example is a comic book. It's a world of boxes and panels where two-dimensional figures have adventures among other two dimensional figures. They live in a world where each panel of their life is bordered on all sides by margins. But, since they are inside their world, they never see the margins. As far as they are concerned, the margins don't exist. They are quite content, these two dimensional beings.

"Now, imagine a three-dimensional being decided to visit. Since the being can move in three directions, including going up and down, it can intersect the flat world of the comic book, or not. If it is above the comic page, it can see everything inside that page from above and never been seen itself. It can even look inside people or buildings. If our creature intersects a comic book page, it can talk to the two dimensional beings, who only see a small part of the bigger creature. But most of it remains hidden in the fourth dimension. The thing to remember is that this entity can exist entirely in the third dimension and never be seen by creatures of the second dimension."

"I think I understand," said Jake. "Our world has four dimensions. If a person could somehow climb up into that fourth dimension, he'd be able to observe everything that happens on Earth from his vantage point in the higher dimension. Plus, if the world was constructed in similar fashion to the two dimensional world, where every moment is captured in an instant of time, forming a bubble of happening, like the panel of a comic book, he'd be able to listen in and learn every secret, ever hidden truth known to man. As you said, it would make him like a god."

Then, Jake frowned. "But who the hell knows how to climb up into another dimension? How did you learn to build that ray gun of yours? And," his voice grew cold and low, "who or what are the Hounds and how did they make their way into the world of the fourth dimension?"

"Now you have passed the simple things and you are asking the truly important questions," said Professor Salt. "The fourth dimension has existed for all eternity. It is merely an extension of our three dimensional world into curved space. It has been here before man began and will be here long after man is gone. The fourth dimension is a dead place, a location without substance. It is the empty framework in which our three dimensional world rests. Again, think of our universe as a comic book and us as the characters in the comic. The fourth dimension is the blank area outside each panel. It is the empty space between the margins."

"That explains everything but the Hounds," said Jake. "Where do they come from?"

"The margins that keep our world separate from the fourth dimension are fairly strong, but sometimes they bend or break. A high energy wave or vicious storm sometimes opens a doorway into the fourth dimension. For a few instances, a man or woman can walk through from our three dimensional world to the fourth level. It's happened throughout history. Strange disappearances, people vanishing and never again being seen. Pity them. Pity the hapless souls who find themselves in a world without time, totally empty and barren. Most of them die there within a few days."

"Most?" said Jake, picking up on the one word.

"Most," said Salt, with a shudder, "but not all. A few determined ones, the very angry ones, the totally insane ones, don't always die. Instead, they undergo a hellish transformation. They *retrogress* into a more primitive form. They lose their humanity. They become monsters. They become Hounds."

"Then, those monsters who hunted me in the restaurant and served Maureen . . ." said Jake.

". . . are humans, stripped of all humanity," said Salt. "Cannibalistic creatures, they feed off warm life. Remain too long in the fourth dimension, and you begin to mutate. Your shape changes, your body flows together, your teeth grow long. You become a living appetite, a Hound. There aren't many of them, but they roam the fourth dimension searching for those people unlucky enough to fall through a hole in space and time. Creatures of no-time, they cannot exist for more than an instant in our world. When there's a break between dimensions, time stands still for a moment. That's when the Hounds feast, devouring anyone in their immediate area. Only to dissolve once time starts running.

"That's how Maureen kills the unfortunate people she thinks of as her enemies. She uses the gun to puncture the boundary between the fourth dimension and our world, opening a doorway into the room where her victims are. The Hounds enter, kill the people in that room, and then in turn, are destroyed when reality returns to normal. As you've seen, it's the perfect crime. There's no way to actually catch Maureen in the act. Besides, as long as she stays hidden in the fourth dimension, she's untouchable by any law officers."

"Before, you said you were the only one who could stop her," said Jake. "How?"

"I have a plan," said Salt. "It relies on the fact that Maureen has spent so much time in the fourth dimension that her mind is starting to slip. She's not as smart as she once was. The only thing is that this plan requires two to make it work. On my own, I can't stop Maureen. I was lucky she didn't send her Hounds after me. But, with your help, I think I could put an end to her killings. Realize this. Until Maureen is dead, you will never rest easy."

"Yeah, I know," said Jake. "Tell me what you want me to do."

"I thought you might agree," said Professor Salt. "Come with me. I have a bottle, a very special bottle to show you."

5.

Little is known about Abdul al Hazred, a mad poet of Sanaa, whom is said to have lived during the period of the Omayyad caliphs of the eighth century. He was rumored to have spent ten years meditating alone in the great southern desert of Arabia known to scholars as the Roba al Khaliyeh, or "Empty Space." During his later years, al Hazred dwelt in Damascus, where he wrote his most famous book, Al Azif, *also known as* The Necronomicon. *According to Ebn Khallikan, al Hazred's 12th century biographer, the writer was seized by an invisible monster in broad daylight in the marketplace of Mecca and ripped apart and devoured before a large number of horrified spectators.*

The trap, for in simple, most direct terms, that was exactly what it was, they decided to assemble the next morning, after they had a good night's sleep and a huge breakfast.

After a final cup of coffee, Jake rolled the huge ten foot tall plexiglass bottle that Salt had prepared through a whole into the fourth dimension. They emerged in a quiet spot of nothingness, surrounded as usual by hundreds and hundreds of transparent bubbles of the present and future. Carefully, the professor and Jake lowered the bottle until it rested on one side. Following the professor's instructions, Jake then used the portable blow-torch he had brought with him to soften the neck of the bottle, so he could twist it fairly easily. Looping it in the fourth dimension, Jake turned the neck so that it extended into the bottle and bonded with a hole in the bottom of the vessel. It was a move impossible in three dimensions, but easy enough to do in four. The first part of their trap was complete.

"Now what?" asked Jake.

"We wait for Maureen and her Hounds to arrive," said Salt. "It shouldn't be very long. In the fourth dimension, very far and very near are meaningless terms."

Several dark marks appeared in the distance. Jake didn't need the professor to tell him that Maureen and her Hounds were approaching.

"They should be here in a few moments," said Salt. "Keep your spears ready."

The spears, thin pieces of plexiglass ending with six inch incredibly sharp needles were another one of the professor's inventions. They wouldn't kill the Hounds, but they sure could make life unpleasant for them. Jake carried two dozen with him. The professor carried an equal supply. Neither of them thought that Maureen could control a pack any larger. Jake hoped they were right.

"They're getting pretty close," said Jake. 'Maybe now's the time for you to reveal your plan?"

"Not yet," said Salt.

"Professor, Maureen Trevor and her hounds will be here in less than a minute," said Jake, starting to feel like a pancake in a pancake shop. "What do you want me to do?"

"Do? Keep the Hounds from entering the bottle, Jake. I want Maureen in there with me, nothing else. Fortunately, Maureen hates me, feels I betrayed her. And, she's crazy. She won't be able to resist following me. You'll see."

And, before Jake's astonished eyes, Professor Salt climbed head-first into the huge Klein bottle. In seconds, the scientist was sitting in the middle of the bottle, smiling at Jake.

Maureen Trevor arrived a little more than a minute later. She came to a stop five feet in front of Jake and the bottle. A half-dozen of the Hounds swirled around her feet. "What's Salt doing inside that contraption? It's time for me to send that geezer to his last reward."

Salt, in the center of the bottle, waved pleasantly at Maureen. "If you want me, Maureen, you'll have to come get me."

Maureen sneered. "Hiding behind a sheet of plexiglass won't help you," she declared. "I'll smash this bottle and then smash you."

Ten minutes of pounding did absolutely no good. The plexiglass was stronger than it looked. Plus, the mouth had a strange curve that was difficult to follow. Staring at the bottle too long gave Jake a headache. Totally forgotten, he stood ten feet away from the bottle and watched as Maureen and her Hounds did their best to destroy the plexiglass surface.

The Hounds, unable to do any damage with their teeth, and kept at a distance by Jake's spears, grew bored and wandered around. After fifteen long minutes, Maureen finally gave up as well. Reaching into her suit pocket, she pulled out a six-inch steak knife. "I've relied on the Hounds to get my revenge. Looks like today I'll have to do the work myself. There's not a lot of room in that bottle, Salt. But somehow I think we'll manage."

Taking hold of the rim of the bottle, Maureen slid her legs into the huge mouth. Then went her torso, and then, finally letting go, the rest of her body.

Clustered around the bottom of the bottle, The Hounds waited and watched. Watched and waited. Salt was inside, as was Maureen. Her hand holding the steak knife was raised up in the air. Her face was twisted into a horrible mask of rage. Or was it really rage? Looking closer, Jake had the oddest feeling it wasn't anger but frustration. Salt sat with his legs crossed, seemingly relaxed, a few feet lower in the bottle than Maureen. He didn't seem the least amount concerned about the woman and her knife only a few feet away.

"It's a Klein bottle," Salt called out to Jake. "A four-dimensional shape, not possible in our normal world. The inside is outside and the outside is inside. The shape makes for some bizarre twists and turns. Nothing is exactly what it seems. As Maureen has just found out. The problem with a Klein bottle, is once you get in you also get out. Your body becomes twisted in space. No matter which way you move, you remain inside and outside. Breaking the bottle results in even a bigger mess. Do that and your body is scattered all through the dimensions.

"But, you-you're trapped in there with her," cried Jake. "That's not fair."

"I was the one who foolishly released Maureen Trevor on the unsuspecting world," said Salt. "If not for my work, she would have harmed no one. I deserve my fate. Besides, neither of us will be harmed in here. Time is stopped, so we will remain like this for all eternity. Or until something interesting happens.

"Leave me, now, my young friend. Use my inter-dimensional gun for the last time. And let the Cut and Run Killer rest in peace."

Having no real choice, Jake did exactly what Salt commanded. Coming up with an explanation of where he had been for three days and how he had lost part of one foot required a lot more imagination than Jake ever knew he possessed. Amnesia and foreign spies proved good alibis. Since the Cut and Run Killer never struck again, the case was never officially closed. Poor Phil died from a massive heart-attack on the way to the hospital, proving that being a cop and drinking was a bad bad combination.

Jake finished telling the story of *Sleeping Beauty* to his twins. He was happy to be back with Cindy and the girls and he swore that he'd put in for a desk job sometime in the near future.

Late at night, when everyone else in his house was asleep, Jake took to sitting by an open window, staring up at the stars. Now that he knew all about the fourth dimension, one question he didn't ask Professor Salt remained in his mind. It's a question he can't answer but wished he could.

If life in a three dimensional world is like a comic strip, complete with margins that keep the world separated and safe from the fourth dimension, then who's the artist? Who draws the Margins?

WORMWOOD

TIM CURRAN

"And the name of the star is called Wormwood."

—*Revelation 8:11*

1

REACTIVITY

THE NUCLEAR GRAVEYARD . . .

On April 26, 1986, the Chernobyl region of the Ukraine was pronounced dead.

Unlike Sleeping Beauty, it was put to dark slumber not with a curse, but a searing kiss of atomic fallout that seeped from the broken carcass of a failed reactor like a silent, wasting pestilence. And in its toxic shadow, the villages went to ruin, the fields went fallow, the cities became ghost towns. Then there was only the smoldering of bones and the moan of irradiated winds, silence and time pulling dryly into themselves.

But in the reactor core itself, that invidious womb of nuclear hell, there was activity. Awareness. A pall of nebulous evil growing and gestating, waiting to open its eyes and stretch its crooked limbs.

Then some twenty years after its death, it did just that.

2

THE ZONE OF CONTAMINATION

In the back of the old Soviet truck, Chalmers kept staring at the map, something doing the slow crawl in his guts. The map showed the Chernobyl Exclusionary Zone. Brilliant red triangles indicated the location of the four deactivated Chernobyl RBMK reactors, all of which were just outside the city of Pripyat, not Chernobyl itself which was roughly eleven miles away from the site. Orange and yellow belts illustrated the dispersal of radioactive fallout from the original accident and dozens of black dots marked the location of deserted villages.

The team sat in the lead-lined, riveted rear compartment of the truck on benches bolted to the walls. Besides Chalmers and Stansfield from the NRC, there was a thick-necked, dead-eyed MVS colonel named Uri Krekov. A Ukranian biologist, Leonid Kuratova, and a Russian theoretical physicist, Ilyana Porsekoi. One of Krekov's MVS troopers rounded out the company. All of them, save the trooper up front, rode in the back in blue rubber Delta anti-radiation suits, helmets on their laps, dosimeters clipped to their belts.

They were a tense bunch and with good reason.

In the past few weeks, The Zone had been completely sealed off to both laborers and health workers. And, once again, it was because of the infamous Number Four reactor.

Number Four was the one that suffered the now famous catastrophic steam explosion in 1986. To contain the radioactive emissions, some 5,000 metric tons of lead, boron, sand, and clay were dropped on the blazing structure to shield it and a concrete sarcophagus was hastily built over it as a permanent enclosure. Problem was, the sarcophagus was erected mainly with remote industrial robots because of the radiation saturation and through the intervening years, it had been decaying rapidly, cracks and holes appearing it. Water was leaking into it and radioactive dust seeping out.

The thing that had everyone scratching their heads was that the reactor was pouring out emissions equal to and possibly surpassing the original fallout and no one knew exactly why. But something was happening.

Something incredible.

Something just not in the books.

Nobody knew that better than Chalmers. He'd been with the NRC some twenty years now. Before that he'd worked in the private sector with Spiradex, a company that specialized in the clean-up of nuclear accidents. And before that he'd been a civilian reactor operator after he got out of the Navy where he'd cut his teeth on the nuclear reactors of the Trident-class subs. He knew reactors. He knew what they could do and what they could not do.

And they could not power themselves up . . . particularly after exploding.

And the Chernobyl Number Four reactor *had* blown up. And what hadn't erupted in the massive steam explosion was completely destroyed in the ensuing nuclear meltdown. There was nothing left but core fragments, tons of radioactive dust, irradiated sludge, and a nuclear lava made of reactor fuel and melted concrete and steel. Very dangerous stuff. But there was nothing left to the reactor itself that could be deemed remotely operable. It was dead. Dead as graveyard soil.

Yet, she was putting out high levels again.

Even with the decay of the Sarcophagus, that just didn't make sense.

Five days ago, a team headed by Vitaly Boreta and a few select members of the International Atomic Energy Agency went in. They spent some six hours in the region, gathering information, then promptly vanished.

Nobody knew what to make of that either.

And that's why Chalmers and the others were going in.

As they approached The Zone, the silence was thick with apprehension like maybe it was the night before doomsday. Chalmers sat there, wondering what kind of tea party Stansfield had gotten him invited to. He stared out the windows at the Ukranian countryside rolling by. Even though it was November, that colorless month of dead browns and drab grays, the landscape was scenic. Hilly pastures and dairy herds, huge collective farms. A heavy snow was beginning to come down, blanketing the pines in white.

It could have been the Midwest back home.

But it wasn't and he knew it.

Because they were getting close to The Zone. And that's where it had happened all those years ago. That's where the burning demon of atomic fission had been set loose to breathe fallout over the countryside.

They passed a checkpoint and into The Zone they went.

Right away things started to change. There were yellow radiation signs everywhere and double rows of razorwire fencing. Deep ditches began to appear to either side of the truck. They'd been dug, Chalmers knew, to prevent cesium and strontium fallout that had saturated the marshy soil from draining off into the Dnieper River basin where millions of Ukranians got their drinking water.

You could almost feel the change. The desolation, the despair, the haunted aura of the place that reached right into its black marrow. Something that was not helped by the Geiger Counters. They were all beeping now. Radiation levels were climbing from 15 microroentgens per hour to nearly fifty.

About that time, they started to see the first abandoned villages.

Decaying collections of houses and graying buildings sat on overgrown lots wild with bushes and creepers. Roofs were collapsing, doors peeling, windows empty with blind indifference. The snow continued to fall like ash, entombing these graveyards beneath cold white shrouds. You could almost feel the presence of ghosts drifting in shuttered attics and ruined cellars. Chalmers wondered what such places might look like at night when they held darkness and stark memory thick in their bellies and only shadows walked the uneven floors and weedy byways.

If any place in the world was haunted, this was it.

"Okay," he said to all gathered. "Any last words?"

But there were none, just that quiet desperation settling into the team.

So he just sat there, not liking the feel of this, unable to get past the fact he was not being told the complete truth. Going into a hot zone like this was always dangerous, but what he was seeing in the eyes of the team was something else. Fear, maybe, like a bunch of kids about to step into the neighborhood haunted house.

3

Ghost Town

When Chalmers first caught sight of Grojaz in the falling snow, he thought it looked like one of those little Medieval European towns from a Hammer vampire movie . . . though not quite as cheerful. All those little houses and trim cottages and all of them empty as coffins. The truck pulled to a stop and everyone hopped out, now donning full protective gear including helmets. They carried air tanks, but for the time being they were just using filters. The scientists and inspectors carried portable radiation spectrometers and Geiger Counters, which continued to beep, telling them that the earth under their feet was putting out nearly fifty roentgens.

Grojaz had been the first stop of Vitaly Boreta's original team.

Like everything in the zone, it was contaminated.

When the Number Four reactor went up, it scattered clouds of fallout over the entire zone, principally strontium-90, cesium-137, and radioactive iodine. The soil soaked up these unstable isotopes like a sponge where they were absorbed by plants and mushrooms, the various insects and animals that fed upon them, thereby entering the local food supply, ending up in the milk, the meat, the vegetables and fruit.

Chalmers looked around in the falling snow, noticing that most of the houses were made of wood as were most in The Zone. And that was bad, too, because wood was a magnet for radioactivity.

As he stood there, feeling a sense of oppression he could not catalog, he thought: *Just look at this place, will ya? It's bad right to its black roots and you know it. Not just a radioactive dead zone, but a land of tall, shadowy gingerbread houses haunted by witches and bleak radioactive forests where the big bad wolf waits behind every steaming tree with gleaming yellow teeth for Little Red Riding Hood.*

He knew that was crazy, but the images just hatched in his head and he could not dismiss their malignant pull.

Krekov and Vasilev took the lead, moving through the village, the wind whipping around them. Rain gutters rattled on roofs and rusting gates creaked. Although the snow was accumulating now in powdery drifts, it was all too easy to see the desolation growing everywhere. Cottages and sheds were consumed by wild creepers. Pools were filled with dank, ice-scummed waters. Children's toys were abandoned in overgrown yards. A baby carriage sprouting leaves and bird's nests was pushed up to a half-open door. And the houses themselves, rotting and dirty, the blackened windows staring out with vapid amusement.

Oddly enough, what struck Chalmers most was a boy's bike. It lay rusting on a sidewalk, perhaps abandoned there the day the village was emptied. Wheels maybe still spinning as the military emptied the town, forcing frightened mothers and crying children onto trucks before the clouds of fallout rolled over the horizon.

Jesus, but the place had a bad feel.

The atmosphere was heavy, almost leaden. Maybe it was the suit he wore and maybe it was his imagination, but he could almost feel the weight of that awful place settling over him like a tomb lid. Everything was decaying and crumbling—fences and garages and houses. Shingles were torn off roofs and shutters hung askew, windows were dusty and cracked, doorways warped, tangles of unpleasant black shadows spilling out.

"Over here," Krekov said, his voice tinny over the helmet radio.

Vasilev had located a house that showed signs of recent occupation: a car without flat tires and a few plastic bags of garbage.

In they went.

They used flashlights because the shadows were thick inside, pooling and flowing. Dust lay over everything, cobwebs spun over light fixtures, dead flies gathered on windowsills. The radiation count had increased. It was like a crypt in there, grim and uninviting, and Chalmers could just about imagine what it might have smelled like . . . vaporous decay and age and corruption. He was glad for the mask on his face.

Krekov and Vasilev went upstairs, while the others looked around the ground floor. There were signs of recent occupation. They found a bowl of shriveled apples, a wedge of cheese, a few bottles of wine. All of them covered in a layer of dust. Grime covered a mirror into which somebody had scraped simple crosses, at least a dozen of them. There was something very disconcerting about that.

While they were soaking up that dread, empty atmosphere, Vasilev came bolting down the stairs. He was breathing hard and his eyes were wide and wet like reflecting pools behind his visor. He said something to Stansfield and then everyone followed him back up.

Krekov was standing outside a little bedroom.

It was nothing much inside; just a bed, threadbare curtains moving over a broken window, black-and-white photographs in frames on the wall. But what drew their attention was the body on the floor.

At least . . . it looked like a body.

There was something definitely unusual about it.

Kuratova, the biologist, said that it was the body of a middle-aged woman, Caucasian. Yes, it was a woman, but she was disfigured, almost blobby in appearance like a great pile of white dough fashioned to *look* like a woman. Her face was flattened, her features grotesquely exaggerated like they were stamped in Silly Putty and pulled in every which direction. Her limbs flaccid lumps.

"What in the hell?" Chalmers said.

Kuratova took one of her arms and held it in his hands. The limb was rubbery and limp like a piece of wet spaghetti. Krekov placed a boot on her chest and pressed down . . . there was absolutely no give. The woman trembled and undulated with gelid waves like a waterbed. Kuratova, beneath the glare of the flashlights, took skin samples and body fluids, the usual, then he opened her lengthwise, from sternum to crotch with a scalpel. Thing was, there was nothing but flesh and meat inside, no sternum, no ribcage, no nothing.

Chalmers was sweating now. "No bones . . . there's no bones in her."

"None," Stansfield said.

"But that's . . . that's not possible."

"If we see it, Mr. Chalmers," Krekov said, "then it must be possible."

"Sure, but *how?* Where are her fucking bones?"

No answers. Not a one. And what started to really eat a hole inside Chalmers was that nobody seemed surprised. Not the scientists, not even Stansfield. And that really bothered him. Because he was thinking that he'd been invited to a party, but nobody told him it was a Halloween bash.

They went back outside and Vasilev found another house.

In the living room, two more bodies.

They had been there much longer. Whereas the other had been an expanse of white flesh, these two were simply gray, mummified things thick with a furry down of mold. Kuratova informed them that they were the bodies of an adult man and woman, but how he could tell that was a mystery. Just mounds of decayed flesh, roughly human in form with ghoulish caricatures of faces, is what Chalmers was seeing. Laying there in such close proximity, they looked like they had grown into a single mass like fruiting bodies.

Chalmers stayed over by the window while the biologist did his grisly work.

While Stansfield filmed it all with his camcorder, Kuratova and Porsekoi made a thorough physical examination. They took the required samples and still photos and then they opened the bodies up. They slit first one, then the other. A black sap ran out and Chalmers had all he could do not to lose his lunch. They sorted about in the various cavities, but it didn't take an anatomist to see that there were no bones in them. Chalmers had seen victims of radiation poisoning, plenty of them, but the bones were never missing.

"What's doing that?" he finally asked. "What's stealing the bones?"

"Something intensely radioactive, I should think," Kuratova said.

Porsekoi was scanning the body with her handheld spectrometer. She was picking up cesium and cobalt, even traces of plutonium, but no strontium.

Again, they knew things that they were not saying. Chalmer's job was clean-up, essentially. They would need his expertise at the reactor site, but not here.

Finally, he pulled Stansfield aside in the corridor. "Okay, what gives?"

He just shrugged in his suit. "We're not really sure, Mike. We're guessing that the bones are being taken by some kind of predator."

Kuratova came over. "We cannot be sure of anything," he said.

"But those bodies . . . they should be ripped to shreds if something yanked the bones out," Chalmers said.

Kuratova shook his helmeted head. "No, no. No one said the bones were being *yanked* out, for that implies violence, yes? This is much more subtle. We are thinking of a specific agent which dissolves the bone and allows for it to be . . . *withdrawn* through numerous punctures."

Chalmers swallowed.

What the hell was going on here?

"Listen," he finally said, "how about some answers?"

But Stansfield shook his head. "We don't have any, Mike." He checked his Geiger counter. "It's getting pretty hot in here. Everyone out."

Chalmers was fine with that. He moved down the stairs with Vasilev at his back. He passed a window and let out a cry.

"What the hell was that?"

Vasilev shook his head. "I saw nothing."

"What's the matter, Mike?" Stansfield asked.

But Chalmers wasn't sure. Through the parted curtains he saw . . . thought he saw . . . something white peering in, something like a distorted and disembodied face, eyes flickering red then almost a purple before winking out. Whatever it had been, it was grinning.

And then it was just gone.

"I guess I'm seeing ghosts," he finally said, not believing that for a minute.

Krekov chuckled over the radio. "Our Mr. Chalmers saw a ghost."

Chalmers got out of there as quick as he could, something unfolding now inside him. Something cold and white and brittle.

After that, he clung tight to Stansfield. They went into a couple other houses, but found no more boneless bodies. Just age and abandonment and silence. People had left the town in a hurry, leaving their belongings behind. Books and TVs and clothes and toys and photo albums and you name it. Not only did they leave their belongings, but their *lives.* These people had been moved out forcibly by the Soviet military with nothing but the clothes on their backs.

The team moved down the street, the shadows beginning to lengthen, the storm throwing snow around that sounded like sand against the houses. It was then that someone screamed. They let go with a shrill, ear-splitting report. This time it wasn't Chalmers.

It was Vasilev.

He was so scared, he'd lost the ability to speak in English. He rambled on in Ukranian, pointing and gesturing. Krekov took him aside and shouted at him. The boy was petrified. He spoke in a high, broken voice.

"What the hell is it, Marty?" Chalmers finally asked, feeling the emptiness closing in around them.

Stansfield shrugged. "He's . . . he's saying he saw a little girl standing there, between those two trees. She was just looking at him."

"A little girl? In this place?" Chalmers said. "Can't be."

But even if it had been, so what? Just a girl.

Then he saw the area between the two trees that Ilyana Porsekoi was sweeping with her spectrometer. An even blanket of snow was laid down and there were no footprints in it. Maybe something had been standing there, but it had been no girl.

Nothing substantial. Nothing made of flesh and blood.

"Must be that ghost, eh?"

Krekov ignored him.

They moved on, came to a green clapboard house and this one had smoke coming from the chimney.

"Jesus Christ," Chalmers said. "Somebody's living in this morgue? What are they still doing here?"

Krekov explained that they were *samosely*—old men and women primarily— that refused to leave. The authorities just gave up. "You can't keep them out," he explained. "You take them away and a week later, they've slipped back in."

Chalmers stopped, breathing hard now in his suit. Feeling its weight, its confinement, the very confinement of that awful town. "Even after the reactor started pissing out the juice, you guys left these people here?"

Krekov had stopped, too. "And what would you have us do?"

But Chalmers had no answer for that. This wasn't America. He had to keep that in mind. This was a far different place.

Krekov knocked at the door.

What a bunch to find on your doorstep on a snowy afternoon in a ghost town, Chalmers thought.

But the old man who opened the door, simply smiled and beckoned them in. He was a trusting sort. But why not? It would not be the first time he saw men in radiation suits.

"Christ," Chalmers said, "he looks almost happy to see us."

"Maybe he is," Stansfield said.

And Chalmers just nodded. Sure, why not? You live in a graveyard, you're happy to see the living again. And that's what it must have been like living here. Like living in the middle of a cemetery. And if what he'd seen at that window had actually been there—and he was very certain of that—then it must have been a very lively cemetery after dark. One haunted by something that sucked the bones out of people.

They all went in.

Chalmers waited in a living room just outside a tiny kitchen while Dr. Porsekoi and Professor Kuratova spoke with the old man by candlelight. He was a thin old guy, not much to him. Looked like he was thrown together out of coat hangers and rags. He smiled and chattered, said his name was Anotaly Cherberka. The only time the smile evaporated from his face was when he looked at Krekov.

Stansfield was translating what was being said, but Chalmers wasn't listening. The old guy had acute radiation sickness and there was no getting around that. Most of his teeth were gone, his hair had fallen out, his face was sallow and blotchy. He seemed to be having trouble standing up.

"He's saying that he does not want to leave," Stansfield interpreted. "He is seventy-seven years old and has lived in Grojaz his entire life. If he had allowed the Soviets to resettle him to the dreary housing projects in Kiev all those years ago, he would have died. He knows he is sick. Better to die at home of radiation, he says, than of homesickness in an unfamiliar place."

Chalmers understood or thought he did. At one time, he knew, there'd been some 200 people living in The Zone, mostly elderly, defying the ban. They and their people had lived in the region for centuries, it was all they knew. A tree might die slowly on blighted land, but if you yanked it up by the roots, it would die that much faster.

Cherberka didn't seem interested in talking about himself.

A true Ukranian, he was interested mainly in the comfort of his guests. Though he had very little, he wished to share what he did have. He offered his guests smoked carp and beet salad, vegetables from his garden, even homemade cheese and apples.

Although he could not accept any of it because of the contamination factor, Chalmers felt almost heartbroken by this guy. He was sick, he was barely surviving, yet he wanted to share his food. And that's how the Ukranians were, he knew. They had suffered under the Czars and the Nazis and the communists, but it had never really broken their spirit. They were generous and kind to a fault. Wasn't that something?

After a brief rest in a rickety chair, the old man started on again, smiling and laughing, though his eyes were filled with tears.

"His wife is upstairs," Stansfield said. "He wants us to meet her."

Chalmers just shook his head. "Jesus Christ, Marty, he's dying. We have to get him out of here. Check your Geiger. This house is hot. I'm reading almost 200 roentgens."

And maybe Stansfield was going to comment on that, but something else happened. Something that froze the little group in silence. They looked at each other through their visors, but nobody dared move.

You see, there was a knocking at the door.

Slow, heavy, insistent. And another sound, something like a voice, but making a howling, lonesome sound like wind blown through a conchshell. And that more than anything told everyone there that this was no neighbor come to call, but something else. Something you might not want to invite in.

Chalmers looked over to Krekov. He was the tough guy, the guy with balls . . . why didn't he go see who it was?

But Krekov was not moving. Nobody was. The house seemed suddenly cold, unbearably cold. A tomblike, creeping damp had invaded now and it was coming off what waited behind the door.

The old man cocked his head to one side like he was listening.

But for *what?*

Suddenly, like some half-ass séance gone wrong, there was not only a knocking at the door, but a rapping at the windows, thudding at the walls. Everyone was slowly pushed closer to one another. And just as quickly as it had started, it stopped.

The old man looked very nervous.

Krekov swore under his breath, unslung his AK-47, and charged at the door. He threw it open and that must have taken some real guts.

But there was nothing out there.

Flashlight beams found only the gathering dimness of twilight, snowflakes, nothing more. No footprints but their own.

The old man started talking and Stansfield looked like he did not want to translate this. Everyone in the team looked very apprehensive. Chalmers waited and Stansfield told him. Cherberka claimed it was only his daughter, that sometimes she visited after dark. Chalmers thought that was fine and dandy until Stansfield said that the old man's daughter had died twenty years before. She had been an engineer at Chernobyl Reactor Four the night it went up.

The old man brought them all into the darkened living room, lit up the wall with a candle. He started talking again and Stansfield translated.

"He . . . Jesus . . . he says that she started coming a few weeks ago. One night, while he and his wife were sitting here, she came to them. She walked right through the wall."

And that's what Cherberka was showing them now.

A little altar had been set up complete with crosses, wilted flowers, melted candles, and even badly yellowed photographs of a young woman. And right above, is where she came through the wall. The wall itself was made of some pale stucco-like material and burned into it was the blackened image of a woman with her hands held out to her sides, fingers splayed. It looked like the image of a saint, almost. The hands held out benevolently. But what came through there, Chalmers figured, was nothing benevolent.

The image was perfect . . . and downright spooky.

Whatever had left it had been fiercely radioactive, yet ethereal like a ghost. Porsekoi had her spectrometer out and was getting readings of strontium, cesium, cobalt. But where the walls around the image were giving off readings of roughly 200 roentgens, the image was cooking at nearly 600.

The old man seemed pleased with his altar.

But Chalmers wasn't. *Something burned through that wall, something like a ghost.* Things were maybe starting to make sense and the more sense they made, the more incomprehensible they became.

Then the old man took them upstairs to meet his wife.

Kuratova, Chalmers, and Stansfield went up there. Chalmers was right behind the old man as they climbed the narrow stairway, their flashlights bobbing and creating lurching shadows. The old man led them into a bedroom and then he started screaming.

Chalmers saw it.

The others did, too.

A white arm, almost phosphorescent, pulled away through the wall with a crackling sound and disappeared, leaving an oval blackened area like the image downstairs. On the bed was Cherberka's wife . . . or what was left of her. Yes, in general shape it was that of an elderly woman, but one perhaps exposed to an intense heat. She was gray like cigarette ash, brittle and disintegrating. And the most horrible thing of all was that she was *alive.*

Chalmers gasped.

She moved and as she did, one of her arms flaked away to powdery fragments and then her entire body just collapsed with a puff of dust that sent cremated fragments spinning in the air like dust motes.

It was enough, by God, it was more than enough.

The entire team got out of there then. The old man would not come with them. He staunchly refused. And despite his deteriorating physical condition, Chalmers had a pretty good idea that he would have fought them to the death if they tried to take him by force. So the team went out into the snow and moved up the drifted streets where the shadows were growing long and sharp like teeth. And that's when they saw it, when they all saw what should have made them pack it in and forget it.

They heard that lonesome, mournful howling again.

Then they looked back at the old man's house. It was incredible, but there it was. Chalmers looked and what he saw hit him with almost physical impact. His eyes went wide and he nearly choked on the saliva in his own mouth.

Stansfield, at his side, simply said, "Jesus."

For above the old man's house, on the roof, there were ghosts.

There was nothing else they could have been.

Just nebulous white shapes that burst out of nowhere like spores from a puffball and became the glowing and electrified forms of men, women, and children. They just floated there, faces skullish and eyes huge and black like bullet holes. A crackling of energy came from them like that of static electricity.

Chalmers said it before the others could. "Ghosts . . . goddamned ghosts."

4

DARK MATTER

Down the road from Grojaz a piece, when he finally got some wind in his lungs, he said, "All right. I've had enough of this bullshit. Tell me what I just saw back there. Tell me what fucking ghosts have to do with that goddamn reactor."

Stansfield stared morosely at the map on the wall in the back of the truck. "I guess it's time. I guess it's time at that."

Nobody said anything for a time, then Dr. Porsekoi sighed, said, "Are you familiar, Mr. Chalmers, with an installation known as Chernobyl-Two?"

"Never heard of it."

"No reason you would have," she said. "It was a former Soviet space communications center. Now, precisely one hour before the accident at the Number Four reactor, a seismic event of two-point-five magnitude was recorded. It has never truly been connected to the Chernobyl accident and that's because those in power prefer it that way."

"But it has something to do with it?"

"It has everything to do with it," Porsekoi explained. "Because that event occurred at Chernobyl-Two."

Chernobyl-Two was much more than a Soviet space communications center, it was essentially a highly classified research facility probing into the vagaries of the physics of propulsion, according to Porsekoi.

"That sounds harmless enough," Chalmers said.

Krekov and Porsekoi just looked at each other as if they were amazed at Chalmer's stupidity. Maybe they were.

"This is very difficult to explain," Porsekoi admitted.

"You're doing just fine."

Well, the first thing that he had to understand, she said, was that much of this was still classified. What she would tell him was half fact and half theory. At Chernobyl-Two, the Soviets became interested in something that was known in theoretical physics circles as Shadow Matter or Dark Matter. Dark Matter or Mirror Matter or even Alice Matter—as in *Through the Looking Glass*—exists, hypothetically, in our universe just about everywhere. Only five percent of the mass of the universe is visible, the rest may be made of Dark Matter. Which in itself may be the remnants of an earlier universe.

"Okay, I've heard something about that before," Chalmers admitted. "Something about there being an earlier explosion or what not, that allowed the Big Bang to take effect."

"Yes, yes exactly," Porsekoi said.

She explained that there was no point going into the mathematical jungles of M-theory or String Theory which state that the building blocks of space and time as we know them are actually composed of countless tiny vibrating strings which are interconnected and hanging upon them are as many as eleven parallel dimensions. The event she was referring to was before the Big Bang when conceivably there were only two dimensions and for reasons poorly understood, these dimensions collided with incredible force and created Dark Matter. And sometime thereafter this earlier splitting came the Big Bang itself, an immense eruption of matter, energy, and mass that created the universe as it was currently understood and at the same time, completely ruptured those earlier Shadow Matter universes. And in doing so, absorbed most of their mass. Most of it.

"But in a severely altered form, Mr. Chalmers," Porsekoi said. "Yet, it is believed that there is still existing a pocket dimension of this original Shadow Matter out there somewhere. Now, the Soviets became very interested in this. Because, technically, just a fragment of Shadow Matter can contain immense amounts of pure energy like nothing we know or can know."

The Soviets decided that this Shadow Matter could be the sort of power source that could fling a spacecraft at speeds up to that of light itself. What they did was to build the Chernobyl Collider, perhaps the world's largest particle accelerator. Beneath the Chernobyl-Two facility there was a circular tunnel that ran some thirty miles in length and in it, particle beams were accelerated to extremely high velocities and smashed into each other fifty million times a second. This would not only create a brief snapshot of the Big Bang itself, they thought, but possibly create Shadow Matter for the briefest of instants. This would allow them to study it and possibly harness its energy. It sounded good in theory. And when these particle beams were intensified by ultrahigh magnetic fields and exotic matter-energy fields, the results were incredible and unforeseen.

"I'm afraid you lost me," Chalmers said.

Porsekoi sighed. "They succeeded in creating Shadow Matter and the results were absolutely devastating."

Chalmers still looked puzzled.

Stansfield stepped in. "They blew a wormhole open into this original Shadow Matter universe, Mike, and something crawled out. Something that was hungry."

Chalmers just sat there looking at them all, one after the other. "That's what these ghosts are? Living Shadow Matter?"

"Hardly," Porsekoi told him. "They are but a . . . side effect? When you plant a garden, Mr. Chalmers, weeds grow next to your flowers, do they not? Unplanned, but very pervasive. But forget about that, please. There are theories that life may exist completely alien to anything we can understand. Crystalline life and anti-matter life and life possibly based upon radioactive plasma . . ."

What she told him was basically this: that the original Shadow Matter universe was essentially a living thing, not just a collection of exotic matter and energy, but something sentient, something with the will to live. When it collided with that other lifeless dimension, it was nearly destroyed. It existed only as a pocket dimension after most, if not nearly all, of its mass was absorbed during the Big Bang. But it did continue to exist, its very reality slowly being compressed out of existence by the expansion of our own universe and others like it.

Stansfield said, "You can picture it can't you, Mike? This wormhole is opened up and this matter slips through, hungry, wasted, but intelligent and like any other living thing, it has the will to survive, to increase itself by any means necessary."

"And this . . . this *thing* coming through caused that earlier seismic event?" Chalmers said.

"Exactly," Porsekoi told him.

This Shadow Matter entity would have figuratively and quite possibly *literally* starved to death in our world. The matter of this universe would have destroyed it if it could not instantly increase its mass and stabilize its field. To do that it needed food: fissionable materials. When it came through, it destroyed the Chernobyl Collider. But it quickly latched onto something else. The Soviets were running a series of RTGs at their installation. Radioisotope Thermoelectric Generators. Simple electric generators that obtain their power from radioactive decay. The Shadow Matter entity found them and absorbed their piles, assimilated them.

"Imagine it as a living organism, Mr. Chalmers," Porsekoi said. "A living thermonuclear furnace. And like any sun, its waste products—gamma rays—are its own food. It is completely cyclical. Yet, to increase its mass and stabilize its field, it must have fissionable materials to feed upon."

"So it went to Reactor Four?"

"Yes, there it glutted itself, creating the explosions which were like buffets to it. Then . . . I don't know . . . it must have went into some sort of dormancy within the remains of the reactor core itself."

"Until recently?"

"Yes, until recently."

Chalmers licked his lips. "And the ghosts?"

"These ghosts as you call them are entities formed of radioactive plasma, hotter than anything you can imagine," she said. "Not mere ghosts, but living entities that are partially corporeal and partially energetic in form and mass. Why they've fashioned themselves in the forms of dead men and women I do not know. All we can know is that like this Shadow Matter creature, they feed on radioactivity. And that's why they go after bones, you see. For certain isotopes and particularly strontium-90 are absorbed by bone tissue and marrow . . ."

But Chalmers knew that.

These people in The Zone were eating the vegetables they grew and drinking the milk their cows produced, eating the fish and fowl, and thereby absorbing huge amounts of strontium which ended up in the bone. Sure, it all made sense to a certain extent, but he was not really convinced.

Science fiction.

That's what this was.

It couldn't be anything else and part of him railed against it. Was even pissed off at this nonsense. Sure, Poreskoi was a theorist, her head was filled with over-intellectualized, egg-headed bullshit. Maybe Chalmers himself had seen ghosts and bodies without bones, but that did not mean he had to jump on this highly speculative bandwagon of over-ripe pseudo-scientific claptrap. But even as he thought these things, a very tiny and very unshakeable voice in the back of his head began to speak very calmly. It said, *Yes, Mike, this is what happened and down deep, you know it. The Ruskies created a controlled anti-matter explosion of sorts that ripped open a wormhole to the primal cellar of time and space. And something, a Shadow Matter boogeyman, born in that black void crawled out and ate those RTGs and then it wanted more. It was still unstable, so it attacked the reactor core at Chernobyl Four and bathed in the nuclear core inferno. And now it's had a good nap.*

And when it finishes eating the fissionable materials in the reactor, it will be hungry again.

Then it will have to seek out other atomic piles, chewing on them one by one and scattering their bones . . .

"So what happens when this fucking entity has exhausted the elements in the reactor core?"

But nobody wanted to answer that one.

Of course, they didn't have to. The thing would grow exponentially in mass and energy as it fed on one reactor after another. And by the time it was done, its very existence would poison the world, turn it into one immense Exclusionary Zone.

A nuclear graveyard where the only things that would be able to exist in the saturation of deadly fallout would be the ghosts themselves, picking at the scraps. Not even ghosts, but evolved life forms of pure radioactive plasma.

5

Wormwood

If Grojaz was a ghost town, then Pripyat was a cemetery.

Here was the so-called Red Forest, a large pine forest near the atomic power plant, the trees of which had absorbed so much radiation that they turned red and their needles fell off. They had to be bulldozed down and buried they were so radioactive. And here also were dozens of auto graveyards that contained thousands of trucks, cranes, and even military helicopters that had been used in the clean-up and were still far too hot to be touched. As they passed the river, they could see the rotting wharves with dozens and dozens of ships and barges that had been abandoned because of contamination.

The whole city was like that.

It looked like the set of some post-apocalyptic movie, just deserted houses squatting beneath moldering roofs, overgrown courtyards, weed-infested thoroughfares. Trees had pushed up through the broken pavement alongside deserted buildings. Storefronts were dirty and yellowed, refuse scattered through the streets, and everywhere, abandoned vehicles and machinery rusting away. There were bus stops and cab stands, grocery stores and little cafes. Ragged washing still hung from lines and bicycles were locked in community racks. You could not look upon it and remain unchanged. You could not see the utter desertion and hear the silence and feel the memories and not have something inside you twist tightly.

For this . . . this was an atrocity.

Pripyat was a tombstone erected to the death of an atomic city.

When the town siren had gone off that dread Sunday morning, the police and army had stormed the town, evacuating everyone. Nobody was allowed to take a thing with them. Everything was left behind . . . vehicles and appliances, antiques and family heirlooms, motorcycles and children's toys. Everything. They left with the clothes on their backs and, several hours later, were processed through army decontamination stations where they stood beneath the sprays of chemical showers. And this was how everyone of them—man, woman, and child—started their new life: naked, confused, frightened, and empty-handed.

The truly tragic part was that the evacuation order was not given until a full thirty-six hours after the accident. In fact, it was said, on the very day of the accident, the people of Pripyat gathered on the roofs of the highest buildings in town and watched the shining cloud of radioactive steam that had gathered over the ruined reactor building. All of them exposed to deadly ionizing radiation.

48,000 people had once lived here and now there was no one.

Pripyat was a modern industrial city of high-rise apartment buildings that were still splashed with badly faded communist propaganda. And ultimately, this is where the Soviet Union finally died. In this intensely radioactive dead zone. This sowed the seeds that brought the giant down.

Chalmers saw it all as they came into the city and toured its dead streets. He felt like some kind of graveworm investigating a huge decomposed carcass.

"We should go to the cemetery," Kuratova said. "Before we investigate the reactor site, we need to see the cemetery."

"This whole place is a cemetery," Chalmers said to him.

But Kuratova insisted. "The cemetery . . . I believe it will be important."

Chalmers didn't ask why, but then he did not have to. He knew what was in the cemetery. The entire city was restricted, but particularly the power plant and the cemetery, because it was there that much of the radioactive graphite nuclear core was buried along with the dead. It was so hot, it could not be left above ground. Even today, its emissions were lethal. But that wasn't the reason Kuratova wanted to go there.

"I fail to see the point of visiting that place," Stansfield said and you could almost hear the pounding of his heart.

Chalmers looked over at Krekov and Krekov seemed to understand, just as Dr. Porsekoi did. "He wants to see those ghosts, Marty. He's got to get a look at the things and not only them, but the ground they were birthed from."

"Yes," Porsekoi said. "It fits . . . does it not? All those dead buried there for so many years. The Shadow Matter entity must have sought out not only the reactor, but the buried core in the graveyard. Probably recently and that set about some incredible chain-reaction that brought our ghosts into being."

"Not merely ghosts," Kuratova said. "Something beyond ghosts. These things are living entities of radioactive plasma. They wear the faces of the dead, but they are so much more than that."

Chalmers had to wonder what sort of chain-reaction brought the dead back. Some people claimed to see ghosts all the time, sensitive types, mediums even. Most people could see or feel nothing when these other select few saw ghosts everywhere. Maybe they did see ghosts. And maybe places like graveyards were full of them. Like the Pripyat graveyard, for example. Only there, something had absorbed these harmless essences, these reflections of the dead, reconfigured and reconstituted them into something else. Something born of the same Dark Matter that had given it birth.

The truck wound through the city streets, avoiding wreckage and abandoned vehicles, and then, as darkness began to fall and the snow continued to whip, it pulled to a stop. Chalmers looked out his window and all he could see was the snow falling, the wind pushing it up into drifts. At the edge of the glare from the truck's headlights, he almost thought he saw vague shapes pulling back into the gloom.

"Is this it?" he said.

"Yes," Krekov said.

Kuratova looked very excited by all of it . . . as if he did not sense the terrible danger they were all in. Maybe it was his boundless scientific curiosity and maybe it was something else entirely.

"I must see," he said, rising and donning his helmet. "I must see."

"You're putting us all in harm's way," Stansfield said. "Do you realize that? Do you realize what you're doing?"

But he didn't seem to care.

He opened the rear doors and stepped out into the storm. By then everyone had donned their helmets, Geiger Counters beeping madly now. The wind blew snow into the back of the truck.

"He's out of his mind," Stansfield said.

That was a pretty fair assessment, Chalmers figured.

"You must understand," Krekov said over his helmet intercom. "It is more than science now for Professor Kuratova. Much more. You see, his sister died in the reactor incident and she was buried here."

That made something go cold inside Chalmers.

Is that what this was really about?

Kuratova was thinking, maybe, that his sister would be one of the resurrected. And who wouldn't want to catch such a glimpse? But not like this. Jesus, not like this. Chalmers had seen those things hovering over the old man's house in Grojaz. They were not people . . . they were horrors, they were wraiths.

They all followed Kuratova out into the gathering night then. The wind found them and tried to bowl them over, throwing snow against their visors. It was blowing so hard they had to lean into it and even then it was no easy thing moving in those bulky suits with equipment strapped to them and air tanks on their backs.

Kuratova was off ahead of them, out of range of the intercoms, but they could hear him on the external mics crying out in Ukranian, his voice broken and despairing. In the headlights of the truck and the beams of their flashlights, they followed. The cemetery was just ahead. It was surrounded by iron gates, a noose that held a hilly expanse of monuments and crypts in check. Dark trees rose up amongst them. Everything shrouded in white.

"He's out of his fucking head," Chalmers said.

He was at the gates before they could hope to stop him. They were chained shut and the fence itself was high and jagged. He was not getting in, but in his desperation he shook the chains again and again.

The Geiger Counters were registering well over 500 roentgens per hour now and climbing. In the center of the graveyard, it would be five times that. And below ground . . . a thousand times more.

"Look," Porsekoi said.

Hanging from the fence uprights just down from where Kuratova was, there were two bodies. Or, rather, two dark rubber radiation suits that looked to have bodies in them. Everyone momentarily forgot about Kuratova. They moved through the storm to the bodies. Vasilev, being young and athletic even in that cumbersome suit, climbed up and dropped the bodies down.

There was no point in unzipping the bodies from their suits or removing the helmets. Krekov assured them that these two poor individuals were members of Boreta's original team. What they were doing here, nobody knew. But as to what had hung them high on the fence, they could only guess. The suits themselves were terribly charred and melted and the bodies sloshed around inside, completely without bones.

"I think we had better go," Porsekoi said.

There was no argument on that.

They started away and Chalmers just stood there, somehow transfixed by the cemetery and what it might contain. The snow slammed into him and made him teeter in his suit, the headlight beams of the truck and his own flashlight filled with swirling white flakes and eerie flying shapes. He was looking not just at the snow and the cemetery, but perhaps to something black and painful and grim far beyond the boundaries of death itself.

"Come on," Stansfield told him.

He started to move, wondering vaguely how long he might have stood there if Stansfield hadn't jerked him out of his fugue. Maybe until he was frozen dead and silent like the tombstones in the distance. The wind wailed and screamed and he could almost hear a freezing voice beckoning him into the cemetery.

Krekov went over to Kuratova and said, "Come now, this is enough. We must go."

But Kuratova just ignored him. *"Svetlana! Svetlana! It is your brother Leonid! I am here! I am here!"*

They all rushed over to him, maybe afraid that something out there would hear him. Krekov had become bored with these games, he took hold of Kuratova and Kuratova fought back, shoving Krekov on his ass.

"SVETLANA!" he called, his voice completely hysterical. *"SVETLANA!"*

"Make him stop," Stansfield said. "I can't take any more of this shit."

Yes, yes, they all felt what he was feeling. The shadows. The night. The yawning graveyard. That awful storm of blowing white death. It was all gathering around them, huge and malefic and bleak.

Porsekoi, Vasilev, and Krekov took hold of Kuratova, speaking to him in Ukranian, telling him that there was nothing to be had in this place but a horrible, lingering death. He fought at first, but then he seemed to understand and allowed himself to be helped to his feet.

"Thank God," Stansfield said. "Thank G–"

"Shut up," Chalmers said. *"Listen."*

At first there was nothing, just the howl of the wind in their external helmet mics. They stood about stiffly, waiting for they knew not what. Chalmers had heard something, but he wasn't saying what. He was sweating so badly he thought his suit might slide right off him. But it didn't and then the sound came again, an unearthly, shattered echo like a voice coming through miles of iron pipe.

"What the hell was that?" Stansfield said.

And what came next was laughter . . . bitter, demented, and echoing. But not the sort of laughter a human voice could produce, but something shrill and splintered and eldritch.

"*Svetlana?*" Kuratova said.

Something was coming out of the blowing darkness of the cemetery, a shade, a creeping shadow that gained solidity and became the form of a woman that blazed with a cold blue fire and at the same time was as white as corpse flesh. It was the image of a woman, but one that had been in the ground a long time . . . a stick-limbed apparition, ragged and windblown, a thing so decayed it was hard to tell what was shroud and what was bone. Wisps of steam blew off it, funneling and fuming like fog in a wind tunnel.

And she was speaking.

No one there could be sure what that wavering, weird voice was saying, for it sounded as if it were echoing from a great distance.

As everyone but Kuratova fell back and away, she drifted ever forward, passing right through the fence with a crackling sound of static. Her mouth was a huge obscene blowhole, her eyes like melting rubies that could burn right through you. She was no dead sister come back to life, but a malignant thing, an atomic pestilence that fed on bones and stuffed itself with strontium-90.

"Everyone to the truck!" Porsekoi called out.

They all started backing away as that thing moved in on Kuratova. Krekov, brave to a fault, unslung his AK-47 and started popping rounds into the ghost. They had no effect whatsoever. She was formed of superhot radioactive plasma, Chalmers knew now, and the bullets would have vaporized the moment they made contact.

Finally, even Krekov gave it up.

Kuratova called out for Svetlana and whether this thing was the image of his dead sister or not, nobody knew. Only that it came on with hunger and malevolence. There was nothing anyone could do. The ghost poured forward in a hissing cloud of irradiated steam, moaning and burning and flaking apart. She hovered and then fell on him, dropped down on him like a glowing spider from a high crevice. The instant she touched him, they could hear the sizzling of his suit. He screamed as smoke rolled off him and gouts of fire belched up.

What came next, nobody knew, because they ran for the truck.

Chalmers stumbled along with the others and it was almost comical to see them trying to run in those suits. They fought through the storm and refused to listen to the terrible sounds behind them. When the truck was only a dozen feet away, Chalmers turned and looked, certain that burning red-eyed revenant would be right behind him, grinning and reaching out for him with gnarled, luminous fingers. But it wasn't. It was still attached to Kuratova like a leech, hands to either side of his head and mouth burning right through his helmet. The two of them blazed like a match head.

But Chalmers didn't pay too much attention to that, for the graveyard was alive now.

Alive with *them.*

There was not just the one ghost feeding on Kuratova, but dozens and dozens of them now rising up amongst the tombstones and burial vaults. They came swarming out of the frozen earth like a flurry of phosphorescent, deep-sea fishes swimming up from the abyss, pulsing and glowing and agonized. A whirlpooling fog of radioactive smoke came with them. They howled and shrieked, exhaling clouds of toxic steam. Like the woman, they burned right through the fence, sparking and crackling, their cadaverous faces screaming, electrified hair sweeping around them, hands held out, the circuitry of their exposed entrails lit up like high voltage lines.

The Geiger Counters were reading over a thousand roentgens by this point and the readings were still climbing.

The truck.

Vasilev jumped into the cab and Porsekoi made it into the back, Chalmers and the others stumbling forward, trying to get away from those things and knowing that they never would. Chalmers slipped on the ice and found his feet and slipped again and it all seemed so hopeless, so completely hopeless.

Vasilev screamed and both Chalmers and Krekov saw why.

Another one of the ghosts had appeared, this one in front of the truck. Vasilev was behind the wheel, ready to burn rubber once everyone was inside . . . but that wasn't going to happen. The ghost—that of what appeared to be a young girl—dropped onto the hood out of the sky in a trail of supercharged particles. Her aura was so bright it was blinding. She reached her hands right through the windshield with that crackling sound of ghost matter intersecting true, three-dimensional matter. She threw off so much heat that the glass of the windshield actually began to liquefy, the paint on the hood of the truck bubbled and blistered and ran like wax.

Vasilev never had a chance.

Long before those hands found him, the intensity of her radioactive emissions pierced his suit like knives and cooked him in his own skin. Then those radiant fingers reached right through the visor of his helmet and took hold of him.

Stansfield had been about to jump into the back of the truck, but now he threw himself back as more of the ghosts came through the walls of the rear compartment and took hold of Porsekoi. She didn't even scream. They swarmed on her and the back of the truck was illuminated like a sun.

"We have to get away!" Krekov shouted over the intercom. "Now!"

He didn't even wait for that to register with Chalmers and Stansfield. He shoved them before him, not listening to their complaints or cries of terror. There was simply no time for that and as an old military man, nobody understood the politics of survival better than he.

Chalmers tried to run with the others, but he was clumsy at best. Moving down those black, winding streets, hemmed in by rising apartment complexes to either side, he felt like he was trapped in some surreal nightmare. He wanted to run, to flee as fast as he could, but the suit made that impossible. It was like one of those dreams where you're chased, but your feet are concrete blocks and your legs are rubber.

Krekov seemed to know where they were going, even if Chalmers and Stansfield didn't.

Fifteen minutes later, they were far from the cemetery.

Chalmers had no idea where they were, but they seemed to be safe. At least he thought so until he saw more ghosts drifting about in blazing mists. They were suddenly gathered all around them like buzzards anxious to peck at some gamey red meat. Krekov wasted no time in steering them into the lobby of what might have been a hotel once. As he did so, Chalmers saw several ghost children—one of them an infant—crawling up the high walls of the building overhead, backlit by their own luminous anatomies.

It was insanity, sheer insanity.

Stansfield was moaning like a sick cow and Chalmers was having trouble stringing two words together. If it hadn't have been for Krekov they would have both died out in the streets. As it was, Stansfield was in rough shape. Krekov got them into what might have been a small conference room at one time and they slid down the walls, resting while they could.

Chalmers and Krekov still had their flashights, but they kept them off to conserve power.

But after five minutes of that, the darkness just thick and dank and creeping, Krekov switched his on. They could see the mustard-colored paint peeling on the walls, the dust and dirt and decay.

Stansfield was gasping and groaning.

Krekov said, "We must reach the reactor site. Once there, I can radio for a pickup."

"Radio for it now," Chalmers said, knowing that Krekov had a radio in his pack.

"No, we have to complete our mission. We must reach the reactor to see what is happening there."

"You're out of your fucking mind," Chalmers told him.

But it was pointless to argue. Krekov had been in the security services far too long now. He only understood duty. He would see it through even at the cost of their own lives. Chalmers could just imagine the intensity of the radioactive emissions at the reactor. Right now, in the building, the Geiger Counters were reading about 500 microroentgens. A safe level, as long as their suits held out. But God only knew how much radioactivity they'd been exposed to at the cemetery and from those nuclear ghosts. Even the suits couldn't have protected them. Chalmers' teeth were aching at the gums, his limbs felt sore, his stomach rolling with waves of nausea. All signs of acute radiation sickness.

They had to get out of Pripyat right away.

"I can't go," Stansfield said.

"You have to, Marty," Chalmers told him.

"I can't," he said. "My heart . . . I can't do it. Feels like somebody's standing on my chest. I think . . . I think I had a heart attack back there."

Krekov put his light on Stansfield's visor. Stansfield's face was pinched and yellow and sweaty. He did not look good at all.

"Then we'll carry you," Krekov said.

"No, no, just get away . . . you have to get away. Don't you see that? Don't you see what's happening in this fucking town? It's an incubator, a goddamn atomic incubator," he said, breathing hard. "Don't you see? It starts here. It starts here. Wormwood, Wormwood, Wormwood . . ."

Chalmers was going to ask him what the hell he was talking about, but the chance never came.

For the wall directly behind Stansfield started to glow. The paint bubbled and flaked away, some of it running like tears.

"Marty . . ." Chalmers began to say.

But Krekov dragged him to his feet and pulled him across the room. Stansfield didn't bother trying to escape. The ghost burned right through the wall with the telltale crackling of hot particles. It came through the wall with a thermonuclear glow, an old woman by the looks of it. She floated three feet off the floor, a wizened and skeletal thing, ashen and radiant. Her hair snaked around her head in coiling loops like the locks of Medusa. Her hands were held out before her in grotesque claws, the fingernails long and curled like corkscrews, trails of uranium vapor coming off them in wisps of smoke. Her mouth was opening and closing like that of a beached fish, her eyes burning radium, radioactive steam blowing from her.

Stansfield didn't even scream.

He was beaten. Completely beaten.

She smiled at him with a grin of seething isotopes and floated down on him and they could hear his suit melting.

But Krekov yanked Chalmers from the room before he could see any more of it. They had to get away. Get away while that smoldering ghoul was otherwise occupied. Yes, Krekov pulled Chalmers away, but not so fast that he could not hear the sizzling of Stansfield's suit, the liquid rending noises, and then that awful hollow sound of his bones being sucked out.

As Krekov led him out into the streets, Chalmers thought: Wormwood.

Wormwood.

Wormwood.

It was familiar, yet he could not place it in the screaming confusion of his mind. It meant something. It meant something very bad and that's what Stansfield had been trying to tell them.

Wormwood.

6

The Furnace

With absolute terror comes clarity, a widening of perception. Everything, all the safeguards and protective baggage of adulthood that keeps people sane and does not let them see the crawling shadows in the corners of the world, is stripped away and laid bare as bone. And that's exactly how it was for Chalmers as they neared the reactor site. He recognized that there was true horror in the world just as he had when he was a child. He knew there were monstrous things under the bed and drooling, perverse nightmares living in the closet. That old houses were invariably filled with spooks and dark woods were haunted by monsters that fed on human flesh and human suffering. He knew, he accepted, he finally understood now that the blinders were off. Adults took these absolute truths and re-channeled them into myth and fairy tale and harmless campfire tales, but they did it out of sheer self-preservation, so the knowledge of the creeping, morbid things would not drive them insane.

But Chalmers was beyond all that now.

He saw the world for what it was and he saw Pripyat—that pestilent, haunted ghost town—as the world's Pandora's Box whose lid had been irrevocably blown off by man's exploration of the forces that held together the universe. Yes, the lid was off and there was no going back and all the dark malignancies of creation were slinking out and that was one cat you'd never get back in the bag again.

And it was because of this clarity of vision that he remembered Wormwood. Remembered what Stansfield had been trying in vain to tell them. Yes, Chalmers remembered it from Sunday school. Wormwood was something out of the Book of Revelation which foretold the end of the world:

". . . and there fell a great star from heaven, burning as it were a lamp . . .

"And the name of the star is called Wormwood: and the third part of the waters became Wormwood; and many men died of the waters, because they were made bitter . . ."

Yes, Pripyat was Wormwood or, more appropriately, the reactor itself. For that was the burning star which would bring about the end of the world. For the end started here and it started now.

Moving through the falling snow, Krekov led them across the bridge. From here you could've seen the reactor if it hadn't have been for the night and the storm. Chalmers remembered that it was here, on this very bridge, that people had gathered the day after the accident. From here they could see the ruptured containment vessel of the reactor and catch a glimpse of the glowing nuclear core as it saturated them with X-rays.

Jesus.

Krekov led on and neither man spoke. The landscape was industrial and bleak. They came to a sprawling park and trudged through the snowdrifts, the wind howling around them. It was an amusement park that was built just before the reactor explosion. It was set to be opened for the upcoming May Day celebration that never came. Here were rusting cars on tracks, rides and recreations, a huge silent Ferris wheel rising above it all, its cars creaking in the wind. Children had come here to play on the day of the accident and it was said that parents had to fight their way through clouds of atomic smoke to find them.

The Geiger Counters were beeping madly now.

Soon, the emissions would be right off the scale.

In the darkness with only two feeble flashlights, they should have not been able to see the power plant, but they could. The entire area was lit by the pulsing luminosity of the reactor itself . . . or maybe by something which was *feeding* on its remains.

"Oh my God," Chalmers said, everything in him just running wet now.

He saw the reactor buildings. He saw all of it rising before him and the stark, absolute immensity of it all withered him and squashed him flat. It took away his breath and made his head swim and drove him right down to his knees in the snow. He could see two looming red structures surrounded by the rusting masts of cranes which he knew were the unfinished fifth and sixth Chernobyl reactor units. Behind a high fence were the deactivated hulks of reactors Two and Three. He saw huge power lines above held by skeletal derricks, high voltage transformers, a maze of steam piping, and there, backlit by the glow, the giant black reactor blocks of Chernobyl Four, smokestacks climbing into the sky.

And yes, there it was, the sarcophagus itself.

About the size of a basketball court, it was a tomb of rusting iron and gray concrete that was badly cracked now, holding in its belly some 216 metric tons of uranium and plutonium . . . the very stuff the Shadow Matter entity was even then feeding upon and, in the course of which, sending out an unimaginable amount of intense gamma rays. There was a total radioactivity in the melted core of something like 18 million curies. Enough to vaporize a man in a split second.

When Krekov started toward the sarcophagus, Chalmers said, "You can't be serious! Jesus Christ, we can't get any closer! That thing will fry us!"

"We have to," Krekov said. "We have to see this thing. It's what we came for."

He was mad. Absolutely fucking mad. The Geiger Counters were registering something like 1500 microroentgens as it was. Beyond this point, radioactivity had to be measured in rem. There were a million microroentgens in one rem and inside that building, they would be looking at something like 2,000 rem. As deadly as deadly could be.

Krekov was going and Chalmers followed him.

He saw no point in not going. He'd already absorbed so much ionizing radiation that he would probably be filled with tumors by the end of the month. What was the point of staying alive for that?

He followed Krekov to the plant's entrance, tossing aside his Geiger Counter now. At this point, trying to keep track of the radioactivity you were getting hit with was like trying to gauge the velocity of a bullet as it punched through your head. There was a bust of Lenin near the door and Chalmers laughed at that. The great father figure of Soviet Russia.

In they went.

Krekov knew his way around just fine. The reactor building was in good shape and well shielded. Until just a few weeks ago when the trouble started, technicians had been working here monitoring the melted core. They went down a set of stone steps and into a rubber-floored ready room where radiation suits hung in lockers.

Now they were going into the sarcophagus itself.

Chalmers was far beyond ordinary fear now. What had taken hold of him was raw and black acceptance, the way one must feel as they wait for the hand of death.

They went down another stairway plastered with yellow radiation warning triangles and emerged in front of the shell of the sarcophagus. Up close, it was an ugly patchwork of concrete and metal plating, crumbling and set with huge gaps from which a steady pulsating glow emanated. Inside, through a narrow staircase near the old turbine hall, they entered the shell. Everything here was highly contaminated with radioactive dust.

"Move quickly," Krekov said.

They went into a shielded control room and this was, essentially, as far as men *could* go. Here was the hot cell itself where nuclear fuel rods could be handled with remote manipulators. But they hadn't come for that. Most of the instrumentation had been stripped away, but there was still battery power. Krekov turned on the lights and activated cameras which would allow them to look into the core itself.

"Now," he said, "we shall see what no man has ever seen."

They were looking down into the remains of the reactor itself. A maze of collapsed ceilings, melted iron and concrete, heaps of debris, and, yes, the glowing nuclear core itself.

It was very bright, but not so bright that they could not see things moving about in there. The ghosts of children. Maybe a dozen of them, white and shining things drifting about like a storm of luminous corpse-flies. Many of them were settled right onto the glowing nuclear waste, shoveling handfuls of fissionable material into their mouths as they looked up at the camera with eyes like burning purple-red bloodclots.

"Dear Christ," Chalmers said. "They know we're here."

"Yes," Krekov said.

"Let's get out of here. Now. Call in your helicopter."

But Krekov shook his head. "You are very naïve, Mr. Chalmers. There is to be no helicopter. When I press the button, the radio will send a signal that will bring in an airstrike that will decimate this place."

Chalmers just stood there, his guts sinking. "So that's it, eh? You're a fucking fool if you think that will stop this. All you'll do is spread radioactive waste across the countryside."

"Precisely. The bombardment will be absolute and devastating. It will scatter the core and its radioactive components for miles around. And in doing so, perhaps starve the thing which lives off them."

Sure, it would scatter the contamination to the four winds. It would kill thousands, but there would no longer be any centralized nuclear materials. Just fragments tossed in every direction. Scraps that the Shadow Matter entity would have to hunt high and low for and, in doing so, would probably be phased out of existence.

Very clever.

"Look," Krekov said.

The camera was filled with a blinding light now. They could not look at the screen.

"It comes," Krekov said. "The entity shows itself."

"Come on, Krekov!" Chalmers said, taking hold of him. "We have to get the hell out of here! Let's go!"

Krekov just shook him off. He wanted to see. He actually wanted to see the thing.

Chalmers just backed away from him, his cup running over with madness. This had all gone too far. Krekov was insane. Utterly insane. Chalmers did not want to leave him. The humanity in him demanded that he not do this. But something else made the decision for him.

The wall nearest Krekov suddenly broke out with what looked like beads of light and then it began to glow and sizzle and one of the ghosts drifted right through it. That of a boy. Hands extended like a beggar, he floated forward, a mummy, an apparition caught in an incandescent blue-green field of energized particles, his mouth yawning open, his eyes like dying suns. He was naked, Chalmers saw in that split second before he ran, and composed of a white luminous flesh charged with lethal radioactivity. In that ethereal, atomic mist, he looked like some phosphorescent corpse seen in the depths . . . moving with slow, liquid undulations: rising and falling like a puppet, mouth opening and closing, limbs stretching, fingers reaching and contracting. An absolute horror that was withering and fraying, ropes and strands of that ectoplasmic tissue fluttering out around him and behind him like kelp caught in a deep-sea current.

Krekov brought up his rifle, his training getting the best of him.

To his credit, he fired off a few shots and then the ghost had him, it moved at him with a slithering motion, mouth opening wide and exhaling a steam of burning fog that struck him right in the helmet like a breath of frost. The effect was instantaneous.

Krekov's head melted.

It actually melted. The helmet collapsed and ran like hot butter and his entire body followed it, melting like wax, oozing into a pool of bubbling flesh and rubber.

Chalmers ran out of the control room.

He fumbled up stairways and down corridors until he was out of the sarcophagus and out of the reactor building in general.

He ran and ran and ran.

Through the blowing snow and driving wind. He kept going until he reached the bridge, some childish urge for survival in him telling him he could actually escape what was coming.

But it was hopeless.

He fell face first on the bridge and then looked up through his dirty visor in time to see the Number Four reactor building completely engulfed in a flickering thermonuclear glare.

It was coming.

The reactor building had melted into a sea of atomic sludge now. The entity was rising from its gutted, charred remains. It was immense. Absolutely immense. The Shadow Matter entity was a chaotic cloud of intense radioactivity, a living breeder reactor, a primal sentient evil born from the hot cosmic wastes before the Big Bang. This was the Devil. This was the ultimate evil and men had invited it in. It rose up with a swarm of attendant plasma ghosts, hungry to suck the world dry of radioactive materials. It would eat nuclear bombs and atomic piles, increasing its deadly mass as it leeched every nuclear reactor in the world and spreading a rain of fallout a billion times worse than anything imaginable, turning the entire planet into one huge smoldering graveyard.

And it was coming for him.

Wormwood. That blazing, falling star that presaged the end of the world. It had been born in that godless dimension of black mists and brought to term in the hot irradiated womb of Chernobyl-Four, feeding on unstable isotopes and white-hot radionuclides and bathing in the thermal fusion of enriched uranium and plutonium. And it had risen now from the searing, smoking reactor pit.

Wormwood.

Chalmers looked upon it as it rolled forth with a hurricane wind that flattened and incinerated everything in its path, a mushroom cloud of vapor rising above it. Yes, he looked upon it and knew that it was aware of him. That churning, hideous mind of hot particles and radioactivity looked into his own and destroyed him at that moment.

And as it emptied his mind, he was bodily sucked into the catastrophic vortex of superhot plasma that was its heart. As a million billion white needles perforated him and his mouth was filled with a taste of cold yellow metal and he was literally vaporized in an atomic steam of molecules, his disintegrating mind wondered how many nuke plants there were in the world. How many stores of isotopes and stockpiles of concentrated nuclear waste? This thing, this Shadow Matter devil, it would eat them all until it was whole again as it had been before the Big Bang, until it had turned the sum of creation into a cold, sterile womb of blackness like the one that had given it birth.

As it was in the beginning, so it would be in the end.

A darkness without form, a void without body.

Wormwood.

WHEN THE SHIP CAME

JOHN SUNSERI

THE SHIP SET DOWN in a clearing in the woods near Five-Mile Creek, not far from the Albertsons' Christmas tree farm. When it touched down, the mud squelched beneath it, and it settled a few inches into the soft ground. A couple of deer, not having heard the thing approach, were startled at its sudden appearance in the field and bolted, their white tails disappearing into the woods like wills-o'-the-wisp.

The ship waited.

"So it's us, then," sighed Tom Traylor.

"Seems like," said Isaiah Havercamp, sitting forward on his barstool, staring blankly into his beer.

"Shit," said Traylor, taking a sip of his own. The bar was packed, more people crowding in every few minutes as word of the ship spread through the town. Every table was full, and men and women stood in the hall and in the spaces between furniture, talking animatedly, most of them with dazed expressions stamped on their faces. Rick and Vicki, the Tap's two bartenders, couldn't keep up with the orders, and had instead taken to just filling up pint glasses and setting them on the bar, where someone would take one and pass it to someone, who would pass it to someone else, and so on, until everyone who wanted one had one. Of course, at the rate people were drinking, it was a never-ending cycle — by the time another pint got to you, you were five minutes past your last one. It reminded Tom of something he had heard one time about the Chinese — that if you lined them up, arm in arm, on their border with Russia, and stacked them as deep as you liked behind each other, then started marching them forward — well, with the amount of them, and their birth rate, that human tide would just never stop coming. You could march Chinese from now to doomsday, and they would just keep coming . . .

"Might not be so bad," said Havercamp. "I mean, we don't know why they want us. Maybe it's something good — like winning the lottery."

"Maybe," said Traylor, but his tone was doubtful. "What do *you* think?"

"I think we're screwed," said the older man. "But I could be wrong."

"I don't think you are," said Traylor. "*Shit!*"

"No point bitching," said Havercamp. "We can't do anything about it, now. You know who *I* feel sorry for?"

"Tricia Salvi," said Traylor.

"Well, *her*, of course. No, I was talking about that guy over there — got a flat tire a mile or so up the road and hiked the rest of the way in, was having a drink while Justin took the tow truck out to get his car. Now he's stuck here with us."

"Where's he from?"

"Portland. He was coming back from a business meeting down in Eugene, and decided to take the scenic route home."

Traylor laughed, a hollow, mildly desperate sound. "Wrong decision, buddy," he said.

"Yeah."

"Christ," said Traylor. "Now what do we do?"

"We wait," said Havercamp. "We wait, and in the meantime we get drunk."

At the churches the scene was similar, though without the alcohol. At the Catholic church, St. Anne's, Father Pete Lorenzini was serving mass, and the Protestants were all sitting in the meeting hall at Greater Glory, drinking coffee and talking nervously.

"They won't need me," Tricia Salvi said worriedly to her neighbor, Lucy Redmond. "They can't expect me to go . . ."

"Oh, honey," said Lucy, shaking her head, "you heard what the President said on Tuesday."

"But I *can't*," wailed Tricia, tears rolling down her cheeks, her hands clasped protectively around her massive stomach. "Not with the baby coming soon, and Ed still over in the Middle East! There's got to be some kind of deferment or something!"

"Oh, baby," replied Lucy, "you poor thing. We'll all help you — you know that." Lucy Redmond was one of those women actively involved in Church matters, always ready with a helping hand for those less fortunate. Some of the wagging tongues around town suggested that her propensity toward delivering charity was a clever ploy meant to give her access to the best gossip, and it seemed that she *did* always know what was going on with the families that filled out the lower half of Calamity Falls's economic bracket, but she wasn't malicious about any of it — and though the Falls's one currently pregnant woman didn't particularly *like* Lucy, that didn't stop her from accepting the woman's matronly hug.

"What do they *want* with us?" she asked plaintively. "Why *us?*"

"The Lord moves in mysterious ways," responded Lucy Redmond.

"Well, *fuck* the Lord!" cried Tricia, and it is to Lucy's credit, gossip or not, that she held the poor woman tighter as people around them looked up from their own conversations with expressions aghast and disapproving, and held the crying, shaking thing for a long time until she settled down.

"Amen," echoed the congregation. The Catholics were a little more formal, and they had waited until Mass was over, everyone having partaken of the Sacrament, before they got together in the grade school auditorium next door and began to debate the consequences of the ship's arrival. Coffee urns were set up, and they had raided the school cafeteria for cookies and sheet cakes, which were thawing on some of the tables next to the badge projects of Boy Scout Troop 507 while the talk raged.

"The President won't let it happen," argued Trevor Rask. "He'll send helicopters or something — jet fighters . . ."

"You been watching the news?" asked Manuel Vega, sipping his black coffee. "Helicopters and jet fighters won't make a dent in the thing. Maybe even nukes wouldn't do the trick."

"*Something*, then," said Rask, looking around for his wife, a little annoyed that he was having this discussion with Vega. The two of them didn't get along so well, and he tended to avoid the man at church, which is the only place the two of them saw each other, save for Grange meetings.

"Oh, I agree the government'll try something," said Vega, smiling as his own wife joined them, cookies balanced on a flimsy paper plate, "I just pray they don't piss off the aliens while they're doing it."

"Manny!" said Lupe, shocked. "Your language!"

"The Good Lord will forgive me a 'pissed' every once in a while," said Manuel, taking a ladyfinger and crunching half of it into his mouth. Lupe set the plate on a nearby table, and the three of them huddled closer together to avoid the traffic around them. Trevor kept looking for Missy, but without much hope — his wife was probably still over at the church, calling families that might not have heard the news. She was a chronic volunteer for stuff like that, seemed to spend half the time at the school and the church, running bake sales and organizing bingo nights . . .

"Okay," whispered Missy Rask, "that's the worst thing we've ever done."

"We've made love before," protested Jake Wilson.

"Never in the *church!*" she snapped, re-hooking her bra, shooting a glare over her shoulder. Jake jerked his head back, surprised. A minute ago, the woman had been as clingy and needful as any hurt child, and now she was yelling at him — in whispers, true, but the *tone* of her words was a yell.

"It doesn't matter," he said. "Church, my house, your house — it's just because we love each other."

"Oh, for God's sake," she said, bending to pick up her blouse and slipping into it. "Let's not start with the love talk again, Jake."

"Why not?" he asked, standing as well. "This might be the last time we get to talk to each other alone, Missy! There are some things we need to figure out . . ."

"No!" she said, eyes blazing. "No, we don't! Listen, kid — you're getting your rocks off on a regular basis. For most boys your age, that'd be plenty, but you — you want to make some freaking *opera* out of this!"

"I'm not a boy," said Jake, his hands clenched into fists. "You're only ten years older than me . . ."

"Thirteen," she interrupted.

". . . and I'm old enough to know what love is," he finished. "I love you. Let's not go into this thing lying to ourselves, Missy."

"Jake," she said, finishing with her blouse and pulling the little mirror out of her purse to begin reconstruction work on her — thankfully short — hair. "I like you a lot. We're good at sex. But that's it. I don't love you — I love my husband."

"Then why aren't you with him right now, Missy?" asked Jake, his heart a mess of contradictory impulses. "Why didn't you go get fucked by *him*, you love him so much?"

There was a short pause as the air electrified.

"Oh, you little bastard," she breathed, looking up from her contact with an expression that would've been at home on a harpy. "You unimaginable little *prick!*"

"Oh, I'm a prick, now?" he asked, feeling two things — the most hurt he had ever been, and gleeful that he was hurting *her*, too. "Ten minutes ago I was a fucking stud, and now I'm a prick?"

"You're a stupid little boy," she replied, flinging the compact back into her purse and rooting through her pocket for the wedding ring she had placed there before she and Jake had began their rutting, "who doesn't know when to leave well enough alone."

"Maybe you're right," he said, moving toward her, his penis shriveled in the cold air. "Maybe I'm so stupid I'll just go have a little talk with your husband about you, maybe tell him what we do while he's up in Portland negotiating with the grocery stores . . ." He stopped moving when Missy stalked over to him. She got within inches, looked up into his face, and, in a deadly quiet tone, began to talk. Her words were quiet, yes, but their impact was undeniable.

"You go ahead, Jake Wilson," she began. "You go tell Trevor that we've been sleeping together. He'll probably even believe you. But, you know what he'll do? Do you?" Jake, uncertain, feeling suddenly vulnerable in his nudity, shook his head. "He'll kick the shit out of you. High school football is nice, you know, but Trevor's a *man*, Jake, and he'll mop the fucking floor with you. Then, I'm sure he and I will fight, and we'll argue, and it'll be a tough, sad thing . . . but we won't get divorced. Trevor and I love each other, and we'll never get divorced. The marriage won't be the same, afterward, but it'll still be a marriage. And *then* do you know what'll happen?" This time, she didn't wait for a headshake. "Then, Jake, *I'll* come after you, I don't care if we're on an alien ship, I don't care if we're in another *galaxy*, Jake. I'll come after you, and *I'll* kick your little immature, juvenile ass too. And I'll do it worse." Then, finished, she swept up her purse and stormed out of the room, the white gold of her wedding band glinting in the light from the lamp over the door of the vestry.

Jake slumped back down onto the couch, and, his hands still tightly balled, the veins bulging on his forearm muscles, he began to cry.

Victor Spielman sat in his root cellar, wondering whether he should kill himself. He had the shotgun in his hands, had been holding it for an hour, now, and his arms were starting to hurt. His dog, Lady, was down there with him, and they were listening to the idiot white-noise hum that came from the radio, Lady sensing something horribly wrong with her master, trying to help with her physical contact. Vic appreciated it — he loved his dog as much as he had ever loved a woman, and he had been married three times — but nothing was going to help, right now. About the only thing that would make him feel better would be if that damned ship changed its mind — just up and took off, found another town to kidnap.

Finally, he stood up and went to the shelves where he kept all his preserves. Selecting a jar of tomatoes, he brought it over to his workbench (the shotgun still in one hand) and opened it. He ate the tomatoes standing up, conscious that the window behind him had been only hastily boarded up, and when the aliens came, they would get right through the plywood if they wanted. But they would make noise, and that would give him enough time to fire off a couple shells at them, and save one for himself. Unless they had some kind of mind-control device . . .

He shivered. Lady, seeing that, began to whine a little, like she used to do when she was a puppy. He looked at her, smiling a small, sad smile, and said, "you need to take a shit, sweetie? Is that it?"

The dog lay down, her big eyes looking hopefully up at him. She didn't understand his words, but the fact that he was talking to her at all was a reassurance to the animal.

"Sorry, sweetheart," he said, glancing at all the boards over all the windows. "We're down here for a while. If you gotta, take a dump on the floor. I won't hit you."

The dog's tail thumped.

Sam Wells and Rebecca Albertson were trying to lose their virginity, but his thirteen-year old equipment, though functional, wasn't responding right. He didn't think it was fair — he got hard-ons ten, twelve times a day; every morning, every evening, in fucking *math* class, for God's sake, but now that he had an actual *partner*, a forchrissake *girl* naked in front of him, it was scrunched up like a dried sponge, socked into his fuzzy little patch of pubic hair.

"Maybe if I touched it again," began Rebecca, who was just as scared as Sam, but didn't have the shrunken penis to show for it — instead, she felt a roiling ruckus in her guts she hadn't felt since she and her mom had moved away from Gary, who used to beat them. That's how she thought of it, when she thought of it at all — Gary-who-used-to-beat-us was always said clinically and quickly in her head, as if by slapping a definition on the past she could denude it of its power, exorcise the memories of hiding under her bed up in the apartment in Portland, trying to hide from Gary but never succeeding . . .

"Never mind," said Sam, fighting valiantly to hold back the tears. "I guess I'm some kind of homo or something."

"That's not right, Sam," said Rebecca, speaking from her authority as an eighth-grader. True, she was only fourteen, a year older than the boy next to her, the boy in whose barn they were currently hiding, trying to have sex, but still. "You're not a homo. Trust me, I know. When I was a girl, in Portland, we had homos next door to us, and you're not like them at all."

"Really?" asked the boy, still staring at his little member, though now he sneaked a glance at the barely pubescent figure of the girl sitting naked on the hay before him. He flushed again — he had been blushing a lot in the last half-hour or so, and was starting to get used to the feeling of the hot blood rushing to his face.

"Oh, yeah," she said. "Homos act like girls, Sam. They're always talking in these real high voices and giggling, and they . . . they cook a lot, and listen to that classical music stuff that Mrs. Van Wormer's always making us listen to in class. They're not like *you*, Sam."

"Whaddya mean?" he asked, his shame being replaced by a kind of fascination at hearing about life among the homos up in Portland. He sat down carefully, and looked back up at Becky, knowing instinctively that he shouldn't stare at the small mounds of her breasts, the little discs of her nipples, but unable to completely drag his eyes up to meet hers. Thankfully, she didn't seem to mind.

"You're a real guy, Sam," she said. "You play baseball, and you know how to build a fire — you remember, when you got that magnifying glass in the Scouts, how you burned that hay?" He remembered, all right. He had been trying to impress her, but she had been with her friend Laura McKinney at the time, and they had both made fun of him, asked if he couldn't just go out and buy a lighter . . . he nodded.

"No homo would know how to do that," she proclaimed, the authoritative voice of knowledge. "No, you're straight as they come, Sam."

"Then how come," he began, one hand gesturing toward his groin.

"Maybe you don't think I'm pretty," she said. This was her real fear, of course, and it was the hardest thing she had ever done, admitting it to him. She knew that she was considered plain by her mother, but she had always sensed that some boys found her desirable — Sam included, dear Sam who was always showing off for her, teaching her how to use a slingshot, taking her out with his .22 and trying to shoot squirrels with her, and she *had* been impressed when he had crouched over the pile of hay last summer with his glass, carefully, steadily focusing the sun onto it until a small puff of smoke had appeared . . . but Laura had made some crack, so she'd had to follow suit . . .

"I do *so* think you're pretty, Becky!" said Sam, so shocked he stopped looking at her breasts and stared straight into her eyes. "I thought so since you moved into the old Barnes place next door! You're the prettiest girl I've ever seen — even prettier than Jennifer Lopez." This was high praise — she had seen the posters on Sam's bedroom wall. She felt a warm flush suffuse her, tempering some of the fear she had felt since her mom had told her about the aliens landing and torn off to town to collect supplies.

"Really?" she asked.

"I think you're beautiful," he said, solemnly.

"Thank you, Sam," she whispered. "Sam?"

"Yeah, Becky?"

"What do the aliens want with us?"

"I don't know," he said, troubled, for the first time not thinking about his performance problems. "Dad says they can't be up to any good, floating around in orbit like they are, not coming down to show their faces, but I'm not so sure . . ."

"Tell me what you think," said Becky, slowly moving over to him, scootching on her butt across the hay, moving slowly and quietly, like she would with a stray dog on the road so as not to startle it.

"What if they want us for some kind of zoo?" he asked, a flare in his eyes as he pronounced his idea. Sam was a reader, whenever there wasn't a ballgame to be got up, and on his shelves was a good hunk of science fiction. "What if they want to take us back to their planet, take the whole town, and study us? It'd be like us going over to Africa and picking up a bunch of monkeys, then bringing 'em over here and putting them in a big cage. Like in the zoo up in Portland."

"That's a great idea, Sam!" she said, truly excited. It was a *lot* better than the ideas *she* had been having since the ship had landed — of course, the extent of her knowledge about aliens, up until Tuesday, had been stuff like *Independence Day* and *Signs*, where the aliens wanted to come down here and kill everybody. Sam's notion opened up a new world of hope in her heart, and she reached out and grabbed his hand. "Do you really think that's what they want?"

"I think so," said Sam who, in truth, had only considered the idea as one among many, including the death-from-above scenarios, but who would now stick with *this* one, seeing how much joy it caused Rebecca. "It's what *I* would do, if I was an alien. Just come down here, grab a town full of people, and bring it back with me. And, you know what?" he asked, suddenly excited by a new idea. "You know what the cool thing is? If we're in some kind of zoo, like the monkeys up in Portland, just think about all the *other* animals in the zoo with us! Why, we'll be able to see aliens from all over the universe, I bet! And maybe they'll let us kinda make friends with them, you know? Go to the next cage over, and there'll be like talking trees or something, and maybe on the other side there'll be intelligent cows . . ."

"Smart cows!" Rebecca laughed, scooting over further and putting her arm around the thin, bare shoulders of the boy. "What an idea!"

"Why not?" he asked, smiling, happy that he was making her happy. "And intelligent dogs, and squirrels, and, and . . . sharks . . ."

"Not sharks," she admonished.

"Okay, not sharks," he said, giving in gracefully, "but maybe cats, and . . ." At this point, Becky leaned over and gave him a kiss — a warm, soft, urgent kiss, with a hesitant tongue darting into his mouth. He kissed back and reached for her, holding her tight, and when they finally broke their clinch most of the fear was gone and they felt like kids again.

She looked down at his lap, and shook her head, but there was nothing mocking in the gesture. "Maybe it wasn't a good idea anyway," she said. "I mean, if we're gonna be in a zoo, we'll have a lot of time to . . ."

"Yeah," he said, more regretful than embarrassed. "So, Becky?"

"Yes, Sam?"

"You wanna go steady?"

The mayor of Calamity Falls, Linda Grady, led the delegation out to the ship. Since it had arrived, and been spotted by Jack and Edgar Michaels, there had been a police cruiser parked on the field fifty yards away from the thing, and Al Hendricks and Terry Ransome had been sitting there, smoking and watching it. Their guns were unholstered and within easy reach and the radio was on, though nothing but white noise came through — since the landing, no radio or television reception had come in anywhere in the Falls, though some local telephone calls were getting through. It made for a nervous vigil, not being able to talk to Marcia back at the station, so Mayor Grady had made sure to send the occasional car out with hot food for the cops, or just so they'd have someone to talk to.

The delegation was twenty strong, most of it men, most of *them* armed, though they had all heard the President's speech on Tuesday, talking about how invulnerable the things were, and how futile it was to shoot at them. There had been some nuclear weapons fired at the ships in orbit, but to no noticeable result, and no country was claiming responsibility for the missiles, though anyone with half a brain could have told you where the responsibility for them lay, even without proof. It's not like China or Russia had that kind of precise technology, after all . . . so when the American President came on the air and told the world that the aliens would soon be landing a ship to collect a town's worth of people somewhere in the world, and that resistance would bring a terrible cost . . .

"And, rest assured that, if this town happens to be an American one, the American government will never stop until we have secured your release from this bondage. Just as in World War II, when, with courage and conviction, thousands were rescued from Dunkirk in France, so will it be with . . ."

"Pencilneck," Patrolman Ransome had said, watching the President on TV on Tuesday night. "No way those bastards should land in the first place, America or not."

"Well, what's the man supposed to do, Terry?" his wife had asked, sitting on the edge of the couch next to him, a Virginia Slim in the corner of her mouth. "We can't hurt their ships . . ."

"We can't hurt the ones in *orbit*," Terry had pointed out. "Who's to say we can't knock their dropship out of the sky on the way down? Then, we get our geeks in the government going on analyzing the wreckage, and pretty soon we'll have a chance to beat the bastards."

"We're not at war, Terry," started Jeanette, but he kept going.

"No fucking way should the American President *ever* give up his citizens without a fight. *Never*. You show weakness, eventually you'll get stomped. It happened to Europe in the Big War — you start negotiating with a Hitler, eventually you'll wake up to sauerkraut for breakfast and swastikas all over the damn place while the Jews head off to the showers. *God* I'm glad I didn't vote for that guy!"

"You didn't vote for anyone, Terry," said his wife. "You haven't voted since that cougar-hunting thing was on the ballot."

"Well, I *wouldn't* have voted for him," he said, grousing. Jeanette sensed the nervousness in his tone and scooted closer to him, placing a calm, cool hand on his thigh. He kept watching the TV, where the talking heads were having the same discussion he and Jeanie were, but with bigger words. "Hell, what if they pick Calamity Falls?"

"Not much chance of that, lover," said his wife.

"Yeah, they're probably saying that all over the world right now," he responded, "but, you know, they've gotta pick *someone*."

The delegation was at the ship now, and everyone was at a loss.

"Should we knock?" asked Rick Reilly, town council chair and smartass.

"Yeah, you go ahead and do that," said Mayor Grady. "Tell 'em the welcome wagon's here."

"Sounds good," he said, and walked even closer to the ship, knuckles extended.

"Hey, dammit!" shouted Manuel Vega, representing the Grange. "What are you doing?"

"I'm doing *something*," responded Reilly, and though his tone was casual, the others could see sweat pearling on his face as he turned to talk. "Or would you rather wait some more, have some more fistfights, like we've been having in town all afternoon?"

"We should try to leave again," said Pamela Corbett, kneading her hands together. "Maybe if we're going fast enough when we hit the force field . . ."

". . . then the car'll just *explode*, rather than bouncing off, like those idiot Edwards boys did," finished Reilly. "No, hon, we're in this to finish it. And the only way to do that is for the aliens to collect us, run all their anal probes, and drop us back off."

"Do you really think that levity is appropriate right now?" asked Mayor Grady, frowning.

"Appropriate?" laughed Reilly, contorting his features into a pained smile. "Hell if I know. All I know is, it's keeping me from falling to the ground, babbling like an idiot." And, with that, he knocked on the dull gray metal of the ship's hull.

A door opened.

". . . and, as you all know, the aliens landed near a small town in Oregon this morning," said the President, "named Calamity Falls. As of this evening, everyone in that town had disappeared, along with the alien ship. The town is still there, and so are all the people's possessions. As I speak, teams of experts are sifting through all the evidence, looking for clues as to why the aliens chose this little community of fine Americans to abduct, and I'm sure, with their technical expertise and their devotion, they'll find the answers we're all looking for, and I guarantee all of you that I, and the government I represent, will work unceasingly to bring these men, women, children and pets back to Earth at the earliest possible time . . .

. . . though we are no longer in contact with the alien vessels which have, apparently, left Earth orbit, I am assured that we will be able to track them and restore communications . . .

. . . God bless America."

Two weeks later there were still no answers — the empty town had been gone over as if it were Atlantis risen from the depths, every square inch photographed, microanalyzed, Geiger-countered and chemically tested, and it was still as dead and silent as the Mary Celeste. The first team into Calamity Falls after the force field disappeared found some interesting data — a couple of Remington shells in a basement and a scattershot pattern of holes in the cellar wall, along with several dozen broken, oozing jars of tomatoes and beans and corn. A used condom in the vestry of St. Anne's. A black, melted spot on the front seat of a police cruiser where a cigarette had fallen and burnt itself out. But no evidence that could tell any of America's brightest minds exactly what had happened, or how.

That night, two weeks later, a smooth silver object the shape and size of a basketball fell to Earth, streaking through the atmosphere at a constant speed, unaffected by friction or gravity, and smashed into the ground in a rice paddy near Birgani in southern Nepal, throwing up a geyser of dirty water a hundred feet tall. Nearby water buffalo shifted uneasily at the loud noise and violent splash, but after a couple of seconds they settled down and went back to their ruminative sleep.

In the morning, Sonam Khadka discovered the disturbance in his rice field, a wide spot where the tender plants had been bruised, bent or smashed, but attributed it to vandals from the town and took no more notice. That night, however, on his plodding trudge back to his mud-and-dung shack, he noticed that the damaged area was larger than it had been that morning — it had been a rough circle five meters across, but now it was twice that large, and the grass at the edges of the blight drooped and had turned black.

Khadka felt despair looking at the affected area, and cursed quietly to himself. The area had suffered the catastrophe of rice blast a few seasons before, and he'd had to sell two of his four buffalo to feed his family that horrible year — and if this was some new kind of fungus, he thought he just might have to kill himself.

Perhaps it would be better in the morning.

More of the silver balls slipped into Earth's atmosphere the next day, one of them bulleting into the ground in north Congo and obliterating half a mile of jungle, another burying itself in a hillside in Guatemala, a third ripping through a lake near the Minnesota-Canada border, yet another splintering a few trees near Tunguska in Siberia, more scattering themselves across the world's oceans and glaciers, where they burrowed into the ice and dirt and rock and began doing their work.

Sonam Khadka's eldest son, Pem, woke that next night trying to breathe through lungs suddenly constricted and flat, and fought to his elbows on his rough mat of jute, straining to suck in enough air to feed his pounding heart, blinked a few times in the heavy darkness as he fought for oxygen, and saw his father lying on the mat next to him, barely visible in the starlight.

The skin had stretched taut across his Sonam's bones, contorting him into a rough fetal position, pulling his lipless mouth open into a rictus; his eyes had collapsed and burst in their sockets and the meat of the older man's body had desiccated and almost dissolved. Pem tried to scream, but his throat would not work and soon his vision went entirely black and he collapsed back onto his mat, his flesh hardening and shrinking, and the jute fibers curled and twisted as they began to dissolve.

The next morning the hut stood alone in a five-mile circle of devastation and dead rice grass, stinking, oily water, the blackened bones of the two buffalo and a poisonous dark haze that gradually billowed out against the wind as the perimeter of the phenomenon continued to creep outward and outward.

More balls fell, one of them almost striking a Japanese whaling ship in the Bering Sea, another shattering the fragile ice crust near the North Pole, a third destroying a skua nest on Macquarie Island and causing nearby albatrosses to squawk in alarm and flap heavily into the frigid skies, yet another careening off the Rock of Gibraltar into Catalan Bay, and instantly a hundred dead fish rose to the surface, glistening white in the morning sun.

And everywhere the balls hit, the corruption began to spread. Within ten days it was over.

And the ship accelerated through the void of deep space carrying a taken town, heading toward strange and alien constellations, leaving behind a planet blackened, blistered and dead.

THE MANUSCRIPT IN THE DRAWER

GREG BEATTY

"JUST ONE MORE QUESTION Mr. Ellis, if I may, and then we'll be done." The interviewer from *Inside Books* looked around the room in a pleased but dullish way. It was essential that all award nominees be interviewed, but some authors, like Robert Ellis, had been prodded and queried from all directions till there was nothing left to ask, and an interview boiled down to a pleasant evening in an overheated book-lined room where all the answers to all the questions were already known.

Ellis was a good sport, though. He played along, gesturing with his pipe for the interviewer to continue. "By all means, Steven. You've been most patient with an old man's maunderings."

"Oh no sir," Steven said. "It's you who have been kind. Alright then, my final question deals with your early writing. Lots of writers have juvenilia left over from the time before they published, the archetypical 'manuscript in the drawer,' so to speak." He gestured air quotes around the phrase. "Do you have any unpublished writing sitting around that might embarrass you?"

"Embarrass? No." Ellis did a curious thing then. He laughed, and drew the curtain closed, shutting out the light of the rising full moon. "Other things, sure, but not embarrass."

Steve leaned forward; was this actual news he saw breaking before him? "Me thinks thou doth protest too much, Mr. Ellis. Is there a story here your readers would want to know?"

Ellis tugged the curtain's hem, as if making sure it would stay closed. "A story? Yes, but I don't think it's one you'll want to share with anyone."

"Why don't you let me be the judge of that?"

Ellis glanced around, setting his dying pipe in an ashtray. "Well Steven, I'm not sure that's wise, but we'll see. I started writing in 1955, and–"

"'55? But you didn't publish anything until early 1961!" Steven inched forward to the edge of his chair, circling the number " '55 on his note pad. "After that stay in the sanitarium due to your parents' divorce."

"Indeed," Ellis said. "And . . . no. You see, I wasn't a poet in those early days. Nor did I think of trying to revitalize verse drama in America, as I've tried to do in recent decades. Instead, well, I was young. I was drunk on comic books and H. P. Lovecraft."

"The tentacle guy? That horror hack?"

"The same. That's what I wanted to write." Ellis laughed again, looking at the mirror in the corner of the room that was angled so that it reflected nothing at all, but only bounced light at odd angles. "You know how obsessed I was with Lovecraft's work? I went from library to library, trying to check out the *Necronomicon*."

"But — Lovecraft made the thing up, right? It doesn't exist."

"Didn't. That's right. I was so disappointed." Ellis sighed, and for a moment his lined face was young again, young and fey with angry disappointment.

"So, that's the story?" Steven said. "You wrote some stories modeled after Lovecraft? I can see why you wouldn't want those–"

"My dear boy," Ellis interrupted. "I might be content with that now, reworking a genre initiated by another. As a brilliant teenager not yet familiar with limits, that wasn't enough. I didn't write a pastiche, no 'Concert Out of Memory' here."

Chastened, Steven waited; Ellis did too, but with the air of one disappointed in a student. Finally, Ellis broke down. "I didn't write about the *Necronomicon*. Once I found out it didn't exist, I wrote it."

Steven rose from his chair. "But this is incredible! America's reigning master of the sonnet, wasting his time scribbling pulp horror inspired by pulp horror! Do you still have it?"

"Oh certainly," Ellis said, gesturing to the lowest drawer in the oak desk beside them. "The manuscript's never been more than thirty feet from me since I wrote it."

"The critics! Your fans! You — may I see?" Steven took a step toward the desk, fingers working in mid-air.

"Steven, you speak as if you already have. Take care."

"I — I don't understand." He took another step almost unconsciously, only half listening.

"Clearly, and I don't think you want to. Like many today, you mistake the medium in which a work of art is produced for the quality of the work itself. Trash via the computer? Still trash. Genius via the pulps? Still genius."

"May. I. See. It?"

"I wouldn't."

"Please!" The request rose to the level of a plea.

"I warn you for a third time; you do not want to do this," Ellis said, but he was already reaching for the drawer's handle, as if certain of the outcome.

"I do, though!" Steven insisted.

Ellis pulled the drawer open. The dust atop the manuscript testified that it had not been touched in some time. Disturbed by his proximity, it rose in a vague gray cloud as Steven knelt to peer into the desk drawer. Peer, then read. Read, then stare. Stare, then fall into an unmoving state that approached catatonia.

"Steven. Steven?" When the spittle pouring from the interviewer's lower lip had matted the last of the swirling dust into a flat gray puddle, Ellis stopped calling the younger man's name.

Closing the drawer gingerly with his foot, Ellis plucked a telephone from its cradle on the desk. He dialed a number from memory. "Hello? Providence Sanitarium? Yes, I'll hold."

Soulless music poured out of the phone, and Ellis pulled it back a bit from his ear. He sighed. "These interviews," he said to the air, "they always end the same way."

Then he shoved the drawer with his foot again, as if making sure it would stay closed.

SPHERES OF INFLUENCE

RON SHIFLET

JODY HOLLINGS CLUMPED THROUGH the thick underbrush, looking over his shoulder every few minutes. Stopping, he listened but could hear nothing but the usual array of sounds one would expect to hear in the woods. He took a grimy red bandana from his back pocket, sighed and wiped the beads of perspiration that threatened to coalesce and run down his forehead. A light breeze ruffled his frizzy red hair — the strands that remained — and felt refreshing to the overweight man.

Stuffing the bandana back in his pocket, he grunted and continued on the circuitous route to the location of his brother's still. Edgar, his brother, had warned him to be careful and make sure that he wasn't followed and he damn sure didn't want or need his brother climbing up his ass. Jody was almost to the site when something struck a tree branch above him with a loud crack and fell into a pile of damp leaves about ten feet in front of him.

"Shit," he muttered, looking over his shoulder for signs of being followed. Seeing and hearing no one, he turned his attention to the spot where the object landed and walked forward.

I'm pretty sure it fell over here . . . whatever the hell it was . . .

He stirred the pile of leaves with his boot, eventually rolling his boot sole over a round object about the size of a golf ball. "There you are," he whispered, bending over to pick it up. He touched the shiny blue object tentatively, knowing that meteors and such things were always heated upon falling to the Earth. *Yeah, but this thing don't look like no damn meteor. It's all blue and shiny like some kind of a Christmas tree ornament. It ain't hot but is cold like an ice cube.*

He peered intently at the strange sphere, rolling it around the palm of his meaty hand. Bewildered, he dropped it into his pocket and felt its cold surface cooling this thigh through the material of his denim pants. Remembering his errand, he temporarily forgot about the object and made his way through the trees to where Edgar was monitoring the temperature on the still.

Jody walked into the clearing and waited for Edgar to notice him. After several moments of silence, he said, "Edgar, I'm here."

Without looking up, his brother answered. "It don't take a genius to figure that out. I heard you stomping around out there at least five minutes ago. At first I thought maybe Barnum and Bailey had lost one of their elephants but then I realized that only you could make that much noise in the woods."

Jody blushed. "I wish you wouldn't always make fun of my weight problem."

Edgar finally looked up and frowned. "Weight problem. Is that what they're calling it these days? Hell, little brother, look at you! Looks like you bought those clothes at Knoxville Tent and Awning."

Jody frowned. "Doc says it's a thyroid condition."

"Thyroid condition my ass!" Edgar exclaimed. "It's an eat every thing in sight condition is what it is. Now, did you bring the money?"

Embarrassed, Jody looked down and fished his wallet from his back pocket. He took out seven twenties and a ten, and handed them to Edgar.

"Thanks little brother," Edgar said, taking the folded bills. "This will keep my ass out of a crack, at least for a little while."

"You late paying Sheriff Bentley?"

"Yeah," Edgar grunted. "Lost a bunch of money in a card game over on Tyson Fork."

Jody nodded his understanding and stood silently.

"Well yeah . . . what?" Edgar asked impatiently.

"Nothing," Jody replied. "I just thought I might hang around a spell if that's okay."

"Well it ain't! Not today anyway . . . I got too much to do and you'll only be in the way."

"Sure," Jody whispered. "Maybe I'll stop by and see if I can do anything around the place for Helen."

"That sounds like a plan," Edgar replied, checking the copper lines on the still. "Just don't be flapping your gums to her about loaning me this money."

Offended, Jody said, "I wouldn't do that!"

"Fine, see that you don't."

Edgar returned to tinkering with the still and Jody headed back into the woods.

Jody stopped to catch his breath and wiped a tear from his cheek. Edgar had made him feel completely worthless and Jody cursed himself for not being used to it by now. *It ain't never been any different. He's been ugly to me since we were kids.*

He thought of Helen, his sister-in-law, and smiled. She had always treated him kind and his niece and nephew seemed to adore him. Reaching into his pocket to see if the hard candy he'd bought for the kids was still there, he felt the smooth cool sphere and smiled.

Maybe it'll bring me good luck.

Taking the object from his pocket, he looked at it and felt his mind begin to fog over as if he were dreaming. In this trance-like state, Jody saw his brother picking himself up from the grimy pavement of a dark alley. Two brawny men laughed at Edgar as he rubbed his wounds. A third man walked up and grinned at him.

"It'll get a lot worse if you don't come across with the money."

Don't worry Slim, I'll get the money . . . I swear."

"See that you do, asshole. This is your final warning."

"Please believe me," Edgar pleaded. "I'll get it from my brother. He ain't got the brains God give a piss-ant . . . I'll get it from him."

"I don't care where you get it," the man called Slim replied. "Just get it to me by next week."

The scene faded and Jody frowned. *That's not why he told me he needed the money. He said he needed it to pay Sheriff Bentley to look the other way. Why would he lie to me? I'd have still given him the money.*

"Yeah, but why tell me the truth?" Jody whispered. "I ain't got the brains God gave a piss-ant."

Feeling low, he walked through the woods, never thinking about what prompted the disheartening vision. Slipping the blue sphere into his pocket, he frowned and took his time reaching Edgar and Helen's house on the other side of the mountain. *What's the hurry? She'll probably just work me like a dog.*

"You jerk," he chided himself. "Helen's always nice to you."

A faint smile returned to his face as he whistled his way through the woods and over the mountain.

Jody finished his second piece of pie and pushed the plate away. "No more," he sighed, rubbing his ample belly.

"Well, I baked three of them," said the petite brunette, dressed in denim jeans and one of Edgar's old work shirts. "I know you can eat more than that."

Jody smiled. "Really Helen, that's plenty. Besides, I'm trying to watch my weight."

"Oh Lord," she said, "I bet Edgar's been giving you a hard time again hasn't he?"

Looking sheepish, Jody said, "Now Helen, you know how he is. He didn't mean anything by it."

"Don't mean anything by it my foot!" she exclaimed. "I'll have a talk with him. He shouldn't tease you the way he does."

"That's sweet of you," Jody replied. "But don't trouble yourself over it. You know how he is. No need to get him mad at you."

"No, I suppose not," she said. "I just wish he wasn't the way he is about some things."

"I don't figure he can help it," Jody answered. "He takes after Pa."

Helen cut another wedge of apple pie and placed it on Jody's plate. "Here," she said, pushing the plate toward Jody. "I know you can eat at least one more slice. It'll give you energy to cart off all that junk behind the house."

"Junk?" Jody asked.

"Oh," laughed Helen. "Didn't I mention it to you the other day?"

"Yeah, probably," Jody said. "I guess it slipped my mind." *Because heaven knows God didn't give you the brains he gave a piss-ant. You'll be working all afternoon and what will it get you? Three lousy pieces of pie, that's what.*

"You okay Jody?"

"Huh?" he answered, not hearing the question.

"I said are you okay?"

Blushing, Jody answered, "Sure . . . yeah . . . why do you ask?"

Smiling, Helen said, "I don't know, you looked sort of strange there for a second. Like you was pissed off or something."

"I'm sorry," Jody responded. "I'm fine . . . just felt dizzy for a bit."

A look of concern crossed Helen's face. Patting Jody on the shoulder, she said, "Maybe you should take it easy and haul that stuff to the dump some other time."

"No!" he answered, more sharply than he'd intended. "I said I'd do it . . . so I'll do it."

"But if you're not feeling well, then . . ."

Before she could finish, Jody got up from the table and was out the door.

Jody grunted as he strained at the bent steel wheel, wedged into the ground. Something had packed it deep when the soil was muddy but once the ground was dry it was damn near impossible to budge. He tugged on the mattock handle but couldn't move the embedded wheel. "Damn," he gasped. "Why in the hell did Edgar let it get this way?"

Don't you know pal? Why not let the yard go to Hell in a hand basket? After all, he's got a shit for brains brother he can bully into cleaning up the mess. You might as well hang a big sign around your neck like one of them homeless fellows. Will work for pie.

Sighing, he planted his broad ass on a five gallon paint can and stared at the back of his brother's house. Laughter emanated from the kitchen, indicating that Randy and Jenny were home from school. "Shoot," he mumbled, "it's later than I thought."

He reached for his bandana to wipe away the sweat and felt the cold metallic object in his pocket. Grabbing both it and the bandana, he wrapped the sphere inside the sweat-stained material and rubbed it across his forehead. It cooled him quickly and seemed to whisper words of comfort that he was only vaguely aware of hearing.

"Yeah, that feels better," he whispered, returning the bandana-wrapped object to his pocket.

He sat back down on the paint can and stared at the house. His niece and nephew were usually eager to see him and always made a point of swarming him whenever he came to visit.

Wonder why they ain't been out to see me? Surely they know I'm here. Yeah, but they're getting older and smarter every day. Maybe it's finally occurred to them that their uncle's got the brains of a piss-ant.

With resentment in his heart, Jody stood up and surveyed the cluttered area, not understanding why he hadn't accomplished more in the time he'd spent outside. The metallic sphere in his pocket whispered to him and told him not to worry about it.

"Right," he mumbled. "I've done enough work for one day. Hell, I'm on vacation and this ain't even my place."

Throwing the mattock in the tool shed, he pushed the door closed and walked back to the house. Stepping inside the kitchen, he spied Jenny reading a book at the table.

"Hi kiddo," he said, walking to the kitchen sink to wash his hands.

"Hi Uncle Jody," she replied, barely bothering to look up from her reading.

Hurt by the lack of affection, Jody distractedly rolled the paper towel between his hands and started to speak again but thought better of it.

See? She's like all the others; only cares about you when she stands to gain something from it. She's just like Edgar and Helen. You know they say the apple don't fall very far from the tree.

"What you reading?" he asked.

Jenny grunted an unintelligible answer, causing Jody to frown. He started to say something but Helen entered the room before he could speak.

"Just ignore her, Jody," Helen said, shaking her head in disgust. "She hasn't been doing well in school and is pissed at me because I'm making her do her homework before allowing her to do anything else.

"Oh," Jody replied. "Is Randy home?"

"He was here a minute and took off. Big doings with his best friend. I doubt if he even realized you were here."

Yeah, why would he? He's like everyone else, couldn't care if I live or die.

"No big deal," Jody answered.

"You must've really been busting your hump to finish out back so soon!"

"Finished?" Jody said. "I never said I was finished. Edgar's thrown so much crap out there it'll probably take the rest of my vacation to finish."

"Do you feel okay, Jody?" Helen asked, seeming concerned by the disagreeable tone that Jody had taken. It was so unlike him.

"Not really," he replied. "I'm going home and rest."

Helen smiled, placing her hand on his shoulder. "Yes, that's probably a good idea. You may be coming down with something."

Jody stared at her, brushed her hand away and turned to go. Without uttering a word, he left the house and started walking toward the dirt road leading to his own modest home.

Helen watched him go and shook her head in dismay. "Well I'll be damned."

Jody lay in bed, his mind in a state of confusion. He couldn't understand why it had taken him so long to discover how his so-called loved ones *really* felt about him. Turning off the light on his nightstand, he stared at the weirdly glowing ball that he'd found earlier in the day. The shimmering glow relaxed him and made his thinking clearer. After finding the object it was as if a veil had been removed from his eyes, enabling him to see for the first time. Reaching for the nightstand, he removed the glowing object and clutched it tightly in his hand. It was no longer cold but instead suffused his hand with a comforting warmth that made him feel strangely secure.

Jody flexed and unflexed his hand, maintaining a peaceful rhythm that made him drowsy and which finally lulled him to sleep. He dreamed he was in a shiny spaceship like in the movies he liked to watch. He was surrounded by small men, all wearing the same face. They were friendly, spending much time laughing and patting him on the back. They spoke in a strange tongue that Jody was unable to understand.

On a large video screen, he watched the actions of several similar ships as they swooped low and fast over a huge city with buildings that towered higher than those in New York or Chicago.

Cool, this is just like watching one of Randy's video games. Of course I ain't figured out what the object of the game is.

Continuing to watch, he saw the ships disperse thousands of the shiny spheres over the city and the surrounding countryside. The video then speeded up as day turned to night and then back again. This process encompassed several days and when the video resumed normal speed it was once more day in the city. But changes had occurred; major changes.

The city was now in flames and hordes of people battled among themselves in the chaotic streets. Acts of barbarism, perpetrated by both individuals and groups seemed to be the order of the day. Jody stared in horror as the video focused on random acts of cruelty, lingering for moments before going on to the next scene. Jody wasn't the sharpest knife in the drawer but it was clear to him that the metallic spheres were somehow responsible for the carnage on the video. Turning to the ship's crew, he watched their faces melt away, revealing porous and loosely connected bone through which glistening, warm tendrils emerged and quivered obscenely before him.

Jody woke with a terrible headache and the sense of dread that usually follows nightmares. He tried to remember his dream but only snatches of it came. *Something about a spaceship . . . like in those movies . . . but I can't remember much of it.*

He found himself still clutching the metallic ball in his right hand. It began to grow warmer, washing away his uneasiness and filling him with a sense of well-being. It imbued him with a confidence usually lacking and provided him with insights that he hadn't known before.

He hadn't told anyone about his discovery of the shiny metallic ball, deciding it would be his secret.

What they don't know won't hurt me. Huh, what the hell does that mean?

Letting it drop, Jody got out of bed and walked to the bathroom. While on the throne, he contemplated returning to Edgar and Helen's place to finish cleaning the yard but thought better of it. "Let Edgar do it," he muttered. "It's his shit."

But he'll probably have Helen do it. So? I don't know why she can't . . . she sits around there on her ass all day long!

He shaved, got dressed and went to the kitchen. After making coffee, he sat at the table and decided not to do a damn thing that day. *I'm on vacation so I might as well start acting like it. Lord knows I work hard enough at the quarry during the rest of the year.*

The day passed, Jody spending much of it watching old re-runs on one of the satellite stations. He napped periodically, dreaming of spaceships and metallic spheres. Each time he awoke, the post-nightmare uneasiness was upon him though the dreams were fragmentary and quickly forgotten. During these periods of unease, he felt compelled to clutch the blue metallic sphere which consistently alleviated his fear and anxiety.

Through the door of his trailer, he saw a red pickup drive slowly down the dirt road running in front of his property. It looked similar to Edgar's truck and the thought of his brother caused his stomach to knot. *Edgar's probably wondering why I didn't finish hauling that trash away. I bet he's really pissed. Well let him be pissed . . . he ain't my boss.*

His bravado vanished as he heard a vehicle pulling onto his property. Headlights cut through the gloom, dancing briefly on the wall behind his sofa before being extinguished by the driver. Sighing, Jody walked to the door and looked out, almost certain whose vehicle he would see in the driveway.

Shit, it's him!

He tried to remain calm as Edgar left the truck and walked to the front door. Jody opened the screen and said, "Hi Edgar. I didn't expect to see you."

With a sour expression, Edgar replied. "Is something wrong with your goddamn phone?"

Taken aback, Jody stammered, "My phone . . . what about my phone?"

Edgar entered the trailer and plopped down on the sofa. "The phone that you ain't been answering this afternoon. That's *why* I'm here."

"Because of my phone?" Jody asked, bewildered.

"Yeah," Edgar replied. "Helen's been phoning you ever since you left the house. She's been worried sick since yesterday when you left. She nagged me until I agreed to come over here and check on you."

"Geez, I'm sorry," said Jody. "I must've been sleeping and didn't hear the phone . . . sorry you had to drive over here."

Edgar grunted but said nothing.

"And," Jody continued, "I'm sorry I wasn't able to finish clearing out that stuff in back of your place. I'll try and get to it tomorrow."

"No need," Edgar answered. "Randy's got a school holiday tomorrow so I'm going to put him on it. It'll knock him off the high-horse he's been on lately . . . damn snotty kid."

"Well okay," Jody replied.

Edgar rose from the sofa and hiked up his pants. "Oh," he said, "before I forget it, I'm supposed to invite you over to the house on Saturday. Helen's cooking up something special and wants you to eat with us."

"That sounds great. Tell her I said thanks."

"Yeah," said Edgar, placing his hand on the door. "Little brother, it looks like it might be a spell before I can get that money back to you. You know how it is."

"Yeah," Jody answered, "I *know* how it is."

Jody got ready for bed, relieved that he would be able to sleep late the next day. It would be Friday, the last official day of his vacation and at least he wouldn't be spending it clearing away trash. He'd have another day of total relaxation and then eat a nice meal with his brother and family on Saturday. While getting into bed, Jody spied the metallic sphere on the nightstand where he'd placed it when napping earlier. He suddenly had a strong compulsion to feel the object in his hand. It seemed of the utmost importance though he couldn't imagine why. Snatching the item from the table, he sighed in relief, much like an alcoholic satisfying his craving for booze.

Oh yeah, I feel better now.

He turned on the clock radio that sat on the same nightstand and listened to the twin fiddles of a western swing band. Humming along to *Faded Love*, he closed his eyes and dreamed.

"I don't want the fat slob here either," Edgar said, "but we got to toss him a bone once in a while."

"I suppose so," Helen replied. "But he makes my skin crawl. Have you ever noticed how he's always staring at my boobs?"

"What?" Edgar growled. "I'll kick his lard-ass up one side of this mountain and down the other!"

"Don't worry about it, Hon. Do you think I could possibly give a second thought to that blubber butt?"

"Blubber butt! Blubber butt!" sang Randy and Jenny in unison. "You guys must be talking about Uncle Jody. The kids at school are always ragging on me because I'm his nephew."

"Hey, someone's pulling into the driveway," Helen said, pushing her chair back from the table. "Looks like Scooter Rollins from over at the quarry."

"Well let him in," Edgar demanded.

Helen ushered the crew-cutted man into the house and Edgar offered him a beer. "What's on your mind Scooter?"

Scooter took a seat and popped the top on the beer. "It's about that lazy, no account brother of yours."

"What's that fat shithead done now?" Edgar asked.

Scooter lit a smoke and answered. "Just the usual screw-ups."

"How?" Helen asked. "He's on vacation."

"Yeah," Scooter answered, "that's why it became so clear to me. I noticed how smooth things have been running these last two weeks."

"Are you gonna can Uncle Jody?" Randy asked.

Helen stood up and said, "You kids get on out of here now and let us grown-ups talk."

"Ah Man," Randy whined, leaving with his sister after seeing the look on his mom's face.

"Now, that's better," Helen said, sitting back down.

"*Are* you going to can him?" Edgar asked.

Scooter flicked an ash in the tray and smiled. "Edgar, I know he's your brother and all but I just don't see how I can afford to keep him on any longer. Truth is he's more trouble than he's worth. I just wanted to let you know first, you being my best friend and all."

"I appreciate that Scooter," Edgar replied. "I'm honestly surprised that you've kept him on this long. He's pretty hopeless. No hard feeling on my part."

"I'm glad to hear it," Scooter said, standing.

"Hey," Helen said, "he's going to be eating with us on Saturday. Why don't you come over and join us? You can give him the news after supper."

"Yeah," Edgar agreed. "Nothing will bother him after he fills that big gut of his."

Helen giggled and said, "I just hope I can cook enough to fill that gut!"

"I'll do it," Scooter said, smiling as he walked to the door.

"Good," Helen said, "we'll see you Saturday."

Scooter shook Edgar's hand on his way out and said, "Thanks much. I'll see you folks Saturday."

Jody woke crying, his hurt and anger a force beyond his control. He looked at the clock beside the bed and smiled. *Plenty of time to do what needs to be done.* He found himself still clutching the metallic ball and felt stronger and more confident that he had felt in years.

The breeze cooled the sweat forming on Jody's forehead. He had walked over the mountain and was tired from the exertion. From his vantage point on the tree-covered ridge, he could see his brother's house clearly. The blue metallic sphere seemed to vibrate in his pocket, suffusing him with warmth and a feeling of expectant satisfaction.

He lifted the binoculars hanging from his neck and peered through them. Adjusting the focus, he smiled upon seeing Helen pass one of the windows. *She must be getting everything ready. It takes a lot of cooking to fill up my big gut. Yes sir, it sure does.* He lowered the binoculars and patted his belly, somewhat regretful that he wouldn't be partaking of the fine meal that Helen was cooking. That was one thing he was truly going to miss. Thinking of Randy and Jenny, he experienced a moment of doubt but his resolve was strengthened by the feel of the metallic ball in his jeans pocket. He checked his watch, knowing that he was expected at any time.

Yeah, but they're gonna get something they don't expect.

"Right," he mumbled, "there's gonna be some big fireworks around here directly."

Peering through the binoculars again, he smiled at the sight of Scooter Rollins' pickup pulling in front of the house. "This just gets better and better," Jody whispered.

He watched his boss leave the truck and go inside. Checking his watch, he began the mental countdown. He'd stolen dynamite from the Rollins quarry and had planted them when Edgar, Helen and the kids had gone into town that morning. It was surprising really; the metallic blue sphere seemed to have made him smarter. He had never worked with explosives before but somehow he just seemed to know what to do.

What I should've done a long time ago.

He clasped the metallic ball tightly, becoming more agitated as Randy and Jenny stepped outside, unfurled a banner and smoothed it out. Jody couldn't read the banner from his vantage point and was also distracted by what Scooter was carrying in from the truck. Jody dropped the shiny sphere into his pocket and raised the binoculars. He frowned.

It's a box . . . the kind that holds cake. What the . . .

He watched Scooter disappear into the house and turned his gaze on the children. They seemed satisfied with their efforts and turned to go inside. As they circled and turned, Jody could read the words on the banner.

Happy Birthday Uncle Jody

Oh Christ! They invited me over for a surprise party!

Jody glanced at his watch, feeling the blood drain from his face.

What have I done?

The mountain shook with the force of the explosion, almost knocking Jody to his knees. With tears streaming down his face, he turned away, devastated by the horrible realization of his actions. The blue metallic ball grew uncomfortably cold in his pocket and filled him with a sense of revulsion. Reaching into his pants, he removed the sphere and hurled it into the stand of trees at his back. Falling to his knees, he vomited, unable to believe what he'd done.

It all started with that damn shiny ball! The blue metallic ball!

Jody sat on the plaid couch and loaded his pistol. It was an old Army issue .45, given to him by his Uncle Frank. Killing himself wouldn't set things right, but it would at least put an end to his own unbearable despair.

He lifted the weapon and paused briefly as the television anchorman reported on the statistically impossible spike in violent crime that was afflicting Knoxville, Nashville, and other cities and outlying regions in recent days. In an obviously unrelated story, the same talking head chuckled about the large number of citizens who had reported strange metallic balls falling from the sky.

"Undoubtedly dropped by UFOs," smirked the anchorman.

"Undoubtedly," said Jody as he held the gun to his head and squeezed the trigger.

A MONSTER IN THE LAKE

MICHAIL VELICHANSKY

SAM STILL WALKED BY the lake at night. The park had aged along with him, and like him there was no money for repairs. Cracks ran through the cement walkways, and the grass had been worn down. Gang signs covered the walls of the old community building; they had even sprayed the trees. It wasn't a safe place for an old man. But Sam still walked by the lake at night.

Even if no one else cared about the park, Sam did. This was his place. At least at night he could walk without seeing how low the water was, without the urge to count the plastic bottles. At night he could pretend he was alone. A breeze blew across the lake. Water splashed where the ducks' harsh quacking broke the silence. Sam liked to watch the ducks in the evening hours. He had seen them move gracefully on the water's surface, and he had seen them fight over the refuse thrown into the lake. Once, he had seen several mallards try to mate with a single hen; they tore the feathers from her neck trying to hold her and grab her away from the others, until finally their numbers forced her beneath the water. Her drowned body later floated to the shore.

Sam couldn't see them now, for all the streetlamps that once lit up the park had burned out. Even with a bright moon, Sam didn't notice the shape approaching him until it was already close. He supposed he could still run, if he had to. But the man was hunched over, and had a shambling gait; he shivered in the folds of a trench coat though the air was warm. Dark hair stuck out from under a baseball cap, covering the man's eyes.

"Are you the keeper of this place?" the stranger asked.

Sam took a step back. "Um, no. I don't think there is one anymore. They used to clean it, but that was years ago."

"This is your place. You claim it more than anyone."

Sam thought the man was probably crazy. He said, "It's the city's."

"They've abandoned it. The other workers who built it are gone, and the visitors look away." The man's voice cracked wetly. Maybe he was sick. "You were here from the beginning. You watched it grow. You walk here, days and nights."

Sam wondered if he could outrun this man. He'd been a runner once. And the guy did sound pretty sick. But he decided to stay. *No need to rush*, he thought. He didn't like to let anything interrupt his time by the lake, and his bad knee would go on strike if he ran. Megaphones and picket lines and everything.

"Does it matter where I walk?" Sam asked.

"Your race is stupid to forget the power that ties people to the land. But it will help me. Only you lay claim to this place. If you let me stay here, it cannot keep me out."

"I don't know what race you mean. You're the same color as me." Sam looked around. "Listen, if you need a place to stay, I'm not going to stop you. But there's a shelter a mile south, they'll take you in if they're not full. The nights aren't getting warmer. And this isn't the best place anymore." *And you should be somewhere where they'll actually call an ambulance for you.*

Sam hated when bums slept in the park. He liked his lake. He liked his chess tables, though they were covered in crayon and spray paint. "Hey. There are some benches down that way, kind of out of the way. Probably nobody'll see you there."

The stranger clutched his coat collar. "Give me the lake. I need a place where I can hide and eat. Let me have it." He lunged at Sam, pressed his fingertips against Sam's head. Sam couldn't pull away.

Help me.

The voice in Sam's head was not his own. Something was in his mind, terrible and huge. It hurt to hear it.

I'll make this place quiet again.

The stranger had no eyes behind his hair. His nose was only a lump of flesh without nostrils. Only his mouth seemed real. Yet Sam couldn't remember if it moved when the stranger spoke; he found himself afraid to see it open.

I can consume you. Help me. Let me stay.

But then the stranger shuddered and slipped out of Sam's mind, as painfully as he had entered. He fell to his knees, palms flat on the cement.

"Don't you have anywhere else to go?" Sam whispered. He felt sick.

"I need your leave. It's in your head — you want your park silent and empty and untouched. I won't eat your mind. I can't. Too weak even for that."

Sam hesitated. He wanted to walk away. Instead he bent down and helped the stranger up. Sam felt only bone beneath the leather. "Jesus. You're starving."

"Yes."

"What do you need me to do?"

Faintly, Sam heard the voice whisper, *Understand.* He felt the body dying as the emptiness ate away at it from inside. When the body died, the thing that spoke inside his head would live on. Ravenous, it would crawl on at the edges of reality, feeding where it could. It would grow to fill the lake, but could never be satisfied. With only a slight effort, Sam lifted the stranger into his arms. The man was light — only the trench coat he wore had any weight at all. It trailed on the ground as Sam carried the stranger to the lake. Sam said, "Sometimes I feel so old. Like the world's been gnawing on me, like a dog chewing on a leather hide. That's me. Good for the teeth."

Lake water soaked into Sam's shoes. He kneeled, and set the stranger down on the water. "That's not really the same thing at all, is it?"

The creature asked, "How will you call me?"

"I won't," Sam said. He wanted to imagine that there would be no consequences to this. As long as he didn't think too much, he could believe that.

"You must have a name to call me."

"I'll call you Andrew. I've never known an Andrew."

Andrew smiled. He floated on the water, out toward the center of the lake. His hat came off and dark hair spread out around him. Then Andrew vanished in the darkness. Somewhere, a duck took off from the lake with a quiet splash.

Sam stayed away from the park the next day, and the day after that. When he did come, he came during the day. He avoided the lake, and sat instead at the chess tables, sometimes playing against others, sometimes against himself. People still came to the park as they had before. Only now, sometimes, they didn't leave. Often, now, Sam caught people staring at the lake, oblivious to things around them. It became a place for suicides. A mother drowned her five-year-old there, then herself. Teenagers sat by it and touched and kissed without ever seeming happy from it. The bums stopped sleeping within sight of it at night, then stopped sleeping in the park at all. The families, the joggers — those who didn't come to stare stopped coming.

After a while the park became an empty, quiet place. Even the ducks had gone. It was as though the city as a whole had decided to ignore it. But Sam came more and more, until after a while he found that he hardly ever left. He felt anxious and dissatisfied anywhere else. When he could, he went without food. Sometimes the suicides would bring a lunch with them only to forget it on the benches. Sometimes they threw money into the lake, as though in payment, and Sam found the soggy bills waiting for him on a chess table stool. He felt loathe to leave the park now. This was his fault; this was his place.

A duck waddled up the path toward him. Metal hooks protruded from its bill. Its wings were stripped of feathers; jointed feelers made of gray metal were grafted to the flesh, and the wings jutted out instead of laying flat against its body.

"You are Samuel, the keeper of the lake?"

The duck's voice was soft and vaguely toned, belying its metallic visage. Sam jerked up from the chair he had been sitting in. Until it spoke, the duck had had no impact on him, as though it were a daydream. He tried to settle himself.

"Sure. That's me. Call me Sam."

"The monster in the lake. You let it stay here — you will make it leave."

Sam regretted his answer. He didn't want the duck knowing his name; names brought you too close to people. "I can't make him leave. I have no power over him. What are you?"

"Another victim of the vile thing you let into the lake."

"His name is Andrew," Sam said.

"Its true name is not pronounceable. It would break your mind to know it. The name you know is a name only for the lie it let you see."

"There was no lie. I knew what he was, mostly. Enough."

"Then you know what it has done since then."

"He has his lake," Sam said. "I have my park. It's quiet here."

"It's grown, and so has your park. The space you see is an illusion." The duck quacked. Sam flinched, unprepared for such a harsh sound relative to the duck's soft voice. It went on, "Are you so careless? We have hoped you ignorant, at least."

"I couldn't be. I had to know, or he couldn't take the lake." Sam looked over at the lake, but soon turned away, staring instead at the moss growing on the base of his chess table. "Have you ever seen someone starving? Picked them up and felt how light they were — how pathetically, sickeningly light?"

"Yes," the duck said.

Sam shuddered. "I hadn't. Not till he came to me. I really felt it then, like I was starving along with him. Was I just supposed to leave him with no place to go? Even monsters should be allowed a place of their own, shouldn't they?"

"No. Not if it feeds off everything around it. Not if it can only corrupt and destroy. There is no home for such a thing. It must be driven out."

"Starved?"

"Do you think it is sated now? How can hunger know anything but hunger? It grows more ravenous when fed. Do you want to see what it has done to your park?"

Sam flinched. "Of course I don't. But I'll go with you."

"And once you see, you will go to the monster and tell it that you take back what you once gave it."

The duck waddled toward the lake. Sam followed. It asked, "When was the last time you walked by the lake?"

"A while now. I don't know. The days all start to blur together. I used to walk by it all the time, but — it's cold there. I didn't feel like going anymore." The duck waddled on. Sam felt nothing of the chill he'd just described.

The air before them rippled and the duck disappeared. A moment later, one more step, and Sam knew why. A vast wasteland stretched before him. Sam kept himself steady; he couldn't let his heart beat so quickly. Some ways off, in the heart of the wasteland, light glittered on the lake's surface. He tried to relax.

"The monster has grown stronger," the duck said. "It's filled your park with its hunger, with the hollow landscape of its being, and all the while it hid it from your eyes, and the eyes of your kind. Soon the monster will be too vast. Nothing of your park will remain except as an illusion."

I liked my park, Sam thought. He knew of no other way to respond to the sight before him. "How far did you come to see me?" he asked the duck.

"Farther than it looks. There are holes in the landscape leading to the remains of alien worlds your monster carried here. We found one of them, and in it the machine pits. Metal and wood starved for flesh to carry it. The metal weighed us down. We couldn't fly away. Instead of flight the machines gave us voices. They took your language, from those lost in the monster, thinking it would be familiar to us. Soon this season's ducklings will hatch, and we must toss them into the pits as well."

The duck stared off at something Sam couldn't see.

"Well?" the duck said. "Will you do as I ask now that you see what it's done to your park?"

"You make me sound like the monster. As if I didn't care about the people he's hurt."

"Do you?"

Sam didn't answer. He didn't know. He should care, he knew that much. He had cared when he met Andrew. He'd never spoken to any of the people Andrew hurt. *If I act like I care, it'll be the same thing. It'll be the right thing to do, and that's what matters. Hopefully.*

"Come on," Sam said. "Show me how to get to the lake."

They walked for a while. Sam asked, "How can I take the lake back? I gave it to him."

"You have remained close to it," the duck said. "You still think of it as your own, and you still exist."

"Why wouldn't I?"

"There aren't many things here that still do. No thinking things, at least. The monster hungers."

"Then how did you survive?" Sam asked.

The duck stopped. It ignored his question. "I took too long. We will be met by others. Be cautious. They may stand against us."

Sam squinted. There were more ducks, blocking the way to the lake. Their feathers were gray in the alien light; the metal in their flesh glittered harshly. "We could go around," Sam offered.

"No. The geometry is broken here. We can only approach the lake one way. Well — you may as well meet my people."

Soon, the other ducks stood before them. One of them stepped forward; its walk looked heavy to Sam, as though it loathed to approach them. Its mouth was held open by wire, and the space was filled with a web of fiber optics. Looking at the ducks, Sam wondered if their machines had gone mad.

"There was a time," the approaching duck said, "we thought we would all act together." Static hissed behind its monotone voice.

"So we did," Sam's duck said. "We all agreed the monster was an evil thing, and we would drive it away if we could."

"We were frightened. The machines still hurt us, and we had not yet learned to live without flight. What will we do now without the creature? What will we do without the machines? You give no thought to our future."

"If we cannot be what we once were, we should not be at all. The thing in the lake turns everything we do to vileness. An evil thing."

"The eggs?"

It took Sam's duck a moment to respond. "Yes. The eggs. They will not go into the pits."

The second duck said, "We're no longer what we were — if the small ones do not become like us, then our kind will have died. How could I let you do that?"

"It's not so hard," Sam's duck whispered. The other duck said nothing. "You will try to stop me, then? Has it come to this?"

"The only thing I see that's truly vile is your obsession with our past, your hunger for things that can never be returned to you. Hunger is the death of thought."

"You do not speak for everyone."

The other duck didn't answer, but turned instead to Sam. "What will you do if we bar your way?"

"I hadn't thought about it," Sam said. "I thought this was the right thing to do."

"Maybe for your kind it is," the other duck said.

Sam whispered, "I don't really like my kind." He hesitated. "You could show me the machines. I've never talked to ducks before. Or whatever you are now." Even as he said it Sam felt guilty. He should care more than this. He had cared a moment ago. He must have, or he wouldn't have come. When had it become so hard to know if he felt anything at all?

"You are as vile as your monster," the first duck said.

"What do you want me to do? Everyone needs help, and everyone wants something different." He rubbed the palms of his hands against his eyes. "Is there a right thing to do if everything you do makes someone miserable?"

"Do something. Only the dead are still." It looked at the other duck, and the feelers on its wings began to move. All the other ducks stepped back. The two that remained, Sam's guide and the other speaker, stared at each other. They strained to hold their wings up. The metal wriggled faster and faster. A hum filled the air, filled Sam's head. He clutched his forehead.

"Stop this," he said. "It's ridiculous. Stop it!" He couldn't hear his own voice for the humming in his head. Then something slammed into him, knocking him back several yards. The two ducks stared at each other; the air around them blurred, as if heat rose up from the ground.

The hum rose in pitch and peaked. Then the second duck screeched and crumpled to the ground. Sam's guide stared down at its opponent as the other ducks moved closer. A trickle of blood oozed out from under the metal grafted to the dead duck's flesh.

We're all starving, Sam thought. *We'll tear each other to pieces, like dogs.*

Without looking up, the duck said, "Do any of you still doubt that we should die?"

In silence the other ducks formed two diagonal lines behind Sam's guide. It turned toward the lake.

"You'll follow us," the duck said to Sam. "I've made things simple for you. There is no choice now. There is a vile thing in us all, Sam."

The ducks marched. A moment later, Sam followed. The lake glittered brighter than it had before. His eyes watered. The ground became soft under his feet, and when he looked down he found he was walking on grass. Something moved near him, but the lake's reflected light was too bright to see clearly. He could make out the ducks, and the figure of a man — the same figure, repeated again and again — bending over each of them.

"Andrew!"

Each figure stood. Each figure looked at Sam. Andrew's hair was dark; the rest of him was too bright to look at.

When the light died, Sam stood near his chessboards, facing the lake. The bodies of the ducks lay scattered along the water's edge.

"No," Sam said. "I can't stay here. Not after all that. I have to do something." Sam walked toward the lake. This time, nothing happened to the air. The lake was as close as it appeared. "I'm sorry, Andrew."

The water rippled. The figure Sam had seen rose out of the lake. Water ran down Andrew's skin. His ribs pushed against the skin of his chest. Sam remembered how they had jabbed his side as he carried Andrew to the lake.

"Hasn't it helped at all?" Sam asked.

"There is less pain. I'm stronger now." Andrew's voice sounded like it came from underwater. "Your ducks were more powerful than they seemed. They might have driven me away without your help, at one time."

"Are you strong enough to stay even if I no longer want you here?"

"No. But I am strong enough to destroy you once our bonds are gone. Do you think you will do as they asked, Sam?"

Sam nodded.

"I'm hungry," Andrew whispered. "There are never enough souls. Not in the park, not in the city, not in any world."

"Don't say that," Sam said. "Don't talk about souls. You destroyed their minds, that's all."

"You knew what I was."

"I knew."

Andrew's feet disappeared beneath the surface of the water. Sam got the impression that Andrew filled the lake.

"I want my lake back, Andrew. I want you to leave."

Andrew nodded. The water shifted. Andrew set one bare foot down on the grass, then another. Ripples ran down the surface of the water. Andrew walked up to Sam, wrapped his arms around him. Sam let himself be pulled into the embrace. He was still so thin. . . Sam could feel that something had changed in the park. The lake no longer belonged to Andrew.

"I'm sorry," Sam said. And he was. "Will I at least sate you for a moment?"

No, Andrew whispered in Sam's mind. Andrew opened his mouth. There was nothing there. No teeth, no tongue, just a hollow emptiness. Andrew's fingers pushed into Sam's skull; Andrew's lips covered Sam's mouth. Sam tried to breathe, but the air was leaving his lungs, he couldn't hold it. The world dimmed. Sam wanted to say something, some last word, but he had nothing to say. Then his skull felt as though it would explode, and he thought he would scream. There was no air. There was no strength to struggle with. Then the pain, too, died away. For a moment, he could see out of the emptiness of Andrew's mouth. Sam watched his own body fall into the lake. He never heard the splash.

THE CLOCKMAKER'S DAUGHTER

E. SEDIA

I LEARNED EARLY ON THAT the moment you put a frog on an anthill and watch the steel-jawed ants take it apart, leaving nothing but a scattering of small, white bones, people start looking at you funny. Like the frog was something precious, not refuse from biology class, and you were this messed up monster, not a girl who happened to find an anthill in the schoolyard. I mean, honestly. The frog was dead, and I just wanted the skeleton. Twelve-year-olds fancy those sorts of things sometimes. Especially the daughters of clockmakers; I suppose we appreciate the intricate structures and neat interlocking parts more than others.

My father was the only one who did not see anything particularly weird about the skeleton. He even promised to put it back together for me, and told all the concerned teachers to bug off, his daughter did not need to talk to any professionals, damn it. Don't worry about them, sugar.

I smiled at him, happy and secure in my knowledge that there was this divide in the world, with my father and me on one side of it, and everyone else on the other. This knowledge warmed me as the two of us sat in his workroom, high above the street that wailed with sirens and glittered with neon. The clocks ticked in unison, and my father's long, thin fingers fitted the bones together, furnishing them with ball bearings the size of an ant's head, and springs coiled like miniature cobras. It seemed much more interesting than his usual clockworks.

"What's that for?" I asked, leaning closer to the polished wood of the table.

"That," he said, "is to make it dance."

I sighed. I just wanted a skeleton, not a toy. But my father had been looking for things to do lately. Damn electronics, he would say. Everything is digital nowadays, and disposable too. How the hell is a craftsman supposed to make a living in the world of disposable digital crap? No one wanted to buy his handcrafted clowns that howled with a high-pitched laughter, or graceful dancers.

So he amused himself by putting tiny wheels and bearings into a skeletal frog, until the clocks struck ten, all together. I froze at the discordant chiming, piping, and tolling of my bedtime.

Father looked up, and pushed his glasses higher on the thin bridge of his nose. "I'll tuck you in," he said.

I rushed to my bedroom. I wouldn't be caught dead outside of it past ten, the time when the Boogeyman came. He had the footsteps and the voice of Uncle George, father's friend, but after ten he ceased being a benevolent, lumbering behemoth of a man, and turned into a sinister creature, whispering in the workroom late into the night, sometimes interrupted by my father, who also sounded different — scared. Sometimes father cried. Their night dealings were decidedly different from the daytime ones.

I changed into my pajamas and jumped into bed.

My father smoothed the blanket around me, kissed my forehead. "Good-night, sugar." He stood. "Go to sleep. And stay in bed, or the Boogeyman will getcha."

The words filled me with quiet dread as I lay in the darkness, listening to the squeaking of the floorboards under father's feet. There was a knock on the door, and my heart beat faster, almost choking me, as the front door squealed on its hinges, and Uncle George's heavy footsteps padded along the hallway. They approached my door and I bit down on my blanket in order not to scream. When I was little, I believed in the Boogeyman; I guessed his identity only recently. But still, the dread remained. The footfalls stopped, and I heard the doorknob turning.

"What are you doing?" my father said.

A soft laughter. "Just messing with your kid. She's afraid of me, isn't she?" And in a different, hollow voice: "Caaaasey . . .."

I pressed into the pillow, trying to disappear, to be absorbed in the darkness and the linens, away from the Boogeyman. I sobbed silently, waiting for the terror to let me be.

"C'mon," father said. "Leave her alone."

"She's mine, too," Uncle George said, but followed father in the workroom.

I didn't need a reminder. The thought of Uncle George's ownership weighed frequently on my mind. Without him, I wouldn't be at all, he was always quick to remind me. My mom did not want me, and father did not have enough money to persuade her. This was when Uncle George had stepped in — he covered all the hospital bills, plus a little something extra for mom. The bank listed him as my stakeholder. I was grateful to him, in the daytime. At night, when everything changed, I was horrified of his power over me.

I couldn't sleep that night. The sirens wailed outside my window, and fat lazy drops of rain slithered down the windowpane, turning the neon signs outside into a flowing jumble of acrid pinks, blues, and greens. In the rare moments of silence, I could hear the voices from the workroom, underscored by a low percussion of the rain.

"The human mind is not digital, it's analog," Uncle George said. "So is seeing, and hearing. CDs and DVDs are bullshit."

Father mumbled something in the affirmative.

The wheels turned. The gears clicked. Something whirred.

The Boogeyman cleared his throat. His words were drowned in the howling of a police car outside, and hoarse shouting, somewhat muffled by the rain. A window broke somewhere down below.

The siren paused long enough for my father to say, "Please, not her."

The cacophony resumed, and I sat up. There was only one "her" in father's life, and it was I. I sat transfixed, terrified of staying in bed, horrified of getting up. Something whined quietly in the corner, something shuffled under my bed. I jumped to the floor and raced for the door, the floorboards singeing my feet with cold. In the hallway, I paused, listening to the ticking and whirring from the workroom.

A discrete clack-clack-clack rose over the cacophony, quiet but demanding attention. I stood in the dark hallway, listening.

"Nice," the Boogeyman George said. "What the hell is it?"

"It's Casey's frog," father said.

I peered through the doorway, jealousy triumphing over caution. I was supposed to be the first one to see the frog skeleton.

The skeletal frog hopped up and down, all its little joints straightening and bending, its muscles made of springs coiling, its empty eye sockets and gaping mouth full of blackness. The frog stopped, and father twisted a small key that wound it up again. He set it on the worktable and watched it hop, absent-mindedly.

"You have a brain on you," Uncle George said. "Do something useful with it."

Father breathed an uneasy laugh. "Let it be, George. I want no part of it."

"But it wants a part of you." The Boogeyman looked pleased with himself, his jowled face carved into black and white triangles by the light of the lamp. Everything was black and white, shadow or brilliance, nothing in-between. "This toy is a fine start."

"Please, George." Father sounded tired, as tired as the earth itself. "Don't make me do this."

Uncle George grinned, the darkness spilling forth from his mouth, flooding his eyes, until his eye sockets looked as empty as those of the frog. "Now, you're forcing my hand here. I don't want to take her away from you — I don't even know what I'd do with a kid, frankly. All I'm saying, I've been making the payments on her, not you. And you give me no other choice, do you now, Jack?"

I was afraid that the pounding of my heart would give away my eavesdropping, but the Boogeyman did not seem to notice. Perhaps he was used to the idea that he was the one lurking in the shadows, not his victims.

He rose, solid and heavy as a millstone, and I bolted back to my room, silent on my bare feet, finding my way around the piles of junk and old bedding. Uncle Boogeyman walked down the hall, and the door opened and shut behind him. Back in my bed, between the cool covers, I let out a slow breath. The sirens wailed. My father cried. I wished I could make him happy.

The next morning, I stared into the bowl of soggy cornflakes and kicked the table leg. We usually ate in the workroom, since it was the only space besides my bedroom still free of barricades of clockwork parts, piles of papers, old sepia photographs, dry flowers, dusty feathers, broken glass, and eviscerated mattresses.

Father was quiet, and didn't even look at the skeletal frog that hopped across the table and back.

"What's the matter, Dad?" I said.

He heaved a sigh and hunched over, his thin fingers entwining, his face pained. "Nothing, sugar. Eat your breakfast; you'll be late for school."

"It's Saturday."

He nodded as if not even hearing me.

"What did Uncle George want?"

He gave me a tormented look. "He has this project he wants me to work on, only I'm none too keen. Don't worry about it."

He cleared the remains of the breakfast off the table, and started work. Wheel bearings and aluminum strips and jagged teeth of the wheels occupied his attention, and I wandered to my bedroom. The rain hadn't stopped since last night, and even the yelling outside sounded soggy and placid. It was dark enough for the cockroaches to grow bold and squeeze between the peeling wallpaper sheets. They scuttled about, like tiny brown glossy cars, and I watched them for a while. These were not your ordinary cockroaches, but the ones father and Uncle George made together. They called them AI, and used to be proud of the fact that the roaches scattered the moment you shone a light on them. That's all they ever did, and the novelty had worn off years ago. Still, they lived, incapable of dying.

The day dragged on. The clanking from the workroom blended in with the usual shooting in the street, and high-pitched voices and sirens. I heard the door open and slam, and voices in the hallway, Uncle George's and someone else's he brought with him.

"It won't hurt," Uncle George said. He then peeked into my bedroom. "How are you, sweetie?"

"Okay," I said. I wasn't afraid of him during the day.

"Listen, Casey." His eyes shifted, following the roaches around with almost paternal disillusionment. "Your dad and I, we've decided that you should come stay with me for a few days. A few days with your uncle — what do you say?"

The breath caught in my throat, and tears burned my eyes. Could it be it? Did father agree to give me up, just like one of his clockworks? "No," I said. "Why?"

"He hasn't been feeling well. The man I brought with me, he's a doctor. Your daddy needs rest, and I'll take care of you. Just for a little while." He opened his arms, smiling, and advanced, determined to give me a hug.

I twisted from under his sprawling arms and ran to the workroom.

Father sat by his table while the man in a green lab coat stooped over him, looking at his eyes. Father smiled once he saw me.

"Dad! You're not giving me away, are you?"

"Of course not, sugar." The wrinkles around his brown eyes deepened as he smiled. "The doc here says I've been working too hard. My eyes are going, but he'll patch me up. Meanwhile, you're better off with your uncle."

His words worried and comforted me at the same time. At least, I was not going away forever, and the doctor would make him better. I picked up the skeletal frog, and put it in the front pocket of my overalls guiltily. It was my fault his eyes were getting bad. I should've never asked him to put the stupid frog together. I was ready to crush the fragile, white bones that poked through the fabric.

"It'll be okay, sugar. Just remember that I love you more than anything."

I nodded and went to pack.

Uncle George's house lay in the outskirts, and we had to take a taxi. I stared through the windows as we rode, at the gray haze that softened the sharp edges of buildings and people alike, and at the few pedestrians who seemed to swim through the rain, like grotesque bug-eyed gangly fish in murky water. Soon, the tall crumbling buildings receded, and we entered the unkempt sprawl of the suburbs. The rain washed away some of the dust, and trees and grass turned green. Still, they were green under all the gray.

Uncle George's bulk trembled in unison with the cab's lurching and bottoming out in the potholes, like a jellyfish. When we arrived at the tall iron gates, he paid the cabman and squeezed out through the doors. "Here we are."

I followed him along the gravel driveway and across the overgrown lawn into the house. Once, it used to be beautiful — maybe a hundred years ago or so. Plaster columns at the entrance peeled and threatened to tip over and bring down the octagonal roof of the porch. The glass in the front door was broken, and Uncle George unlocked the door by reaching through the hole and turning the knob from the inside.

The roof in the hallway leaked — dark spots spread over the white ceiling like leprosy, and the hardwood floors buckled under dripping water. An array of my father's clockworks greeted us — father had given them to Uncle George. I didn't mind much, as long as I got to keep the frog.

Ballerinas and butlers, and things with many legs, and a cuckoo clock with a single blazing eye in place of the clock-face all gathered to say hello. A harlequin whirred by, bowing and laughing. He was the creepiest of all father's clockworks, since his face and movement were so humanlike. I found that the clockworks that looked like monsters or toys were much more tolerable. I recoiled.

Uncle George touched my shoulder. "There, there," he said. "They are not real." There was sadness in his voice, as if he regretted that my father's creations were no more than toys.

"Are they all AI?" I asked.

He nodded. "They are A all right, but not much I. Unfortunately. See, this digital crap just doesn't cut it."

I just stared at him, since I had no idea what he was talking about.

He smiled. "Sorry, kid. You hungry or anything?"

The clockwork maid brought us sandwiches, while the rest of the mechanical menagerie just hung out around the table, staring at us with their shining metal eyes. They seemed drawn to people, but unsure of what to do once they got close.

Uncle George grew talkative after eating. "See their eyes?" He pointed with a butter knife. "Just little cameras. See better than any human eye, but not the same. All digital, all in little zeroes and ones, you know?"

I nodded, even though I had no idea. He kept talking and my mind wandered, to the slow rain outside, to the whirring and clicking of the clockworks, to my father. I worried about him.

Uncle George stood. "Well, make yourself comfortable," he said. "I'll go check on your old man."

I thought it odd that I was safe in the Boogeyman house — at night, he went somewhere else, leaving me among the ticking and clacking of his toys, in the darkness and moist air of his old house, alone and safe.

Uncle George had been gone for two days, and I grew worried. There was no one there to take me to school, but the clockworks brought me food when I asked for it, and made my bed even when I didn't. I played with my frog and looked through the window. The world outside seemed to have drowned in an endless gray deluge, and I imagined that Uncle George was washed away, and would never come back, and my father would never find me. I cried when I thought about that. And I cried when I thought what would happen to me — I was a clockmaker's daughter, and I knew that the wheels would lose their teeth, that the ball bearings would break down eventually, and that the whirring of the clockworks would stop, and then I would have no one.

On the third day, I could not take it any longer. I threw on one of Uncle George's jackets, and went outside, into the drizzle. The harlequin and the ballerina walked me to the door, their faces impassive, their joints bending silently, their mechanical hearts whining softly. The harlequin held the door for me, and watched me descend down the steps with his camera eyes. His green and red outfit seemed gray through the rain. I plodded through the sodden grass, and turned again at the gate. The ballerina seemed to wave at me, her white dress the only bright spot on the dark façade of the house.

I walked along the road slick with rain, trying to flag down a cab. They were rare in these parts, and my clothes were heavy with water when one stopped.

The cabby gave me a long look of his squinting eyes. "Got any money?"

I didn't. I groped through my pockets, in the vague hope of finding something of value. My pruned fingers closed over the frog skeleton.

The cabby watched as I wound up the springs and let the frog hop on the palm of my hand.

"It'll do," he said. "Hop in."

All the way back, I gnawed on my fingernails. The frog, my lucky talisman that had absorbed a great deal of my anxiety over the past few days, was not mine anymore. Without it, I felt defenseless.

It was dark when the cab stopped in front of our house. The light was on in the workroom window, and I dared to breathe with full chest. I ran up the stairs and opened the door.

There was a strong smell of medicine inside.

"Dad?"

I heard a heavy rolling and scraping, as if someone dragged a sackful of metal parts across the hardwood floors.

"Dad?"

I sighed with relief as my eyes locked with my father's, soulful and brown. The hallway was dark, and it took me a moment to realize that his eyes were level with mine. I stepped back, mute with terror. The thing that stared at me was not my father — it had a poorly made body of aluminum sheeting, and I could see the whirring of the wheels inside its hollow chest. The arms — spindly metal shafts operated by springs — pulled it along, and the legless body made the scraping sound I had heard earlier. The metallic voice came from the gaping hole of the metal mouth. "Caaasey," it said.

I gasped in horror, trying to comprehend why this incomplete, ugly clockwork had my father's eyes.

Uncle George appeared from the workroom, guilt evident in his little smile. "Sorry, Casey, we got carried away here. Lots of work, very exciting."

I was unable to speak, and just pointed at the thing.

Uncle George grinned. "Oh? That? It's not finished yet, but it'll be great." His eyes grew dreamy. "You know what the problem with AI is? It's all digital. I needed an analog sensor, and there's none better than a human eye. Window to the soul, literally. Your old man needed to be convinced, but I managed."

My voice returned to me, although high-pitched and dry. "Where's my father? What have you done to him?"

Uncle George motioned toward the workroom and I ran there, circumventing in a wide semicircle the thing with my father's eyes.

Father lifted his head from a set of wheels he was fitting together. Silvery cameras framed with clotted blood shone in his face. "Hi. How'd you get back?"

I backed away. It was my father and yet it wasn't; his eyes were not the only thing that had changed about him. He sounded distant, and did not stand up to hug me.

There was scraping behind me, and the legless AI thing crawled into the workroom. I stood transfixed, between the man who was no longer my father, and the atrocity that had his eyes. The clockwork propped itself upright and extended its metal arms toward me. "Don't worry, sugar," it said. "I will take care of you."

MAGIC FINGERS

JAY CASELBERG

IT WAS THERE AGAIN, nagging away at the back of his consciousness, multi-faceted, streaming, and there was little Jase could do to alleviate it. His head seemed to be full of things to make him go: hmmmmm? Yeah, yeah. Next thing he'd be talking to himself. Guaranteed to drive you insay-ay-ay-ay-ay-ayn. Flashes, snippets, images tumbled one after each other in staccato reality inside his head. You lived and learned though didn't you? Well, he thought he had.

Jase tried to shut off the inner noise and concentrate on what he had to do for the rest of the afternoon, but the docusoap running behind his left eye kept dragging at his attention. It might be okay if there was anything but crap on. Problem was, there seemed to be a devaluing of quality that went with the level of accessibility. Much of the stuff was LCD driven, but that was the marketplace, wasn't it? Lowest Common Denominator all the way. Really, he loved the stuff; he just wished there was something better on the feeds. The media were the iconic voiceprint of the age and everywhere he looked, there were the patterns in what he saw. The problem was, he saw it inside.

Jase had been one of the first to invest in the linkstream technology that fed stuff straight into your head. It was better than satellite, better than cable. And after they'd installed the signal repeaters on the transport networks, it got better still, apart from those annoying commercial interruptions. He'd always been a one for toys and gadgets. Toys for the boys. He just hated the way he had to keep tonguing his volume molar to kill the noise every time there was an ad break, but what could you do? He didn't understand why the ads had to be louder anyway. Wasn't it enough that they got right inside your head? It seemed that apart from the new infrastructure and the technology drivers, the old marketing rituals held true. Slam something into somebody's consciousness and they had to pay attention.

He glanced across at the old guy sitting opposite. Middle aged, gray, slightly disheveled and red-faced, with a half-vacant glaze across his piggy eyes, he was chuckling to himself over in the corner. Probably some comedy show, Jase guessed. He played games with himself like that — trying to work out what was playing on people's individual inner screens. Better than dreams. He couldn't remember the last time he'd had a proper dream, though he was sure he'd had them once upon a time. He knew he had.

The tube pulled in to a stop and he huddled back in the corner, pulling his feet back flat against the front of the seat. You had to watch stray limbs these days. Far more people, caught up in their own inner realities, were likely to tread on the stray foot or trip over your ankles. Jase had learned. People shuffled in. No eye contact. But then there'd never really been actual eye contact in the city, proper. The more into the urban forest you got though, the more people were likely to be wired up. The brokers and dealers had found linkstream to be a godsend. Immediate access to the global boards twenty-four hours a day. It couldn't be good for you though could it?

Some idiot further up the carriage was singing out loud, completely tunelessly, no doubt to a clip inside his head. Jase frowned, giving him a hostile glare, then sighed and merely tongued his own volume back up. The guy carried on, oblivious. Jase pressed his molars on the other side, browsing through channels to try and find something halfway decent to grab his attention. Maybe he'd just blank. But then the whitenoise was just as distracting, so he settled on an animal documentary. Don't think of an elephant, Jase, he thought to himself. But there it was. And at the moment it was doing something unspeakable inside his head.

As the tube pulled into his stop, and he headed for the exit for his normal lunchtime routine — there was a small park, populated by office workers on fine days like this one — he was thinking about it, thinking about the way everything had changed. Back at the office, when linkstream had first emerged, they tried banning it. There'd been a whole lot of scare tactics about mind control and interference with individual freedom, but in the end, it was like the web. Businesses had tried to ban internet usage at work when it had first really taken off. Most of them eventually bit the bullet and decided that their employees were going to do it anyway, so why not maximize the benefits? Of course there were firewalls and forbidden sites and institution of usage monitoring and audits, but the thing was, they couldn't audit linkstream; they couldn't get right inside your head — well, at least not yet. He wondered briefly what would happen when they did. They were bound to find a way some day. Not that they'd ever found a solution to smellovision, and not that you'd want them to anyway. It was bad enough watching some stray pachyderm doing things inside his head without having to smell it too. But then, maybe there were some who'd get off on that as well. It takes all kinds to make a world.

He reached the park, located a vacant bench and took up position, his arms draped over the back and his head angled back to catch a few rays while the sun still shone. He used to do this before linkstream — what was that, B.L.? — but then he'd watch the dappled red and orange patterns the sunlight made through his lids. It was a different time. A different sense of reality. He thought, maybe, there were more things they could be doing with linkstream, many more opportunities to exploit. There was the whole education arena for a start, but they hadn't allowed kids to have it yet. He couldn't imagine that it would be too long though. He wondered briefly what the implications of that particular step might be. Would the whole family unit break down as a result?

"Hey, Jase. How you doing?"

Jase opened his eyes and squinted against the glare. "Hey, Carl."

Carl was someone he knew from work circles, a friendly acquaintance. They often ran into each other in the park at lunchtimes. Carl's office lay close by. He took up a spot next to Jase on the bench and proceeded to lever open his plastic sushi container. He didn't bother with the chopsticks, squirting soy from the little plastic fish and then popping pieces of maki one by one into his mouth with thumb and forefinger. He scanned the park as he sat there vaguely watching with half an eye, not really displaying any interest. Jase watched him in turn.

"So," said Carl around a mouthful of raw fish, rice and seaweed. "What's up?"

Jase tongued his inner volume and frowned. "Not much really. Same old. You?"

Carl shook his head. "Seen anything good?"

There it was, Jase thought. Conversation immediately turned to the feeds, the conversational gambit of the technologically initiated. He plucked at his lower lip, before replying. "No, not really. Seems to be all crap these days. Did you catch that new series on the SF feed though? Looks promising."

"Yeah. Managed to catch a bit of it while I was flipping through. You're right. It doesn't look too bad. They seem to have gone overboard with the effects budget."

Jase nodded. "We'll just have to wait and see. Might be nothing more than gloss. Show you the best bits and then all the rest is crap. But you never know . . ."

He turned back to the park's occupants. Now that he was thinking about it, there didn't seem to be much conversation going on. Over near the corner, on a free patch of grass sat an obvious couple. The guy was leaning back, his arms propped behind him. She lay, one arm covering her eyes. They weren't talking. They weren't eating. They weren't doing anything except staring into space.

"So, Carl," he said, turning back to his companion. "What about you? You been up to anything interesting?"

Carl shrugged, folding his sushi container closed on the bench beside him after balling the paper napkin and popping it inside. Rather than answering, a semi-glazed expression slipped over his face. It stayed there for a few seconds, and then he seemed to come back to himself.

"Wow!" he said.

"What?"

"You must have missed it. Wow." He shook his head. "That was some clip. This new ad. It's like . . . ." He spread his hands. "It's like you're being sucked into a black hole or something. His hands closed. "Man."

Jase stared at him. Carl was still slowly shaking his head.

"What were they advertising?" asked Jase.

"Shit, I don't know."

"Hmm, I'll have to look out for it." That was funny. He wouldn't exactly be looking out, now would he? But then, who was these days? How effective could advertising be, if the medium of delivery overwhelmed the message? He wondered briefly what the advertising guys were thinking. What had that MacLuhan guy said? Something about the medium . . . He shrugged to himself. It was probably just a random thought anyway and he tucked it away for later.

Carl reached for his container. "Well, that's me done," he said.

He stood, holding the empty container awkwardly in one hand, glancing around for somewhere to deposit it, then apparently deciding to take it with him, tucked it under one arm as he stood looking down at Jase. "I'll catch up with you later," he said.

Jase nodded. "Yeah, see you, Carl," he said.

As he watched Carl's tall, thin frame exit the park, Jase realized that their conversation had been a non-conversation. There was nothing there. Nothing of substance at all. He glanced around the park. There wasn't too much activity happening there either. Clumps of people staring vacantly, captivated by their inner eye. Jase sat forward and brushed his hands together, preparing to head back to work and the rest of the afternoon, wondering if perhaps he was on to something. He wasn't quite sure what it was yet, but there was something niggling away in the back of his head and he was determined to put it in its place.

The headspace might have changed, but the transport system hadn't. There was dirt and that ever-present musty smell that came with tightly enclosed spaces in the underground. The scents lingered, and as Jase took up position in the corner of the carriage, he mused about what else lingered in his environment. Maybe that's what the advertisers were banking on. With a shake of his head, he sighed and flicked channels, looking for something else to watch.

At the next stop, his day-daze was rudely interrupted by a group of youths piling into the carriage. Street clothes, street cred, street tough. He suppressed an uncomfortable squirm but was forced out of the pretence as one of them tripped over Jase's knees, forced forward by his companions piling in behind. The others laughed.

The kid — he was no more than a kid — pushed himself upright and rounded on Jase.

"Hey man, what you fink you're doing?" he said.

Jase gave a little shake of his head and looked away.

The youth, spurred on by the laughter of his pack pressed forward, leaning over, pushing his face in close.

"Hey man. I is talkin' to you. What you fink you're doing?"

Jase tried to press himself further back into the seat, avoiding eye contact. If he ignored it, the kid might just go away. He glanced further up the carriage, but no one was paying attention. They were all locked in their own special reveries, or at least pretending.

"Sorry," mumbled Jase.

The kid leaned in closer.

"What's that? You sayin' somefing?"

"Yo, leave him, man. He's just another stupid fuckin' chiphead." This from another of the group.

Jase was feeling distinctly uncomfortable and at that moment, the tube chose to grind to a halt, right in the middle of a tunnel. There was no way out.

"Look, I'm sorry, okay," said Jase to the kid confronting him. "I don't want any hassle." He swallowed. Just right now, he wished linkstream was a two-way affair. Maybe they should have a panic tooth or something.

Something you could press in cases of emergency. He didn't know what else to say to the kid.

The kid stood up, turned around and spread his arms wide, playing to his audience. "You hear that?" he said. "Chiphead don't want no trouble."

Jase closed his eyes, and surreptitiously bit his lower lip taking a deep breath through his nose. With a lurch, the train struggled in to life again and a partial sense of relief washed over him. Wouldn't be long now. His was the next stop. The youth was still performing and hadn't turned his attention back yet, but he was bound to.

Jase started counting the seconds, waiting, trying to ignore the other noises going on inside his head. His assailant turned back.

"Hey, chiphead. You think you're special, man. You think you own this place. Hey?" He was leaning in close again. "You don't own nothin', man. You don't even know how to be like people no more."

Jase frowned. The youth's companions had gone silent. And inside his head, some woman was talking about dishwashing powder.

"You don't know nothin', man. You *is* nothin'."

"Look, I . . ."

At that moment, they pulled into a station, the lights forming strobe flashes along the length of the carriage as they broke out from the tunnel's darkness. Jase, whatever he was going to say cut short, quickly stood and pushed past the kid and out the door. He was followed all the way to the platform exit by a wave of laughter. He glanced back to see one of the kids pushing a finger into his temple and making an idiot face. As the doors hissed shut behind him, a wash of cold relief swept over him.

You don't even know how to be like people no more.

The words followed him as he left the station and headed for his offices. Maybe the kid was right. Was that what was happening?

He spent the rest of the afternoon tapping with his fingers on the top of his desk, wondering, the boy's words coming back to haunt him.

That night, slumped back in the armchair, staring at the inside of his head, he wondered more. He didn't read newspapers anymore, so he hadn't seen anything that might indicate there had been any problems with linkstream, but the kids on the tube had told him something. There was resentment out there. The pre-packaged entertainment stream was a mark of the consuming haves. It cost. Jase wasn't rich, but he had the means. He, personally, did all right. There were others who didn't. Did he, did they, any of them, know how to be people any more, really? Or had they marked themselves as the consumer haves, an idiot layer of society with little more than the means to consume? It wasn't an image he really liked to think of for himself, but maybe what the kid had said was right.

He'd never even considered it before, but he wondered if he had the capability to turn it off. Would they even let him? He remembered the prep lectures before the implant procedure, but they were nothing more than a foggy haze, bits and pieces dribbling through about the operation and the risks and how he had absolved linkstream from any liability on the process. Standard contractual garbage. It was like the old software license agreements. How many people really read them? You glanced over them and pressed the button that would take you to the next screen of the signup process. That was how it had worked for years.

The following morning, Jase struggled into awareness, the vestiges of some advertisement threading through his half-awake consciousness. They followed him around, catchy jingles, sexy images, slick designs. They followed him around even when he wasn't going anywhere. He scratched the back of his head as he sat up in bed and grimaced. What had he become? What had they all become? What had life been like before linkstream? He didn't really know, couldn't remember, really, but he was starting to think there were better options. Had there really been a time before linkstream? He really couldn't remember if there had. He grunted and shoved the covers off, swinging his legs out of the bed before padding out of the bedroom to get ready for another day. Automatically, he tongued the channel for the early-morning news program and adjusted the volume until it suited him, washing over the external noises as the city staggered into to its own sort of consciousness around him.

He watched the morning bulletin, stumbling around the kitchen, making breakfast, pouring a bowl of the latest smart cereal. Full of grainy goodness, it was also supposed to enhance your brainpower. Jase picked up the box and looked at it dubiously, taking a couple of moments to read through the ingredients. It had to be one of those chemical names. Damned if he could see that it was having any effect. He wasn't sure if he even liked it. Slowly, he lowered the spoon back to the bowl. He couldn't remember even making the decision to buy the stuff. He left it sitting there, going soggy, half-finished, the spoon resting in the milky sludge. He showered and changed, still thinking, a knot of tension beginning to form between his shoulder blades despite the pounding of the hot water.

The linkstream feeds lingered all right. The specials, the advertisements, the lifestyles, they all crept around the inside of his brain and prodded him, pushing him to make purchases, pushing him to do certain things, make certain decisions. How many more were there? How many more would there be? And he was not the only one. As the technology got cheaper, more and more were taking the plunge. A hostile face, the kid from the tube, floated up in his memory and he pressed his lips together firmly. At least there were some who hadn't gone there yet. Despite the hostility, the naked aggression, somehow, Jase thought that each one of them, the kids on the tube, would end up that way too. It wouldn't be long, he thought, before they started lowering the age of consent, and then the technology would sweep through them, just like cell phones had so many years ago. Cell phones and iPods, those were the things he remembered, and linkstream was no different, really. It carried its own badge of status with it, but one marked by a semi-vacant gaze. That was as much designer label as you needed these days. The question was, did he really want to live with that branding himself? It was a hard call.

Before he finished getting ready, on a whim, he headed for the phone. He looked up the number and called. He knew they operated a twenty-four hour service.

"Hello, Linkstream? Yes. I'd like to talk to someone about the implant."

"Of course, sir. We can offer you several different packages, according to your budget and your needs. Do you like sport, for instance?"

"No," said Jase. "I don't think you understand. I don't want to talk about getting an implant. I want to know what I have to do about getting an implant removed."

There was a lengthy pause on the end of the line, and then finally, the woman spoke. "I'm sorry, sir. This would have been made quite clear to you at your initial meetings. The Linkstream consultant would have gone through this with you in detail. Implantation is a one-way procedure. Your consultant would have detailed the risks of tampering with the implant. Linkstream holds no liability if the client later decides to change his or her mind. This is spelled out quite clearly in your contract. Would you like me to send you an information pack? The terms and conditions are stated there quite clearly in the material."

"Um, no. That's all right. But is there nothing . . . ?"

"I'm sorry, sir."

"Excuse me?"

"I'm sorry, sir. I'm afraid I'm unable to assist you. Perhaps if you spoke with one of our consultants about altering your package . . ."

"Um, no. Thanks. I kind of thought that might be the case. Thanks for your help."

"Linkstream is happy to be of service, sir. Have a nice day."

Slowly, slowly, Jase replaced the receiver.

He stood staring at the phone, not moving for several minutes. Finally, he turned away, tongued the volume to hear the rest of the news and grabbed his things. He could think about it on the way to work. Somewhere, somehow, he remembered a news item, an article about someone who had tried tampering with their implant, but the details were vague. Maybe it had been a documentary on the linkstream feeds themselves. Anyway, all he could remember were the warnings of dire consequences. Do not try this at home. Yeah, right. He paused at the door, struggling to dredge up the details from his memory, but it was to no avail. The only thing he could think of was an old woman in a back alley with a coat-hanger, and that was something he didn't want to think about at all.

On his way to the office, Jase paid special attention to his fellow passengers, to the other pedestrians walking alongside him, to the people standing in shops and coffee bars. One by one, he saw the infinity gaze written on their faces, spelled out in the blandness of their expressions. And with every face, every lack of real expression, he felt the cold growing steadily inside him.

The day passed like most days, and despite some searches online, he'd come up with very little on the side-effects of the implants. It was as if no one had done any work on it at all, which seemed strange. You could find anything you wanted online if you looked hard enough. It was almost as if they all avoided the subject. He'd tried broaching the subject with one of his co-workers, but Ben had looked at him like he was crazy, so he'd backed out of the conversation, laughing the whole thing off. Of course there could be nothing wrong with the implants. How could there be? Remember what life was like *before* linkstream?

The problem was, Jase couldn't.

The rest of the afternoon, he sat at his place, hands folded on the desk in front of him, staring into space, trying not to notice the flickering landscapes intruding on his awareness from inside his head. Though try as he might, they remained. And by then end of the day, as he packed his things away, he had come to some sort of a decision. He didn't know how he was going to do it yet, but there had to be a way.

As he walked down the street approaching the tube station, amongst his fellow linkstream-glazed commuters, snatches of an old, old song ran through his head, overlaying the images sliding colorfully past his inner eye.

"I can't get you out of my head. I can't get you out of my head."

"La-la-laaa. La-la-l-laaa-laaa."

But that was disjointed too, just like the other snatches of information that paraded through his skull.

He swallowed, took a deep breath and headed down into the station. Maybe Thailand. Maybe, somewhere like that. He remembered seeing a news item about specialist surgery been done in those other countries, places where they weren't bound by the regulations, where if you had the money, you could get what you needed, whatever surgery you might require. He'd seen an ad about Thailand. Yeah, Thailand. That might just be the answer.

Maybe Thailand.

He'd have to save up for it though. And that would take some time, he thought.

A FAMILY AFFAIR

WILLIAM C. DIETZ

SUB-LEVEL 38 OF THE Sea Tac Residential-Industrial Urboplex is a sprawling maze of corridors, passageways and tunnels some of which are part of the original design and many of which are not. Maybe that's why some of the walls sweat, bulge, and eventually give way.

Anyway, it helps to know your way around. Partly due to the somewhat iffy infrastructure but also because of the thieves, jackers, addicts, whores, androids, scammers, pimps, pushers and corrupt cops who prey on the weak, cater to the weirdoes and screw the few honest citizens we have left.

The slime balls were everywhere as I made my way along the litter strewn corridor. Leaning against the cold, clammy urine drenched walls, gathered in tightly knit groups, screwing in doorways, barfing into garbage cans, dancing to bar music, and, in the case of one poor soul, sitting dead on a plastic chair. The Takers, robots with permanently sad faces, would collect the body during the night and take it to the death train. They say the machine is black, like death itself, and about fifty cars long. It stops in the smaller plexes too, and while some people get on, nobody gets off. Not till they arrive in North Dakota where endless rows of graves take up more than a thousand square miles.

I turned a corner, stepped onto "the vard," short for Norley boulevard, and headed north. Most of the people I passed could be divided into two groups: predators and prey. The predators watched me the ways predators always do, through sleepy half-lidded eyes, and the tension generated by their never ending hunger. Most of them lose interest. After all, why tackle another predator, when there's plenty of prey?

The prey, which is to say regular citizens, travel in protective groups, avoid eye contact with dangerous beings such as myself and maintain a brisk purposeful stride. Partly to discourage the scammers but mostly out of fear. Most but not all of the cits make it home in one whole piece.

It doesn't work for vendors though, people who, like my friend Bobby Wang, make a living off the fleshy river and are forced to stay in one place all day. Bobby owns a taco stand, a sort of wagon that he and his wife constructed themselves. Each morning they get up, shoo the kids out of their tiny kitchen, and prepare the necessary ingredients.

Once the cart is loaded Bobby kisses Chris goodbye, rolls the wagon out into the hall, and starts his long grueling day. It begins with a walk through dimly lit, graffiti splashed corridors to the point were "Tunnel F" intersects the romantically named "Passageway 123." That's where Bobby hooks up to an illegal power tap, locks the wheels in place, and opens for business.

The local cops, also known as Zebras, or Zeebs because of the skin tight striped body stockings they wear, arrive first. Two breakfast burritos. That's the price they charge for strolling past the stand once an hour.

Then comes a long uncertain day during which business may be moderate, bad, or just plain crappy, none of which matters to the preds who assume it's good and want a cut. That's where I come in. The trouble with being a seven-foot, two-inch bodyguard is that nobody wants to hire you. Not when there are pretty bio-sculpted models to choose from. It's a struggle to pay the rent on my crummy apartment and feed my two-hundred and fifty pound body. Still, it's all I have, so that's what I do. All of which explains why I tend to show up in the vicinity of Bobby Wang's taco stand about 5:00 p.m. or so. He gets an armed guard, which he definitely needs, and I get four or five tacos, or, if business was slow, a couple of left over burritos. My personal favorite.

On this particular afternoon I side stepped the remains of a recently stripped messenger droid, wondered who had been stupid enough to send the poor piece of shit below Level 10, rounded a corner and noticed that Bobby had company. Not the good kind, like old friends, but the bad kind, of which there are plenty.

Three men, all dressed in leather and lace, surrounded the stand. The largest had a knife. The kind that comes all gussied up with a custom handle, blood gutters, and fancifully curved blade. He appeared to be explaining the weapon to Bobby, who, judging from his expression, was extremely interested.

Bobby isn't very big, maybe five-foot eight or so, and looks even smaller. That, plus a light frame, receding hairline, and cheap eye glasses all scream "victim" in letters ten feet tall. The problem is that appearances can be and often are deceiving. Bobby has the heart of a lion. A wonderful trait — but one that could get him killed.

The alpha thug gave Bobby a shove, and, contrary to good sense and the dictates of the subterranean food chain, Bobby shoved back.

The street thugs were amazed. There was a script, a good script, in which they shoved and other people didn't. Except this guy hadn't read the script, or didn't want to follow it, which made them angry.

The guy with the knife damned near fell, heard someone laugh, and turned bright red. I winced. It was personal now. Bobby was toast.

The thug growled like an animal, assumed what he believed to be the correct knife fighting stance, and shuffled forward.

Bobby, brave to the last, grabbed the only weapon available: a pair of tongs.

That's when I reached inside my jacket, grabbed the .38 Super, and waved it over my head. "All right, break it up, and leave while you still can."

Now, this may sound ineffective, but it requires a license to pack heat, and the little bastards are hard to come by. Unless you're a corpie, or work for the corpies, like I had.

The knife fighter stopped where he was but one of his buddies went pocket diving. Maybe he needed to scratch what itched, or grab a piece of gum, but I didn't wait to find out. The .38 jumped in my hand, the thug jerked as the slugs hammered his chest, and a 9mm disposable clattered to the pavement. Its owner landed on top of it.

The thugs hauled butt, all except for the guy with the knife, who looked to me for permission. I nodded and he ran like hell.

I looked around. Not a Zeeb in sight. Fine with me. They make you fill out forms when you shoot people. A whole lot of them . . . and that makes my head hurt. Passersby averted their eyes, gave us a wide berth, and walked a little faster. Good idea. I motioned to Bobby. "You ready? Let's get the hell out of here."

It took but a moment to roll the body over, collect the 9mm, and give it to my friend. "Here . . . if the guy with the knife comes back shoot him. What were you thinking anyway? Pushing the guy like that."

Bobby shrugged. "I was tired of taking shit."

"Yeah? Well, that's real nice except for the fact that you have a family.

Chris is gonna kick your skinny butt. Now come on, let's haul."

It took the better part of forty-five minutes to escort Bobby home, tell Chris what an idiot her husband was, and collect my tacos. She was still chewing his ass when I left.

Maybe it was the tacos, which I ate while I walked, or maybe it was the brain damage, or maybe, and this seems most likely, I had gotten lazy. Whatever the reason I forgot one of the most important precepts of personal security: vary your routine.

That's why I was strolling along, licking the grease off my fingers, when a pair of very burly androids converged from left and right, grabbed my arms, lifted my size thirteens right off the pavement, and carried me away. Plenty of people saw it and none of them said a word.

The one on the left looked like a zombie that someone had forgotten to bury, and the one on the right wore white-face and a black grim reaper outfit. They were supposed to look intimidating and they did.

My first thought was that the thugs had located me and were bent on revenge. That didn't make sense though, since they couldn't afford machines like these, and wouldn't use them if they could.

No, the knife fighter and the rest of his posse would want to get close and personal. They would want to see their fists hitting my face, feel the way my flesh split beneath their knuckles, and hear me beg for mercy.

So, who did that leave? The corpies that's who. The handful of men and women who ran all of the major corporations, enjoyed the perks that went with the guarantee of lifetime employment, and used freelancers to handle the grunt work. Millions, no billions of people who eked out whatever living they could working for an hourly wage. Competing with each other, robots, and automated machinery for what little work there was. But which ones? And why?

The machines carried me around a corner and into one of the ubiquitous lift tubes that no one ever seemed to use but were plastered with decals that read "for official use only," "high voltage," and "danger!" All of which was bullshit, meant to keep subterranean scum such as myself from trying to hijack them. The droids turned me around so I could see my own image in the shiny doors. "How 'bout putting me down?"

The zombie looked at the reaper, I imagined that a high frequency conversation took place, and they put me down. The zombie had a voice like a gear box filled with gravel. The same clowns who had dressed the machine in graveyard chic had customized its speech patterns. "You make trouble I rip head off."

I had every intention of offering a snappy rejoinder but the platform coasted to a stop and the doors slid open. It was dark topside, but there were plenty of lights, and a limo floated not ten feet from the tube.

A greenie had spotted the vehicle and summoned some of his or her buddies. Call them what you will, "Earth firsters," "tree huggers," or just plain nuts, the greenies oppose the corporations and advocate what they call "demechanization," and a return to the land. Land which the corpies just happen to own.

I considered calling on them for help, realized that they didn't give a shit, and ducked as a bottle crashed against the wall above my rather reflective head. The zombie gave a 300-pound nudge and I took the hint. We stepped out onto the pavement. The air stank of sulfur, ozone, and all the other crap that the corpies continue to pump into it. It made me cough. The robots were unaffected. The reaper pointed a long bony finger toward the limo. "Get in."

There seemed to be very little point in debating the issue so I did as I was told. Something smashed against the roof. The interior smelled of leather, stale cigar smoke, and the faint scent of a woman's perfume. I didn't know what the stuff was called but I liked it.

The zombie planted his steel plated ass in the seat next to me, the reaper took his place next to the empty driver's seat, and the limo lifted off. The air car's on-board computer guided the vehicle upward, demanded a slot commensurate with its owner's status, and was integrated into the carefully managed flow of traffic.

Sky scrapers rose all around. They were more like monuments than office buildings, since the corpies didn't need much space, and those freelancers fortunate to cop a few hours of work did most of it from home. Still, you had to stash your computers somewhere, and the high-rise boxes, towers and cylinders functioned like silicon silos.

The limo banked to the left, skimmed an aluminum clad pyramid, and headed south. Logos floated past. There was Droidware Inc., better known as "the big D," Elexar Corp, Trans Solar, Seculor and a half dozen more. Individual pustules within the concrete acne that started in Vancouver and stretched south to Ensenada. An endless sprawl of refineries, tank farms, slums and haz dumps. All leaking their various toxins into the planet's underground bloodstream.

Something beeped, the limo started to lose altitude, and I scanned the buildings ahead. There were plenty to chose from. Which were we headed for? Then, as if to answer my question, a luminescent blue X materialized at the center of a flat-topped roof. The name Alfano Inc. was spelled out in twenty foot high red letters and circled the top of the building like a dog chasing its tail.

It's weird about my memory, how I have days when I can't remember where I live, interspersed with moments when everything is so clear. I knew, don't ask me how, that Alfano Inc. was the 900-pound gorilla in the terrestrial freight business, and that everyone knew the Alfred Alfano story, partly because it was interesting, and partly because the old fart never stopped talking about himself. "The last self-made billionaire," that's what the audio pops claimed, and maybe it was true.

The limo kissed the center of the X, the door whined open, and the zombie slid off the seat. I followed. It was breezy outside, breezy enough to blow the worst of the stink off toward the Cascade mountains, and cut through the fabric of my lightweight jacket. The roof was open, and with the exception of boxy elevator lobby, flat as a pancake.

There were heavies standing around, not bodyguards like myself, but paramilitary types complete with chemically assisted bodies, urban camos, assault weapons and a lot of attitude. Just the way I used to be when I was a big, bad Mishimuto Marine.

One of them, a woman with a light machine gun cradled in her arms, wore a purple crew cut. She eyed my skull plate as if wondering where she could get one installed. "You pack'in?"

"Yeah. Under my left arm."

She nodded. Her voice was level. One pro to another. "No offense . . . but we gotta check."

I assumed the posture, arms out, legs spread. One of her troops ran a metal detector over my body, confirmed the .38, and got the predictable beep off my head.

"Okay," the woman said. "I ain't got no instructions about your piece . . . but keep it holstered. Andre handles internal security and he runs a tight ship."

I gestured toward her team. "What's the deal? You expecting trouble or something?"

She grinned. "Of course I am! That's what I get paid for."

It was a good answer, the kind any pro might give, but I thought I saw something in her eyes. A sort of expectant wariness, as if a shit storm was on the way, and might arrive at any moment.

The reaper escorted me across the roof to what looked like a one-story box. It had been fortified with sand bags. More evidence that something was cooking.

Doors slid open, I entered, and found myself standing in front of a full length portrait of Alfred Alfano. The family patriarch looked like a man who should've been bald — and would be if he stopped rubbing stuff into his scalp. He had dark penetrating eyes, the kind that look right through you, and that some women find interesting. Alfano's nose looked normal enough, but there was something about his mouth, a quality I couldn't quite put my finger on. What was that expression anyway? A smile? Or a sneer? There was no way to be sure. "Mr. Maxon?"

I turned around. The elevator had arrived. The rather polite use of my name stood in marked contrast to the manner in which I had been abducted. The android sounded female but looked androgynous. "Yes?"

"Please follow me. Mr. Alfano is waiting."

It was tempting to say "So what?" Or to make some other withdrawal from my vast store of witticisms, but I managed to resist. I was alive which meant Alfano wanted something. Something for which he would pay. Or so I hoped. "Of course. Lead the way."

The elevator was a luxurious affair complete with walnut paneling and some sort of nondescript music. And there was something else as well, the faint but unmistakable scent of expensive cologne, the same perfume I had noticed in the limo. Who was this elusive female? And what would she look like? The guy in me wanted to know.

The platform coasted to a stop and the robot gestured toward the door. The outer part of Alfano's office was quite imposing. A single individual sat behind a rosewood barricade. She looked up from a computer and frowned. She was far too homely to be a robot — and looked a little bit like the portrait I'd seen. A relative? Probably. Corpies use nepotism like glue. In any case, the woman looked more like a guard than a secretary. "Yes?"

"Mr. Maxon here to see Mr. Alfano."

I was surprised when the desk nazi nodded toward the inner sanctum. "Mr. Alfano is on the com right now . . . but go on in. He'll be free in a moment."

Ever obedient, and curious as to what the whole thing was about, I circled the desk and passed through double doors. The room was mostly the way I had expected it to be. A lot of dark wood, shelves full of books that Alfano probably hadn't read, and a forty acre desk. There was an old fashioned hinged picture frame. Ornate silver circled two holo stats, one of a young woman so beautiful that she could have been a model, and a second of a woman who, though well made up, was handsome rather than pretty. Alfano waved a half-smoked cigar toward one of the guest chairs and continued to talk. "So, what are you telling me? That he doesn't want her? Who the hell does the punk think he is?"

I took a chair and tried to disappear. Alfano listened to the other person's answer, said, "Yeah, yeah, yeah," and shook his head in disappointment. "All right Marty, thanks for trying. I'll see you at the shareowner's meeting."

The com set clattered in its cradle and Alfano turned his attention to me. I noticed that the patriarch was smaller than he appeared to be in the portrait and a good deal older. The eyes were the same however — and seemed to drill their way into my head. "I'm a busy man Mr. Maxon . . . so I hope you'll forgive me if I get straight to the point. Do you know what a shareowner's meeting is?"

I shrugged. "It's an opportunity for the corporation to provide shareowners with information regarding how the business is doing."

"Exactly," Alfano replied. "I have enemies, lots of'em, and the meeting would make the perfect place for a hit. Everybody knows I'll be there. That's why we hire some freelancers each year, men and women like yourself, to beef up the team."

"Why?" I asked stupidly. "You have plenty of security."

The eyes looked flat and hard. Alfano wasn't used to questions and didn't much care for them. "Think about it Mr. Maxon. We have to defend the building even when we aren't in it, especially when we aren't in it, and still move enough muscle to handle the gathering."

I nodded. "Hobbletygorp."

He looked the way most people do when I say something like that. Surprised, confused, and a little bit annoyed. Can't say as I blame them. The shrinks can't explain the nonsensical words and neither can I. Odds are that they have something to do with the headaches and the weird repetitive dreams. The worst of which involves some sort of operation. There are doctors, the harsh smell of antiseptics, and a general sense of disorientation. That's when it starts. The general sense of inflow, a virtual blizzard of words and numbers that seem to bury me alive, and choke off my air. That's when I escape from my body, hover just under the ceiling, and watch them bring me back. I forced a smile and pretended to clear my throat. "Yes, sir. Thanks for the clarification. Who will I report to? Andre?"

There was a change in Alfano's eyes, as if the mention of his Security Chief indicated that there was some hope for me. He pointed toward the more homely of the two women. "Yes, where the big picture is concerned. But your job is to guard my eldest daughter. That's why I chose to interview you myself."

The words rattled like stones on concrete. They sounded false but I couldn't say why. I nodded. "Yes, sir. I'll do my best."

"Good. We leave in the morning so you won't be able to go home. Find Andre and draw anything you need. He will introduce you to Pru."

"Pru?"

"Prudence, my daughter."

"Yes, of course."

Alfano nodded, examined the end of his cigar, and stubbed it out. The interview was over.

I showed myself out of Alfano's office, requested directions from the desk nazi, and proceeded down the hall. Now, left to my own devices, I realized how empty the building was, with lots of dark empty offices, unpopulated work cubes, and sterile common areas. The place felt haunted, as if the ghosts of a million laid off workers still roamed the corridors, taking meetings, kissing ass, and, when things went well, making products that people needed and used.

The Security Chief was where you might expect him to be, on the same floor with the boss, but comfortably removed. To provide the alpha male with some privacy? Or to escape the blast in case a bomb went off? I put my money on number two.

I stepped through the door, and entered a completely different world. Steel, plastic, and vinyl had replaced the brass, wood and carpeting that typified the rest of the building. Security monitors, literally hundreds of them, tiled three long walls. A rack of radios, lights rippling, murmured to one side, while weapons, at least half a million credits worth, waited in racks.

Andre, assuming he and the man in front of me were one and the same, was a surprise. Rather than the hulk I had expected to see, he was small, very small, standing no more than about four feet tall, not counting the power assisted stilts. Most people would have assumed that he was the victim of a hereditary birth defect but I knew better. The Mishimuto Marines included an entire battalion of gene manipulated men and women, so called "specialists," designed to function as crew for exotic weapons systems. "Normals" tended to look down on them, to refer to them as "freaks," and I was no exception. Not till I became one myself. Maybe that's why I took a liking to him. He had a pretty good build for a little guy, brown hair that was pulled back into a pony tail, and level green eyes. "So, who the hell are you?"

I shrugged. "Max Maxon. Mr. Alfano hired me to protect his daughter."

Andre's eyes narrowed. "Which one?"

"Prudence."

"Hmmm," he said. "Interesting."

"How so?"

The Security Chief ran his eyes the length of my frame, brought them back, and met mine. "Tell me something . . . How good are you? Compared to the very best?"

I didn't care for the question and decided to stall. "Like what? On a scale of one to ten?"

"Sure," the Security Chief answered easily. "On a scale of one to ten."

I swallowed. It was tempting to exaggerate, to build myself up, but something held me back. The look in Andre's eyes? The knowledge that I couldn't back it up? It didn't matter. I went with the truth. "Maybe a five."

Something changed deep within his eyes. Something subtle but important. He was silent for a moment. When he spoke there was respect in his voice. "That took courage Maxon . . . more than most people have."

He looked around as if to verify that the room was empty. His voice was little more than a whisper. "Tell me something Maxon . . . if your daughter was in danger, and you could afford the very best, would you hire a five?"

"No," I said slowly, "I guess I wouldn't."

"Neither would I," Andre replied softly. "So a word to the wise: watch your six. Who knows? You might live long enough to get paid."

Pay! Something I should have asked Alfano about but had failed to do so. "So," I said casually, "how much is the pay? Assuming I live to collect it?"

"Five hundred credits per day," the Security Chief replied cheerfully, "plus expenses. Not bad, huh? You need anything?" He gestured to the weapons racked along the wall.

I tend to carry at least two back up mags for the .38, but ammo is damned expensive, so why not? "You got any boxes of .38 super hollow point express laying around?"

Andre nodded. "Yeah, not much though, most of the team prefer 9mm. Let's take a look." The power assisted stilts made a whining noise as he crossed the room. The Security Chief checked the shelves, and, like so many things in life, found the stuff he was looking for on the top shelf. There were four boxes of fifty. A nice little bonus. I took every single one of them.

"So," Andre inquired. "You ready?"

"Reckon so."

"All right, then. Let's pay a visit to Miss Prudence. We leave at oh-dark thirty . . . so you should get acquainted."

Servos whined as the security officer made his way down the hall.

Now, viewed from the back, I saw Andre had stuffed a 9mm down the back of his pants. Tried it once but damned near blew my ass off. Stuck with holsters ever since.

We entered an elevator, dropped two levels, and got off. The first thing I noticed was the change in décor. The almost sterile feel of the floors above had been replaced by a beige sort of beauty replete with thick off-white carpets, beautifully crafted wood trim, carefully chosen brass fixtures and paintings. Lots of paintings, abstract things mostly, executed in bright primary colors. I liked the one that fronted the elevators, but hey, part of my brain is missing. Andre must have noticed my interest because he nodded toward the jumble of brightly colored shapes. "Miss Pru likes to paint."

The tone was neutral, and his face was blank, but there was no denying the underlying judgement. Andre considered painting to be a waste of time, and judging from the fact that Alfred Alfano's office boasted bare walls, the old man did too. The Security Chief pointed toward the far end of the hall. "Both Miss Pru and Miss Linda have suites at the far end of the hall."

I raised an eyebrow. "What? You're bailing out?"

Andre smiled. "She's all yours Maxon . . . use the radio if you need reinforcements."

"Will anyone come?"

The little big man laughed. "Maybe, if we're in the mood." Servos whined, doors closed, and the Security Chief was gone.

I grumbled to myself as I trudged the length of the hall, still finding time to make note of side doors, exits, windows and the building across the street. The sky scraper was a big hummer, equal in size to the one I was in, and just as empty. A few rectangles of white light showed where some poor slobs were working late while most of the offices were dark.

The hall ended in what amounted to a small lobby. There were two sets of white enameled doors, one to the left and one to the right. It might have been confusing except for the fact that some extremely thoughtful soul had mounted brass plaques next to both. The one on the left read "Miss Linda," and the one on the right said, "Miss Pru." I rang the bell and spoke into the intercom. "Max Maxon here to see Miss Prudence."

The voice sounded tinny. "Come in."

I tried the door, found it was unlocked, and shook my head in disgust. I mean doors won't stop the poppers, not the more determined kind, but they do slow 'em down. And seconds, even a few, are damned nice to have. I entered the suite, secured the door, and went looking for my client. The color scheme was very much like that found out in the hall, complete with more splashy paintings, and Beethoven's Piano Sonata No. 8 in C minor beckoning me on. How did I know that? Good question. I wish I knew.

I passed through an entry hall, entered a sparsely furnished sitting room, and followed the hardwood flooring. It led me past a nicely equipped kitchen, some doors that might have led to bedrooms, and out into a solarium. That's where Miss Prudence was, sitting behind a baby grand, eyes out of focus.

She sensed my presence, or I thought she did, but kept on playing. Her hair was dark, her nose was too large, and her mouth was small and determined. There was nothing wrong with her body however; it appeared to be in good shape and featured bumps in all the right places. Her clothes were simple but stylish. A white blouse, some nice jewelry, and black slacks. Finally, after the last note had died away, Miss Pru looked up. She started to smile, gave a start, and turned white as a sheet. "Are you the man father hired to protect me?"

I'm used to some double takes, what with the skull plate and all, but this seemed excessive. "Yes," I replied cautiously, "I am. Is there some sort of problem?"

Slowly, as if afflicted by old age, she stood. "I wanted to be sure that's all . . . I had hoped, well, it hardly matters what I had hoped. It's over now."

My eye was drawn to the building across the street.

I ran toward the piano, launched myself into the air and yelled, "Dork Nop!" at the top of my lungs.

It was supposed to be "Watch out!" but I don't suppose it made much difference as she heard the shout, saw me hurtling straight at her, and threw herself backward. Glass shattered a fraction of a second later.

Having established themselves in the building across the street, and gone to the trouble of setting up tripods for their custom made rifles, the poppers had been presented with an irresistible opportunity. Here was their mark sitting in what amounted to a well lit bubble. What more could any assassin want?

Popper number one, who was almost certainly an apprentice, had the relatively easy job of breaking the glass. Glass, which, if left intact, might deflect the second shot by the journeyman, thereby giving the victim a second to escape. Now, as I harvested that second by landing on top of my already supine client, I grabbed and rolled her toward the wall.

Frustrated, and blessed with twenty or thirty shot clips, the assassins began to hose the area down. The piano jumped and made strange thrumming sounds as armor piercing slugs tore through the highly polished wood and buried themselves in the floor.

Prudence, who was understandably frightened, wrapped her arms around my neck and pulled me close. This turned out to be a rather pleasant experience since she was not only well put together but smelled divine. That's when I realized that it had been her perfume that I had detected in the limo and elevator.

My thoughts were interrupted by a muffled explosion. The firing stopped. Five or ten seconds passed. Her tone was dry. "Thank you Mr. Maxon . . . but you can release me now."

"Yes, well, I suppose I can. I'll check. Please keep your head down."

I sat up, rolled onto my knees, and poked my head up over the sill. Smoke poured out of a rather sizeable hole in the building across the street. That's when I remembered the woman up on the roof. She, or one of her camo clad mercenaries had detected the attack, prepped a rocket launcher, and nailed the poppers with one shot. Prudence stirred at my side.

"You saved my life. How did you know?" she asked.

"No big deal," I said as I stood and offered my hand. "Some idiot turned a light on. They turned it off two seconds later but the damage was done. I saw the tripods, guessed what they were for, and took to the air."

"You're not much of a bird," she said while brushing little beads of safety glass off her clothes.

"No? Well, you make one helluva landing pad."

Prudence laughed. Not a little chuckle, but the sort of gut buster you don't hear very often, but tend to remember. She was still laughing when Andre, plus a couple of his security people, entered the room. They looked at me and I shrugged. Women. Who can understand 'em?

The better part of three hours had passed before the window was boarded up, the broken glass was removed, and the two of us were left alone. The first thing I did was to ensure that the steel shutters that Prudence hated to use were extended and locked in place. Once that was accomplished I headed for the entry and a semi-comfortable chair. Comfortable chairs are a bad idea since I tend to fall asleep in them. Especially when I'm tired . . . which I was. Prudence intercepted me. "Got a minute? I'd like to talk."

I shrugged. "Okay, but I'm not much of a talker."

"We were talking before the shooting started."

I nodded and followed her into the sitting room. She pointed toward a chair and asked if I wanted a drink. I shook my head "no," and waited while she built one for herself. Ice clinked as she sat down. I watched her choose the words. "No offense, Maxon, but in spite of what you did for me earlier, you are what Andre would call 2nd or 3rd rate talent."

This was the second or third time someone had told me how pathetic I was within the last five or six hours and I was getting tired of it. She must have seen it in my face because she raised a hand. "No, I haven't forgotten who saved my butt, so put your ego in neutral. I have something to say."

I nodded, wondered why I was holding the short end of the stick again, and tried to look attentive. Pru frowned, summoned up an expression that made her look a lot like her father, and started to talk. It seemed that she and her father had never been close, especially after her mother's death, and his subsequent remarriage.

Though brilliant during his youth Alfano had made some mistakes of late, picked the wrong deals, and lost a substantial amount of money. No, the empire wasn't about to crumble, not yet, but repairs were in order. Serious repairs, the kind that require millions of credits, and, depending on where you get them, can result in a loss of control. Something the old man wasn't willing to consider.

That left the other possibility, an alliance, or a merger that left him in control. It seemed that there were numerous ways to structure such a relationship, including the ever popular arranged marriage, which given some time, would almost certainly create blood ties. Kind of like European nobility used to do hundreds of years before. Anyway, what with a whole room full of disappointed shareowners to deal with, the old man needed a fix.

Pru sipped her drink and I remembered sitting in her father's study while he discussed what? A potential husband? Who didn't want "her?" Whoever she was? Now I thought I knew.

"So," Prudence said flatly, "I think we can assume that my father tried to arrange some sort of marriage, couldn't find anyone who would take me, and made the obvious decision. Kill me, market Linda, and close the deal."

I remembered the picture of Linda, figured there'd be plenty of takers, and wondered how she felt about all this. I'm a gentleman though, well sometimes, and tried to soften the blow. "You're being too hard on yourself. It's a business deal remember? If you're correct, and that's a mighty big if, chances are that the numbers didn't compute."

Pru shook her head. "Thanks, Maxon, but no thanks. You took your medicine and I'll take mine. You're a five . . . and so am I. Have you seen my father since the poppers attacked? No? Neither have I. Let's be real. He hired the poppers or had someone do it."

She had me there. "Still," I replied, "why kill you when he has your sister?"

"She's pretty," Pru responded, "but I'm the one with the stock."

"Stock?"

"Yes, stock in the company given to my mother on their wedding day, and passed to me. He needs my block to negotiate a deal — and I won't give it to him. Not without some sort of insurance policy."

"But not your sister?"

"No, because she has a different mother. Or had, since Elaine was killed by a car bomb two years back."

"You could change your beneficiary," I said brightly, "so there's no reason to kill you."

There was pity in her eyes. "You really don't get it, do you Maxon? There would be no one to protect me if I did that . . . greed makes a pretty good motive."

"So," I said doubtfully, "what's left?"

Pru took a long hard pull on her drink and looked out over the glass. "Beats the hell out of me. Your job is to keep me alive until I find an answer."

"What about the meeting?"

Prudence looked thoughtful. "I think we'd better go. It's dangerous, but no worse than sitting here all by ourselves."

I got to my feet. "Yes, ma'am. I'll be ready."

I napped till dawn, got my hands on enough stuff to make myself presentable, and reported for duty. The entire household mustered on the roof at 0800. There was Alfano, puffing on a cigar, Prudence, with circles under her eyes, Linda, who no one thought to introduce, whining about how early it was, and Andre scanning the skies.

Prudence and her father seemed determined to stay as far away from each other as possible and not a word passed between them. She looked at him though, as if hoping for some sort of communication, which I found to be surprising until I realized what it was. In spite of what he'd done, or tried to do, Prudence still loved him. And in her own corpie way, understood his motivations. After all, he had tried to make a match, had tried to make it work, but been unable to do so. It was then and only then that the contract went out. Sweet, huh?

The Alfanos traveled in separate air cars, so one missile couldn't kill them all, and so they wouldn't have to spend any time with each other. Though slow when compared to real aircraft, the limos took only three hours to reach SF Urboplex. Prudence produced a com set, dialed a number, and caused a partition to drop between our seats. I tried to think of something useful to do, failed, and took a nap. It ended when the car settled onto the Hilton's roof. The partition had been raised and Prudence stared out the driver's side window. It was a busy place, thick with parked vehicles, and people wearing sunglasses, weapons and a lot of attitude. Most of the shareowners were corpies — and the meeting was about to begin.

It got a little weird after that as Alfred Alfano, Linda Alfano and a dozen bodyguards all made for the elevator lobby leaving Prudence and I to pretty much fend for ourselves. Androids handled the luggage. I maintained a sharp lookout as we checked in via the roof top lobby, made our way down to the 27th floor, and entered her suite. I searched the place and found three listening devices and two vid cams but no bombs, booby traps or homicidal robots.

Then, with that out of the way, we keyed the door pad to our fingerprints, and made our way down to main level where the actual meeting was scheduled to take place. The lobby itself was quiet as a tomb, but outside, beyond the heavily armored glass, a mob had gathered. The signs said it all: "Down with Alfano Inc.!" "Back to the soil!" "Earth first!"

The greenies seemed to surge forward, an army of Zeebs reinforced by security people pushed them back, and Prudence stopped to watch. She was calm, very calm, as if nothing much mattered anymore. Then, as if I were the one who had stopped to look, she nodded toward the far side of the lobby. "Enough standing around Maxon . . . the auditorium is over there."

The lobby had been furnished with chairs that people rarely sat in, glass topped coffee tables, and enormous tropical plants. We made our way between them to emerge on the other side. Andre had guards on the doors. They damned near growled. I nodded in reply.

The auditorium was large, much larger than it needed to be in order to accommodate the forty-odd shareowners who actually showed up. Smartly dressed waiters dispensed appetizers and drinks. One of them spilled something, received a wicked tongue lashing, and backed away.

Prudence nodded to some of the shareowners as we made our way down the aisle and were shown to our seats. They had pre-printed cards on them. Hers read: "Prudence Alfano" and mine said: "Assistant."

Linda took a seat nearby but didn't look our way. There was no sign of Alfano senior. Pru touched my arm. "Maxon . . ."

"Yes?"

"No matter what happens, no matter how my father reacts, don't kill him. He may be a first class dyed-in-the-wool shit but he's still my father."

I was about to ask her what she was talking about but didn't get the opportunity. Martin Zawicki, the company's Chief Financial Officer, took the podium and called the meeting to order. Once that was out of the way there was a good 30 minutes worth of holo charts and financial mumbo jumbo before the CFO brought the presentation to a close. That's when Alfred Alfano made his appearance, delivered a surprisingly effective speech, and opened the meeting to questions.

There were a couple of soft balls, tossed by friends of the family, but the sharks were waiting their turn. A woman with a nurse at her side sucked oxygen through a mask and removed it so that she could speak. Her voice was high and wheezy. "I join those who laud Mr. Alfano for past achievements — but am forced to look to the future. Why has Alfano Inc. lost 4% market share during the last 12 months? And what steps does he plan to take?"

Here it was, the moment when Alfano would have announced a deal, had there been one in the making. He forced a smile, hinted at new but unspecified initiatives, and pointed to a man in the 4th row. "You, sir. Did you have a question?"

The shareowner's suit looked a little too large, as if he had recently lost some weight, or borrowed it from another man. His eyebrows were bushy and untrimmed. Bright blue eyes peered out from under them. "Why yes," the man replied, "I did. My name is Hoskins, Mark Hoskins, a one-time employee of Alfano Inc., presently serving as Regional Manager for Green Party. We would like to know when you plan to cut your reliance on fossil fuels, address global warming, and provide benefits to freelancers."

Blood suffused Alfano's face and his jaw started to tighten. "This meeting is for stockholders Mr. Hoskins . . . Andre will show you out."

"Oh, but I am a shareowner," the greenie replied tightly, "and a rather important one at that. Isn't that correct, Ms. Alfano?"

Every eye in the place swiveled between Linda and Prudence. I felt something cold trickle into the pit of my stomach and allowed my hand to drift under my jacket. Prudence stood. "Yes," she replied, her voice strong and clear. "I joined this morning, and, to demonstrate how sincere I am, donated all of my shares to the party. From this moment forward the Greens control 14.1% of Alfano Inc."

It was an audacious move, one that put the screws to her father, and purchased some pretty good protection. They might be looney, but the Greens were well organized, and very well armed. And, thanks to all the press her conversion would generate, the tree huggers had every reason to protect her. It was a deal worthy of her father.

The crowd sucked air, Alfano reached inside his coat, and I shot him in the knee. A jet of blood sprayed outward, he crumpled, and all hell broke loose. A bullet whizzed past my head, the waiters produced sub-machine guns, and fired them into the ceiling. That froze everyone in place. Gun smoke drifted beneath the lights.

Hoskins stood and side stepped toward the aisle. His movements were calm and precise. Once there he turned to look at the audience. "It isn't too late. Earth can be saved. Miss Alfano? Are you ready to leave?"

It was nicely done. Just like he had practiced in front of a mirror. Prudence nodded. She made her way to the aisle and I followed. The waiters covered our exit. Hoskins led us into a restaurant and through the kitchen. A row of employees, all gagged and bound, lined one of the walls. We followed Hoskins out onto a loading dock. An unmarked delivery van waited with opened doors. We stepped inside, took our seats, and strapped in. The driver knew her stuff and the corpies never came close.

Prudence gave me three days pay plus a bonus. Not bad, all things considered. I never saw her again except on the holo, speaking for the greenies, or when they run a piece on her paintings. The critics seem to love them and she smiles a lot.

Her father sent three different poppers after me, got tired of paying for services he never received, and eventually gave up. As for me, well, the money ran out a couple of months ago, but Bobby's still out there and the burritos are good.

THE MORTIFICATION OF THE FLESH

ALEXIS GLYNN LATNER

WITH A SLIGHT SHUDDER, the lander settled onto the cracked concrete of an ancient spacefield. The landing team stood up, unfastening safety webs, and double-checked the seals on their environmental suits.

Captain Suorro appraised his subordinates. Rula's envirosuit concealed her stocky female figure. Golt's suit overtly displayed his weapon — a big pulse rifle holstered at his side. CS Tau-62 wore no envirosuit at all, just coveralls the same silvery color as its hair. An ecologist, one guard and a computer scientist. It was a small contingent with which to conquer a planet. But, in Suorro's experience, it was sufficient.

Suorro exited the lander last, under a sky that looked as hard as blue glass. Heat from the lander's blazing descent through the atmosphere shimmered around its hull. Suorro led the way toward the deserted field's only hangar.

The antiquated hangar was huge and sturdy. A tangle of native vegetation had grown up against the sides of it, as though piled there by the wind — thin, leafless vines that looked rubbery and, for all their abundance, cast only sketchy shade. "Native, not terran," Rula said over the suit-to-suit link. She snipped off a tendril, dropping it into one of the collecting glasses that hung on her utility belt.

The spacefield ended where the bluff on which it was built tumbled into a valley. Suorro walked to the edge. He liked views, however harsh or desolate — the high perspective was what he always wanted. This time, though, he gasped in amazement at what he saw.

Shrubs and bushes carpeted the valley's sides. Further down, trees lifted dense green canopies. The grassy bowl of the valley floor held a blue glaze of water where sable-coated antelope dipped their heads to drink, silver horns flashing in the sun. It was far better than Suorro had expected on the basis of remote sensing from orbit. This was an oasis, a relief to star-struck eyes.

The landing team joined him. "Very abrupt transition from xenobiota to terrabiota," Rula murmured. "It's . . . beautiful down there!"

"Houses?" Golt pointed toward low, cottagelike structures on the other side of the lake.

"Yes," Tau-62 agreed. Atmospheric wind ruffled its silver hair. "What next, Captain?"

Suorro's stomach knotted with sudden sick dread. His answer came out like a retch. "Plunder the colony, exploit the colonials. The usual."

Rula gave him a shocked look from inside her clear helmet. "It meant, what's our next action!"

"Estimate the population," Suorro ordered Tau-62.

The android stared at the distant cottages, its eyes in far-seeing binocular mode. "No more than fifty, if all the dwellings were inhabited, but there are many signs of disrepair and no colonists visible. I'd say the colonists have died out."

Suorro welcomed the words like fresh air in a bout of flight-sickness. Maybe this time it would be simple — claim an abandoned colony in the name of the Redux Hegemony, along with whatever mineral ores the old colony had been attracted to in the first place, but have no inhabitants to deal with. A Suorroville reclaimed without sorrow. "It won't be the first time a colony's died out," Suorro reminded the team. The usual reasons were famine, bad planning or radiation-induced damage to the human genome. But other, more ominous possibilities existed. "There could be pathogens here. Suit integrity is top priority. If you're exposed to the environment, you might spend weeks confined to quarantine."

Golt gave Suorro a loose salute, while Rula nodded. Suorro told them, "You two descend to the lake. Analyze the water." Standing with Tau-62, Suorro watched them weave their way through the bushes just below the bluff, shade dappling their white envirosuits.

"Another colony is ushered out of the Isolation with no objections," Tau-62 said. Its bloodless sense of humor was showing. A colony that had failed, leaving no survivors, would indeed not object to being reclaimed.

From space, the planet had looked like a moldy orange. Marginally breathable atmosphere, desert conditions, sketchy vegetation. Terrible place for a colony. But then, almost all of them were. And most of the old colonies had degenerated to subsistence levels and were easy to reclaim.

This one, though — it wasn't like anything Suorro had seen before. There was a strangeness about the scene below. Even with a vigorous colony in place, terraforming wasn't usually this successful. Or this neat. The verdant valley was so unique on this world, so perfect, so little like the usual meager footprint of a colony on a barren planet, that it looked unnatural. Even allegorical. It reminded Suorro of imagery from his disavowed childhood religion, of scriptures adorned with luminous medallions of plant and animal design. Disquieted, he turned away from the valley.

They found the main hangar door rolled shut. "I would assume this was a typical colony," Tau-62 commented, removing the cover from the control panel beside the door. "They built this structure out of the guts of their ship at the end of their starward journey."

When Suorro had studied history in school as a boy, he'd been astonished by the bravery of people in the old days before the Isolation. Desperate to leave a polluted, perplexed, dying Earth, they had mustered the courage to leap across a yawning gulf in technology. True star flight hadn't been invented yet. The colonists left the solar system in *space* ships, in slow flight, knowing no return would be possible. At their disparate destinations they cannibalized their ships to build their colonies. Thus they plunged into the Age of Isolation. Which was over now, thanks to the interstellar exploration hegemony called Redux. Suorro's command, the *Redux Explorer*, presently in orbit and maintained by its own artificial intelligence, was a true starship. The journey from Earth that took this world's colonists nearly five centuries had been made by the *Explorer* in less than a month.

Thin tendrils of native plant had pried their way into the door control panel. Tau-62 picked them out with its fingers, then whipped out a tool, which it used with speed and dexterity that a human could never match, to override the control mechanism. The door slid ajar with a faint scream, discarding flakes of rust.

The hangar was a cavernous dark emptiness. Tau-62 stepped in and the motion-sensitive emergency lights came on.

"Find the control computer," Suorro told the android.

An antique space-to-ground shuttle hulked in the dark hangar bay. Thin vines twined around the shuttle, vegetation that had crept in under the main door. On this sun-blasted world, plants would seek shade as determinedly as plants on Earth sought light and water. Ducking under the shuttle's wide wing, beside the hangar wall, Suorro noticed a rumpled piece of material on the floor. A blanket.

Suorro picked the blanket up by a corner. A fibrous substance like the strands of a cocoon stuck the fabric to itself. Suorro's gesture pulled the inside folds of the blanket apart, tearing the fibers. Gummy green fluid oozed out. Repelled, Suorro dropped the blanket. Maybe a plague had killed the colonials and maybe the blanket was fouled with the flux of it. Safe inside the envirosuit, he felt an urge to wash his hands anyway.

Rula's voice unexpectedly came over the communications link. "Captain, we've got findings."

"What?" Suorro demanded, expecting to be informed of rotted human remains.

"None of the valley vegetation is terrestrial."

A visual transmission from Rula flashed on the clear faceplate of Suorro's helmet, faint images he recognized. Rhododendrons and evergreens. Rula showed him a shady vale, a cup of frilly greenery surrounding a clear bubbling spring. "But those are–" The word *ferns* died on his lips when he noticed pink flowers. It was a lucid impossibility. It reminded Suorro of religious iconography again. "Ferns don't flower!"

"They certainly don't! In addition, the foliage is anomalous at the structural level. It doesn't have the vascularity of terrestrial foliage. There's a fine fibrous architecture, almost like a mesh."

"Why the resemblance to terrestrial plants?" Suorro demanded.

"The ingenuity of the colonists," Tau-62 answered, its voice distant and hollow. "I've found the control room with their log. They created some interesting biologicals in their day."

Suorro told Rula, "Proceed to the lake. Be advised that you may find plague victims, dead or alive." Hopefully dead, Suorro thought. For all concerned, it would be a more merciful universe that way.

But Suorro knew too well that the universe wasn't merciful. Mercy could not exist without its equal opposite, and it had been centuries since the universe was wild enough to be a merciless antagonist of humanity.

During the uneventful intervals of his star travels — it took days to go from one destination to another, and little ever went wrong — Suorro often pondered ancient history. Bloody, yes. But glorious in the hyperbolic ascent of science and technology. Nature, fickle and almighty, sometimes merciful and often merciless, had challenged humanity to scale ever more lofty heights of science, technology, medicine. The breathtaking trajectory of science climaxed with the invention of star flight.

Then everything went utterly wrong.

The Redux Hegemony was a cultural and political entity as well as a monopoly on star flight. It located old colonies, planted new ones, terraformed the worst worlds, tamed the wild ones. A thousand new worlds and a hundred reclaimed colonies since its inception, Redux ruled an ever-widening realm of stars. It was an irresistible force meeting a malleable galaxy. Meanwhile civilization essentially stopped evolving. Stagnated. Maybe Redux was the infinite-looping end of history.

Or maybe Redux was Earth's civilization compulsively seeking something it failed to thrive without — something more important and less attainable than mineral resources or even scientific knowledge. The one thing always expected out among the stars, but never discovered there, was alien intelligence.

Redux incessantly explored the universe. Searching for — friendship? Communion? Suorro thought not. Human civilization craved opposition. A new incarnation of the often merciless Other. A new player for the role originated by nature when it challenged humanity to evolve from Paleolithic spear-throwers who lived in dirt and germs and gaped at the lights in the night sky to Star Captains like Suorro, who strode across the galaxy in easy steps across sands of stars, and reclaimed lost worlds at will.

The control room, entered through a door from the main hangar, contained a console and a wide screen. The colony's log scrolled across the screen too fast for the human eye to follow. Tau-62 summarized it for Suorro. "The usual seeding of crops, optimism supplanted by despair, a drought or two, a plunge in population, rejoicing at emerging from the first precarious days, and hope that the worst was behind them."

"The usual," Suorro agreed bitterly.

"Then they found a tiny, indigenous life form which held promise of being adapted to aid in terraforming." Tau-62 stopped the log. Displayed on the screen were several views of a thin, wormlike creature. It had a disproportionately large head dominated by two round eyes.

Expression appeared on Tau-62's face: a neatly furrowed brow. "What the colonists called weaver-worms are variable in size, mostly quite small, on the order of nematodes or pinworms. Eating organic matter, they excrete a matrix of stiff fibers in which algae-like photosynthetic cells grow. Such is the true nature of most apparent plants here, including the vines we encountered earlier. It's a symbiotic arrangement, rather than flora on terran lines."

"That's what Rula found. But it looked damn terran."

"The weaver-worms were genetically altered by the colonists. Instead of the native vinelike habit, the architecture of the matrix produced by the altered worms approximates Earth foliage."

"Approximates? To the naked human eye, it looks perfect," Suorro said slowly, his thoughts launching toward his own most secret and compelling hope. "Rula might say we've found a *biological ore*. And she might be right." This had the earmarks of something Redux would want. And for which it would reward the discoverers with a share of profits.

For some years now, Suorro had longed for early retirement. A share in a gold mine of biological ore would make it possible to quit Redux gracefully and with a decent future. He couldn't imagine himself doing what he'd seen one of his own captains do. He'd been a junior officer at the time. His then-captain, fed up and burned out, walked away from Redux on a marginal colony world to live out the rest of his life trapped under a watery blue sky.

"The altered weaver-worms were called 'our changers.'" The android brow remained furrowed. Computer scientist Tau-62 did not understand the worms to its satisfaction and was, for a super-intelligent machine, taking a long time to think the matter through.

"Forward the log," Suorro said impatiently.

Tau-62 narrated, "The changers multiplied, producing matrixes shaped like broad-leaved vines and trees and, yes, flowering ferns. Thus the valley was terraformed. In my opinion, the colonists cheated."

"Captain!" Rula's voice on the comm link sounded shrill. "We've found the populace."

The words hit Suorro like a physical blow that spun him half around. "Where?"

The answer came in his heads-up visual display. It showed the meadow beside the lake and a group of people arrayed in a circle there. Suorro heard a lilting sound background in the link. The colonials sang and danced, unaware of Rula and Golt spying on them.

"Mutations?" asked Suorro. "What do you see?"

"No signs, sir. Do you have my signal?"

Suorro held his head still to steady the picture from Rula's suit-mounted recorder.

Clothed in simple tunics, they were light-skinned, dark-haired males and females, of different heights and ages, children and young adults. No graybeards. All physically perfect as far as Suorro could see. And pretty. *Damn. Damn!* Reclamation was easier when the colonials were deformed, degenerate, miserable. Suorro broke out in a sweat.

The dance crescendoed unexpectedly, with the dancers all tumbling in the grass together, laughing, as uninhibited as river otters.

"We could apprehend and examine one more closely," said Rula.

"I'll do the examining," said Golt.

"Physical contact with the colonials is ruled out by protocols," Suorro snapped. But Suorro knew it didn't matter. Golt, like his colleagues, had adapted his character to his work. Golt used tools for doing what he pleased to colonials. Sweating, Suorro felt feverish, almost sick. It wasn't climatic heat or real fever. He knew what was wrong with him. It was conscience. Nothing more serious — or less inexorable — than conscience.

He'd started out as a prospect specialist. That posed a technical challenge: combing the old data banks and current astronomical surveys to identify the stars that might reward a visit by a reclamation ship. Suorro was good at deducing where the colonists had chosen to settle.

It had taken years for Suorro to learn what "reclamation" sometimes meant. By then, it had been too late to abandon his career. By now, he had become a mighty nomad, criss-crossing the stars like grains of sand under his feet. He seldom acknowledged the ugly side of reclamation. Only when he occasionally stepped into the noxious excrement of it all.

Unwittingly captured in Rula's transmission, the colonials were repeating their carefree dance. The beauty of the dancers horrified Suorro. Elsewhere, he'd distanced himself from plunder, rape and murder by assuming that the lives of misbegotten colonials on miserable worlds mattered little. That self-deception wouldn't work here. Suorro felt nauseous as he shut off the link to Rula, *per* reclamation protocols: minimize long-range transmissions until the temperament of the rediscovered colony was known.

"Captain," said Tau-62, "I am able to translate the colonials' song. It's in a dialect of Old Panglish." The android cocked its head, in a very human attitude rendered with superhuman precision. "They sang about the worms."

The amalgam of innocent colonials, imminent reclamation and alien worms jarred Suorro. He breathed deliberately to regain his composure. "Anything factual?"

"It's a very simple verse, like a children's chant:

"Changer worm weaves roses and leaves
"Changer worm made flower and shade
"Skin crawl and hair fall–

"What?" The nape of Suorro's own neck itched with apprehension.

Tau-62 mechanically shrugged. "I can't explain that line. Captain, I think the colonists misunderstood their little changers. 'Worm' was a misnomer for an accidental similarity–"

Suorro interrupted. "Get on with the log."

A moment later, Tau-62 halted the picture again. It showed this very place — the control room. But the walls glistened. The camera focused in on the gloss, and it resolved into writhing fibers. Hair-thin worms shrouded the walls, the floor, the desk. "It seems the changers got out of hand," said Tau-62.

The screen displayed a man who slapped at his clothes and at his own bare, glistening arms.

"*Skin crawls!*" Suorro cursed. He activated the link. "Attention team! We've found evidence of dangerous xeno-biologicals. This may be a red zone. Make no physical contact with the colonials, the dirt, the air, anything."

"Oh, but this isn't a red zone," said Rula. "It doesn't have the signatures."

Suorro stoppered his reply before it poured out of him like acid: *You're new at this. You haven't ever seen a red zone. The textbooks specify neat signatures, but this is reality.* "Proceed with water analysis," he grated. "With all precautions. Golt, cover her, in case the colonials interfere."

Transmitting, Rula walked toward the lake. "The ground is solid enough for the lander."

The colonials noticed her and Golt then. They broke their dance circle and scattered, whether startled by the mere presence of strangers or alarmed by Golt's big gun, Suorro could not guess.

Rula stooped to sample the lake water, held up her flask in the display and reported the flask's readout. "The water is pure, with traces of dissolved minerals." She looked up. The transmission from her helmet-mounted visual recorder showed Suorro what had caught her attention: Golt advancing toward a slender girl with his rifle cradled in one arm, the other extended.

In his gloved hand Golt held out a data crystal that sparkled in the sun. The expression on the girl's flawless face was wary but intrigued, like a fawn watching a wolf sidle toward it.

"No. Please. Not again," said Rula, her voice trailing off weakly.

Suorro had thought Rula confined her narrow attention to ecology, and that Golt's crime during the last reclamation was ruled out of her notice. Maybe not. "Golt, do your job. Watch out for adults," Suorro ordered with a razor edge to his voice. "Ones that might be armed."

"Captain, don't worry so much." Golt closed his gloved hand over the crystal and then revealed it again, tantalizing his prey. "They're harmless. I can tell."

Suorro gritted his teeth. On the last reclaimed planet, he couldn't discipline Golt for the rape and murder of a colonial. It was unwritten Redux policy to tolerate such crime when it conferred the advantage of undermining local resistance. He'd since learned that Golt had amused himself in the same fashion on several planets before, under other commanders.

But Golt was getting addicted to his blood sport. Like any addict, he'd grown careless. This time Suorro could discipline Golt for endangering a colleague by dereliction of duty.

Suorro's conscience, in the remembered tones of religious instruction, interjected: *What should reward YOUR career, Redux Captain?*

To Suorro's relief, the girl skittered away, not seduced by the sparkling crystal after all. He shut off reception of the transmission.

"The colonials' song was incomplete. Or, rather than words, the completion was enacted," said Tau-62.

"What?" Suorro replied. "When they fall onto the grass and get back up?"

"Yes. I would guess that the enacted words were *all fall*, but I am puzzled, because they laughed and seemed merry. For their ancestors, it was no laughing matter."

Tau-62 stopped the log at a close-up view on the screen, the image of a man. The man did not look old, yet he was hairless, his skin jaundiced. Suorro's eyes riveted to the man's hand, clenched in front of his breastbone. The hand and forearm were shriveled — no — stripped down to bone coated with oozing, bloody pulp. Stretched between ravaged fingers were fine fibers like spiderwebs.

"The altered worms had a high metabolic rate and they consumed flesh as readily as dirt," said Tau-62, its voice as tranquil as ever.

The head jerked toward the viewers, lips pressed together in a twist of agony.

"He was one of many. The colonists suffered horribly. They had no choice but to be devoured and changed."

"Changed?"

The man's eyelids spasmed open, revealing eyes of an indescribable color. It took Suorro a disjointed instant to realize that the tormented man's eyes were iridescent. Inhuman.

Shocked, Suorro ripped his own gaze away from the screen. His heart pounded as he remembered the discarded blanket lying in the hangar, empty and foul like a loathsome cocoon. Suorro snapped on the communications link. "Red-zone protocols are in effect," he said harshly. "Withdraw from the colonials. Keep distance. Preserve suit integrity at all costs."

"The changers xenoformed human flesh." Tau-62 turned from the screen. "Captain. I assume you know what a Dire Red Zone is."

Suorro gripped the counter to steady himself. "Theoretical. Ultimate danger. Intelligent alien pathogen."

"Even though the individuals are tiny, the species seems to have sentience. I fear that it was not so much passively altered by the colony's scientists, as informed about terran biology."

Suorro shivered, the marrow of his bones flash-frozen with dread. "Where are the altered worms now?"

"Potentially everywhere, in apparent plant matter, in the dirt, in the dust."

Suorro snatched his gloved hands off the counter, which was thick with dust. He violently slapped his hands against each other. Then he forced himself to slow his breathing, damping down panic. "Is there any hope?" He'd never asked Tau-62 for hope before, and wondered if the android understood.

"Your envirosuits and my metaskin keep viruses out, and the worms are much larger than viruses. Without punctures, or other breach of integrity, we can go through decontamination in the *Explorer*, and be pronounced clean and safe in the end."

The frozen image of the worm-riddled man on the log screen flickered — a lapse of some interval of time. Now the man looked straight out of the screen with those iridescent eyes. Fingers and lips were no longer clenched in pain. But the face looked cadaverous, as though the flesh under the skin had been carved down the bone.

Whatever the man had become, it could talk. With effort, it uttered words incomprehensible to Suorro. And then the screen went dark. End of the log.

"It greeted us," Tau-62 said.

"What??"

"Its Panglish was distorted but understandable. It said, 'Well come, long travelers from home. We wait you.'"

"Captain!" Rula's transmission sounded panicky. "Help! Golt is — he shouldn't–"

"Let's go," Suorro told Tau-62.

Outside, under the remorseless sun, Suorro ran toward the edge of the bluff. Tau-62 matched Suorro's pace. The act of running seemed to help Suorro's shocked brain function. *Used Panglish. Knew about space flight. Expected arrivals from Earth sooner or later.*

The things digested the colonist's mind.

And understand.

Suorro halted above the green valley with his heart racing in his chest. Tau-65 paused with Suorro, its pose expectant. It was not programmed to feel fear.

Suorro hurriedly activated his virtual control panel, displayed inside his helmet, initiating data relay through the lander up to the *Explorer*. The *Explorer* would transmit the team's findings back to Redux HQ on Earth even if none of the landing party made it back to the *Explorer*.

By brute force of will, Suorro made himself move on, down the slope into the fragmented shade under ordinary-looking trees. *This is it. Dire Red Zone. The human race may have met its match.*

Finally.

They followed the route Rula and Golt had taken earlier. But those two had veered toward the lush, attractive vegetation. Suorro and Tau-62 shied from it.

The ground underfoot, coated with dry fallen leaves, slipped under Suorro's boot. He caught himself by grabbing a branch of scimitar-slim leaves that imitated eucalyptus. Some of the leaves tore off the branch. Silky and fibrous, the torn edges writhed. Suorro hurled the pseudo-leaves away.

Tau-62 reached the fern-flower spring first. The soft moist bank trampled by Rula and Golt was slick as oil. Tau-62 lost its footing, skidded and fell forward into the ferns. It got up, wiping globs of mud off its hands onto its coverall.

The most direct way downhill was to follow a stream that overflowed the spring. Golt's big bootprints and Rula's smaller ones marked the bank of the stream. The indentations were full of glossy fluff like spun silk.

Suddenly a shrieked call came through the link. "*Captain!*" Visuals from Rula came up, blurry until Suorro stopped moving. Then he could make out the image of Golt with a dark-haired colonial girl struggling in his grip. Suorro felt his anger blaze up into fury so hot that it burned cold. He hadn't intervened in time to save a blonde girl on the last reclaimed world. Now, Golt could be stopped. For deviating from DRZ protocols, Golt could be summarily executed.

The dark-haired girl, a faint image painted on his faceplate, blurred. But Suorro was standing stock still — it wasn't his own movements blurring the picture. The girl's skull melted under her skin and hair. Suorro stared, incredulous. She metamorphosed into a creature with a long, pointed face and a black mane. From her head sharp silver horns erupted in front of Golt's gape-mouthed face.

The antelope/girl twisted. Slashing silver horns pierced Golt's suit. Golt's scream came over the link loud enough to hurt Suorro's ears.

Then there was no impossible antelope/girl in the image, just Golt lying on the ground in his envirosuit, clutching his gut with both hands.

Running up beside Suorro, Tau-62 used a clenched fist to indicate a direction. "That way. Hurry."

Suorro angled downhill, clumsy with disbelief. Maybe he'd just seen a false transmission. Or a hallucination. Neither could deceive Tau-62's binocular vision. "Did you see what happened to Golt?"

"The girl changed."

"Those horns must have been sharp as knives!"

"Yes, even though the girl's shape shifted in less than a minute. Needless to say, the colonials are not remotely human any more, appearances to the contrary."

Suorro groped for comprehension. "Then what are they?"

"Unprecedented. There are known biologicals capable of morphing in a similar scale of time, but not so–" The android actually paused to think about what to say next. "Creatively."

Biological ore. Deadly radioactive biological ore. Suorro called up the virtual control panel. By moving his real hand, he put a semitransparent virtual finger on the largest blue button that floated on the transparent faceplate of his helmet.

Trailing behind him, Tau-62 said, "You've summoned the lander? Good. It may not be too late for you."

Startled, Suorro spun around.

Tau-62 held up its arms, besmirched with the glistening gray mud it had fallen onto uphill. The android's hands were claws of mangled, sparking circuitry. "The worms are more invasive than I'd hoped."

Suorro panted. His head felt light, but the pit of his stomach was solid ice as he ran the rest of the way. He found Golt on the ground beside the stream from the hillside spring, wide and shallow where it met the lake. Golt moaned with every breath. Blood seeped out of his white envirosuit. Rula crouched beside him, wringing her gloved hands. "The girl — thing — sharp horns–" Rula stammered.

"I know."

On the other side of the lake, a group of human and antelope simulacra stood together. The skin on the back of Suorro's neck crawled. Then the roar of the lander rippled over the valley. The simulacra fled, disappearing behind trees and rocks.

"Captain! Captain!" Rula demanded Suorro's attention. "I can save him with first aid if I break suit integrity!"

At that moment, Suorro realized that his feet itched insistently. So did his fingertips. Suorro's soul turned to black ice, hard, cold, numb. He looked at Rula crouched beside Golt, her boots coated with glossy mud. And knew that there was no hope for her either.

"Well?" she demanded.

"Go ahead," Suorro told Rula.

The lander hovered overhead, its pulse thrust flattening the grass. Suorro put a virtual hand on the control panel. Automatically enacting his dire-emergency training — the last resort that a captain hoped never to need — he uncapped the red button in the panel. He put a ghostlike finger on the button and pressed it.

Rula had opened Golt's suit and was attempting to stop his bleeding with pressure to his stomach. Clear collecting jars dangled from her utility belt. One of the jars contained the looped tendril she had cut from the vines beside the hangar.

The tendril's tip had swollen in size, and stood upright in the jar. The thick tip pointed toward Suorro, staring at him with two round changer-worm eyes.

Suorro stifled a scream, thrust it back into the ice inside him, where it froze.

Tau-62 stood erect with useless hands at its sides, gazing at the hovering lander. It was listening to the machine-code communication between the lander and Suorro's control panel. Tau-62 said, "You've acted in accordance with the protocols, Captain. Your career is ended with distinction."

Time slowed as the remaining seconds tolled in his brain, with infinite chasms of suspense between them. Rula, busy trying to save Golt's life, did not know that the lander was about to explode and incinerate them all. She would die without foreknowledge or fear. Suorro felt both, ripping his self-control like fanged jaws.

He saw the cracks in the lander's bulging engine cell the instant they first appeared, lines of brilliant fire that lanced his sight and spurred his reflexes.

He leaped into the water.

Suorro raised his head out of the water, rivulets streaming down the clear faceplate in front of his eyes. He lay sprawled on his stomach in the shallow stream.

Globs of fire guttered on top of the water, floating away into the lake. The grass beside the stream smoked. Suorro gaped at the burning wreckage of the lander and, closer, the charred corpses of Rula and Golt and the melted, sparking mass of circuitry that had been Tau-62.

Pain thrust itself into his consciousness, a dim but relentless recognition of pain from his back and his right hand. Shaking violently, Suorro saw that his right glove was smoldering. His back and hand hadn't been submerged when the exploding lander spewed flaming fuel on him. He was on fire! He rolled over, plunging his back and hand into the water, which sizzled around him. But he couldn't hear it. His ears rang from the blast. He could hear only the ringing echo of destruction.

The terrible pain eased as though reluctantly washed away. He'd extinguished the fire on his flesh. He was badly burned. But he was still alive.

Alive!?

Suorro hysterically cursed his weak will. He profaned himself for staying alive, until a new sensation silenced him. It felt like needles pricking the perimeter of his burns. Suorro jerked his dripping gloved hand out of the water.

Scorched, bloody flesh showed inside the curled black edges of the envirosuit. But gossamer fibers already fluttered on the wound. "*God–!*" he cried out. In that shattering instant, Suorro knew why he'd inflicted life on himself. Fiery death wasn't enough to purge his conscience. He'd chosen a biological fire, a remorseless one that would sear and scour the humanity out of his veins, out of his cells, while he lived to feel it.

The hard blue sky above sealed him off from the stars like the curve of a glass jar. He sobbed, helplessly waiting for the changers' next move.

The first pricks had been tentative assessment. Now his back arched in shock at a hundred hot needles of pain.

When the pain ebbed, he gasped, sagging back into the water, and prayed for the first time in decades. Suorro desperately prayed for redemption in the end. The *Explorer* would send a warning to Earth. Redux would come in arrogance, ready to explore and exploit as always. But the changers would sift Suorro's brain by then. They would learn everything he knew. Mankind would find its long-awaited match waiting here.

The changers orchestrated their attack. He convulsively embraced the slick, teeming mud, and screamed. A group of human and antelope forms stood on the meadow nearby, watching Suorro's last and first agony with iridescent eyes.

PREDICTING PERDITION

Paul Melniczek

MAYOR WISTON STOOD UP at his desk and stared through the open blinds of the solitary window in his office. The sky was sullen, heavy gray clouds hanging above the small town of *Rakerville* and throwing it into a premature twilight.

He frowned, stroking his brown mustache for a moment, then sipped at a cup of water. The liquid tasted flat and metallic, but he drank more anyway. Overweight by thirty pounds, the mayor felt uncomfortable — he always felt such lately — and he stepped outside onto the cracked sidewalks of the town. *His* town.

The streets appeared empty. Only a few people ambled about, most of them shuffling forward, looking at the sky at times and moving along on their various errands. He arched his neck upward again, trying to remember the last time it had appeared any different, something other than the oppressive carpet of gloom hovering above. The mayor gently shook his head. It had been a long time ago, he decided.

He walked down Main Street, nodding to the familiar faces, greeting them politely. A lean middle-aged man passed him carrying a burlap sack slung over one shoulder.

Potatoes, the mayor mused. The man's name was . . . Jarold? He thought so.

"Hello, Mayor Winton. How are you?"

The mayor paused at the pronunciation of his name. Instead of correcting the man, he merely nodded and exchanged the greeting. "Hello. Fine, I guess. And you?"

Jarold placed the sack on the ground. "Potatoes," he said, pointing to the bundle.

"Thought so." Mayor Wiston pursed his lips.

"Heard the pond is getting low." Jarold's eyes were narrow slits as he whispered, his face bony, the skin pale.

The mayor frowned for a moment, a puzzled look on his face. "Ah, yes. Trecker's reservoir. It *is* getting low, matter of fact. I need to go out there today."

Jarold approached him. "That should never have been emptied. The stories . . ."

The mayor hesitated. "We all know the stories, Jarold. I don't think anyone needs to worry. That's all they are, just stories."

"Everyone says something bad is under the water, real bad for this town."

"Nonsense."

Jarold persisted. "There's a lot of worried folks talking."

"Let them talk. They'll see soon enough." The mayor waved to a pair of elderly women who stared at him from across the street. They both wore long dresses, their hair set in buns, and one of them pushed a cartload of groceries along the uneven cement. "Isn't that the Mayberr sisters?" He asked Jarold.

The other man turned, nodding. "Yeah, I think so."

Mayor Wiston coughed. "I have to go — business, you know."

Jarold grabbed his sack. "All right, mayor. But the pond . . . it shouldn't be disturbed."

"Take care." The mayor stomped away.

A half hour later, the mayor walked past the elementary school.

The playground was strangely quiet, and he stared at the monkey bars. Why were they called that, he wondered? And where were all the children? The school itself appeared deserted. To be a child again, what would it be like? Swinging carelessly on a swingset, riding the see-saw, romping around with the other kids, playing whimsical games . . . His thoughts wandered for a moment as he gazed toward the darkened windows of the building.

He leaned against a huge hickory tree, its leaves a faded green. The trunk was strangled by a thick growth of unhealthy-looking moss, the color a pasty orange. He felt repulsed by its touch, and pushed quickly away.

The mayor tried recalling his own childhood days, in pursuit of a satisfied look appearing on his face. "Coming along rather nicely."

"Yes, it is." The teacher dropped his gaze to the ground.

The mayor instinctively followed the gesture, looking at the bare patches of earth between the brownish grass. Why did it look so dull?

"A lot of people feel uncomfortable with the reservoir being emptied, you know." The teacher tapped his booted foot absently on the ground. That small act disturbed the mayor for some reason, although he didn't know why.

"So I've been told. No cause for concern. Seems there's a lot of superstitious folk around here. I guess it's always been like that."

Lerder shrugged. "Maybe you're right. Talk of monsters, that sort of thing . . ." He stared at the mayor. They locked gazes for a moment, until they both broke away. The mayor felt his shirt sticking to his back from sweat. The teacher continued. "Still, there's truth behind a lot of folk tales."

The mayor snorted. "Don't tell me you believe in such nonsense? Being a teacher yet." He gave Lerder (was that his name?) a look of disappointment.

The man's eyes widened. "Who said I was a teacher?"

They both stared at each other strangely for a moment before ending the conversation. The mayor swallowed heavily, approaching the dam.

The brief discussion left him feeling empty and confused. But he had other things which demanded his attention, so he quickly forgot the episode.

A concrete stairs led to the head of the dam, and he slowly made his way up. When he reached the top he turned, staring at the dwindling pond. Another day, two at the most, and it would be entirely drained. Most of it consisted of only mud and bottom-growing water plants. A drying, barren crater — the uncovered gorge of Trecker's Pond, looking strangely revealed to the world. A gradual incline leveled out toward the middle, where the remaining water lay in what wasn't much more than a large puddle.

Certainly by tomorrow it would be all gone, the mayor concluded. With no dark secrets laid bare, only muck and rocks. Hardly enough to raise the unsubstantiated fears of the townspeople. He would return the next afternoon. The mayor looked above the treetops. The sky remained unchanged except for becoming even more gray, nightfall leaking its darkness into the forlorn horizon. A mantle of gloom, impenetrable and overwhelming.

The men waved to him, now working at the head of the canal where

Trecker's Stream was being diverted. Everything appeared to be going smoothly.

The mayor's stomach grumbled. He was eager to return home. There was nothing for him to do out here anyway. Turning, he scanned the clearing. Several people still paced about aimlessly, a few of them leaving and heading back up the path. The mayor knew that there would most likely be a small crowd here tomorrow. That was fine. Everyone would see that no monsters lived beneath the water. Foolishness . . .

The mayor descended the stairs. When he reached the bottom, he realized something which greatly upset him, causing him to stop in mid-stride.

He hadn't the faintest notion as to why they were even draining the pond . . .

The mayor sat in a swivel stool at *McClen's Pub,* finishing a plate of food and drink. Dangling ceiling lamps gave off a dim light. Pictures hung on the paneled walls, depicting figures of unknown people. A few customers sat at scattered tables, engaged in muffled conversation. At times, he caught snatches of their talk.

". . . clouds, can't recall when they last broke."

Another: "And Maybel, forgot to attend church service she told me. Funny, I didn't even know there was a church in town . . ."

From a young couple, holding hands uncertainly, the man, trimmed beard with a sweeping mustache: "Wish they wouldn't drain it, something bad's going to happen, mark my words." The woman, shadowed face beneath a dusky cowl: "I'm frightened for some reason, but I don't know why."

More:

". . . spoke to the mayor, yesterday, I think? Wenton isn't it?"

"Everyone's nervous. I don't like it."

The mayor listened to the surrounding voices with mild interest as he sipped his drink. It tasted bitter, lacking any real flavor as it trickled down his throat, leaving him with a hollow feeling inside. Even the bread was flavorless. The topping non-descript, the meat unfamiliar. He couldn't even recall what he'd ordered, come to think of it. Working too hard, he thought to himself. The reservoir. After tomorrow, things would go back to normal. He almost smiled at first, quickly frowning instead. He failed to grasp what the word 'normal' really meant. The word was vague, lacking any meaning to him. Sometimes he wondered what his position as mayor even stood for.

Or a more chilling revelation.

What did his life even stand for . . .

◆◆◆

Another day.

The mayor dressed in his small apartment room, yawning as he rummaged through the dusty dresser in his bedroom. He pulled out a pair of long socks, the material faded and thin. He searched for a shirt in his closet, pulling out the closest one within his reach, more out of habit than anything, not lending the action a second thought. Trousers were next, and numerous pairs hung on his right hand side. Clicking his tongue, he was indecisive for a moment. He grabbed the third one down, pulling it gently out.

Every pair was the identical make and shade.

He shaved in the small bathroom, splattering water on his face to clean away the soap. Water, he thought. That reminded him of something. Yes, the reservoir. Today it would be entirely drained. And the townsfolk would be there, waiting to see what would happen.

Waiting.

For nothing.

They would all be wasting their time, he told himself. No monsters lurked beneath Trecker's Pond. A child's fancy.

Despite trying to maintain his confidence, he felt a twinge of doubt, a tiny seed of uncertainty. All the stories, all the comments, whispered and spoken forthright. He was definitely convinced there were no monsters — here or anywhere — no such thing. He almost smiled. But the reservoir struck him as a bit odd for some reason, and *that* made him feel genuinely uneasy.

The mayor finished in the bathroom, shuffling toward the solitary window. Outside, a somber sky, swollen with a rage of gray clouds. Another dismal morning. Certainly a dismal day. When would it change? He felt a cold brush of fear for a moment.

When had it ever been different?

With that nagging thought lodged in his mind, and shards of nervousness inching toward his heart, the mayor soon left his apartment for Trecker's Pond, his lumbering figure swiftly swallowed up by the cement sidewalks of his town.

It seemed half the townspeople waited along the reservoir.

The mayor worked his way through the subdued crowd, at times nodding or exchanging brief greetings. Dozens of eyes met his own, each of them asking the same unanswered question. What would they find at the bottom of Trecker's Pond?

He didn't pursue the thought, instead pushing ahead, determined to fulfill his obligations as mayor, whatever they would be.

Several of the township workers were there, staring into the receding waters. As the mayor reached the edge, the ranks of people let him through, silently moving aside and keeping a respectful distance from the pond's edge.

The mayor glimpsed the face of the man with whom he'd spoken to before, was it yesterday? The teacher? He wasn't quite sure. Lerner, perhaps . . .

The mayor stopped.

Barely a puddle remained. A long hose had been thrust into the murk, and he heard the last drops now being siphoned out. He gently shook his head, wondering what could possibly have made the townsfolk so worried. A harmless body of water, home to fish and plants. He spotted a small one even now, flopping in the mud. Suffocating. The sight disturbed him, and he gestured for one of the workers to save it. The man plunged forward with a bucket. They had been prepared to save any fish that escaped the drain tube. The mayor watched as the man picked the fish up and tossed it into the container. He nearly slipped in the soft mud, but caught himself at the last minute.

The mayor felt a wash of calm spread across his body. The pond was drained, and nothing strange or malevolent had materialized. Of course not, he chided himself. They had all feared for nothing. He would give a short and polite speech, encouraging them all to return to the town and back to their individual pursuits.

Nodding quietly, he turned around to face the onlookers, his sense of relief quickly transforming into alarm as people pointed back toward the empty reservoir, shouts of terror ringing out, many of them rushing away from the edge in dismay.

The mayor froze, dread clutching his chest, fearing the unspeakable.

He turned mechanically, steeling himself for what everyone else was looking at. Willed his muscles not to twitch. His heart not to pound. Holding his breath, the mayor followed their gaze and looked upon the focus of their stricken attention.

Sticking up from the middle of the pond was a gray object, round and metallic.

Perplexed, the mayor stood mutely for long moments, finally remembering to exhale. Amazed, a bit frightened, he stared at the strange object.

It didn't look very big, or at least from what he glimpsed it didn't look too large at all. Spherical in shape, smooth. It appeared to be some type of metal. But it was directly in the middle of the pond, where so many people had feared something bad existed. A monster, some had said. Surely, this was a bizarre circumstance, the discovery of something previously hidden within the depths of Trecker's Pond. Weird, unexpected maybe. Monster? No.

He held up his hands, peering over his shoulder at the townsfolk. Many had already fled. A number of them hovered at the edge of the woods, the township workers with them. He spotted the teacher there as well. Lerner, was it?

"Friends . . ."

He started to speak, then realized he had nothing to say. What could he say? Absolutely nothing until the nature of this thing was revealed. And he had to be the one to do it. Mayor. His responsibility. Whatever the consequences, he was their leader, and he had to assure them they were not in any danger. Reveal the threat as something common, he thought. Familiar.

Yes, that word again. Familiar. It resonated inside him. There was something strangely *familiar* about the object, but he couldn't place the memory. Few other memories as well . . .

He wiped his moist hands on his trouser pockets. He knew what needed to be done. Stepping gingerly at first, he waded into the soft mud. He sunk a few inches into the muck but it wasn't too bad. Much had dried already. His gray boots went above his ankles, but it wasn't concern over getting dirty that bothered him. This object, although it certainly didn't appear to be a threat in any way, *did* bother him.

Never looking back, he eased his way deeper into the drained reservoir. The sky, as always, was overcast and solemn. No wind blew, the air stagnant. His eyes skimmed the perimeter of the pond, and he noticed a few varieties of flowers, although he couldn't recall their names. Subdued colors — grayish brown, pale white, light tan. No aroma weaved through the air from the vegetation. He now considered it a strange thing. Didn't plants smell like . . . something? Pleasant?

These ideas held a strong degree of truth, but he was astonished by how quickly his mind raced to divert attention from the real matter at hand — the object unsurfaced before him. Was it subtle distraction?

Or something much deeper and profound?

The mayor surged forward, stopping several yards from the object. Without hesitation, he proceeded until he was directly before it, within hand's reach. The metal gleamed dully, nothing striking about its appearance other than the very *existence* of it in that most unlikeliest of places.

Trembling, he placed a tentative palm upon its surface. Cool to the touch, he tried moving it, and found that it was smaller than he'd originally thought. He stared down at it for well over a minute, noticing a crease around the top.

An opening.

Very strange, he thought. Yet . . .

He pressed on the rim, and felt it give way beneath the pressure. A lid snapped open, and he saw that it was hollow inside. A compartment.

He finally turned to glance back, feeling the eyes and minds of the townsfolk bearing down on him. His people. He had to look after them. Their mayor. They waited, and some of them had approached the edge of the pond. He glimpsed the man there again — the teacher, wasn't it? The mayor waved to them in assurance. None of them waved back.

Disturbed, but undaunted, he leaned down, peering at the unusual object. To his surprise, there was a manuscript of some type inside. He gently reached down, taking it in his hand and uncurling it, bringing it higher for better viewing. Read the first three words.

This time capsule . . .

And stopped in absolute horror, recognition crossing his face.

He wanted to scream. Run. Waves of terror engulfed him, wrenched his stomach into revulsion. He felt terribly sick, both physically ill and grief-stricken. But there was nothing in the world that could have pulled his gaze away from that most horrifying of messages, and he absorbed the following words as if they were poison forced upon his consumption.

. . . is placed here as testimonial of our plight. Mere words are inadequate, meaningless. Snatched away, but from where, there is scant memory. And to where, there is no knowledge. By what means or purpose, we have long-since stopped asking. All things are blurred, our very existence and meaning. Past, present and future are intertwined into one inescapable prison. We lack for nothing and everything. Desire nothing and everything. Hope for nothing . . . and everything. Whoever reads this, I pray beyond all hope, has been released, and the cycle is broken, sparing you of our fate. Even now, the meaning of what I've just written slips my mind, and I've lost the purpose behind this script . . .

wasteful pleasures. What games had he played? He felt frustrated, as no memories materialized within his mind's eye. Aloof they were, stretched across the chasm of his recollection. He was depressed by his inability to remember anything at all from his youth. Instead of dwelling on such thoughts, he continued ahead, leaving the schoolyard behind, along with his elusive memories.

The mayor walked for a short distance, reaching a forest of mixed hardwood and pine trees. A stone path cut through the grove, and he trudged forward, glancing at the scattered acorns and nuts which lay strewn beneath the eaves. Like the town, the forest also appeared subdued. He stared up into the branches, wondering what made him feel so uneasy, if that was the proper word. He noticed several birds hopping from branch to branch, but they too were silent. The mayor brushed a hand across his brow, wiping away the sweat. He continued.

After a few hundred feet, the trees opened up before him. A clearing sat in the midst of the surrounding forest, and within this area was a small body of water, more a large pond than a lake. A dam rose up to his right, an aged structure which held back the waters of Trecker's Pond. A canal cut its way along the pond's side, and he heard the flowing channel as he drew near. A drop of perhaps five feet led to the surface of the stream, and it was moving along quite well. He watched as two men emerged from the dam breast, both of them carrying a small tool pouch.

That must be . . . he thought for a moment. Ravers and Duncan? Yes, that sounded right. They worked for the township. The mayor then noticed several other people milling about the path which continued around the pond, none of them at the water's edge though. He walked along the footpath, crossing the canal over a small stone bridge.

A young man approached him. He was lean, his thin face cleanly shaven, tufts of curly blond hair sitting on top of his head, most of it concealed by a hat so weathered that the original color was impossible to distinguish. The mayor recognized him as Lerder, a teacher at the elementary school.

"Hello, Mayor. Weston, isn't it?"

"Um, yes." The mayor brushed off the incorrect greeting, feeling a bit uneasy, but unwilling to pursue the matter.

"The water's getting real low." The teacher pointed, some of the other townspeople staring over at them questioningly.

"Should be drained soon enough." Mayor Wiston crossed his arms,

He reeled back in horror, nearly falling.

Understanding crushed down on him, drowning even the grains of hopeful possibility, devouring any chance of its taking root and sprouting.

Inevitability. Despair.

They were all just another name for reality.

And so he gently placed the manuscript back inside, tears running down his face, his lip quivering. Sealed the object, almost reverently. He knew that the contents could absolutely *never* be revealed to the townspeople. He would play upon their other fear instead, as a diversion. The lesser, superstitious one, which was immensely dwarfed by the harsh and unforgivable elements of their true destiny. Yes, he knew what needed to be done. He was, after all, their mayor. He pushed the time capsule deeper into the mud.

Mayor.

And he fully understood his obligations, the unwavering demands placed upon his shoulders alone. He always did what was best for his people.

Always had.

And always would.

No, they must never be allowed to read the ancient manuscript and discover the identity of its creator.

Himself.

Who had only ever done what was best for his people.

WHEN THE STARS FELL

William Jones

An unrelenting storm of missiles rained down upon the surface of Amara, leveling its cities and scarring the countryside. The blasts spewed spirals of smoke into a gray and dead sky.

"Focus on the light," a woman said.

A bright spot danced left and right. A hand, firm and warm gripped Iason Rhan's shoulder. His left leg blazed with pain.

"Iason, you're going to be fine." This time the voice was deep and familiar.

The circle of light vanished, and a jigsaw world pieced together.

Iason lay on a cot inside a rectangular gray-walled room. A young woman perched next to him, gliding a handheld scanner over his leg.

"No breaks or fractures," she said. "The cut will take time to heal." She looked at him. "How bad is the pain?"

Iason tried to remember what had happened. A sky blossoming in orange and red like a flower unfurling in the morning sun floated in his mind. That was the first attack. Then the missiles came.

He sat up with a groan; acid pain seeped into his leg.

"Don't move," the woman said. Her tone was gentle like Leena's.

"You are safe." Again the familiar voice. Iason looked up to see a stocky man with close-cropped blond hair and an angular face towering over him. He wore a military uniform, black with a high collar, and white piping tracing his broad shoulders. The rank insignia of Colonel was emblazed on his arms.

"Joris?" Iason said.

A tight smile formed on the man's lips. "You remember me," he said. "I admit, it took me longer . . ." He hesitated.

"What's going on?" Iason asked, easing back onto the cot. "Did the UW troops arrive? Who hit us?"

Joris Quinn lowered to his haunches. Beyond him, Iason saw maybe ten or more people moving about the room. The lighting was dim, and though several terminal interfaces were scattered throughout the room, none seemed to be active.

Immediately, Iason queried his neural interface. Images and numbers appeared like ghosts, overlaying his vision. *Severe laceration to the left Vatus lateralis,* the biological computer nestled on his spine told him. *Low grade nanocites detected. Seek immediate medical attention. Spectrum network not responding. Unable to contact medical response unit.*

"Everything is offline," Joris said, obviously recognizing the blank expression on Iason's face. "It's safe to use the NI in here — we're sheltered. But the network is down. You'll have to set your NI to manual. We can't risk it attempting to broadcast."

For nearly a century, humanity had been genetically engineering the synaptic cluster that was rooted to the human spine. Since his retirement, Iason had used the neural interface less and less. The biological computer burrowed tendrils deep into the human nervous system and brain, allowing for conscious interfacing with the body. Sometimes it made him uncomfortable, as though someone were watching him. He mostly used it for communications. The cluster was capable of producing a low-level microwave pulse that connected to the spectrum network.

The warning continued to repeat in Iason's mind. He quickly dampened it. "What the hell's happening?"

"Cédee," Joris said to the woman, "can you give him synthine for the pain?"

Her brown eyes flashed in the dim light. "Yes," she said softly. Short black hair framed her face. Just above her collar, Iason noticed the tattoo. "It will make him sleep."

"Wait a moment," Iason said. "Are we fighting, Joris? Are the UW troops here? What's going on?"

Joris gestured for Cédee to leave. He turned to Iason, leaning forward. His temple twitched — just as Iason remembered it did when Joris was troubled. "There are no United World forces here," he whispered, his smile vanishing. "As far as we can tell, Amara was the only world attacked. The communication sats were taken out with the first blast. Within twenty-four hours the planetary defenses were completely eliminated."

"That's not possible," Iason said. "We're a frontier world, but when I was serving, we had over ten-thousand soldiers stationed here. And the defenses . . ."

"True," Joris interrupted. "And since yesterday, nearly every human and indent on this planet has been exterminated. There is no military now, except for the few survivors like us."

Iason stared at the dark ceiling. Its pitted surface reminded him of the scorched city he'd stumbled through trying to find this bunker.

"Who hit us?" Iason said.

"Don't know. The tech is too high for one of the Unitary planets. And they know there would be retaliation." Joris shook his head. "I think it's someone new. A new species."

During his twenty years in the military, Iason had seen countless worlds with only the ruins of civilizations — advanced and primitive. Never in the history of the United World Confederation had an intelligent alien species been encountered. The prevalent thought was that intelligent life either advanced to a point of self-destruction, or lacked the advancements to survive natural destruction. Not once had there been any indication of outside contact. Certainly there were plenty of worlds with alien life, but sentient beings had never been encountered.

"Has anyone seen or contacted them?" Iason said.

"No. We've only seen what we think are remote assault drones. They're scorching the planet, but not using radioactive weapons."

Iason inhaled sharply at a spasm of pain in his leg. *Seek immediate medical attention*, the NI announced. He formed a mental command to hush the alarm, feeling the muscles in his face go slack — a clear sign of someone accessing.

"I know you wanted out," Joris said, shaking his head. "That didn't mean you couldn't keep your NI upgraded. We scanned you, and that's the same one you had when you left the service ten years ago."

"I didn't trust it then, and I still don't."

Joris smirked. "You need to rest. We're in contact with several other shielded sites, and the protected landlines allow communication. Until we're sure, the chatter is limited. Whoever or whatever is out there can smell electro-magnetic radiation, and with NIs, that makes nearly every human a target."

"Except the unplanted indents," Iason said, nodding toward Cédee. "I saw the tattoo. How many others are here?"

"Eleven," Joris said. "And two genned, counting you."

"And you don't think it was a Unitary planet that hit us?" Iason said sharply.

"Indents with the aggression inhibitor implants were also killed in the attacks. Only those who'd served their indentures are down here. More planted indents died than our kind. Why attack and kill mostly your own? Doesn't make sense. Besides, you know they couldn't think up the tech for this."

"Colonel Quinn," someone called. "One of the sites is sending a data burst."

Joris placed a hand on Iason's shoulder. "Get some rest. I'm working on a few things, but I'm going to need your help, so let the nanocites heal that leg."

He stood and motioned to Cédee. "Give him the synthine."

As she approached, an endless stream of thoughts and memories stormed through Iason's mind. He'd retired early, not because he'd had a stomach full of the military, but because every day it became more difficult facing the indents, working with them. They were humans who refused genetic enhancement, a people who wallowed in their primitive nature. Most dwelled on planets outside the United World Confederation, isolated from the rest of humanity. But those who didn't, lived in squalor in UW cities, unable to do anything except menial labor, unable to restrain their aggressive behavior. They were the residue of the human species.

At one time, only the criminals were implanted. Eventually every non-genned human was given the inhibitor implant at birth. They served years as indentured laborers. The hope was to tame them before they were unplanted.

Cédee lowered her rangy form onto the cot. "I'm going to place a synthine derm on your neck. It will let you sleep and accelerate your healing." She reached out, pressing a finger lightly against his neck. The spot felt cold.

Synthine detected. Spectral digits appeared before him. They were ratios and bio-statistics, all meaningless to Iason. *Induce adrenal response?* Iason disliked the NI nearly as much as he did the indents. *No.* The thought let the drug carry him into the embrace of oblivion.

In the darkness, he found Leena — before she'd left. They were together, before the uprisings. She was always there when he returned from off-world missions. But then came the bitterness for what he'd done. That gnawed at her, until resentment festered in her . . .

Incoming link. Iason knew he was dreaming. Sometimes the NI caused lucid dreams and followed the unconscious flow.

He opened the transmission. It was always the same. The last message from Leena. The NI replayed it flawlessly each time.

Assistance will secure your sanctuary. Provide the locations of other humans. That is the only request.

It wasn't Leena. There was no image, only voice. It possessed a mechanical pacing as though translated by a machine. The NI had no reference, no link identifer, so it used a generic voice, cold and inhuman. Panic seized him. He commanded the NI to block the link.

"You're dreaming."

Iason jumped at the words, pushing himself upward. Razors danced along his leg. Cédee sat next to him. She patted his brow with a cloth.

Dread lingered in the distant depths of his mind. "How long have you been watching me?" His tone was sharp.

"I haven't been *watching* you. You were restless. Sometimes the synthine causes bad dreams." She stood abruptly. "And sometimes guilt causes them." She turned, walking away.

People jostled about the room, muttering to terminals and each other. Some were packing cases with equipment. Joris stood nearby, his visage slack, clearly accessing his NI.

Iason climbed from the cot. It took a moment for his balance to return.

He shuffled forward, navigating over the bundles of cables crisscrossing the floor. He legs felt heavy, and the left one still throbbed. *Activate adrenal and endorphin response.* He issued the command to the NI — the first direct request he'd made in years.

Stimulating system, came the reply.

The effect was immediate. The room brightened, sounds became crisp, and the biting pain in his leg diminished. He also felt the familiar edginess — borderline anger. With practiced effort, he brushed aside the emotion. Years of relying on the NI in combat had taught him to manage the anger, use it as a tool.

Iason's gait steadied as he approached Joris.

"You look like shit," Joris said, the far-away stare vanishing from his eyes. "Why'd you stop the re-gen treatments? That leg would be better by now."

"I don't like shots," Iason said. "Guess that's why you didn't recognize me at first. I look older." He felt old, too. "What's going on? Looks like an evac."

Joris shifted, using his bulk to isolate the rest of the room. Lines creased his face. Iason knew that the next words would have gone over the NI if possible. They weren't intended for the indents.

"We're moving to a new location. Another group made contact with us and said they had access to the Proconsul's shuttle. It's functional and in an underground hangar."

Iason nodded. "So not just an evac from here, but from Amara?"

"Yeah," Joris said, rubbing his temple. He stole a glance over his shoulder before continuing. "There's a problem, though."

"What?"

"Our passive sensors detected broadcasts coming from inside this bunker." A smirk flashed across his face.

Iason's dream resurfaced, bringing with it tendrils of panic.

"Your NI is old, Iason. You know the synaptic structure degrades without re-gen or retro-viral alterations." He leaned closer, the voice detached, flat. That had been the way Joris spoke years ago, when they discussed going *beyond* their orders in halting an indent uprising on Helena Prime. Back then, Joris had been a captain under Iason's command. "I think your NI is bleeding data. Broadcasting without your knowledge."

"You think I'm giving away our location?" Iason struggled to maintain a balance between the edginess and swelling panic.

"That . . . maybe more," his voice still flat, eyes cold. "You know it works with the subconscious. It's possible to leak information you're not even aware of — stuff floating in the back of your mind."

A low thrumming shook the bunker. Iason felt the vibration climbing his legs, tingling in his spine.

"Power!" someone called. A black shroud fell over the room.

Low frequency sound waves detected, the NI informed Iason. *Prolonged exposure could result in bone, joint, muscle, and cerebral damage. Auditory . . .*

Hibernate, he ordered, knowing his tell-tale expression wasn't visible.

"That's a buzzer," Joris said. In the darkness he sounded closer. "When one passes over, the engines — at least I think they're engines — send concussions through the ground. The buzzers are the drones that hunt us. They're the only contact we've had with the aliens, and Amara is swarming with them."

Long moments passed before the rumbling faded. The bunker blinked to life. Terminals winked on, and everyone returned to work.

"It's not me," Iason said finally, but doubt lingered in his words.

"All of the indents here are unplanted. Can't be them." The edges of Joris' lips curled. "They already suspect you, and I have to be honest, Iason. Your record with indents isn't buying you anything. Most of them were young during your Court Martial. They grew up knowing about the killings, about you."

"That has nothing to–"

"You were exonerated. We both know the reasons — *they* don't." Joris ran a hand through his stubby blond hair, peeking at the others. "Maybe that's why you stopped the re-gen, to look different, be forgotten? They still remember you, and they don't understand how things were then. They *can't* understand. They don't have the intellect to understand."

It didn't make sense. Everything went crazy twenty years ago when the uprisings started. Somehow the truth became fuzzy; it was something only the experts could understand. Iason hadn't been genned as a politician. He was a solider who killed for a living. Death was his craft, and it became easy. No one questioned him so long as the rebellions were quelled. He simply did his job.

"So what do we do?" Iason asked, exhaling deeply. His leg ached.

"Synthine," Joris said. "You still need to heal, and enough synthine should keep your NI dormant."

"And enough will kill me."

Joris placed his hand on Iason's shoulder. "We fight together. I'm doing this to maintain order here. Once I know the shuttle is functional, I'll come back and we'll leave *together*."

Muscles knotted in Iason's stomach. He stepped back, letting Joris' hand fall away. "You're putting me to sleep in a bunker full of indents who think I'm a murderer?"

"They like to be called *Naturals* now." Joris grinned, and nodded toward the others. "I'm not going to send one of them to scout the hangar. I have to go."

A buried fear clawed to the surface of Iason's memory. He turned, focusing on a wall, trying to hide the panic.

"It's the option *I* prefer," Joris said.

The fear instantly ignited into a burning rage. Iason spun, fists clenched at his side. "If you plan to kill me, you'd better do it with the synthine."

"Calm yourself." Joris raised his hands in mock surrender. "Your NI is making you jumpy. All I'm saying is nothing's going to happen to you. I'll find the hangar, and we'll get off Amara."

Without replying, Iason shouldered past Joris, returning to the cot.

"Cédee," Joris called. "Iason needs your assistance."

Iason lay on the cot, wondering if getting away from Amara was going to help. *Whatever* attacked them had superior technology, and the distinct advantage of not having to fight on their homeworld.

Cédee kneeled next to the cot, opening a medkit on the thin mattress. "Colonel Quinn told you how much synthine I must use?"

"He wasn't specific, but his point was clear."

She placed a hand on his chin, turning his head to reveal his neck. Her touch was warm, the fingers rough. "Can your NI simulate sleep?" she whispered. "Just nod."

Anger still flared inside Iason. His neck stiffened. He wasn't sure what games were being played, but he was reaching a limit.

"Please," she said. "If you can simulate sleep, do it when I place the derm on your neck."

From the case she removed a packet, peeling the protective surface away. Her eyes locked on his.

In many ways, she reminded him of Leena. Or at least the way Leena was before she'd left. The years after that he'd spent alone. He'd stopped the re-gen treatment because living seemed less important, and he'd hoped that aging might wash away the memories. *So many memories.* Time had buried them, but never erased them.

He nodded.

Delicately, she placed the derm on his neck, pressing it lightly to activate it.

Joris stood across the room watching, hands clasped behind his back, a tight, white smile on his face.

"You'll sleep now," Cédee said.

Iason closed his eyes, focusing on the NI. In his imagination, he felt the ropey, engineered neurons reaching through his body, snaking into nerve clusters. *Activate*, he ordered, stirring the NI from hibernation. He waited for a flurry of warnings about the synthetic narcotic. Nothing happened.

Induce somatic state, he commanded. *Maintain cognitive functions.*

His muscles relaxed; his head sank into the pillow, eyes closing while his mind and senses remained alert. He focused on the noises echoing throughout the room, even though his mind kept skipping through the past, back to Helena Prime. He'd killed so many of them. And now he waited for his death. He'd always been waiting.

Incoming Link. The message pulled Iason from a dark slumber. The simulated sleep he'd induced allowed him to be swaddled in a restless trance. Remaining motionless, eyes closed, he queried about the transmission, requesting a link ID. The NI was unable to provide any information beyond that it had received a data burst.

With the spectrum network down, the transmission had to come directly from an NI or some other source. But being in a shielded bunker made that impossible, unless there was a secondary relay or booster inside.

Then an idea coalesced. NIs had the ability to produce low-level microwave bursts — strong enough to be detected and amplified by the spectrum network. Normally, NIs only responded to links directly addressed. But over the years, his NI had deteriorated, suffering synaptic loss. It was possible the filter had failed, and now he was receiving unintended broadcasts.

Monitor link, passive mode, he commanded. If his NI was detecting transmissions, it might be possible to eavesdrop. Still, a lurking fear dwelled in the depths of his mind. It might be his sub-conscious activating the communication, broadcasting his dreams to the alien attackers.

. . . clear of the area. The target is ready. I will initiate another link when I've reached the next location.

The words filled Iason's mind, genderless and detached. With an incoming ID, the NI usually synthesized the sound, prowling through associated memories to reproduce the expected voice. General links tended to be a mixture of several remembered people, generic in nature.

Link closed, the NI announced.

Iason realized that this message was different from the first one. It flowed with a rhythm. It had a familiarity of language.

Abort somantic state, he ordered. The brief seconds it took for his body to transition felt like an eternity. Thoughts blurred and folded together. He pushed through the confusion, willing his body to move.

With a lurch he shot up, pushing from the cot. His sudden movement hushed the room, startling everyone, except Cédee who stood before him.

"We need to leave," Iason stammered.

Cédee's face tightened in confusion.

He turned to the others, yelling, "Leave everything! Get out of here now!"

The floor quivered with a faint vibration.

Iason grabbed Cédee by the arm, ushering her toward the door. "They know where we are!" he yelled. "Go to the hangar!"

As he moved forward, a jumble of voices sounded, accompanied by hateful stares. He continued moving with Cédee in tow.

The rumble spread from the floor to the walls, sinking to a low grinding that reverberated from every direction.

"They have to trust me," Iason said to Cédee. "Joris betrayed us." The words had the sour taste of history clinging to them.

Cédee looked at Iason. He fought the urge to turn away, to let go of her arm, to flee. It felt as though she could rip away his flesh and see into his soul.

"Leave," Cédee called. "Form groups and meet at the Proconsul hangar."

In a single motion, Iason deactivated the bunker's lock, pulling the door wide. Stairs led upward into blackness.

"Come on," he said, tugging on Cédee's arm.

She resisted. For an instant, the dead of Helena Prime flashed in her eyes. Like a thing refusing to be buried, the images kept returning.

Iason had ordered the indents to be executed as an example to the rest, to stifle the growing protest, to earn the favor of his superiors.

Cracks snaked through the stonework. Gray clouds geysered from the fractures.

Indents hurried past, dashing up the stairs. The lights flickered, making every movement seem impossibly slow. Iason let the hand holding Cédee fall to his side. There was nothing he could do to change the past. *His past.*

"Go," she said, her hands prodding him onward. "Up."

He climbed the stairs, first one at a time, then two, feeling Cédee continue to push him.

A line of indents flowed from the bunker into a palpable blackness. *Night vision,* Iason sent the thought to the NI. In response, his pupils widened, capturing every remnant of ambient light. In the gloom, he saw indents staggering through the debris. They moved in huddled groups, hands locked together.

Overhead, a vast craft hovered, engines thrumming. Iason's teeth chattered; the sonorous sound resonated through his bones.

Low frequency sound waves detected . . . Iason silenced the warning. Reaching back, he clasped Cédee's hand, leading her through the field of rubble.

Screaming, Iason tried to attract the others. The thrumming grew louder, to the point that he no longer heard his own voice.

A brilliant flash and thundering concussion sent Iason tumbling. Sharp stone ripped flesh as he hit the ground. Staying low, he waited for his eyes to adjust, and then scanned the darkness for Cédee.

Nearby, she slumped against a crumbled wall. Above, the buzzer maneuvered, spinning as though to acquire a new target. Strewn around the area were the dead, bodies bloody and mutilated.

"Cédee," Iason called. He fought the deep-rooted habit to access his NI. Even the long years of disuse couldn't erase the military training. Quickly he scurried toward her. The buzzer droned above. His ears ached, and the pressure from the engines squeezed his lungs.

Using strength he thought had faded, he hefted Cédee to her feet. She glanced around, dazed. Iason motioned for her to follow, leading her through the darkness.

They sat in the shell of a building, watching the lights on the horizon. A staccato series of explosions flashed over the landscape, as rhythmic and repetitive as a beating heart. A thick miasma blotted out the heavens, leaving only a churning gloom that reflected the glare of earthly explosions. The ceaseless chaos created a ruddy hue by which any human could see.

"Why didn't they follow?" Cédee asked, her voice raspy.

"I think they did follow others," Iason said. He stared at the horizon. "Maybe they mistook me for Joris. Both of us have NIs." The words burned in his throat.

Cédee made no response. Instead, she stepped to one of the demolished corners, and bent to peer through an opening in the wall.

"Do you know where the hangar is?" he asked.

"Yes."

"How many others do?"

"All."

Iason moved toward Cédee. "Then they could reach the hangar," he said dully.

"They might. Joris might already be gone."

"I doubt that," Iason said, gazing at the faraway flashes. "There can be no compacts here."

Motion detected, the NI announced. Even though Iason saw nothing, he knew the NI sensed things beyond his ability. *Multiple objects approaching at high velocity.*

"Hide," Iason said.

Cédee turned to speak, but he stepped away, repeating the word.

As he reached the edge of the ruined building, he stepped through the large gap that had been blasted away. Dancing in the sky above were tiny lights, darting up and down, circling.

"If they attack, stay hidden," Iason said. He hoped that the aliens had not mastered the language enough to comprehend his words. He continued to look at the objects as though he were speaking to them.

One after another, with perfect coordination, the spheres of light dropped from the sky, hovering before Iason. With the same uniform motion, they joined together, connecting as though to form a single entity. Now he saw that they did not glow. They reflected the wine red sky. Amazed, he watched as the tiny devices, only a few centimeters in circumference, formed a shape resembling a human. It possessed hands, arms, legs, torso, and a head — a man made of silver spheres.

Iason watched as the alien creation mirrored his movement and posture.

"Can you understand me?" he asked.

An unrelenting roar echoed in the distance. "Yes," the thing replied using Iason's voice.

"Why did you attack us?"

Four decades of military training had instilled the protocols of First Contact. Now Iason ignored those protocols. They seemed pointless.

"I did not attack. I am halting your function."

Iason gestured with a hand. "*This* is not an attack?" The rage returned, but now it was natural, not fueled by the NI.

"The double-strand was created to transform worlds. The double-strand function is complete."

A cold knot formed in Iason's stomach. The growing fury abruptly vanished like a raging fire extinguished by a faint breeze. From across the distant millennia, Iason saw who he was for the first time. What he was. What humanity was. All of the knowledge, advancements, successes and failures, every accomplishment and discovery had suddenly and simply been rendered meaningless.

"That's not possible," he said weakly.

The thing shifted, drawing back. Iason realized it continued to mimic his posture. "I seeded the worlds with the double-strand."

"Where are the others of your kind?" he asked. "Why have they sent you?"

"Kind?" it asked flatly. Raising an arm, it pointed toward the roiling sky. One sphere darted away, disappearing into the darkness. "That is I," the thing said, lowering its arm. "I am all. My consciousness spans this galaxy. I am in many places. I watched the stars rise. I shall watch them fall."

Iason inhaled deeply, tasting the ash and smoke and death. "Why?" he muttered. "You can have any world . . ."

"Yes," the thing interrupted. There was finality underscoring its tone — *his* tone. "Are you Joris?"

Then Iason remembered the link in his dream. He'd overheard the alien granting Joris sanctuary.

"*No*," Iason said, stepping forward.

As though dissolving, the spheres detached, accelerating upward. Iason watched as they vanished into the gloom.

From behind, he heard Cédee approach.

"Do you believe it?" she asked, her voice sounding small.

He faced her. In the ruddy gloom she seemed vulnerable. Again, he was reminded of Leena. Shame reddened his face.

"I don't want to believe it," he said, eyes gliding over the wrecked building, moving to the remains of the devastated city. "I'm not sure I have a choice."

"Then every human on every world dies tonight," she said, the words catching in her throat.

The faraway rumble was joined by a deep thrumming sound. *Low frequency sound waves detected . . .*

"We need to get to the hangar," Iason said. "Joris plans to use the shuttle to escape. He's been buying time — giving away the location of others and running."

Cédee nodded, stepping through the rubble. Iason followed.

The razed Proconsul mansion littered the earth. Giant shards of polished stone jutted upward like fingers grasping at the heavens. At one spot, the debris had been cleared, revealing a ramp sloping downward.

Iason hurried down the ramp, stopping at a reinforced door. Like all military buildings, the shielded structure had a protected power generation system. The lock still functioned.

Pressing an ear to the door, Iason listened. Even with the aid of his NI, he only heard faint sounds. There was no doubt Joris had entered the hangar and was prepping the shuttle.

Cédee appeared at the top of the ramp. Several other shapes moved alongside, shifting hesitantly.

From their stature and shape, Iason knew every skulking figure near Cédee was an indent. The genned were sculpted, engineered and taught to possess and present hubris.

"There are other survivors," Cédee called, approaching. "Joris came here and forced them to clear the ramp. Then he locked himself inside."

For a split-second, Iason wondered if he could convince Joris to open the door, and then they could leave *together*. The idea made him sick.

He'd sunk so far. It seemed impossible to turn around now.

He gazed at the lockpad.

"I know the code," Cédee said.

Iason cocked his head. She stood next to him, fixing him with her piercing eyes.

"There was a relay transmitter in the bunker," she continued. "I was suspicious, so I recorded all broadcasts to it, and the landline bursts. Eventually I got the lock-code." She paused as if to reconsider her words. "I didn't trust Joris . . . I didn't trust you." She tilted her head toward the gathering indents. "They don't trust you either."

"They shouldn't . . ." Iason said, his words fading away.

Booted feet stamped down the ramp. From the corner of his eye, he saw figures with makeshift clubs.

Hibernate, he ordered the NI as a heavy blow landed, forcing the air from of his lungs. He staggered back, bouncing against the wall, raising arms to shelter himself. The ferocious attacks continued, hammering his head and torso. He remained standing for as long as he could. Through pain-glazed eyes, Iason saw Cédee turn away.

They persisted until he crumpled on the ground — until the genned hubris had been smothered. Then they opened the door. Rough hands hoisted him to his feet, pushing him into the hangar.

A fog of pain numbed his mind. He staggered, understanding their intent. He was a diversion.

Above the pounding in his ears, he heard the familiar whine of a gauze-pistol. A red-hot shaft tore through his shoulder. The energy sent him spilling over.

Iason's heart hammered. Raw agony traced a path along every nerve in his body. Slowly, he lifted his head. Before him stood Joris. His uniform was haggard and dusty, but he still possessed the stiff posture of a genned solider, pistol in hand.

"I thought they would kill you," Joris said. The words boomed in the hangar.

"Which *they*?" Iason wheezed.

"Either one," Joris said. "It didn't matter. Both are enemies." The familiar, thin smile crept across his face as he lowered the pistol. "You were the rearguard, Iason. But you turned out to be a hollow, old man."

The desire to activate the NI tugged at Iason's mind. With a grunt, he pushed to his knees, rising to his feet. Blood streamed down his arm, staining his hand, dripping from his fingers.

"You were never good at killing," Iason said in a ragged voice. "You always left if for someone else."

Joris' visage darkened. His temple twitched. "Someone has to lead," he growled. "Someone has to warn the other worlds."

"*Someone* will . . ." Iason said.

Another fiery slug cut into Iason's chest. He lurched and wobbled, and then deliberately stepped forward. The whine of the gun repeated. Hot spikes burrowed into his body, continuing until he collapsed.

Swathed in agony, Iason convulsed. Helplessly, he watched as Joris reloaded the pistol.

A violent crash sounded. Joris fired, shuffled backward. In a flurry, indents rushed past, screaming, swinging metal clubs. Several bodies fell, but others continued forward, piling on Joris, battering at him until he lay motionless on the floor.

Iason let his head roll back, thoughts swirling dizzyingly.

He felt his body being dragged across the hard floor. He sensed it as though he were miles away. They propped him against the wall.

A memory fluttered from a hidden place in Iason's mind. Leena smiling, happy. He'd forgotten that she'd loved him once. Detached from his body, he drifted in a distant universe.

Something small bit at his neck, and slowly he returned to his body.

"Why aren't you using your NI?"

His eyes opened. Cédee kneeled next to him. The glaring light burned his eyes.

"Are they boarding the shuttle?" he asked, coughing weakly.

"Yes."

Through the harsh light, he recognized the observation room, beyond that was the lift-pad where the shuttle would be prepped. "How many?" he asked.

"Maybe one hundred," she said. We've waited as long as we can. The buzzers will come soon."

He pulled his hands to his sides. The pain swelled. It felt as though searing metal poured through his abdomen.

"I can't spare any more meds," Cédee said. "We might need them."

Iason started to nod, but caught himself. He felt something wet dribble down his chest.

"Your NI can reduce the pain."

"No." He tried to swallow, but his throat was dry and swollen. He blinked, focusing on Cédee. Her eyes had softened. Still, no happiness lurked in them, not like it did in Leena's long ago. "How strange we are. Ideas get lodged in our minds and they stay there."

She placed a warm hand against his cheek.

"Where will you go?" he asked.

Her eyes dropped to the floor. She remained silent.

"I understand." He struggled to smile; instead, he gasped at the boiling pain. "There are others . . . Even if every human world is attacked, there will be survivors. We are more than a *double-strand*, more than creatures farming the galaxy. *More* . . . And we have a purpose."

A tear ran down Cédee's cheek. She clasped his hand. The pain made him flinch. He drew in a quick breath and tightened his grip.

"I'm sorry," she said.

Voices babbled in the background. Footsteps approached.

"I have to go." She gently pulled away.

"Remember who we are," he muttered, and coughed, tasting blood.

Iason closed his eyes, clenching his teeth against the twisting pain and the years of anger. In the darkness, he saw the stars rising.

ABOUT THE CONTRIBUTORS

A. A. ATTANASIO lives by his imagination in Hawaii. He is the author of *The Eagle and the Sword*, *The Wolf and the Crown*, *The Dragon and the Unicorn*, *Solis*, *Radix*, and many other titles.

GREG BEATTY attended Clarion West 2000, and any rumors you've heard about his time there are, unfortunately, probably true. Greg publishes everything from poetry about stars to reviews of books that don't exist. When he's not writing, Greg teaches for the University of Phoenix Online.

TIM CURRAN lives in Michigan and is the author of the novels *Hive* and *Dead Sea* from Elder Signs Press. ESP will also be publishing the next two volumes of the *Hive* trilogy. His short stories have appeared in such magazines as *City Slab*, *Dark Wisdom*, and *Inhuman*, as well as anthologies such as *Horrors Beyond*, *Shivers IV*, and *Hardboiled Cthulhu*.

JAY CASELBERG is an Australian writer currently based in Germany when he is not travelling the world for various work commitments. His short stories and novels have appeared in many different countries, publications and media. He can be found online at www.jaycaselberg.com.

WILLIAM C. DIETZ is the best-selling author of more than twenty-five science fiction novels some of which have been translated into German, Russian, and Japanese. He grew up in the Seattle area, spent time with the Navy and Marine Corps as a medic, graduated from the University of Washington, lived in Africa for half a year, and has traveled to six continents. Dietz has been variously employed as a surgical technician, college instructor, news writer, television producer, and director of public relations and marketing for an international telephone company. He and his wife live in Washington State where they enjoy traveling, kayaking, snorkeling, and not too surprisingly, reading books.

C.J. HENDERSON is an Origins Award-winning author and the creator of the Jack Hagee private detective series, and the Teddy London occult detective series. He is also the author of the *Encyclopedia of Science Fiction Movies* as well as scores of short stories, comics and non-fiction articles. www.cjhenderson.com.

WILLIAM JONES is a writer and editor who works in the fiction and hobby industries. His works span mystery, horror, SF, historical, and fantasy. He has edited and appeared in various anthologies and magazines, and he is the author of *The Strange Cases of Rudolph Pearson*. William is also the editor of *Dark Wisdom* magazine, and he teaches English at a university in Michigan.
www.williamjoneswriter.com.

PAUL S. KEMP is a *New York Times* bestselling author of eight novels and many short stories, most of them dark fantasy, and most of them set in The Forgotten Realms setting. He lives in Michigan with his wife and twin sons. To drop him a line, visit his weblog at http://paulskemp.livejournal.com/

ALEXIS GLYNN LATNER'S science fiction novel *Hurricane Moon* was published by Pyr in 2007. Her stories have appeared in the magazines *Analog* and *Amazing* and the anthology *Bending the Landscape: Horror*. She lives in Houston, works in the Rice University library, and teaches creative writing.

RICHARD A. LUPOFF has been a novelist, short story writer, cultural historian, screenwriter, critic, broadcaster and teacher. Not to mention soldier, dishwasher, and a few other occupations too unsavory to mention. In recent years he has been most proud of *Marblehead: A Novel of H. P. Lovecraft*. First written in 1976, this book was caught up in a publishing maelstrom and apparently lost beyond hope. When a copy of the manuscript surfaced in 2006 the book was finally published by Ramble House—www.ramblehouse.com—to high acclaim from *Publishers Weekly, Locus, Ellery Queen's Mystery Magazine* and other publications.

PAUL MELNICZEK has been writing since 2000, with over 100 stories sold to a variety of markets, including *Cemetery Dance, Fangoria*, and several appearances in the mass market *Darkside* anthologies from ROC Books. He is the author of *Frightful October, Restless Shades, A Halloween Harvest, Troubled Visions*, and the collab *Dark Harvest*.

GENE O'NEILL has published 100 plus short stories, including tales in *Twilight Zone, F & SF, SF Age, Dark Wisdom, Cemetery Dance, Dead End: City Limit, and Borderlands 5*. His story "Balance" was a Stoker award finalist in 2007. He has seen three novels, two short story collections, and two novellas—including *White Tribe*—published. Two new novels, *Deathflash* and *Lost Tribe* are at interested publishers. He is just beginning *Fade Away*.

STEPHEN MARK RAINEY is author of six novels, including *Blue Devil Island, The Lebo Coven*, and others, as well as over 90 published works of short fiction. He has edited *Deathrealm* magazine and several anthologies. Mark lives in Greensboro, NC, with his wife Peggy. Visit his Web site at www.stephenmarkrainey.com.

EKATERINA SEDIA lives in New Jersey. Her new novel, *The Secret History of Moscow*, is coming from Prime Books in November 2007. Her next one, *The Alchemy of Stone*, is due from Prime in 2008. Her short stories sold to *Analog, Baen's Universe, Fantasy Magazine*, and *Dark Wisdom*, as well as *Japanese Dreams* and *Magic in the Mirrorstone* anthologies.

RON SHIFLET was born in Ft. Worth, Texas and currently resides in Crowley. He is an admirer of Robert E. Howard and H.P. Lovecraft and first contemplated writing after reading their work. His stories have appeared in *Book of Dark Wisdom, Seasons in the Night, and Dark Legacy*. They have also been selected for anthologies such as *Eldritch Blue, Maelstrom, Travel a Time Historic* and *Goremet Cuisine*.

Winner of the Bram Stoker Award, given by the Horror Writers of America, for his story collection "Black Butterflies" (Leisure Books), JOHN SHIRLEY is the author of numerous novels, including the recent *Demons*, which has been optioned by the Weinstein Group and is in development as a film; other novels include *Crawlers, Eclipse, A Splendid Chaos, The Other End* and *City Come A-Walkin'*. His newest story collection is *Living Shadows* from Prime Books. The authorized website is: www.darkecho.com/johnshirley

LUCIEN SOULBAN (www.luciensoulban.com) is a novelist and scriptwriter living in beautiful Montreal. He's written four novels — *Blood In-Blood Out, Fleshworks, The Alien Sea* and *Desert Raiders* — contributed to numerous anthologies including *The Book of Final Flesh* and has written for various video-games including *Rainbow Six: Vegas* and *Dawn of War*.

JOHN SUNSERI is the co-author (with David Conyers) of *The Spiralilng Worm*, a collection of Lovecraftian Mythos/espionage tales published by Chaosium. He's currently editing a collection of cross-genre horror tales for Permuted Press, and his stories and novellas have appeared in over fifty magazines and anthologies. He lives in Portland, Oregon with his beautiful wife Elizabeth.

BOB WEINBERG is the author of sixteen novels, two short story collections and more than a dozen non-fiction books. He's also scripted comics for Marvel, DC, and Moonstone. Of the approximately 100 short stories he's written, in the past fifteen years, Bob's favorite is "The Margins."

DAVID NIALL WILSON has been writing Science-Fiction, Fantasy and Horror since the mid 1980s. He has thirteen published novels and over a hundred and fifty short stories in anthologies and magazines. David is an ex president of the Horror Writer's Association and winner of the Bram Stoker Award for his poetry.

MICHAIL VELICHANSKY was born in the former Soviet Union, but emigrated with his parents when he was five years old. He was a winner of the *Writers of the Future* contest in 2005. In 2007 he completed his first novel, a young adult fantasy about fairies and hangings.

ALSO AVAILABLE FROM ELDER SIGNS PRESS

PUBLISHER OF QUALITY DARK FICTION, SCIENCE FICTION, FANTASY & HORROR

Now Available
Author: Michael McBride
572 Pages

CHRONICLES OF THE APOCALYPSE: SPECIES

In the final days, humanity faced the final hour of existence. With a whimper they passed from this life and into something inhuman, something monstrous, something alien. In the last hours they longed for a deliverance that would never come — there was only emptiness. But all species are difficult to extinguish, and in humankind there were seven imperfect souls selected for survival. What seemed a blessing was a nightmare. And the dead are unforgiving.

Signed, Limited
Hardcover: $45.00
ISBN: 0-9779876-7-1

Trade Paperback: $17.95
ISBN: 0-9779876-8-X

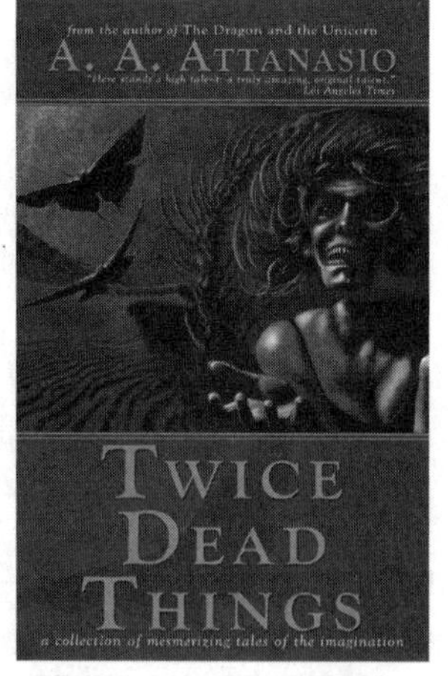

Now Available
Author: A. A. Attanasio
320 Pages

A. A. ATTANASIO'S TWICE DEAD THINGS

Twice Dead Things is a collection of the captivating, terrifying, and poetic writings of A. A. Attanasio, one of today's most powerful and insightful writers. This volume includes many rare and previously unpublished works, and the re-writing of his popular Lovecraftian tales into a solitary narrative. Over his lengthy career, Attanasio has written in many genres, proving a master of each. *Twice Dead Things* is a collection of many of those captivating writings.

Signed, Limited
Hardcover: $42.00
ISBN: 0-9759229-8-X

Trade Paperback: $16.95
ISBN: 0-9759229-9-8

WWW.ELDERSIGNSPRESS.COM

Elder Signs Press, Inc. P.O. Box 389 Lake Orion, MI 48361-0389 USA
248-628-9711 www.eldersignspress.com info@eldersignspress.com